WARRING HEARTS . . . AND HIDDEN DESIRE

"Had I the time or inclination, I might be tempted to tame that terrible temper of yours," Gilbert bit off, "but as I've neither, you will have to content yourself with this."

Suddenly Graeye felt his mouth on hers. Turning away from the insistent voices that urged her to exercise caution, she welcomed the invasion upon her singing senses. When he urged her, she parted her lips with a sigh of pleasure. . . .

Then, as abruptly as it had begun, it was over. In the blink of an eye he had turned from passionate lover to cold and distant adversary.

"I may have fallen prey to your wiles last eventide," he said, "but I assure you I have no intention of paying the price you would ask for such an unfortunate tryst. Your scheme has failed."

"You err," she said, lifting her chin a notch. "Though you do not believe me . . . 'Twas freedom from the church I hoped to gain, not a husband. And that you gave me."

Nostrils flaring, Gilbert gave a short bark of laughter. "Be you assured, Lady Graeye," he said as he adjusted his sword on its belt, "you have failed. For you will return to the abbey . . . even if I have to drag you there myself."

Bantam Books by Tamara Leigh

Warrior Bride
Virgin Bride

Virgin Bride

TAMARA LEIGH

BANTAM BOOKS

NEW YORK   TORONTO   LONDON   SYDNEY   AUCKLAND

Virgin Bride

Prologue

❦

England, Autumn of 1156

She was a vision in virginal white, from the top of her bowed head to the toes of her shoes peeking from beneath the bridal habit she wore. Save for her vast silvery eyes, there was simply no other color about her.

Thinking to calm her racing heart, she lifted a hand and pressed it to her breast, her gaze straying as she gathered her courage.

"Be still!" the novice mistress reprimanded, her deep, masculine voice jolting her charge's slender frame.

Stiffening her spine with well-learned obedience, Graeye sighed—a lack of deference for which she immediately repented. Though not of late, she had more than once felt the sting of Mistress Hermana's strap, for that part of her spirit which had not been broken picked the most inopportune times to declare that this life was not of her choosing. Of the three vows she was about to take, she knew obedience would be the most difficult to keep.

Digging her short nails into her palms, she lifted her chin and slowly slid her gaze up the black-clad woman.

She needn't have gone farther than that square, unmoving chin to know of the novice mistress's displeasure, but she did.

Issuing an unflattering snort of disapproval, Hermana reached forward and tugged on the wimple where it passed from beneath Graeye's chin up to the stiffened band around her forehead.

Her heart sinking further, Graeye lowered her eyes and forced herself to stillness. Over the years she had become painfully accustomed to such ministrations—a vain attempt to conceal the faint stain marring the left side of her face. Starting just shy of her eyebrow, the mark faded back into the hairline at her temple. Though it was not very large or conspicuous, it might as well have covered her entire face.

It was the mark of the devil, Hermana often pointed out. Always the devil in Graeye was responsible for the trouble she got herself into. What might otherwise have been viewed as simple, childish pranks or the foolishness of youth, the superstitious woman attributed to evil.

When the other novices skipped matins, or devised tricks against one another, their punishment was a verbal reprimand and prayers of repentance. With Graeye it was that and more—a strap across her back, long hours on her knees scrubbing floors or pulling weeds, and always humiliation before her peers.

Though she did not believe it was the devil in her that was responsible for her penchant for trouble, Graeye knew too well the curse her physical flaw afforded. It was, after all, the shape of her destiny thus far.

When she was seven, her father, unable to bear the sight of her any longer, had dedicated her to the Church—only days after the death of her mother. The handsome dowry he had provided the convent at Arlecy had insured her acceptance no matter what mark she bore, and no matter her own feelings. And now, too soon, she was to wed—not to a mortal as she might have wished, but to the Church.

On this, the day of her Clothing, she would become a nun, her profession made, her hair sheared, and her only garment a black habit. It burdened her, though her passing into sisterhood would finally free her from Hermana's severe dominance, and that was a blessing. Though Hermana was not a nun, for she had once been wed and her chastity forever lost, she had held the esteemed title of novice mistress for as long as Graeye could remember.

Now, however, Graeye would have a new and kinder master to serve—the Lord. If only she could rejoice in that and be content . . .

The faint sound of music from within the chapel indicated the commencement of the ceremony.

"Eyes forward," Hermana snapped.

Obeying, Graeye began a mental recitation of her prayers—not those devised for a novice preparing to take the veil, but her own pleadings that she be freed from this obligation.

Minutes later, the large oaken doors to the chapel groaned inward.

Squaring her shoulders, Graeye pressed her bouquet to her abdomen, her fingers crushing the delicate stems and leaves. Though she commanded her legs to take that fateful step forward, she found she could not. However, a sharp nudge from Hermana was all that was needed.

"Halt!" The command sliced the cool morning air.

As if joined, Graeye and Hermana whirled about to search out the intruder.

Though the half-dozen knights who emerged from between two of the outlying buildings came disarmed, as was the only permissible entrance to this holy place, a small group of clergy were vainly trying to halt their determined advance.

"You dare enter consecrated ground without permission?" Hermana's voice rose as she stepped forward and placed herself in the path of the intruders.

"Forgive us," a tall, thin knight apologized, though he sounded anything but repentant. He withdrew a rolled parchment from his belt and handed it to the novice mistress. "I carry an urgent message from Baron Edward Charwyck."

Graeye sucked in a breath. A message from her father? Had the letter of appeal she'd written brought about a change of heart? Anxiously, she watched as Hermana turned to put the sun at her back to better read the missive.

The woman's thick eyebrows drew ever closer as she read. Then, abruptly, she lifted her eyes to stare over the top of the parchment at her charge.

Suppressing the desire to wrap her arms around herself, Graeye shifted her gaze to the right. There a young, fair-headed knight stood beside the messenger, his eyes intent upon her. Graeye lifted a hand to the wimple, insuring it was in place and the telling mark covered.

The resounding crackle of parchment broke the silence. Stiffly, Hermana traversed the stone walkway and mounted the steps to the chapel. At the top the abbess waited, having come outside to discover the cause for delay.

The exchange between the two women was hushed. While the abbess, a woman Graeye regarded with affection, listened, the other gesticulated wildly. With a few words the abbess calmed Hermana, then she examined the parchment. More words were exchanged, then the novice mistress descended the steps.

Venturing a look past the stern-faced woman approaching her, Graeye was startled by the abbess's serene countenance. Though she could not be certain, she thought the woman's mouth curved into a smile for the briefest of moments.

When Hermana stopped before her, Graeye raised expectant eyes to her face.

"'Tis your brother Philip," the woman began, unexpected emotion in her voice. "He is deceased." As the words passed her thin, colorless lips, she crossed herself.

Surprised by the news, Graeye could only stare for a moment. Then, remembering herself, she also made the sign of the cross.

Philip dead. Though there was an odd fluttering in her chest, she felt little else.

Contrite over her lack of deep emotion, she offered up a silent explanation that she might not be condemned for her un-Christian reaction. She'd hardly known her half sibling, for he'd been a good deal older than she, and her few remembrances of him were seeped in pain.

She had seen little of him while he'd been in training, first as a page, then as a squire, at a neighboring barony. However, she'd seen enough to dislike the loud, foulmouthed boy with whom she shared a father. He had taunted her mercilessly about her "devil's mark," and played cruel pranks on her whenever he caught her out from behind her mother's skirts.

God forgive her, but she could not mourn one whose memory dredged up old pain, and whom she had not seen for nigh on ten years. He was a stranger, and now would forever remain one. Still, she would pray for his soul.

"Your father has requested you attend him so that your brother might be given a proper burial," Hermana went on, her voice choked, her eyes grown moist.

Graeye wondered at the woman's peculiar behavior. She had never known Hermana capable of any emotion other than anger and displeasure.

"And as you are now his only hope for a male heir," she continued, "'tis not likely you will be returning to us."

Leave Arlecy? Forever? Graeye's heart swelled as she stared into that wizened face, her hand reflexively opening to release the ravaged bouquet. With a soft rustle it fell unheeded to the cold stones.

Her prayers had been answered. She was to be freed of this obligation. A moment later her wavering smile faded. Why had God waited until the last possible moment to grant her desires? Had He been testing her? Had He—

"You are to leave immediately," Hermana said. "I will have your possessions packed and sent on later."

"I must change," Graeye whispered, smoothing the skirts of her bridal habit.

"There is to be no delay," the woman snapped. "You are to leave now, that you might complete the journey ere nightfall."

Graeye had no intention of arguing the matter. Bobbing her head, she grasped the skirt of her habit and stepped around Hermana without another word. Trembling with excitement, she walked quickly to the knight who had delivered the message.

The gaunt man was much older than he had appeared from a distance. In fact, he looked well past twoscore years, every telling groove in his hard face stark against his chalky complexion.

"Lady Graeye," he said, "I am Sir William Rotwyld, Lord of Sulle, vassal to Baron Edward Charwyck." His eyes shone with a coldness Graeye did not care to fathom, though it was impossible to ignore.

Inclining her head, she clasped her hands before her. "Sir William."

"Come." He grasped her elbow. "Your father awaits you at Medland."

Stealing one final look behind, Graeye swept her gaze past Hermana and settled it briefly upon the abbess. This time there was no doubt that the woman smiled.

Chapter 1

A broom in one hand, a dirty rag in the other, Graeye took a rest from her labors to cast a critical eye over the hall. Through her efforts this past month, the castle had seen many changes both inside and out, but none were as obvious as those to be found here.

Gone was the sparse, putrid straw that had covered the floor and that she had slipped on her first day at Medland. In its place lay fresh rushes smelling sweetly of herbs. Immense networks of cobwebs and thick layers of dust had been swept away. The dark, tattered window coverings that had permitted nothing but an icy draught within had been replaced with oiled linen that let the day's light spill beams throughout. The trestle tables and benches that had threatened to collapse beneath a man's weight had been repaired, though they did not look much better for all the effort. Even the old, threadbare tapestries had been salvaged by days of cleaning and needlework.

Still, no matter how hard she worked, Medland would never be grand, Graeye conceded with a wistful sigh. At least it was finally habitable. And it was the castlefolk she had to thank for that. Determined as she had been to set the dilapidated castle right, she could not have accomplished any of it without their help.

It had taken persistence, and a considerable show of interest in the reasons behind the sorry state of the demesne, before the people began opening to her. Finally, setting aside their superstitions about the mark she bore, they told her what had transpired over the past several years.

Four years earlier her father had relinquished the responsibility of overseeing Medland to Philip, and it had proved a poor choice. Unconcerned for the welfare of his people, the young lord had frivolously squandered both time and money.

By the second year his neglect had led to diminished stores of food for the castle inhabitants. Hence he had appropriated livestock and grain from the villagers to meet the demand within the walled fortress. That had greatly weakened the once prosperous people and resulted in winter famine.

Philip had been a cruel master, too, doling out harsh punishment for minor offenses and using his authority to gain the beds of castle wenches and village women alike.There were even whispered rumors that his cruelty had extended to the taking of lives whenever he was displeased, and that was how his late wife had met her end.

Graeye had chosen not to delve too deeply into that last matter, for it weighed heavily upon her conscience. Instead she set herself the task of righting wrongs, and that more than anything else brought the castlefolk and villagers to her side. It had taken courage, but she had opened the stores of grain her father had been hoarding and distributed a goodly portion among the people. Though he and his men had grumbled over her actions, none had directly opposed her.

When she had toured the village and fields outside the walls of the castle, she was relieved to discover that the villagers' crops were in far better shape than their lord's, though she kept this to herself for fear her father might lay claim to the harvest once again.

Through her efforts the harvesting of the lord's sparse crops and the plowing and sowing of the fallow fields were set in motion, though not without a great deal of prodding and coaxing. Still, she knew that even if the fields yielded late crops, it was unlikely there would be enough to last through the long winter that the brisk autumn winds promised. Though the changes she'd wrought were great, there was still so much left to do.

With that thought Graeye straightened and drew the back of her hand over her warm, moist face. She was tempted to remove the stifling wimple, but she immediately squelched the impulse. Several times during the past week she had contemplated discarding it altogether, but the familiarity and security it provided prevented her from doing so. She was not ready to expose herself to greater curiosity than what she had endured thus far.

"Lady Graeye," a voice broke into her reverie.

Propping her broom against the wall, Graeye turned to face the man who crossed the hall toward her. It was the young knight who had caught her notice at the abbey—Sir Michael Trevier. During her first days at Medland he had been instrumental in bringing about the changes to the castle, and helping her gain acceptance among the people. He had been all smiles for her then, always at hand to assist in whatever task she undertook. But that was in the past.

A fortnight earlier he had issued a challenge to the knight Graeye's father had chosen to be her husband. He wanted her for himself and had been prepared to do battle to win her hand. However, Edward Charwyck had remained adamant that Sir William Rotwyld, the messenger who had been sent to escort Graeye from the abbey, was to be her husband.

Angered, Michael had hurled insults at William, pointing out his flaws and great age, which might prevent him from fathering the heir Edward wanted so badly.

Although Graeye would have far preferred marriage to Michael than to the repulsive man Edward had chosen, to avoid bloodshed, she had stood and declared she was content to wed William.

Though she had been successful in preventing the two men from taking up swords, Michael was no longer her champion. He had no more smiles for her, nor kind words to ease her misgivings. He had become conspicuously scarce, practically a stranger. She missed him.

"There is a merchant at the postern gate who says he has cloth for you," he said, coming to stand before her.

"Cloth?" Graeye frowned, trying to remember when, and for what purpose, she had ordered it. "Ah, yes, for the tables." She swept a hand to indicate their bare, unsightly tops. "Don't you think coverings will brighten the entire hall?"

Mouth set in a grim, flat line, he nodded and turned on his heel. "I will send the man to you," he tossed over his shoulder.

Pained by his indifference, she hurried after him and caught his arm. "Michael, don't you understand why—"

"Perfectly, my lady," he said, his gaze stony.

Nervously, Graeye shifted from one foot to the other. "Nay, I do not think you do . Won't you let me explain?"

He shrugged her hand off his arm. "A lowly knight such as myself deserves no explanation."

So that was what he thought. That she had rejected him because of his rank. "You are wrong," she said. "I—"

"Excuse me, but I have other tasks to attend to," he interrupted. Bowing stiffly, he turned and walked away.

With a heavy heart Graeye watched him go. Though she could not say she loved him, he was every bit the brother she had once fantasized having. Perhaps love would have eventually grown from that, but now she would never know.

"He is the one you want, is he not?"

Gasping, she spun around to face Edward. "F-father," she stammered, embarrassed at having been caught staring after the knight.

Edward's lips twisted into a knowing smile.

Trying to gauge what kind of mood he was in, she took in the sour smell of alcohol that ladened his breath, the sound of his shallow, labored breathing, and the gray, sagging features set with reddened eyes. He presented a common enough sight, for he was more often drunk than sober, but she had yet to become accustomed to it.

His mood was harmless, she decided. With every passing day he became more and more genial toward her, but it had not been like that when she'd first come to Medland. Then he had been half-mad with grief over Philip's death. He had called her the devil's daughter and forced her to . . .

She did not want to think of that first night, for it chilled her to relive any part of the memory. Pushing it aside, she nodded to the tables. "The cloth has arrived," she said, hoping Edward would not pursue the matter of Sir Michael. "By tomorrow eve the tables will all be covered."

Edward chose not to let the matter drop. "William will make you a good husband," he slurred. "That pup Michael thinks only of what is between his legs. He knows nothing of responsibility or loyalty. And I assure you he knows little of breeding."

Graeye blushed at his blunt remarks. "Aye, Father," she said, averting her gaze.

"But still you want the young one, don't you?"

She shook her head. "I have said I am content with Sir William. That has not changed."

"Content." He spat the word. "But you would choose Michael if I allowed you. Do not lie to me."

Reminding herself of the vow she had made weeks

earlier not to cower, she lifted her chin. "It is true that Sir Michael is young and handsome, and that he is kind of heart, but—"

"He is a weakling is what he is. He has no castle, no land, and very little coin."

Though it was unwise, Graeye could not help but defend the knight. "He is still young," she reminded Edward. "And what would William have, had you not given it to him?"

Surprisingly, Edward did not anger at her boldness. "True," he mused, "but he earned it. That, Michael has yet to do—if ever."

"Methinks he will."

"Not with my daughter. Nay, I want an heir, and soon. Your union with William will assure me this."

"How can you be so certain?"

He grinned. "William made seven boys on his first two wives—not a single girl child." He let that sink in, then added, "It is a son you will bear come spring."

Now she understood. It was not the knight's possessions, nor his years of loyalty to his liege lord, it was his ability to produce sons that had decided Edward. She suppressed a shudder at the thought of the man making on heir on her.

"Hmm." Hands on his hips, Edward turned to survey the hall. "You have done well, daughter," he pronounced, the first comment he had ever made on any of the improvements.

He had changed topics so abruptly, it took Graeye several moments before she understood what he was talking about. Relieved, she abandoned all thoughts of her future as William Rotwyld's wife.

"Thank you," she said, pleased by his praise. All the hard work had been worth it for just those few words. Had he also noticed the improved foodstuffs that had graced his table recently, or had drinking numbed his sense of taste?

"Methinks I shall have to reward you."

"That is not necessary," she objected, having already found her reward in his acknowledgment.

"Of course it's not necessary," he snapped, his color rising. "If 'twas, I would not do it."

Realizing he was teetering on the edge of one of his black moods, Graeye merely nodded.

Grumbling beneath his breath, Edward studied the floor, then smacked his lips. "A new wardrobe," he declared. "Aye, it would not be fitting for a Charwyck to go to her wedding dressed like that." With clear distaste he slid his gaze down the faded bliaut she wore.

Graeye smoothed the material. Having no clothing other than what she had worn as a novice at the abbey, she had taken possession of the garments that had once belonged to her mother. Though aged, they fit well, for she was nearly the same size as Lady Alienor had been, only a bit shorter.

"I would like that," she said, visualizing the beautiful fabrics she might choose for her trousseau.

"Then it will be done." Swinging away, Edward stumbled in his attempt to negotiate the level floor, sending the rushes beneath his feet flying. By the luck of the devil he managed to keep himself upright, though he looked as if he might collapse at any moment.

Hurrying to his side, Graeye caught his arm. "You are tired," she said, hoping he would not thrust her aside as he did each time she touched him. From the outset he had been averse to her touch, as if he truly believed the devil resided within her.

He looked down at her hand but, surprisingly, did not push her away. "Aye," he mumbled. "I am tired."

She urged him toward the stairs. "I will help you to your chamber."

The wooden steps creaked warningly beneath their feet, soft in some places and brittle in others. What pit of darkness awaited them if the boards gave way and sent them crashing downward? Graeye wondered. A disturbing image rising in her mind, she decided to set some men to replacing the steps as soon as possible.

Up a second flight of stairs they went, down a narrow corridor, and into the lord's chamber.

Tossing the covers back from the bed, Graeye stepped aside. "I will send a servant to awaken you when supper is ready," she said as he lay back on the mattress.

"Supper," he griped. "Nay, send me a fine wench and some ale. That will suffice."

Pulling the covers over him, Graeye made no comment. He asked for the same thing each evening, and each evening she sent a manservant to deliver him to the hall. It was bold of her, but thus far it had worked.

Edward caught hold of her hand as she straightened. "A grandson," he muttered. " 'Tis all I ask of you."

Pity surged through her as she looked down into his desperate, pleading eyes. He was vulnerable . . . pained . . . heartbroken. . . . Aye, here was a man she was no longer frightened of—the man who should have been her father these past ten years. Mayhap it was not too late.

Graeye knew she should not entertain such foolish thoughts. After all, had she not been Edward's last chance to gain a male heir, he would never have sent for her. Knowing this should have been enough to banish her false hope, but she could not help herself.

Bending low, she impulsively laid her lips to his weathered cheek. "A grandson you will have," she whispered. "This I vow."

Lifting her head, she looked into eyes that shone with gratitude and brimmed with tears.

"Thank you," he said, his fingers gripping hers more tightly. Moments later he fell asleep.

Withdrawing from his chamber, Graeye quietly closed the door and turned toward the stairs. She had taken no more than a half-dozen steps when a sound behind her caught her attention. Chills creeping up her spine, she slowly turned to face the small chapel situated at the end of the corridor. As no torches had been lit beyond Edward's chamber, she squinted to see past the shadows that abounded there, but to no avail.

More than anything, she wanted to ignore the noise and return to her chores belowstairs, but she knew she must eventually face the memories that had haunted her dreams since that first night at Medland.

Squaring her shoulders, she drew a deep breath and walked forward. What was making the noise? she wondered, refusing to allow her imagination to believe it had anything to do with her brother's death. A rat, perhaps, or a breeze stirring the rushes about the chapel, she reassured herself.

As she drew near, the sound became that of scratching and quick, shallow breathing. Her heart leaping, Graeye stumbled to a halt and peered into the shadows. "Who goes there?" she demanded, her voice high and shaky.

Silence followed, but was soon shattered when a deep groan rent the air. In the next moment a large figure bounded out of the darkness and skidded to a stop before her.

Her hand pressed over her slamming heart, her mouth wide with the scream of fright that had nearly leaped from her lungs, she stared disbelievingly at the great, mangy dog. "Groan," she exclaimed.

Looking up at her with wide, expectant eyes, its tongue lolling out of its mouth, the dog wagged its tail so vigorously, its backside shifted side to side.

Limp with relief, Graeye sank to her knees and curved an arm around the animal. "You are a naughty dog, frightening me like that," she scolded, turning her face away when he tried to lick it.

As she stroked the dog's head, she smiled, remembering how frightened she had been of the beast when he had introduced himself during her first meal at Medland. She had rarely been around dogs, and certainly never one of such proportions, and had shrieked when he had laid his slavering chin upon her lap. That had gained her nothing but humiliation, for the dog did not move, and her father's men had roared with laughter.

In hopes that he might leave her if she fed him, she had tossed food to him, but always he returned to her. Offhandedly, Edward had advised that if she beat him rather than feed him, he would not bother her. At his callous words a feeling of protectiveness had assailed her and replaced her fright.

Since that day Groan—as she had named him, due to his penchant for making that horrible noise—had attached himself to her side. And he had more than once proved himself valuable.

With a shudder Graeye remembered the night, a week after she'd returned to Medland, when Sir William had cornered her as she'd readied to bed down in the hall. The vile man had taunted her, his words cruel and cutting, his hands bruising as they made themselves familiar with her cringing body. Though he was to be her husband, and it was likely she could not prevent the rape he intended, she had fought him with every ounce of her strength.

It had not deterred him, though. In fact, he had seemed to enjoy her resistance. Even as he had torn her bliaut and laid his hands to her bare flesh, he had threatened that if she bore him a child with the same mark she carried, he would kill it himself.

That had frightened her more than the inevitable violation of her body.

She had been about to scream for help when Groan had appeared. Snapping and snarling, he had circled William, his body bunched as he readied himself to attack.

The man who had thought nothing of exerting his greater strength over a frightened woman had retreated posthaste, leaving Graeye to offer profuse thanks to her unlikely champion.

Conveniently forgetting her resolve to face the haunting memories within the chapel, Graeye straightened. "Come," she said to Groan, "I will find you a nice morsel."

The dog, however, went back to the chapel door and began to scratch and sniff again.

Graeye pulled her bottom lip between her teeth. How much longer could she avoid that place? she asked herself. Sooner or later she would have to go within and brave her fears. Otherwise she would never be free of them.

"Very well," she said. "We shall see what it is that interests you, Groan." Taking the last steps forward, she laid trembling fingers on the handle. Then, swallowing hard, she pushed the door open.

Immediately, Groan rushed ahead, leaving her behind.

It was not like that first night when a shower of candlelight had greeted Graeye—quite the opposite. Today the chapel was dim, its only light coming from the small window that had been opened to air out the room.

Crossing herself, Graeye stepped inside. Instantly her gaze fell upon the high table that stood against the far wall. Her brother had been laid out on that table that first night, his ravaged, decomposing corpse emitting the most terrible stench. She could still smell it.

Though she did not want to, she found herself reliving that night when Edward had brought her here. She'd been unable to cross the threshold for the horrible smell that had assailed her, and he had thrust her inside.

"I would have you see Philip with your own eyes," he had said, "that you might know the brutality of his murder." Pulling her forward, he had swept the covering aside to reveal the festering wounds and Philip's awful death mask.

"See the marks on his hands and chest?" he asked, running his fingers over the stiffened corpse. "These he survived. 'Twas the arrow that killed him."

Fighting down nausea, Graeye asked, "Arrow?" She saw no evidence of such a wound.

"Aye, took it in the back," Edward said. In the glowing light his face turned a horrid crimson and purple as he stared into the sightless eyes of his son.

Anxious to withdraw, Graeye touched his sleeve. "Come," she said, "let us speak elsewhere. 'Tis not the place—"

" 'Twas that Balmaine bitch and her brother!" His accusation cut across her words.

Graeye's head snapped back. Balmaine? Was that not the family under which Philip had done his training to become a knight? Aye, she was certain their properties bordered upon those of Medland.

"I fear I do not understand, Father," she said. "The Balmaines are responsible for this?"

He looked up from the body, the hate upon his face so tangible, it gripped a cold hand about her heart.

"Aye, Gilbert Balmaine challenged your brother to a duel, and when Philip bettered him, that wicked sister of his put an arrow through his back."

Graeye gasped. Though her familial ties were indeed strained by the long years of absence, she was appalled that such an injustice had been done her brother.

"Why?" she whispered.

Edward gripped her upper arm. " 'Twas the Balmaine woman's revenge upon Philip for the breaking of his betrothal to her."

Graeye had not known of her brother's betrothal. Despair over the lost years gripped her fiercely. Mayhap things would have been different had her mother lived and Graeye herself had been allowed to grow up at Medland.

"Why would Philip break the betrothal?" she asked, and flinched when Edward's fingers bit deeper into her flesh.

"She was a whore—gave herself to another man only days before she was to wed Philip. He could not have married her after such a betrayal."

Graeye's hands clenched. What evil lurked in a woman's heart that would make her seek such means of revenge? she wondered. "When did he die?"

"Over a fortnight past."

Looking around her father, she glanced at the corpse one last time. "Why has he lain in state for so long?"

"He was returned to me nine days ago over the back of his horse," Edward said, the corners of his mouth collecting a froth of spittle.

"Whence?"

"One of the northern shires—Chesne."

"The north? But what was he—"

"Be silent!" Edward stormed, giving her a bone-jarring shake. "I grow weary of your questions."

Promptly, she closed her mouth.

"The Balmaine is my enemy—ours!" he bellowed. "Do not forget what you have seen here, for we will have our revenge upon them."

"Nay," she protested. "We must forgive, Father, for 'tis not for us to sit in judgment. That is God's place."

"Do not preach at me!" He threw his arm back as if he meant to strike her. "I will have my revenge."

She shrank from him, her gaze fixed on the hand poised above her. Then, suddenly, he released her.

"You will remain the night here," he said. "I would have you pray Philip's soul into heaven."

She shook her head. It was far too much he asked of her—the horrid smell, the decaying corpse. . . . If there was not yet disease in this small chamber, there would be soon. Panic-stricken that Edward might actually force her to remain within, she spun on her heel and ran for the door.

Abruptly, Graeye pulled herself back to the present. She did not need to relive any more of that night to exorcise her memories. There was not much else to them other than endless hours spent in prayer. Locked in the chapel, she had knelt before the altar and prayed for her brother's soul, and for her own deliverance, until dawn when a servant had come to release her. Since then she had not come near this place.

Groan's bark brought her head around. "What have you found?" she asked.

Crouching low, he pushed his paws beneath the kneeler and swatted at something that gave a high-pitched squeal.

"Is it a bird?"

A moment later she had her answer when a bird flew out from beneath the kneeler and swept the chapel, searching for its escape. Excitedly, Groan chased after it, but it was too fast.

It was a falcon—a young one, Graeye saw as she rushed to close the door so it would not escape into the rest of the castle. Had it escaped from the mews?

It took patience and much effort, but between Graeye and Groan chasing it about the room, the falcon finally found the small window and its freedom.

Holding onto the sill, Graeye watched the bird arc and dip its wings in the broad expanse of sky. She smiled and wondered what it would be like to be that bird. To fly free and—

At once she chastised herself for her foolish yearnings. There was nothing she had ever wanted as badly as to come home to Medland and assume her place as lady of the castle. In spite of all the obstacles she had encountered these past weeks, and the fact that she was to wed a man she loathed, she had never known greater fulfillment.

With the abbey forever behind her, her future was assured. That, no one could take away.

Chapter 2

There were to be no more discussions of Graeye's marriage to William Rotwyld. Simply, there would be no wedding.

An air of import surrounded King Henry's knight as he strode into the hall five days later, his armed retinue following close behind to position themselves about the room. Clothed in chain mail, they wore no smiles, nor congenial air, that might mistake them for visitors simply passing through.

Realizing that something serious was afoot, Edward ordered all, except his steward and William, from the hall that he might receive the king's missive in private.

Graeye had not long to wait to learn what news had been brought to her father, for his explosion was heard around the castle. Thinking it time to intercede, she hurried into the hall, stumbling to a halt when she saw the half-dozen knights clamoring to hold her red-faced, bellowing sire from the messenger.

Eyes wide, she searched out William and found him beside the steward, his expression reflecting the other man's. Shock, disbelief, outrage . . .

She moved forward uncertainly, and looked questioningly at the messenger when he turned to face her. "What has happened?" she asked.

His gaze swept her faded bliaut before settling upon her face framed by its concealing wimple. "And who are you?"

"My lord," she said, dipping a curtsy, "I am Lady Graeye."

His eyes narrowed on her. "Sir Royce Saliere," he stiltedly introduced himself. "You are a relation?"

Graeye's eyes flickered to her father before settling once again on the knight. "I am the baron's daughter."

The man looked surprised, but quickly recovered. "No longer baron," he said with a token shrug of regret. "By King Henry's decree all Charwyck lands have been declared forfeit and returned to the sovereignty of the crown."

Edward roared louder, raising his voice against God as he continued his struggle to free himself.

Feeling as if she had just been delivered the mightiest of blows, Graeye shook her head. It could not be true, she told herself. That King Henry would take from the Charwycks that which had been awarded to them nearly a century past was unthinkable. Surely this was some kind of trickery by which another thought to wrest her father's lands from him now that he was without an heir.

"Methinks you lie," she said boldly.

Sir Royce's brows arched high. "Lie?" he repeated.

"Aye, King Henry would not do such a thing. My father is a loyal subject. He—" The parchment thrust into her face halted her torrent of words.

"Can you read?" Sir Royce asked, his tone patronizing.

"Of course I can read," she replied, uncertainty creeping over her as she stared at the document he offered.

When he waved it at her, she took it, her gaze falling immediately on the broken wax seal gracing the outside. Though she had never seen the royal signet, she knew with certainty that what she held had, indeed, come from the king. Heart sinking, she unrolled the parchment and read the first lines, but could go no farther.

"Why?" she croaked, groping for something to hold to, but finding naught. If the Charwyck properties were lost, what was to become of her father, an old man no longer capable of lifting his sword that he might earn his fortune? And what of her? She would not be needed to produce a male heir—thus, of little value. Certainly William would not wed her without benefit of the immense dowry she would bring to their union.

"For offenses committed by your brother, Philip Charwyck," Sir Royce explained as he pried the document from her fingers before she damaged it.

Graeye swayed, but managed to stay on her feet. Taking a deep breath, she looked entreatingly at the man. "I do not understand. What offenses do you speak of?" She stole a glance over her shoulder to where her father had grown quiet.

"Murder, pillaging . . ."

Remembering her brother's disposition, the accusations should not have surprised Graeye, but they did. "Surely you are mistaken," she said, desperation raising her voice unnaturally high. "'Twas my brother who was murdered. Why do you not seek out the perpetrator of that crime?"

Looking bored, the man rolled his eyes back as if he sought guidance from a higher being. "As I have told your father, Philip Charwyck was not murdered. His death is a result of his own deceit."

"What did—"

Sir Royce held up his hand. "I can tell you no more."

"You would take all that belongs to the Charwycks and yet refuse to tell me what, exactly, Philip is accused of having done?"

Sir Royce folded his arms across his chest. "Your fate

rests with Baron Balmaine of Penforke. 'Tis his family the crime was committed against, and King Henry has given the care of these properties to him."

Graeye barely had time to register this last shocking news before her father erupted again. "Curse the Balmaines!" he yelled, renewing his struggles. "With my own sword I will gut that bastard and his whore sister."

His patience worn through, Sir Royce signaled his men to remove Edward.

Rushing forward, Graeye came to her father's defense as best she could. "Nay," she cried, following the knights as they half dragged, half carried Edward across the hall. Her efforts to halt their progress were to no avail, for she was thrust aside each time she stepped into their path. Neither William, nor the steward, were of any help. As if great pillars of earth, they remained unmoving.

Desperate, she hurried back to where Sir Royce stood watching impassively. "Where are they taking my father?" she asked, touching his sleeve. "Surely he has committed no offense."

"He must needs be held whilst he is a danger to others," he said, looking pointedly to where her hand rested on his arm.

She dropped her hand but continued to stare into his hard, unmoving face. "'Tis a great blow he has been dealt," she said. "Not only has the king taken everything he owns, but he has given it into the hands of my father's avowed enemy."

"Lady Graeye," the man began, running a weary hand through his cropped silvery hair, "I do not fault your father for his anger. 'Tis simply a measure of safety I take to ensure Medland passes into Baron Balmaine's hands without contest."

"Then he will be coming soon," she concluded.

"A sennight—no sooner." Finished with her, he turned and walked to where his knights were gathered near the doors.

So many questions whirled about in Graeye's mind, she thought she might go mad, but she knew that pursuing the matter would be useless. Lifting her chin, she turned and looked across at William and the steward.

"All is lost," she said, pushing the words past the painful tightness in her throat.

At their continued silence she left the hall. Without benefit of a mantle to protect her against the lingering chill of morning, she set out to discover her father's whereabouts.

She knew full well the precipice upon which his mind balanced, and was worried for his welfare. Also, she needed to ask him whether she would be allowed to remain at his side to care for him, or if he intended to return her to the service of the Church.

It was no great undertaking to discover where Edward had been taken, for with expressions of concern castlefolk pointed Graeye to the watchtower.

Along her way there, she became increasingly uneasy by the great number of the king's men positioned about the walls. They were alert, ready to stamp out any signs of uprising. That unlikely possibility almost made her smile. Not only was the number of Edward's retainers considerably depleted from Philip's foray to the north, where he had given up his life for a cause as yet unclear to her, but few would be willing to challenge the king's men for their lord. They disliked him so.

At the watchtower a surly knight halted Graeye's progress. "You would do well to return to the donjon, my lady," he said. "No one is allowed to see the prisoner."

"I am his daughter, Lady Graeye," she explained. "I would but see to his needs."

Shaking his head, the man placed his hands upon his hips. "My orders are clear. No one is allowed within."

"I beseech you, let me see him for but a short time. No harm will be done."

He wavered not a notch, though she thought perhaps his eyes softened. "Nay."

Later Graeye would question what drove her to be so bold. Grasping her skirts, she ducked beneath the man's elbow and managed to make it up the flight of steps before encountering the next barrier. The first knight close on her heels, she came to an abrupt halt when faced with the two men who guarded the room where her father was imprisoned. They had heard her advance, for their swords were drawn and trained upon her.

The knight behind needn't have gone to the trouble of seizing hold of her, for she could go no farther. "You—" He snapped his teeth closed on his next words.

Unable to check the tears flooding her eyes, she looked up at him. "Just a moment," she choked. "'Tis all I ask."

The angry color that had flooded his face receded; then, miraculously, he acquiesced. "Very well," he said, a corner of his mouth twitching in a slight smile, "but only that—a moment."

Releasing her, he motioned for the guards to stand away. They resheathed their swords and stepped back, their eyes never leaving her.

After a brief hesitation, during which Graeye was certain he had reconsidered the wisdom of allowing her to see her father, the knight threw back the bolt and opened the door.

Murmuring her gratitude, she stepped past him and entered the frigid room. She had expected to be given privacy with her father, but the man had no intention of allowing that. His great bulk throwing a shadow across the floor, he stood in the doorway as she crossed to where Edward huddled in a corner of the room.

She lowered herself to the floor and waited for her father's acknowledgment. His forehead resting on arms propped upon his knees, he seemed not to notice he was no longer alone.

Her heart swelled with compassion for the pitiful heap he made. True, he had often been unkind to her, had never loved her, had not once inquired as to her welfare at the abbey, but he was her father. He was a man who had lost everything—his son, the grandson who would have become his heir, his home, and now his dignity. Everything gone. Would the remainder of his mind go too?

Her eyes pricking with tears, her throat tightening, Graeye laid her hand to his shoulder. She wanted to embrace him, yet knew she risked much with just this simple gesture. "Father," she said softly.

He did not move.

She spoke again, but still no response. Was he ill?

Moving nearer, she slid an arm around his shoulders. "Father, 'tis I, Graeye."

Lifting his head, Edward stared at her. Then, suddenly, he came to life. "You! 'Twas you who brought this upon me. Aye! Spawn of the devil." Swinging his arm, he landed his hand to her chest, knocking her over.

Her back to the cold floor, Graeye drew a shuddering breath, surprised she was able to do so at all.

"I should have left you with the Church!" Edward roared, lurching upright to stand over her before she could gain her feet. "For this offense I am to be punished to everlasting hell!"

Glancing at the knight, who remained unmoving in the doorway, Graeye slowly rose and stepped back a pace. "I have come to see to your needs," she said, clasping her hands before her.

"My needs!" Edward spat, then thrust his face close to hers. "And what else have you come for?"

She met his stare. "I would also know what is to become of me," she answered truthfully.

He laughed, a loud, raucous noise that died abruptly. "And what do you think your fate should be, daughter?"

"I—I would stay with you."

"Stay with me?" he repeated, mimicking her voice.

"And of what use would you be now that all has been taken?"

"I would care for you. You will need—"

He seized hold of her. "I do not need the devil on my shoulder."

"'Tis not true—"

"Know you that twice your mother bore me sons? Sickly things that lived no more than a few days? Then she bore me you with the devil's mark full upon your face—strong and healthy. And then no more."

This was the first Graeye had heard of it. Never had her mother spoken to her of those children who had come before. It explained so much of her father's treatment of her. But now that she knew, mayhap she could do battle with it—find a way to reach him.

"Nay," he continued, "you will return to the abbey. As the Church has already received your dowry, your place there is secure. *That* Balmaine cannot take from me."

She pulled free from his punishing hands. "I do not wish to return!"

"Think you I care what your preference is?" he ground out, hate coursing from his every pore as he advanced on her again. "You are ungrateful. Many a daughter would vie for the soft life of a nun. But you— 'tis the devil in you that resists. Nay, 'twill be my final offering to God. You will return."

"You need me!" she declared. Deny it he might, but it was true. What would become of an old man alone in a world so changed from what he had previously known? And what of her? She could not simply wander out into the world without a man to protect her.

"Need you? Nay, I needed but your body. Blood of my blood. A vessel for the heir you would have made with William. Now"—he gave a short burst of crackling laughter—"you may either return to the abbey or go back to the devil whence you came. That is the only choice I give you."

His words—the air of hate they drifted upon—cut

deeply. Hope faltering, dread fear in her heart, Graeye backed away.

"And do not let me see you again without your nun's clothing!" he yelled.

She was surprised when she came up against the knight standing in the doorway. Wordlessly, the man drew her outside and slammed the door closed on Edward. There was silence; then a great clamor arose as the old man threw himself against the door, his curses vibrating through the wooden planks.

"My lady," the knight spoke to Graeye's bowed head, "'twould be best if you returned to the donjon now." At her sullen nod he gently took her arm.

She was grateful for the support he lent, for otherwise she would surely not have made it down the steep stairway, so blurred was her vision.

At the bottom she expected him to send her on ahead, but he did not. Instead he led her past the curious stares of the castlefolk and soldiers and did not relinquish his grip until they stood within the hall.

She offered him a brave smile. "My thanks, Sir . . ."

"Abelaard," he said with a sweeping bow.

Her smile grew more certain, but nonetheless remained a thin, tight-lipped line. "If you will wait but a moment," she said, stepping away, "I will gather blankets that you might take them to ensure my father's comfort."

A thick silence followed that had her turning back to face him. Too late she realized it would be beneath the knight's rank to perform such a duty for her.

"My apologies," she murmured. "I will send a servant."

Looking relieved that he didn't have to refuse her, he offered her an uneven smile. "My sister is a nun," he said gruffly. "'Tis not a bad life she has."

Graeye stared at him, watching as he grew uncomfortable with the effects of his poorly timed, though well-meaning, disclosure. "I fear you do not understand, Sir Knight," she said, then turned and left him.

It was difficult to find privacy where she could vent her distraught emotions, and in desperation she returned to the small chapel abovestairs.

Kneeling before the altar, she clasped her hands to her breast and tried to offer up prayer. However, there was simply no room for such devotions. All of her hopes were dashed forever by the coming of the treacherous Baron Balmaine. She drew a shuddering sob, then cried as she'd never cried before—and vowed she would never cry again.

Chapter 3

With all the extra mouths to feed and bodies to bed in a hall that suddenly seemed inadequate, Graeye had had little time throughout the day to dwell on the terrible misfortune that had befallen her father—and the fate awaiting her.

Now, however, as the night deepened and sleep refused to wrest her churning thoughts from her, she found herself reliving each nightmarish detail. She did not allow herself to dwell on the confrontation between her and her father. It simply hurt too much. Instead she fixed upon the events that preceded and followed that encounter.

She recalled the painful conversation with Sir Royce, Sir Abelaard's parting remarks, the flood of emotions that had assailed her in the chapel, and afterward her encounter with William—one that might have gotten out of hand had she not put a quick end to it.

Amid the preparations for the noon meal, she had come face-to-face with the angry knight who had sought no cover in which to deliver his cutting, hateful words.

Without thought, and before the servants, she had struck him across the face with all the strength she could muster. Fortunately, he had been too surprised to retaliate, allowing her to flee the hall and seek safety in the kitchens.

During supper, the tables overflowing with the addition of the king's men, she had spent an uncomfortable hour beneath the watchful gaze of both Sir Michael and William. Afterward the younger knight had twice attempted to corner her, but each time she had successfully evaded him. No good could possibly come of allowing him too near.

Truly, it had been the most difficult day of Graeye's life. But it was the pity that bothered her the most. It shone from the eyes of the castlefolk, and, surprisingly, many of Edward's knights. Even the king's men cast their sympathy upon her.

Pity, though, was not what she needed. She had already wasted far too much time indulging in that useless emotion. What she needed was a plan, one that would make it possible for her to stay at her father's side. Though it seemed all was well and truly lost, after her time in the chapel she had determined she would not abandon her quest to remain free of the Church. She would find a way. But how?

Twisting upon her bench in an attempt to get more comfortable, she winced at the disgruntled rumble that drifted up from beneath her.

Throughout the day Groan had become increasingly testy at the changes in his home. There were too many people, too much commotion, and the air of gloom that hung over all was as tangible as the morsels the dog had been denied due to the shortage of viands. Nevertheless, he had never strayed far from her side— except that one time when William had cornered her.

He rumbled again, but more loudly.

Frowning, Graeye leaned over the side of the bench and searched out the dog's glowing eyes. "Shh," she breathed, reaching out to him.

"Lady Graeye." A man's whispered voice halted her hand midair.

Stifling a scream that would have awakened all in the hall, Graeye pressed herself back on the bench and peered at the still figure that stood less than a foot away.

Was it William come to seek revenge for the offensive slap she'd given him earlier? she wondered, fear mounting. If so, she would gladly awaken all to avoid whatever the wicked man had in mind for her.

"Who goes there?" she whispered, hugging her blanket to her.

Groan rumbled another warning.

Ignoring the dog's threat, the figure bent down and leaned nearer. "Tis I, Sir Michael."

Graeye was relieved, but still alarmed that he would seek her out in the middle of night. "Wh-what do you want?" she asked, easing her hold on the blanket.

"I must needs speak with you."

"We can speak on the morrow," she said, wishing he would leave her be so that she could return to her search for a way out of her dilemma.

"Nay, we must needs speak now."

"Shh," she hissed. "Do not talk so loud. 'Twill awaken the others."

"Then come with me."

She drew back from the hand that attempted to urge her from the bench. "Be gone, Sir Michael. On the morrow will be soon enough for us to talk."

Without further word the young knight slid an arm beneath her and scooped her from the bench. Though Graeye's immediate response was to protest his boldness, she checked the indignant words for fear of awakening the others.

True, she was angered that Michael would be so free with her, but she did not fear him as she did William. Besides, the scrape of claws over the floor told her Groan was close on Michael's heels and had no intention of leaving her to fend for herself should she have misjudged the young knight.

Resigning herself to the conversation Michael was

forcing her to, she grabbed fistfuls of his tunic and held tightly to him as he picked his way over the sleeping bodies and carried her to the stairway.

Though not of a great height or build, Michael proved surprisingly strong, easily negotiating the stairs to the first landing, where a torch flickered. Grimacing at Graeye's undisguised anger, he lowered her to her feet.

"Forgive me, my lady," he apologized.

After adjusting the chin strap of her wimple, Graeye jerked the blanket closed over her shoulders and glared up at him. " 'Tis quite unseemly behavior, Sir Michael," she reprimanded, comforted by the press of Groan's body against her side.

"Aye, but it seemed the only way."

She stared at him a long moment, then sighed. It was, after all, her own fault. Had she but given him the time he had sought that day, all this would have been unnecessary. "Well . . . speak," she said, impatient to return to her solitude.

He shifted his weight from one foot to the other, then back again. "I would have you go away with me," he said in a rush.

Her eyes widened. "What? Go away with you?"

Oddly encouraged by her reaction, he reached out and laid his hand upon her shoulder. "Aye, there is naught for you here—nor for me. As the fourth of five sons, I have not much to offer, but 'tis more than that abbey can give you. Surely you do not wish to return there?"

She leaned back against the wall for support. "Nay, of course not," she breathed. Was this the answer she sought? "But . . . is it marriage you speak of, Sir Michael?"

"I offered once before and you denied me," he said, bitterness creeping into his voice as his hand slipped beneath her chin to tilt her face up to his. "If I offered again, would you do the same?"

She stared into his imploring eyes. "Surely you know

why I denied you," she said, hoping to erase his hurt. When he did not respond, she forged ahead. "Even had I expressed a preference for you, my father would not have agreed. I did not wish blood to be spilled for a lost cause."

"And you thought 'twould be I who fell?"

Apologetically, she shrugged. "I did not know, but 'twas not worth the risk."

"I am not a child unable to defend myself," he reminded her with great indignation. " 'Twould have been William's blood that was spilled, not mine."

"I am sorry," she said, trying to soothe his injured pride.

As if it had never been, his indignation was swept away and replaced with a smile. A moment later his mouth lightly touched hers.

"Will you marry me, sweet Graeye?"

Surprised at the gentleness of that fleeting kiss, she lowered her gaze, her mind setting itself to furious work. The young knight was, by far, a better man than William. And what he offered certainly held more appeal than returning to the abbey and leaving her father behind to fend for himself among his enemies. Edward ...

She looked up at Michael's expectant face. "What of my father?"

"Your father?" he repeated disbelievingly. "Your loyalty is misplaced, Graeye. You owe him no allegiance. Leave it to Baron Balmaine to decide his fate."

Graeye could not do that, leave Edward to the mercy of one of those responsible for Philip's death. He was still her father, and her only living kin.

"His enemy?" She shook her head. "Nay, I cannot desert him."

Michael took hold of her shoulders. "Graeye, can you not see the evil in him? You my family would accept, but Edward?" He shook his head. "I could not ask that of them. Would not ask that of them."

Her hope extinguished, she eased out of his hold. "I understand," she said, "but I cannot leave him to the greater evil of this Balmaine." She offered him a weak smile, then placed one hand on the wall to guide her down the steep steps.

Groan followed, but Michael made no move to detain her. Clearly, his desire for her was not strong enough to change his mind on the subject of Edward.

Grateful to regain her bench, Graeye huddled back against the wall and wondered if she had made a terrible mistake in refusing Michael. After all, her only other option was to return to the abbey. Whether she went with Michael or back to the Church, the result was the same—Edward would be alone to face the cruelty of Baron Balmaine.

Wasn't there some way to save both her father and herself? She must convince Edward that she belonged at his side . . . or make it so it would be impossible for him to force her back to the Church. The idea that followed upon the heels of that thought thoroughly shook the moral foundations upon which her life had been built.

Chastity. The breaking of that vow was unforgivable. Without it she could not be professed a nun. She clasped her arms tightly about herself as her conscience took up a vehement protest. Wanton! Blasphemous! Ungodly!

Time and again she tried to push the wicked idea aside, but it kept returning to her. In fact, it struck her that, had she not been successful in escaping William when he had tried to force himself upon her weeks earlier, there would now be no question regarding the taking of vows. It would be impossible, and Edward would have no choice but to keep her with him.

Nevertheless, she was still a virgin. And how was she to remedy that? As if in answer she saw again Michael's face and the longing in his eyes. He wanted her, but would he be willing to settle for the possession of only her body?

Chapter 4

⸙⸙⸙⸙⸙

Over the next three days Graeye searched for an opportunity to be alone with Sir Michael. Unfortunately, none presented itself, for the man seemed determined to keep his distance.

Desperate, she considered any number of the knights at Medland, but she simply could not bring herself to approach one. What was she to do? She had no experience with seduction. How, exactly, did one go about capturing a man's desire? If she was to succeed, it seemed it would have to be with Michael.

In the late afternoon of the fourth day following the arrival of the king's men, she was faced with the prospect of seeing her reckless plans forever spoiled when Sir Royce ordered her father's release from the watchtower.

Immediately, Edward sought her out and informed her that arrangements had been made to return her to the abbey the following morning. He was calm—emotionless—until she attempted to convince him to allow her to remain with him. Then he had begun to rage so terribly, he probably would have hurt her had Sir Abelaard not interceded.

She frantically searched for Michael, but he was nowhere to be found, and late that evening a thoroughly defeated Graeye slipped out the postern gate, heading for the one place she knew might offer solace—the waterfall.

She had spent many sunny days there with her mother, before an untimely death had taken the one person who had loved Graeye unconditionally.

She was not running away, for life in the Church had become less daunting than the prospect of being on her own in a world she did not know, nor understand. She simply had to see the falls one last time and relive the wonderful memories left there ten years past. And on the morrow she would carry those revived memories with her on the long journey back to Arlecy.

Her mantle flying in the wind, she left the castle walls far behind and entered the woods. She picked her way down the sloping ground, and soon the sweet melody of falling water led her to the glorious white veil that swept from on high and fell to a large pool below.

For the first time in days Graeye smiled as the childhood memories came to her and urged her to venture nearer. Without hesitation she walked to the edge of the uppermost pool, knelt beside, and dipped her fingers into its cool, soothing water. Almost immediately all her worries washed away, making her feel like a carefree child once again.

She tossed off her habit and underclothes and entered the pool. With the stars and moon the only witnesses to her pleasure, she clumsily attempted the strokes her mother had taught her so long ago. They were not graceful, nor efficient, but they allowed her to cross the deepest stretch of the pool without mishap, and to venture into the biting spray of the falls.

She was so caught up in the enjoyment that, had the horse not whinnied loudly, she might not have noticed the intrusion until it was too late.

The past fell away abruptly, and she treaded water as horse and rider drew even with the grassy bank.

Her first instinct was to flee, but fear of discovery

stayed her. Even with the width of the pool separating them, there would be little to deter the man from pursuit if he chose to give chase.

Shivering as the water lapped her bare shoulders, she berated herself for lingering so long. She glanced up at the moon and saw that it had traveled a good distance since she'd first come upon the falls. Exactly how much time had passed, she did not know, but she should have started back to the castle before now.

Praying the dim light of the moon would not reveal her, she pushed through the water to the protection of the long shadows of the bank. There she knelt in the shallows and trained her gaze upon the intruder.

Who was he? she wondered. Was he one of her father's former retainers, someone who had heretofore gone unnoticed? She did not think so, for she would certainly have remembered such a man—even if she'd glimpsed him only from a distance. And neither did she think he was one of the king's men.

Still, it was hard to be certain. All she knew was that he was no wayfarer. Nay, with his fine vest of chain mail and the well-fitting raiments beneath, he was certainly of the nobility. And his mount, a highly prized white destrier, further attested to that.

For a moment it crossed her mind he might be one of the dread Balmaine's men, but she quickly tossed the thought aside. The new lord of Medland was not expected for three days hence. Likely this was a knight-errant passing through.

Curiously fascinated, and secure in the belief she would not be found out, she used the cloak of darkness to scrutinize the man.

Dark of hair and beard, and sitting tall in his saddle, he appeared every bit the gentleman warrior as he looked around. But gentleman or no, with the breadth and certain height of him, he looked to be a formidable opponent. In fact, his strength, born on a wave of something ominous, was a tangible thing that caused a shiver of disquiet to course her spine.

Beneath the water she rubbed her hands briskly over her arms and pondered what it was he exuded. Anger?

When he suddenly dismounted, smoothly swinging himself to the ground, she nearly gave in to the impulse to scramble from the water and flee. Eyes wide, her breathing ragged, she quelled the urge and pressed herself more deeply into the shadows. He would leave soon, she assured herself.

As he walked to the pool's edge, she thought he limped, but could not be certain. It had taken little more than a single stride to carry him to where he now knelt to quench his thirst. Mayhap he was simply in his cups, she surmised as she conjured a vision of her father.

Straightening, the man placed his fists upon his hips and surveyed the pool.

Did he sense her presence? she wondered as she fought down her rising panic. Surely he could not see her; the shadows were too deep.

At last he turned back to his horse, but he did not remount. Instead he took off his belted sword and draped it over the back of the destrier. Then he began to remove his chain mail.

Dear God, the man intended to bare himself! Mouth agape, Graeye stared in disbelief as he drew the armor over his head. She knew she should turn away, should not cast her gaze upon him, but found herself transfixed by a curiosity Mistress Hermana would have severely punished.

Above the sound of the waterfall came the metallic rasp and glitter of thousands of joined rings as the chain mail was carefully laid aside. Next came the tunic and padded undertunic, leaving nothing save the gloss of night upon a broad, tapering back.

Graeye's maidenly senses protested, but then she reminded herself that he had intruded upon her sanctuary unwittingly. He was oblivious to her presence, unaware he shared with another the dark-mantled sky that danced stars upon the tumbling water.

When moments later she was faced with the sight of bare buttocks and sturdy legs, her pulse leaped unexpectedly, a gasp escaping her lips.

She was given no time to comtemplate her wayward reaction, for the intruder instantly swung around, his sword in hand, his stance challenging. With a snort and a toss of its massive head, the great animal echoed its master's disquiet.

Warrior-alert, the man peered at the cloak of darkness where Graeye hid.

Was it possible he could have heard that small sound above the spill of water? she wondered frantically. Were she to flee now, would he give chase in nothing save his swarthy skin?

After an interminable time that had her chest burning from lack of air, the man finally turned back to his destrier. Muttering something unintelligible, he returned the sword to its sheath. However, he belted a dagger about his waist.

Her breath threading its way into her lungs, Graeye sagged with relief. Only then did her eyes confide to her what they had discovered in their journey over the darkly matted chest to the undulating muscles of the man's abdomen.

She would have liked to look away—knew she should—but found herself unable to. Her cheeks warming, she settled her untried gaze upon that dark place between his thighs. Only just, she sealed her lips against the sound that would have been her undoing.

Seemingly unaffected by the chill that had stolen Graeye's breath earlier, the man entered the water.

Would he keep to the lowermost portion of the pool? she wondered. How long would he stay?

Though his great height had been obvious at the outset, she was better able to gauge his measure when he stood at the center of the pool, his head and shoulders above the surface where she had treaded water.

He would stand more than a foot above the crown of her head, she guessed, and wondered at the sensations beginning to curl her insides. As she watched, he dived beneath the surface.

Now. If he stayed under long enough, mayhap she could . . . She shook her head. Nay, she could not risk it.

At his reappearance she was swept with relief. It did not even bear thinking what might have happened had he swum upstream.

Leave, she silently entreated him. He did not accommodate her, seemingly in no hurry to finish with his bathing.

After a time, when it appeared he didn't intend to explore the uppermost portion of the pool, Graeye began to relax. Submerged to her neck, she leaned back against the sloping bank and followed the man's movements. Unbeknown to her, a smile curved her lips. When he turned onto his back, his darkly furred chest glistening in the moonlight, his lower extremities exposed to eyes fascinated by this new wonderment, her smile grew wider.

How little she understood the heat upon her skin, she mused, realizing she was no longer cold. Not so long past she had been eager to don her clothes again. Now every one of the prickly bumps that had sprouted upon her limbs had softened.

Desire? she ventured a guess, then promptly rejected such absurdity. It was simple curiosity to know that which had long been forbidden her. After all, had she not been pledged to the church, she would have wed years ago.

The smile fell from her mouth. And now, too, she would not wed. Never would she lie in a man's arms, nor hear the laughter of the children she might bear him.

Tears gathered in her eyes. Hopeless. Now that she was no longer a pawn upon which to get heirs, she was to be thrown aside once more. On the morrow she would be returned to the abbey to profess herself a nun. Aye, truly hopeless. There was naught she could—

The thought shook Graeye with its force. Aye, she

realized, here was a man she could offer herself to, an unknown who would not worry about her father's wrath.

But would he be willing? she wondered. Uncertain, she raked her teeth across her bottom lip. If he had been too long without a woman, perhaps.

She thought of the mark on her face and grimaced. How easily she had forgotten it. Surely he would reject her if he saw it.

She glanced at the quarter moon. Perhaps he would not notice. . . . Ah, of course he would. Had he not eyes? She shook her head.

Having nearly buried the whole preposterous idea, she suddenly remembered how her father had recently concealed the mark. He had seemed pleased enough.

Lifting her hands, she pulled the sodden mass of her hair over her shoulder and raked it forward, her fingers guiding it down her temple. Nervously, she lingered over the fall of pale strands, smoothing them as she considered, then considered again.

A shuddered breath left her as she finally gave over to the idea. What she planned was evil, but this man had been sent to her for a reason. Surely God would understand.

By the time she had committed herself, the man had gone to stand in the shallows, his back to her.

With a calming breath Graeye forced herself forward, the silt surging between her toes as if to prevent her from committing the wicked act. When the ground fell from beneath her feet, she fanned her arms out and swam closer.

She was still several yards away, her heart pounding furiously, when he spun about, his dagger violently rousing the air.

Searching the darkness for the being he sensed there, his gaze settled upon Graeye where her chin bobbed upon the surface.

"Who goes?" he demanded, even as his expression

turned to disbelief. He blinked as if to dispel an unexpected vision, then leaned forward to see better.

He stood thus with the moonlight upon him, his short hair not simply black, but pitch—so much that the night bestowed a blue cast upon the unruly locks. Though more attractive than Graeye had gleaned from her hiding place, he looked hard and ... dangerous? Aye, his strength lay in the anger she had sensed.

Battling her fear, she raised her gaze and found herself staring into glittering eyes that held no kindness. Nervously, she wondered what color they might be, and if ever they shone with the light of a smile.

She shifted her scrutiny down the formidable length of his body, and easily found that which made him so incredibly different from her. Heat spilling upon her face and neck, she dragged her gaze away—lower to the thick ridge of a scar that started midthigh and curved downward to disappear beneath the water. So it was, indeed, a limp she had witnessed, and not a state of drunkenness. Still, that did not ease her mind, nor lift the great burden of shame from shoulders suddenly unwilling to support the weight.

'Tis the only way, she told herself as her mind urged her to abandon her plan. She must finish what she had begun. Only then would she be free to remain with her father. Assuring herself her hair still hid the mark, she lowered her feet, crouching so only her shoulders and head were visible above the water.

"Who are you?" he demanded.

Not knowing how she should answer, and wary of other questions he might put to her, she chose silence and only shook her head.

His eyes narrowed on her, his jaw clenching as the silence stretched.

Aye, he was dangerous ... too dangerous.

Her resolve began to fray, causing her heart to pound furiously and her breathing to turn shallow. Then something taut and trembling snapped within her.

Nay, she could not do this thing! She took a step

back, but the man lunged for her, closing a hand around her arm and dragging her up the sloping ground to her feet.

A distressed sound tumbled past her lips as she threw out a hand to balance herself. It found the taut muscles of his abdomen, and though the feel of his warm flesh disconcerted her, she did not drop her hand.

"What are you?" he asked, the warmth of his breath reaching her from that great height.

What? The question confounded Graeye so much that she momentarily forgot her state of undress. Drawing a shaky breath, she dropped her head back and looked up at him.

"Perhaps you are a fairy turned woman, come to tempt me with your wiles," he mused.

She saw the softening in his face, the slight curve of the tight corners of his mouth, and felt his bunched muscles ease beneath her palm. The danger was past.

An inexplicable emotion rushed through her, taking with it the fear and shame that had urged her to flight, and replacing it with something that had naught to do with the reason she had sought out this intimacy.

Her wakening senses were patient with her inexperience, gradually yielding to her their discoveries. Her palm tingled where it lay against his chest. He felt splendid. And there was a scent about him. Not perfumed, but of muscle and sinew. She inhaled it, her gaze sliding over him to his burgeoning manhood. She wondered at that—not understanding, yet somehow knowing. Reflexively, she stepped nearer.

When a hand's breadth was all that separated them, she impulsively slid her hand to his shoulder and trailed it down his arm, her fingers finding his own, still clutching the dagger. He did not resist when she uncurled his fingers, allowing the weapon to fall to the water.

In size Graeye felt like a child before this giant, but in all other ways—from the odd, insistent heat coiling up from her depths, to the curious longing to be held in those strong arms—she felt like a woman come of age.

How to explain it? she wondered. Swept by something she did not understand, she breached the last space between them, feeling the force of that strong, male member rise between them.

Was that her breathing? she wondered, hearing a shallow, raspy sound. What was this incredible song singing through her that made her pulse speed? She reached up and touched his face, threading her fingers through his crisp beard as she focused on the mouth hidden there.

Suddenly, she wanted very much to feel those lips upon hers. Daring to hope they would be unlike William's fumblings, or Michael's brotherly peck, she raised herself onto her toes. Still the man was too tall for her. Curling a hand around his neck, she urged his head lower.

Letting go his held breath, he encircled her waist with one arm and pressed her into the hard contours of his body.

A shiver of pleasure rippled up Graeye's spine, causing every part of her roused femininity to tremble. Without surrendering his stare, she met his lips and felt a jolt of light pierce her core as he proceeded to coax the breath from her. She gave it to him.

They were as two who had been without sustenance for a long time—touching, caressing, each searching the other with wild abandonment.

Not until his hand slid up from her breast and slipped through her hair did the magic fall away, cruelly pulling her back to the present.

Gasping, she jerked her head back and lifted a hand to smooth her hair, relieved to find the mark had not come uncovered.

The man straightened, a frown creasing his brow as he reached again to brush her hair aside.

Again she resisted. Raising her hands before her to

ward off further exploration, she locked her gaze with his and shook her head.

Though his frown deepened, he accepted her entreaty with a shrug. He contented himself instead with running his fingers through the length of hair that swept her hips; then he molded the warm, fluid lines of her to him and lowered his mouth back to hers.

Graeye accepted the caress that slid over her lips and then inside, responding as he had shown her only minutes earlier. Though she was inexperienced in such things, she took this new and wondrous discovery to heart and soon forgot the awkwardness driving her responses.

A sound, animallike, erupted from her as his hands slid over the curve of her buttocks and inward to her woman's secret, leaving trails of flame in their wake. Now she knew ... and wanted more.

Heat rising from the forbidden regions of her body, she instinctively began to move against him, her fingers tracing the contours of his body. Quickly, she learned the hard feel of the muscles bunched beneath his skin, and unconsciously committed all to memory.

Aye, here were the desires too long suppressed demanding a release from their bonds. Though she sinned, she could not stop herself.

Through a haze of warring sensations, Graeye realized she was being lifted, her thighs settled about the man's waist. She clung to him, shivering when his lips trailed down her face and lingered at the sensitive place between neck and shoulder.

A sudden, sharp sensation drove up into her, turning her pleasure to pain. Gone was the promise of heaven and the spreading of wings that longed to fly. Here was the pain of woman the nuns had warned of.

"By my troth!" the man exclaimed.

His words did not register in Graeye's protesting mind. Seeking escape, she arched back and thrust her hands to his chest. The tearing pain did not ease, it only burned more. Tears gathering in her eyes, she closed her lids against the dark.

Why would he want to hurt her? she wondered as she attempted to twist out of his hold.

With little effort he clasped her wrists in one hand and pulled her back to him, holding her firmly against his chest and affording her no chance of escape. Then he began to murmur soothing words into her ear.

Slowly, the burning flame up Graeye's center faded and she found herself relaxing, her spine softening until she became slack in his arms. It crossed her mind that if this was what mating was like, it was a wonder women subjected themselves to it at all.

Had he been in as much pain as she? she pondered, then thought better of it. Nay, he would certainly have withdrawn. He had not, and it seemed he had no intention of doing so.

When she felt his renewed movements and the pain, though less intense, returned, she resumed her struggles. Still he did not release her, apparently determined to make her suffer.

"Shh," he breathed, pressing kisses to her moist face. " 'Twill not hurt long. There is pleasure at the end of it."

She wanted to believe him, but he offered no evidence that he spoke the truth. As his thrusts deepened, she continued to squirm, thinking she might find a way down from the discomfort this brutal giant was causing her.

Intent on escape, she did not notice when the pain subsided altogether. She only became aware of the change when the pleasure he had promised arrived—a sweet, drawing ache that grew to a breath-stealing sensation. Full of wonder, she tried to match his movements, her attempts awkward yet satisfying.

How was it something so painful had turned enjoyable in so short a time?

Finally finding the elusive rhythm he set, Graeye joined him, not quite knowing what to expect, but certain there was something beyond this ... that it was not far off. It was building, lifting her ever higher to soar on those gilded wings she aspired to. It bid her find completion.

He gripped her tighter, his large hands molding them into one as his rhythm quickened. Then, as if from afar, she heard his shout and felt his body shudder violently as he gave his liquid heat to her.

And she was plummeting, her own moment of satiation stolen from her.

The man's chest rose and fell heavily, his breath like a wind through her hair as the calm that followed was broken by the tremors of his subsiding passion. Knowing she had missed something important, Graeye leaned away, frowning her question, but he pulled her back to him and pressed her face into the curve of his neck.

"Forgive me," he said. "It has been ... a long time."

Confused, she settled her cheek to his damp skin, warming to the feel of the strong, erratic beat of blood coursing through his veins.

He had certainly exerted himself, she acknowledged. Impulsively, she touched her lips, then the tip of her tongue, to his skin. She liked the taste of him, and unashamedly ventured another.

She did not realize he had moved until he lowered her to the bank, himself atop her. Her back pressed to the moist ground, she watched as he raised himself above her to search her shadowed face.

Immediately, her hand went to the hair covering the mark. To her relief she found it still in place.

The man's raised brows asked the question before his words. "You are not going to tell me who you are?" he said in those deep, resonant tones she found pleasing.

Denying him her voice again, she shook her head. Then, her eyes lighting, she touched a finger to his chest and cocked her head questioningly.

An unexpected lopsided grin transformed his face

into one of humor. With a bob of his eyebrows, he shook his head.

'Tis for the better, Graeye assured herself after a bout of disappointment. For the first time since she had set herself this course, she reminded herself of her objective. It would be best if she did not know his identity, for she would never see him again. Still, such cool logic did not stop her from wishing it could be otherwise.

She did not flinch when he cupped her chin in his palm, his thumb drawing lazy circles over her jaw and twice dipping inward to brush her parted lips. Turning her head, she laid her lips to his palm.

"You are real?" he asked. "Or are you a spirit come to distract me from my labors?"

She smiled, offering naught but a lazy shrug.

Mild irritation at her continued obstinance had his brows drawing together, but he refrained from further coaxing.

"You are beautiful, little one," he said, his voice deepening as he lowered himself to her and tucked her head beneath his chin.

Beautiful? Truly? She recalled the image she had caught in the pool earlier. Aye, she was not unbecoming, but to be told she was beautiful . . .

It warmed her to know he desired her, and she felt a sudden sadness this could not last—that after tonight she would never see him again. Deciding to spend her last minutes cherishing him, she searched out his body again, feathering her fingers over him and thrilling when she felt him tremble at her touch.

Were it possible, she thought she could stay with him forever. Though she was unfamiliar with the notion of love beyond what she had felt for her mother, there was something here she desperately wanted to hold to.

A noise from the wooded area broke through her dreamy consciousness. Immediately, the man raised his head. A moment later his body followed. Moving so swiftly Graeye momentarily lost sight of him, he retrieved his sword.

She wrenched herself from her stupor and stumbled to her feet. There was no cover for her, though, and the person moving through the woods was making good speed. He would be upon them any moment. Frantic, she stepped back into the water.

"Wait," the man called.

Graeye spared him only a glance, then waded farther out. She simply could not be discovered, especially if the person approaching was one of her father's men—or the king's—come to battle the trespasser. There would be time aplenty to feel the old man's wrath, but now she had to escape.

Looking one last time over her shoulder at the man who had become her lover, she was surprised to find him following. Lunging forward, he caught hold of her and pulled her back to him.

She tried to push him away, but he held fast. Desperate, she met his gaze and shook her head, entreating him to release her.

"My lord," a voice called from the trees.

She felt the man's tension dissolve.

" 'Tis but my squire," he explained in that wonderfully thrumming voice. "You need not fear."

Finding no comfort in his words, she again tried to pull free. It was to no avail, for he had no intention of releasing her.

"Joseph," he called, "come no nearer."

The crackling of leaves ceased immediately, and a short-lived quiet fell over the wood. "But, my lord—"

"Remain where you are!" the man commanded, then looked back at Graeye. "Stay with me," he murmured. "I have yet to give you what you gave me."

It was all she could do not to shout at him and demand her release, but she kept her lips sealed and shook her head.

He searched her face a long moment, then, unexpectedly, recaptured her lips with an urgency that vied with his earlier possession of her.

In spite of her body's yearnings, Graeye was too fearful to respond, remaining still beneath his expert ministrations.

When he finally lifted his head, he wore a puzzled expression. "I will release you that you might seek cover," he said, "provided you vow to stay near until I have finished with my man."

Surprised at his stipulation, Graeye paused before setting herself to a course she prayed God would forgive her for. She placed one hand over her rapidly beating heart and nodded, knowing all the while it was a vow she could not keep. She saw doubt in his eyes, but then his hands fell from her.

Fearful that he might change his mind, she wasted no time in crossing the pool to the opposite side. Without a backward glance she boosted herself from the water and hurried to where she had left her clothes. She snatched them up and sprinted for the shelter of trees. There, immersed in the tall shadows, she peered back at the pool and saw that the man stood unmoving.

She would have donned her clothes then, but she had the most peculiar feeling he was every bit as aware of her location as she was of his. Unmindful of the chill that raised the fine hairs along her arms, she turned and ran deeper into the woods, her vow to the man shredded upon the breeze stirring the leaves.

Leading his destrier into the clearing where a temporary camp had been erected for the night, Baron Gilbert Balmaine headed directly for the large glowing fire at its center. There the messenger he sent ahead awaited him.

Immediately, Gilbert's squire, Joseph, appeared at his side and began a recounting of the messenger's call upon the castle.

Joseph was not the person Gilbert wanted to hear

from. Still irritated that the woman had run off, he threw his hand into the air, bringing an immediate halt to his squire's ramblings. Tossing the stallion's reins to the boy, he curtly instructed, "See he is properly fed and watered."

"Aye, my lord, 'twill be done," Joseph assured him, poorly disguising his frustration at his lord's strange mood. Though he did not understand what had brought it on, the baron's displeasure had been immediately evident when Joseph had interrupted his bathing a short while ago.

" 'Tis an undine I have seen," the baron had muttered, referring to those mythical water spirits who it was said could earn a soul by marrying a mortal and bearing his child.

Joseph had not understood then, and he did not understand now. Shrugging, he turned and led the destrier to where the others had been penned for the night.

Gilbert drew a hand through his damp hair, then began kneading the muscles at the back of his neck as he advanced upon the group of men gathered around the fire. The news he awaited was important, yet it seemed less so since his encounter at the bathing pool. The barely controlled anger beneath his calm surface quickened.

She had deceived him. She of the witching mouth and beguiling curves had dismissed her vow to him and disappeared as simply as she had appeared. Damnation, if she was real, he would find her. If not . . .

Ridiculous! Of soft flesh and warm blood she had been. She was no wraith, but a woman.

"I will have me a leman on the morrow," he muttered as a knight disengaged himself from the others and came forward.

"My lord." Sir Lancelyn respectfully inclined his head. "I bring news from the king's man, Sir Royce."

Setting his feet apart, Gilbert crossed his arms over his chest. "And?"

"All is secure. There will be no resistance. On the morrow all of Medland will be given over to you."

Gilbert considered the tidings, then nodded his approval. "What of the old man?"

The knight shrugged. "Naturally, he would fight you for Medland, but he is without recourse. Nearly all his men have deserted his cause. I am told his vassals are eager to pledge themselves to you."

This pleased Gilbert. He had recently set himself the task of ridding the world of all Charwycks. Edward was the last one. With a grunt of discomfort he shifted his weight off his aching right leg. "Then Charwyck will not give me his oath of fealty?" he asked, his sarcasm just below the surface.

"Not likely, my lord."

Shrugging his indifference, though a corner of his mouth turned up, Gilbert began grinding the heel of his palm into his aching thigh. "Good."

The vassal stepped nearer, urgency etched in the grooves and furrows around his mouth and eyes. "My lord, methinks it best you expel this Charwyck from Medland at the first opportunity. He is certain to prove a difficulty."

Gilbert stilled, his brows arching high. This time he smiled fully. "He is of the same bent as Philip?"

"This I do not know, but Sir Royce believes him mad. He raves incessantly with threats against both you and your sister."

A fire leaped to Gilbert's eyes. "He has been detained?"

"Aye, he was." Lancelyn frowned before he continued. "However, this morn Sir Royce allowed him his freedom. Although he does not think the old man much of a threat, he warns he is not to be trusted."

Gilbert shook his head. "He is old and now without an heir. What can he gain from resisting? Even had King Henry not given Medland into my care, 'twould likely return to the crown upon Charwyck's death."

Lancelyn's face lit.

Catching sight of the man's expression, Gilbert raised a questioning brow. "So . . . tell me."

" 'Tis not as thought," Sir Lancelyn said in a rush. "It seems the old man does have another heir—or nearly so."

Gilbert's face mirrored his surprise first, then his anger. "Baseborn?" he demanded.

"Nay, legitimate."

A muscle spasmed in Gilbert's jaw. "I have heard of no other. There was only Philip."

He said the other man's name with such contempt, Lancelyn winced. Well he knew the reason for his lord's hate of the Charwycks. Still, it pained him to see his baron so eaten with that savage, destructive emotion.

Lancelyn shook his head. "Unbeknownst to all, Edward Charwyck has a daughter."

"A daughter?" This puzzled Gilbert. Penforke and Medland were so close, he was certain he would have heard of the existence of another offspring. "Still a child, then?" he concluded.

"Nay." The knight shook his head, his lips twisting wryly. "A woman . . . and a nun, no less." He gave that a moment to sink in, then continued. "The old man brought her from the abbey more than a month past. It seems he intended to wed her to one of his vassals that she might give him a male heir."

"A nun?" Gilbert echoed, then shook his head. "She would break her vows? What manner of woman is she?" He expelled a harsh breath that misted the air. "I would not think the Church would allow it."

Lancelyn's shoulders rose and fell. "This I do not understand, my lord, but 'tis said she bears the mark of the devil clear upon her face. Mayhap the Church was grateful to be rid of her."

"Mark of the devil . . . ," Gilbert repeated. Though it certainly fit with what he knew of that family, he could not bring himself to believe in the absurdity of such a thing. He curled his lips back and dismissingly waved it aside.

"I will see her returned to the abbey at once," he decided. "Providing, of course, the good sisters will accept her back amongst them after such a betrayal."

" 'Twould seem her father is of the same mind, my lord, for he has asked Sir Royce to arrange an escort for her on the morrow."

Gilbert was satisfied with that. "As it should be," he said, suddenly eager to be finished with this particular subject. "Now, let us talk of the state of the demesne. Is it in as poor condition as I have heard?"

Chapter 5

Not until she arose from a sleepless night did Graeye learn of Balmaine's impending arrival. As the news had surely been brought during her venture to the falls yestereve, she had been none the wiser until she caught a snippet of conversation from the servants.

She was stunned. The man wasn't supposed to arrive for days. Dismay followed a moment later with the realization that she had little time in which to confront her father on the sin she had committed. He would have to release her from the obligation of taking the veil. But how would he take the news?

Not until she returned to the hall following matins did the implications of the baron's untimely arrival fully strike her; so directly, in fact, that had there not been a table nearby on which to brace herself, she would have sunk to the floor.

There was only one conclusion to be had. The man she had given herself to had been one of Balmaine's. Inwardly, she recoiled.

Aye, it was true her father would know soon enough, but the humiliation of so many others possibly knowing of her sin nearly brought her to her knees. What could she do?

A spring of hope surged forth as she contemplated the possibility that the man might not recognize her. It had been dark, after all.

She had no time to think further on it, for her father appeared at her side, drunk from a night of heavy drinking. He smelled foul, the horrid odors wafting from his clothes causing her to suppress the breath she had been about to draw.

"Where is your habit?" he demanded, swaying unsteadily. "You dare defy me in this?"

She looked down at her rumpled clothing. As it had seemed sacrilegious to wear her habit now that she had broken the vow of chastity, she had chosen to wear the brown bliaut. "I—"

"You are to return to the abbey this day, and you walk about as if you've time for a hunt! Go dress yourself now before that bastard Balmaine arrives and starts slavering over you."

The confession hovering upon her lips was quickly swallowed when Edward gave her a forceful push toward the stairs.

She nearly protested, then realized that the habit might well serve as a disguise if the man she had so wantonly given herself to was among Balmaine's. He would certainly not expect her to be a nun. Moreover, now was not the time to confront Edward. Soon, though.

Abovestairs, in the small, darkened room where her mother's meager belongings were kept, she threw back the lid of the old chest and dug down to where she had buried the habit earlier that morning. Dragging it out, she grimaced at its sorry state. Having thought never to don it again, she had bunched the whole thing in a ball and secreted it beneath the other clothing.

She shook it out, the corners of her mouth dipping lower when she held it from her and surveyed the damage. Not only was it terribly wrinkled, it wasn't clean.

She chastised herself for having been so careless with it the previous night. She should not have left it on the bank. Forcing her misgivings aside, she hurriedly stripped off the bliaut and returned it to the chest.

With great reluctance she donned each piece of the cumbersome habit, all the while mumbling prayers of contrition for daring to clothe herself as a bride of Jesus. Nevermore.

When the wimple was in place, she experienced the most awful feeling that she had sealed her fate. Ridiculous, she chided herself. Edward would have to let her remain with him. With that thought she descended to the hall.

The room was empty when she stepped from the stairs, all thought of the morning meal put aside for the time being.

Obviously, the decision had been made to await the baron's arrival, Graeye concluded with sudden resentment. Her brow knit, she hurried across the rush-covered floor and stepped out into the morning air. Everywhere the king's men and Edward's former retainers bustled about in readiness for the arrival of the new baron of Medland.

But where was Edward? she wondered. Had Sir Royce imprisoned him again now that Balmaine's arrival was imminent?

Her father had such an obvious presence that within moments she knew he was not in the inner bailey. Aye, the watchtower was where she would find him. Lifting her skirts, she hurried down the steps and broke into a half run to overtake those surging toward the outer bailey. Though she pretended not to notice the curious stares that followed her, she was uncomfortably aware of them.

Flushed, Graeye crossed the drawbridge to the outer bailey just as a colorful procession of armored and mounted men passed beneath the portcullis. The sight brought her to an abrupt halt.

Balmaine had arrived.

Panic rushing through her, Graeye lowered her head and slipped among the throng of castlefolk who had gathered to greet their new lord. Their voices were loud and raucous as each clamored to view the impressive spectacle. Not until she had found adequate cover, the stark white of her habit hidden amid the dull colors of the peasants, did Graeye dare venture another look.

She grimaced. Though she had managed to make herself less obvious pressed close to the others, because of her short stature she was forced to stand on tiptoe to catch the barest glimpse of the retinue as they surged within the castle's walls. Jostled from side to side, she unthinkingly took hold of a nearby arm and steadied herself. Having gained a small vantage, she scanned the mounted knights in search of a dark-headed, bearded man.

With each elimination she was swept with relief. They were all either too short, their hair too long or straight, or their faces too soft.

"Milady." The tall woman beside Graeye lightly touched her shoulder.

Graeye recognized her as one of the serving wenches from the hall, and was embarrassed to discover it was her arm she clutched. She removed her hand.

"I am sorry," she muttered, and started to turn her attention back to the riders.

"Nay, milady, I do not mind," the woman said. "I only thought to point out the baron to you."

Odd, Graeye thought. She had been too intent upon discovering whether or not her lover was among his men even to seek him out. Flushing crimson, she thanked the woman, took her proffered arm again, and craned her neck to look where the servant pointed.

Her gaze settled upon the great white destrier that stepped to the inner drawbridge before the others, proclaiming by that to be Balmaine's mount. Ice poured into Graeye's veins as she stared wide-eyed at the animal. With its purity of white, it was a rare horse. In fact, she had only ever seen one so untouched with any other color but white.

With dread, she forced her stricken eyes over long, darkly clad legs, a vivid red-and-gold tunic, and up a bearded face to familiar eyes that were staring straight at her.

'Twas he!

Time yawned between them. For those long, torturous moments, it was as if the whole world had paused in its toils to take note of the occasion.

With a muffled cry of distress Graeye tore her eyes free, breaking the thread of recognition.

Landing heavily on her heels, she stumbled backward and collided with the man behind. He steadied her, then loudly exclaimed when she trod upon his feet in her haste to push past him. Intent upon escape, she barely noticed the offense, though she was all too aware of the commotion that followed her slow progress through the crowd of people. As a result she trod upon many more toes in her reckless bid for freedom.

Frightened, she did not spare even a glimpse behind, though she was certain he followed. An opening ahead spurred her on, though she did not know where she was going—did not even consider her destination. She knew only that she had to find a haven.

When she at last broke free of the crowd, the destrier materialized before her, his huge eyes pinning her with their fire. A murmur of interest arose from the people as they directed their attention to this odd turn of events.

A hand to her pounding heart, Graeye jumped back from the menacing beast and nearly collided with someone behind her. She managed to keep her feet beneath her and ventured a glance at the rider. The contemptuous look he swept her with spoke more than words could ever begin to.

Cornered, the quarry of the black-hearted cur who was responsible for her brother's death, Graeye broke the stare and looked around anxiously for an avenue of escape. Beyond, the community chapel stood waiting, and with no more thought she skirted the horse and ran to the building on legs that threatened to give way beneath her.

She mounted the steps two at a time and slipped inside. Pushing the door firmly closed behind her, she leaned back against it as she attempted to regain her breath. Moments later she resolutely pushed herself off and made for the altar.

The sudden appearance of the chaplain directly in her path brought her to a standstill. "F-father," she stammered, then lowered her gaze to her tightly clasped hands.

"What is it, my child?" he asked, his voice proclaiming his usual lack of interest in the members of his flock. "Something is amiss?"

She looked up at him, then quickly away. "I must needs pray," she said, then stepped past him to the altar. She had barely settled herself upon the kneeler and clasped her hands before her when the door of the chapel was thrown wide. It crashed against the wall and issued in a swell of light that rarely knew the darkened interior of the chapel.

Bowing her head, Graeye attempted to block the sound of boots upon the floor with an offering of fervent prayer.

Still, the harsh voice that burst upon the chapel made her start violently. "Out!" the baron commanded the chaplain.

Shuddering, Graeye fingered the knots of her leather girdle, offering a prayer for each that slid through her fingers.

She heard the chaplain sputter incoherently for a moment before falling silent. Though their exchange was unspoken, she knew something had transpired between the two men. A moment later there was a shuffling of feet followed by the door closing once again, taking with it the light and returning the sanctuary to its normal gloom.

Graeye did not falter in her prayers, thinking that by some miracle she might yet find her escape from the inevitable. Mayhap the floor would fall from beneath her knees, or the ceiling yawn open to raise her up and away. . . .

Gilbert Balmaine's presence became a tangible thing as the minutes dragged by. She prayed him away, but his presence persisted. She prayed it was a terrible dream she found herself in, but knew she was fully awake. She prayed herself to another time and place, but found she was still in the chapel upon opening her eyes. In the end there was naught for her except to brave the encounter and have done with it.

Crossing herself, she slowly rose from the kneeler, then turned to face the one responsible for her brother's demise, and to whom she had unknowingly given herself the previous night. The Baron Balmaine.

Legs spread wide, arms crossed over his broad chest, he stood in the center aisle that divided the benches into left and right, presenting a formidable adversary. His partially shadowed countenance hard and expressionless, he slowly drew his gaze from her face and down her disheveled habit.

Graeye forced herself to remain motionless. Still, her insides were churning with a fear she was having far too much difficulty keeping hidden. Her heart beat a wild, frantic tattoo in her chest that made it difficult to draw a full breath.

When at last Balmaine's eyes returned to hers, looking as if they could pierce her straight through, she felt thoroughly degraded. There was no mercy there—not a hint of tenderness for the night now long past.

This, she realized, was not the man who had loved her yestereve, though his likeness was none other's. This was an angry man, a man who looked ready to tear her limb from limb rather than make love to her again. A coldness thrust itself upon her as she waited to hear the deprecating words she knew would come.

As if part of his design to disgrace her, Balmaine allowed the awkward silence to drag out for interminable minutes, until Graeye had clenched her teeth so tightly, her head pounded.

Perhaps he was uncertain as to her identity? She toyed with the far-fetched possibility, but found no consolation in it. Nay, he had placed her, otherwise he would not have pursued her.

"'Tis obvious," he said at last, his voice deep and clear in the silence of the chapel, "you are not accustomed to keeping your vows, Sister—sacred or otherwise."

His words jolted her. Truly, he must see her in the very worst of lights. She had offered her body to him, then made a vow she'd had no intention of keeping. And today she stood before him clothed in the raiments of a nun.

He stepped forward, his limp slight but noticeable.

Graeye mentally armed herself for what was to come. She stiffened her spine, straightened her shoulders, lifted her chin, and instructed herself that she was not to cower.

When Balmaine stood but an arm's length away, he halted. His hands fisted upon his hips, he looked down that long, straight nose of his.

Graeye swallowed hard on the lump of anxiety lodged in her throat as she raised her eyes to brave the wintry stare so far above her. His face no longer shadowed, she was taken aback as she met the most amazingly blue eyes. In the darkness of the night they had disguised themselves as being anything but this vivid hue. Never before had she seen eyes that color.

"By what name are you called, daughter of Edward Charwyck, faithless bride of Christ?" he asked, his upper lip curling.

Graeye pulled herself back to the present. Her mouth having gone suddenly dry, it was some moments before she was able to answer him. "I am—"

"Ah. So you can speak, after all."

Yet another mark against her already maligned character. Feeling a flush of color steal up her neck to inflame her face, she nodded. "I am Lady Graeye Charwyck," she said, feeling her voice was far too husky. Except for a barely perceptible narrowing of his eyes, the baron seemed not to notice. "But I am not—"

"Graeye." He spoke over her words, then rolled the name upon his tongue a second time. "Appropriate," he pronounced with an inclination of his head. "And what is your name in religion, Sister?"

She shook her head, taking a step backward when he moved nearer. Immediately, she chastised herself for the retreat, but could not check the impulse to take another step away from this daunting person. As she did so, it crossed her mind that she was forever running away from those who threatened her. She hated herself for it. Still, as it was the only comfort she knew, she gave over to shielding herself, throwing a hand out before her in hopes of warding off his advance.

"I am not of the sisterhood," she said.

Her words stopped him. His long shadow falling over her, he searched her pale face before commenting on her claim.

"Naturally, I spoke literally when I afforded you the title of Sister," he snapped. "I was not speaking of your genuine disposition. Do we not both know what that is?"

Her eyebrows flew high, skimming the crisp head band at her forehead. She tried again to clarify the misunderstanding. "I am not a nun."

"Certainly not after last night." He took another step forward, and his long, hard leg brushed her skirts.

Dismayed, Graeye found she could retreat no farther from his menace, for the kneeler was against the backs of her calves. "Nay, you do not understand," she said, her neck strained by the angle she had to hold her head to look up at him. "I do not play with words. I speak true when I say I am not a nun. I have not yet made my profession."

When his hands suddenly descended to her shoulders, she nearly shrieked. Grappling with a fear that threatened to shatter her, she dropped her head and stared sightlessly at the bare space between them.

He gave her a brusque shake, his fingers biting cruelly into her—hands so different from the ones that had caressed her in the pool.

One of those hands pulled her chin up, forcing her to look into his hardened face. "If you are not a nun," he ground out, "then why do you dress as one?"

Again she was made aware of how angry he was. Not only the planes of his face evidenced this ominous emotion, but also the tautness of his body where it brushed against hers.

'I am ...' " Her words trailed off as she gave herself a mental shake. Muddling through the words in her mind, she found it difficult to formulate a coherent explanation with him so near. This strange mixture of fear and desire confounded her.

"I was a novice," she managed after a lengthy struggle. " 'Tis my bridal habit I wear." She glanced down at the voluminous folds of material, then back up at him. "I was to have been professed the day my father sent for me."

He looked incredulous. " 'Tis true you have not taken your vows?"

"Aye, 'tis what I have said."

With a bark of laughter the baron released her and swung away. " 'Tis a great burden you have lifted from me," he said, moving to the front bench and dropping down upon it. He stretched his legs out before him and placed both hands behind his head, looking every bit as if he meant to settle himself in for a time.

"For this I thank you, Lady Graeye. Now I may rest a bit easier." His gaze swept the length of her before piercing her once again. "I am certain that if there is a God, he would not have been kindly disposed toward my taking the virginity of his son's bride."

Astonished by his nonchalant words, Graeye took a

step forward. "If there is a God?" she repeated. "Surely you speak heresy."

His mouth lifting in a sardonic smile, he set himself to kneading his thigh. "Heresy?" He shrugged. "I merely question His existence. Do you believe in Him?"

Graeye's fear was suddenly displaced by an indignation so strong, she found herself stepping quickly from the altar to stand before the blasphemous man. "Of course I believe in God!"

The baron's dark eyebrows arced in mock distress. "And I thought I had found myself one of kindred spirit. Tell me." He leaned forward. "Is your sexual proclivity typical of all members of the clergy? For if 'tis, then I vow to question God's existence no longer. I will simply deny it."

The anger that had given her strength for those few moments drained from her, leaving her despondent. He was bent on punishing her. She was horrified to feel the sharp prick of tears in her eyes.

He was not moved.

"If . . ." Her voice cracked terribly, and she paused to take herself firmly in hand. "As you obviously refer to yestereve," she continued, looking anywhere but at him, "I would have you know that what I did was done with the full intention of refusing to take the veil."

"Truly?" He cocked his head and regarded her trembling mouth. "Then you wear the habit today simply for the privilege it affords you?"

She felt her anger spark again, but was not quick enough to fan it to life. Somewhere she found the courage to meet his gaze. "Nay," she said, crossing her arms over her chest and attempting to rub warmth back into them. "Only by my father's order have I donned it. He does not yet know of my sin."

She was completely unprepared for what happened next, though she caught the glimmer of it in the baron's eyes the moment before his hand shot out and caught her habit. Yanking hard, he tumbled her across his lap.

"And when did you think you would tell your father you no longer qualified to become a nun?" he demanded as she struggled to emerge from the excess material of the habit. "Or perhaps he does know of your sin—even condoned it as a means of entrapping me. Was it he who sent you?"

Graeye went perfectly still, his words like a slap across the face. He truly believed that she and Edward had conspired to entrap him by the giving of her virginity to him? That she would whore her body in hopes of gaining concessions? Nay, she wanted naught from this man!

Thrusting aside the veil that had fallen across her face, she glared up at her assailant. "Release me!" she demanded, suppressing the temptation to drag her nails across his face.

Smirking, he forced her into a sitting position upon his lap. "What did you hope to gain by seducing me?"

She threw her hands against his chest and tried to push off him, but for all her efforts, he only gripped her tighter and twisted her about so she faced him. Struck by how attractive he appeared even with that mask of hate firmly upon his face, Graeye ignored how terribly askew her wimple had gone.

"Did you hope to force me to marriage?" he continued, his warm breath fanning her lips. "Is Medland so important you would sell your body for it—perhaps even your soul?"

So that was what he thought! Rage of a kind she had never before experienced flooded through her, suffusing her entire body with heat.

"Nay," she loudly denied, straining against arms that were like steel bands around her. "Never would I marry one such as yourself. Had I known who you were when you came upon my sanctuary, I never would have given myself to you!"

He appeared amused by her outburst. "And I am to

believe you?" He shook his head. " 'Twould seem more likely 'twas you who came upon me and decided to take advantage of the situation."

Further angered by his conclusion, and her inability to free herself from this lover-turned-enemy, Graeye lifted her fists and struck his chest with all her strength. He allowed her to vent her rage, all the while smirking at the ineffectual blows dealt him by one so small.

It was not long before she realized she had little chance of making any dents in him. She had, however, gained a measure of control over the powerful anger that had so suddenly come upon her. Stilling, she plunged her throbbing hands into her lap and stared into his cold eyes.

"You are wrong about my intentions." She attempted to speak evenly, grasping at a calm she did not feel. Whether or not he chose to believe her, she decided he must know the truth.

"By giving myself to you I forever renounced the possibility of becoming a nun. I did not do it that I might capture a husband." She blinked, then settled her eyes to his once again. "I did it so that I would not be forced to take vows I did not wish to. That I might remain at my father's side and help his people—"

"My people," he harshly corrected her.

Aye, they were his now. She nodded. "Their needs are great, their fields—"

"Think you I cannot see to their needs?"

Would he? This man who had shown no mercy to her brother?

"Even if you speak the truth," he continued, "and I was fool enough to believe you, then you would be little better having used me to achieve that goal."

" 'Tis true," she admitted, "and I have repented for having done such a thing, but I cannot change what has gone before." She looked at her clasped hands. "I did not wish to return to the abbey."

"Forgive me if I do not believe you," he said, his eyes probing her face, reminding her of the mark beneath the wimple. "I have heard that life among the clergy is far preferred over the toil of everyday life ... even if it be in the comfort of a castle."

She shook her head. "The abbey is where I have lived since the age of seven," she said, her gaze wavering beneath his harsh stare. "In all those years I knew little but unhappiness within its walls. Mayhap for others 'tis desirous, but for me it was not enviable." Self-consciously, she lifted a hand to smooth the linen about her face.

Immediately, the baron intercepted the movement, pushing her hand away. "How touching your tale," he sneered, then reached up and fingered the chin strap of her wimple.

"Nay," she protested, thinking he intended to snatch it from her. In a poor attempt to evade him she jerked her head back, but his hand came around the nape of her neck and pulled her face near again.

"I was told Charwyck's daughter bore the mark of the devil," he said, his mouth near hers, his thumb stroking her jaw. "Is it this you hid from me yester-eve?"

She swallowed, then nodded.

"Show me." He withdrew his hand and leaned back, his eyes daring her to take advantage of the uncertain escape he afforded her.

At first Graeye was too surprised to do anything but stare dumbly at him. Why didn't he simply do it himself? she wondered. Was it consideration, or merely an attempt to humiliate her further?

Reluctantly, she complied. Gripping the pieces of linen tightly in her fist, she raised her gaze back to his, waiting for the response she was certain would follow.

"Clearer and clearer," he murmured, ignoring her distress as his gaze settled near her left brow. "'Twas a game I thought you played last night. I should have guessed. . . ." He shifted his attention back to her light-eyed stare.

"Necessary," she breathed, ardently wishing she

might be delivered from this heart-rending confrontation. She bowed her head again, her silken curtain of hair falling between them.

"Then you misjudged me," he said so softly, his words started her heart hammering.

Her head snapped up, and for a moment she was allowed a glimpse of that other elusive man she had treasured. And then he was gone.

Smoothly, he slid back into the one she now feared. "You see," he said, his lips curling as he fingered the golden strands of hair pooled upon his thigh, "I have as much belief in the devil as I do God. Nay, perhaps more." He reached up and ran rough fingertips over the faint stain.

Graeye did not flinch, though her heart plummeted further with this new intrusion.

"Still," he said with a weary shrug, "after your deception, I daresay there might well be something to this. " 'Twould seem—"

"Enough!" The anguished cry wrenched itself from her throat. All her life she had been looked upon with suspicion, but now, with her world crashing down around her, she simply could take no more accusations—and most especially from this man ... a man to whom she had given her most precious possession.

Driven by renewed anger, she was unable to check the reckless impulse to wipe the derision from his face. She raised her arm, and a moment later was amazed at the ease with which she landed her palm to his face. With the exception of William, never before had she struck another.

"I am but a human being cursed to bear a mark set upon my face—not by the devil, but by God." In her tirade she paid no heed to the spreading red left by her hand, nor the sparkle of fury that leaped to Balmaine's eyes.

"'Tis a mark of birth, naught else," she continued.

"You have nothing to fear from me that you would not fear from another."

"So the little one has claws, eh?" He made the observation between clenched teeth. "'Tis as I thought."

One moment Graeye was upright, face-to-face with this hard, angry man, and the next she was on her back, that same face above hers as those spectacular orbs bored into her.

"Had I the time or inclination," he said, "I might be tempted to tame that terrible temper of yours. But as I've neither, you will have to content yourself with this."

Temper? But she didn't— Graeye had no time to ponder his estimation of her nature before she felt his mouth on hers. The thought to resist never entered her mind.

When he urged her to open to him, she parted her lips with a sigh and took him inside. Slowly, his tongue began an exploration of the sensitive places within— places he knew better than she.

Turning away from the insistent voices that urged her to exercise caution, she welcomed the invasion and recklessly wound her arms around him, pressing herself to his hard curves. When his hand slid between them to stroke that place below her belly, she arched against it.

Then, as abruptly as it had begun, it was over, and she was left to stare up at the man who had so effortlessly disengaged himself from her.

In the blink of an eye he had turned from passionate lover to cold and distant adversary. How was it he had such control over his emotions when she had none? Was she too long suppressed?

"I may have fallen prey to your wiles last eventide," he said, smoothing his hands down his tunic. "But I assure you I have no intention of paying the price you would ask for such an unfortunate tryst. Your scheme has failed, Lady Graeye."

To gather her wits about her after such a thorough attack upon her traitorous senses was not an easy thing, but the impact of his words made it less difficult than it would otherwise have been. Doing her utmost to put behind what had just occurred, she lifted herself from the bench and stood before him.

"You err," she said in a terribly small voice that made her wince. Drawing a deep breath, she delivered her next words with more assurance. "There is naught I want from you that you have not already given."

His eyes narrowed. "And what do you think you have stolen from me?"

She lifted her chin a notch, refusing to be drawn into a futile argument as to whether she had stolen or been given his caresses.

"Though you do not believe me," she said, "I tell you true that I did not know who you were until this morn. 'Twas freedom from the Church I hoped to gain, not a husband—that is what you gave me."

Nostrils flaring, Balmaine gave a short bark of laughter. "Be assured, Lady Graeye," he said as he adjusted his sword on its belt, "you will return to the abbey. Though you are no longer pure enough to become a nun, there will be a place for you there at the convent. You will go ... even if I have to drag you there myself."

The convent ... She took a step nearer him. "'Tis not your decision whether—"

His hand sliced impatiently through the air. "Ultimately, *everything* that has anything to do with Medland is under my control. You had best accept it and resign yourself to entering the convent."

Her heart began to hammer against her ribs. Was what he said true? Could he, in fact, usurp her father's rights over her? If so, since he was determined to return her to Arlecy, all would have been for naught. Biting her lip, she bowed her head and focused upon the hilt of his sword.

"Then I would ask you to reconsider, Baron Balmaine, and allow me to remain with my father. He is not well and in need of someone—"

"The decision has been made," he interrupted again, then turned on his heel and strode away.

Even if Graeye could have contained the anger flaring through her, she would not have. There was nothing left to lose. "You have a rather nasty penchant for rudely interrupting when one is trying to speak," she snapped. "'Tis something you really ought to work at correcting."

Seething, she stared at his back, willing him to turn again.

He did not disappoint her, returning to tower over her and looking every bit the barbarian. "In future, if you have anything to say to me, Lady Graeye, I would prefer you address my face rather than my back. Do you understand?"

Though she knew he could easily crush her between his hands if he so desired—and at that moment he certainly looked tempted to—Graeye managed to quell the instinct to cower. After all, considering the fate that awaited her, it hardly mattered what he might do. She gathered the last shreds of her courage about her and drew herself up, utilizing every hair's breadth of height she had.

"In future, you say?" She gave a short, bitter laugh. "As we have no future together, Baron, 'tis an entirely absurd request. Or should I say 'order'?"

His lids snapped down to narrow slits, a vein in his forehead leaping to life. "Sheathe your claws, little cat," he hissed, his clenched fists testament to the control he was exercising. "The day is still young and we have games yet to play."

Then he was walking away again, leaving her to stare after him with a face turned fearful.

Chapter 6

It was midday before Graeye finally summoned enough courage to leave the chapel. Stepping out into the gloom of a day shot through with heavy clouds, she saw that the castlefolk had resumed the labors she had set them to weeks ago. She was grateful for this small mercy, but still felt a multitude of eyes turn upon her.

Aye, they were curious as to their new baron's interest in her—something he could not have made more clear by his following her to the chapel. It must have caused a great commotion . . . and a good deal of speculation. Fearing the worst of their hastily drawn conclusions, Graeye told herself she didn't care what any of them thought, but she was only lying to herself.

At least now she had a plan—or the beginnings thereof, she reassured herself as she determinedly put one foot before the other. It had not been easy formulating it, but she had used her time of prayer to ask for guidance, and the idea had slowly come to her. Though not the best solution, it seemed the only one available to her.

With firm resolve she smoothed her wimple and tossed her chin high. She crossed to the watchtower,

certain she would find Sir Abelaard nearby. If anyone
knew where her father was, she was confident it would
be the king's man. He had been given the responsibility
of making certain Edward did not cause further trouble. In fact, if her suspicions proved correct, he had
likely seen the old baron locked up for Balmaine's arrival.

So many new faces, she thought of those she passed.
It appeared Gilbert Balmaine had brought a great
number with him, likely having anticipated meeting
with resistance. It must have greatly amused him to
simply ride in and have the castle handed over to him
without so much as a scrap of opposition. But, of
course, the king's men had made the road smooth for
him.

To her relief Graeye did, indeed, find Sir Abelaard.
He was just inside the watchtower, speaking with another knight who displayed the colors of Balmaine.

"Lady Graeye," he said, disengaging himself from his
conversation and walking over to her. "You are looking
for your father?"

"Aye. He is above?"

"Nay. Baron Balmaine sent for him a short while
ago. He has been taken to the hall."

Already? Graeye had not thought the man would
have turned his attention to Edward so soon. What did
he intend?

"Know you what is to become of my father?" she
asked.

The knight seemed at a loss for words, his brow furrowing as he considered her silent appeal for reassurance. Grimacing, he glanced back, sending Balmaine's
man a questioning look.

The other knight stepped forward. "Lady Graeye, I
am Sir Lancelyn," he said, reaching to take her hand.

Graeye took a step backward, firmly clasping both
hands at her waist.

Her action raised an eyebrow, but otherwise elicited
no response of the kind she would have expected after

such a snub. With a hint of a smile the man drew himself fully upright. "The baron is a fair man, my lady. I am certain he will deal justly with your father."

"My father has done nothing wrong."

He shrugged. " 'Tis up to the baron to determine that."

Frustrated, Graeye swung around.

"My lady," Sir Lancelyn said, "if the hall is your destination, 'tis not likely you will be received within until the baron has concluded his business."

She turned to face him again, but he was so near she had to jump back to see him better. Why was it, she wondered, there was no one she could speak to without straining her neck? "And when will that be?" she asked tartly.

"I fear I cannot say for certain, perhaps many hours yet."

Lips pursed, she turned and left the watchtower, surprised when she was not followed.

A detachment of men-at-arms stood in the open doorway of the donjon, their backs to her. However, so engrossed were they with the goings-on in the hall, none paid any heed to her approach.

From within she recognized the baron's deep voice. She cringed, but refused herself the luxury of retreat. Slipping unnoticed past the men, she entered the hall, which had been set fully to light with torches. Only the deepest corners knew any shadows. She slipped into those shadows, vainly trying to catch a glimpse through the wall of people to discover what transpired beyond.

Balmaine stopped speaking, and a long silence followed that she did not understand. Then Balmaine's voice again swelled around the hall. "Sir Edward Charwyck, will you be the first to give me your oath of fealty?"

Graeye's eyes flew wide. Never would her father make such a pledge. Pushing between two men, she wedged herself a small space. Surprised by her unexpected appearance, they stared down at her, then exchanged looks that she took no time to decipher.

Before the raised dais at the far end of the hall, Edward stood before Gilbert Balmaine. What would happen when he refused? she wondered, her eyes straying to where her father's former retainers waited patiently to pledge themselves to their new lord. Aye, she acknowledged with a rueful twist of her lips, they were eager to take their turns—including her formerly betrothed, William Rotwyld.

The much-awaited reply finally came. "I would sooner die before pledging myself to my son's murderer!" Edward's gravelly voice echoed around the room.

"I have told you, old man—" Balmaine began, but his words died a quick death.

The scene before Graeye distorted as she watched her father rush forward brandishing a long, ugly dagger. She could only stare wordlessly, her mouth agape, as the seconds flew past.

Though he had not the time to evade the attack, Balmaine did have the presence of mind to sidestep, reaching for his sword as he did so. Edward missed his target—Balmaine's heart—but Balmaine took the blade in his shoulder.

With a deafening roar Balmaine threw the man away from him, sending him sprawling upon his back. Then he tore the dagger free of the wound and sent it skittering across the floor.

Hands clasped to her mouth, Graeye fought to regain her wits that she might aid her father, but her feet were leaden and unwilling to carry her.

As the baron's knights rushed to his aid, their anger shouted loudly about the room, Balmaine moved forward with the predatory stealth of a cat and came to stand over Edward, where he lay winded. Muscles bunched, he placed a booted foot upon the old man's chest, lowered the point of his sword to Edward's neck, and motioned his men to stand away.

"I now see from whom Philip learned his treachery," he growled, his face contorted with rage.

Somehow Graeye managed to put one foot before the other and step toward the center of the hall where the two adversaries faced each other.

The baron swung his sword high.

"Do not!" she croaked as the weapon began its slicing journey down. Too late.

Covering her eyes to block the sight of the rushes running with her father's blood, she sank to her knees and buried her face in her skirts.

Silence fell over the occupants of the hall, broken only by the baron's raging a moment later. "What is *she* doing here?" Gilbert bellowed.

No answer was forthcoming, and with another string of invectives, he strode toward the silent form heaped upon the floor. Behind him his men rushed forward to take custody of Edward.

As Gilbert neared Graeye, his interest focused on her to the extent it blocked all sight and sound of the stirrings around him. He was more angry than he'd known in recent times—angrier than the moment he had first understood her treachery.

Had it not been for the pleading of that husky little voice, he would have had done with the Charwycks forever. The father dead with just cause, and the daughter returned to live out her miserable days at the abbey.

Aye, he had known the old baron would not pledge himself, had even expected an attempt upon his life. That Edward Charwyck had not deviated from this projected course had proved convenient . . . and then this woman had laid siege to his plans.

By voice alone she had denied him the drawing of his enemy's blood, causing him to pull up just as his sword had neared its destination. It had spared the old man's life. Thus the curses Gilbert hurled were not only against the Charwycks, but also against himself.

He returned his sword to its scabbard and pressed a hand to his shoulder to staunch the flow of blood, then leaned down to take hold of Graeye's arm. Before he could lay a hand to her, a large, mangy dog bounded forward and placed itself before the lady. Fangs bared, a growl loosed from its throat, its sparse coat standing on end, it thrust its great head forward.

Straightening, Gilbert eyed the animal and lifted his hand to cover the hilt of the dagger at his waist. The dog snarled louder, but maintained its stance.

A movement beyond caught Gilbert's attention. Shifting his gaze, he saw that one of his knights had removed his own dagger and was drawing his arm back in readiness to hurl it. Gilbert caught his eye and gave an abrupt shake of his head.

With great reluctance the man lowered his arm.

"Lady Graeye," Gilbert called to her, making no attempt to disguise his irritation, "you will stand—now."

Lifting her face from her arms, she stared up at him with vast gray eyes that shook him to the core. It was unsettling that she could have such an effect upon him after what he had discovered of her true character. Indeed, it sickened him, the influence of his baser needs.

Without surrendering his stare she reached a hand to the dog and, holding to its fur, raised herself.

Though her eyes were bright, Gilbert saw no tears upon her face. He wondered at that, for he had expected her to be hysterical. What was the relationship between her and her father?

"You are satisfied?" she asked in a tremulous voice. "Or am I to be next?"

"Satisfied?" Gilbert repeated, his brow furrowing. Then, understanding, he stepped to the side and nodded to where Edward was held by two knights. "Nay, I am not," he said, watching for her reaction.

Graeye gasped. Though her father looked near to collapsing, his head hanging down upon his chest, he was alive with not a spot of blood to testify otherwise. Her heart swelling for his need, she took an uncertain step forward.

Balmaine grasped her arm, stopping her. He'd used

the hand that had covered his wound, and a collective gasp went around the room as bright, running blood stained her white habit.

Where he poised between the two of them, the dog gave a terrifying howl of anger. Teeth bared, he drew himself back in readiness to lunge at the one he perceived dangerous to his mistress.

"Nay, Groan," Graeye commanded as she dragged her gaze from the pitiful sight of her father and met the animal's stare. "You had best unhand me," she murmured to Balmaine, running her hand over Groan's twitching neck.

Even with the threat of attack by a ferocious dog, who obviously would have liked nothing better than to tear out his throat, Balmaine did not release her. Instead he tightened his hold.

Graeye looked pointedly to where that large hand held her. The sight of blood coating his skin from fingertips to wrist brought her head sharply up. At his shoulder she saw the tear where the dagger had landed its mark and the soaking of blood through the fine linen of his tunic.

Brow knit, she lifted her gaze higher and noted the deepening grooves that belied Balmaine's hard, unmoving facade. Aye, he was in pain, for it was more than a flesh wound he had acquired.

"Come," she heard herself say, "I will tend your injury."

A flicker of surprise appeared in the depths of his eyes, but disappeared just as quickly, replaced by indifference.

"Methinks you should first call off your dog," he said, inclining his head toward the seething beast.

"Groan will stay with me," she said with firm resolve, having discovered, not for the first time, how valuable his loyalty was.

Balmaine looked ready to refuse her, then shrugged off the stipulation with a lift of his uninjured shoulder.

"Very well," he said, releasing her to press his hand to the wound.

Graeye cast a sidelong glance at her father, then stepped around Balmaine's formidable mass and made for the stairs, Groan close on her heels.

"Take him to the watchtower and hold him until I decide what is to become of his miserable person," Balmaine commanded those holding Edward.

Graeye bit her lip, but did not falter. Stopping in front of Sir Michael, she braved the compassion of his stare and asked that he send one of the servants with a bowl of water, strips of clean cloth, needle and thread, and salve. Then, continuing to the stairs, she mounted them with the baron close behind.

With the coming of the king's men, she had forgotten how badly the stairs were in need of repair, but was reminded of their poor state as they groaned protestingly beneath Balmaine's weight, and that of the squire who followed his lord.

Knowing it to be the most adequate room abovestairs, she led the baron to her father's chamber, turning to glance over her shoulder just as the thought struck her that he would not clear the doorway.

It was on her lips to caution him when he ducked beneath the frame. Clearly, he had grown accustomed to his height.

She was grateful she had seen to the freshening of the rushes within, the cleaning of the sparse furnishings, and the placement of oiled linen over the narrow window opening. Still, it was a gloomy, dank room, the brazier having long since radiated its last ember of comforting heat.

Pulling a stool to the center of the chamber, she montioned for Balmaine to seat himself. He complied, completely engulfing the three-legged stool that wobbled beneath his weight.

Groan's eyes never left the man; he took up a place near the stool, securing for himself a vantage from which to attack, if need be.

Graeye turned to the squire, who had situated himself in the doorway, his distrustful eyes following her every movement. "I will need light," she said. "Fetch me some torches."

The young man shifted his weight, propped himself against the jamb, but made no move to follow her directive.

"Joseph," Gilbert said, "bring some torches within."

Casting Graeye a look of warning, the squire straightened, then turned on his heel and went to do his lord's bidding.

Graeye turned back to Balmaine and noted, with some alarm, the ashen color shadowing his face. Though the prospect of seeing his body bared unsettled her, she knew the tunic and shirt beneath it would have to go. "You must needs remove these," she said, lightly touching the material.

He nodded. "With your assistance, of course."

Her unease must have shown, for his mouth twisted derisively. Removing the belt with its sword and dagger, he laid it carefully aside, then waited for her to attend him.

In a failed attempt to disguise her nervousness, she moved only as close as she needed to in order to grasp the garments. Eyes trained on the task, she drew the garments up, baring Balmaine's magnificently sculpted chest. He made not a sound when the material pulled from the wound and passed over his head, but the sudden tension that stiffened him told her of his discomfort.

She paused, her gaze moving from his most recently acquired injury to a jagged ridge that slashed across his breast, then another lower. She had not noticed them the night before, though well she remembered that which was responsible for his limp. Lord, he had so many scars.

"Hold your hand to it," she instructed. Shaking out the garments, she laid them upon the rumpled bed, grateful for the reappearance of the baron's squire when she turned back around.

Quickly, the torches were placed around the room in the wall sconces, throwing light into every corner of that dismal place.

Returning to where Balmaine was seated, Graeye bent over him and examined the nasty wound. Truly, it was a wonder her father still lived after inflicting it, she thought, her stomach turning.

Though she had spent time in the infirmary at the abbey, she had rarely been responsible for caring for the sick and wounded unless another had first seen to the stitching, medicating, and bandaging. Still, she had watched the sisters perform the duties required to mend such wounds, and was certain that if she could keep her stomach settled, she could see to this one.

"Milady," a young voice called to her.

Turning, she saw that two serving girls stood in the doorway, their arms laden with the items she had requested, their eyes growing wide and round as they fell upon the baron's naked chest. Behind them stood Michael.

"Come," Graeye beckoned to the girls, trying to ignore the young knight's presence.

Their eyes never leaving Gilbert, the two entered, their hips swinging provocatively. Graeye frowned, speculating on how they made their bodies flow so smoothly.

Could she do that? Ashamed of her wandering thoughts, she pulled herself back to the present. And for what purpose? To seduce again this man who thought her the vilest thing? Nay, she would never again subject herself to such humiliation.

"Baron Balmaine," Michael said, stepping just inside the chamber, "with your permission I would have a brief word with Lady Graeye."

Astonished that he would be so forthright with the man who was to become his new lord, Graeye turned to catch Balmaine's reaction to the request.

Save for the narrowing of his eyes and a lapse of several seconds, he gave nothing away. "Be quick about it," he said.

Reluctantly, Graeye stepped out into the passageway. "You should not have done that." She spoke low so none but Michael would hear.

With a hand to her elbow, he urged her from the doorway. "There is no need for you to tend his wound," he whispered. "There are others capable of the task."

Taken aback by his concern, she could only stare at him for a long moment. Why did he seek her out after avoiding her for so long? Had he changed his mind about Edward?

" 'Twas my father who did the deed," she explained. " 'Tis I who should mend it."

Michael sighed. "Still you make yourself responsible for that old man. Is there naught you would not forgive him for? He tried to murder the baron, Graeye."

" 'Tis Philip's death—" As the serving girls exited the chamber, Graeye halted the flow of words to defend her father's madness and took a step back from Michael.

It was Michael who resumed their hushed conversation. "Graeye," he coaxed, taking back the distance she had put between them, "'twill likely be death for the offense Edward has committed. Come with me this night that you do not have to witness his end."

Death? She shook her head. Nay, not if her plan went well. "I have told you," she said with conviction, "I will not abandon my father to the likes of Baron Balmaine."

A mixture of disappointment and frustration coming upon his face, Michael cupped her chin in his palm. "You are being foolish, sweet Graeye."

Aye, she knew that, but she was not going to give up so easily. "I—"

"Are you finished?" Balmaine interrupted.

Eyes wide, Graeye spun around to face him where

he leaned in the doorway, his forearm resting against the frame. Although his brows were lifted questioningly and a tight smile curled his hard mouth, he looked ominous.

How much had he heard? she wondered. It had been unwise to allow Michael to pull her into such a conversation with him so near. Foolish.

"We are finished," she said, stepping toward the chamber. The baron remained unmoving, his great bulk denying her access while his gaze probed both her face and Michael's.

Her ire rose at his arrogance. "If you will step aside, I will tend your wound," she said between clenched teeth.

His eyes, which seemed more black than blue at that moment, lifted from her face and fell again upon Michael. "I will see you belowstairs," he told the young knight, then stood away to allow Graeye to pass before him into the chamber.

She checked the items the serving girls had laid out upon a table beside the stool, then washed her hands, all the while aware of the eyes boring into her back. The tension cloaking the room only grew worse when Balmaine resumed his seat upon the stool, his thigh coming to rest against her leg.

Though Graeye's first thought was to step away, she pushed it aside, determined not to let him know the effect he had upon her. She dipped a strip of the cloth in water, wrung it out, then wound it about her hand.

"Joseph, leave us," Balmaine ordered his man.

"But, my lord—"

"Leave us!"

" 'Tis heartening to see I am not the only one you treat so rudely," Graeye observed once Joseph had gone. Still, she was sure the young man lingered not far down the corridor, prepared to defend his baron should she make an attempt upon his life. That thought nearly made her laugh. As if she posed a threat to a man such as he . . .

Unwilling to meet the stare Balmaine leveled on her, she moved his hand aside and set herself to cleaning the wound. It was only seeping now, the flow having been suspended by the pressure he'd applied to it. Careful lest she start it welling again, she wiped the cloth lightly across it.

Though Balmaine continued to stare at her, she refused to look at him, even shifting her body sideways so the shadow from the postered bed fell upon her face, offering her some protection from those probing eyes.

The wound cleaned to her satisfaction, she picked up the needle, momentarily disconcerted to find it unthreaded. She turned back into the light, holding the needle and thread close to her face. "I have not done this before," she murmured as she attempted to thread the elusive eye of the needle.

"What?" Balmaine bellowed.

She looked at him, then quickly away when she encountered his thunderous expression. "I have seen it done," she said. " 'Tis simply sewing, and be you assured, I am proficient at that."

He did not look assured, but he said no more.

"What is to become of my father, Baron Balmaine?" she asked, touching the thread to her tongue before making a second attempt at forcing it into the small eye.

"You would ask that before laying a stitch to me?" he barked.

Her second attempt failed, and she frowned. "I assure you, your answer will have no bearing on my handiwork. 'Tis what you are implying, is it not?"

"What is your relationship with your father?" he asked, leaving her question unanswered.

She stilled and met his eyes. "He is my father."

" 'Tis not what I asked," he snapped.

Beside her Groan growled low in his throat, swiping his tongue from one corner of his mouth to the other as he regarded Balmaine.

Graeye paid little heed to the dog, though she was

reassured by his presence. "Nevertheless, 'tis the only answer you will have from me," she muttered, returning her attention to the task at hand. "There!" Triumphant, she held the needle up for him to see, the thread dangling from it.

Balmaine suppressed a groan.

"So, what is to be my father's fate?" she persisted as she bent over his shoulder again.

"Stitch first, then we will talk," he said in a voice that brooked no argument.

Swallowing hard against her growing trepidation, Graeye pressed the two pieces of flesh together and pushed the needle in with a hand that refused to remain steady. Miraculously, it easily slid in and out, the only sign of the baron's discomfort witnessed by the rigid hold of his body.

With great concentration, and an easing of her restless stomach, Graeye continued.

"The stitches need not be so small!" Balmaine snapped when she was only halfway through. "Space them farther apart."

Frowning, she lifted her head and looked into his fiery eyes. Her breath caught in her throat as an ache shot through her chest. Quickly, she looked back to the wound.

"You would not want there to be a great, ugly scar, would you?" she asked, continuing with the spacing of her stitches.

"One more will do me no harm. Now do as I say."

It was bold of her, but she ignored his order, and was surprised when he did not pursue the matter.

When she finished, she straightened and flexed her shoulders to ease the tightness that had settled there. Still evading Gilbert's stare, she set the needle aside and opened the pot of salve. The next minutes continued in silence as she finished with the wound.

Once he was properly bandaged, she retrieved his clothing and dropped them onto his lap. "Now I would ask again that you tell me of my father's fate."

Gilbert lifted the garments and inspected the damage to the linen. Then, without warning, he tossed them at Graeye.

Reflexively, she caught them.

"Hold them open over my head," he commanded.

Reluctantly, she stepped near him and lifted the garments high.

Suddenly, his arm snaked out and pulled her between his thighs. She let out a yelp of surprise that had Groan rushing to her defense, snapping and growling.

"Back!" Balmaine roared.

As if he understood the danger this man represented, Groan came no closer, but neither did he retreat.

Recovering sufficiently to see the task through, Graeye held the garments and waited for Balmaine to raise his arms into them, but he did not accommodate her. Instead he urged her more deeply into the vee of his thighs.

Her heart beat so heavily, Graeye thought it might burst. "How—how long do you expect me to hold these for you?" she managed, determinedly fighting the sensual effect he was having on her.

He was silent so long, she finally felt compelled to look at him. It was a mistake. Staring into wide pupils rimmed with incredible blue, she was taken back to the night past. Briefly, she closed her eyes to savor the desire melting her insides.

A deep, rumbling laugh that made her cringe with shame surrounded her a moment later. A man with no heart, she thought, staring into his triumphant face.

Abruptly, his laughter faded. "Has Sir Michael ever touched you as I have?" he taunted. The hand he held her with stroked the small of her back.

Telling herself she felt nothing, that the flames he ignited were only the result of her outrage, she strained back against his hold. "Let me go," she demanded.

His mouth turning grim, he pulled her closer, his hand moving lower to the curve of her buttocks. "Has he touched you?"

She knew there was no escape from this giant's hold, so she grudgingly answered his question. "You know that is not so."

"Do I?" His hand slid to her waist and began a maddening exploration up her side. "I know only that he did not gain your virtue." His fingers splayed wide to brush the side of her breast. "Has he never touched your soft skin nor tasted your lips, sweet Graeye?"

Angry, she met his gaze. "Methinks you are jealous, Baron Balmaine," she retorted.

His eyes narrowed. "You have not answered me."

"And I will not."

He held her stare a long moment, then smiled and lifted his arms.

Grateful, Graeye lowered the garments, then jumped away lest she suffer any further assaults upon her wayward senses.

Balmaine stood and smoothed his tunic down, then retrieved his belt, keeping her waiting as he refastened it about his waist. Then, without a glance her way, he walked to the door.

"What about my father?" she sputtered.

His hand on the frame, he turned and raked his gaze over her. "Ah, yes," he sighed. "Your father." He flexed his injured shoulder. "I have been thinking on that."

"And?"

"I have not decided."

Her mouth dropped open. "You kept me waiting for that?"

He shrugged. "I must needs think on it some more, but for the offense he has committed, it would not be undue punishment to take his life." He let that sit a moment, then continued. "Of course, there are other ways to assure he never troubles me again."

She looked away. "Then I pray God lightens your heart," she murmured.

"Were you true and virtuous, Lady Graeye, I might feel compelled to believe prayer alone could do that. But I fear you will have to look elsewhere for a means of convincing me to have mercy upon a man such as Edward Charwyck."

Graeye did not rise to the bait, though her heart felt as if it were breaking into a thousand tiny pieces that she would never be able to put together again. Turning her back on Balmaine, she leaned down to stroke Groan between the ears.

Gilbert did not immediately retreat. Instead he stood in the doorway and stared uncomprehendingly at her back, acknowledging that he did not understand this enigma who had earned his wrath by her cunning seduction.

He frowned as part of him defended her, pointing out that she appeared the kindest of souls, that the heart in her breast seemed pure and not corrupt as he was so ready to pronounce it. Had not the servants been quick to come to her defense, outspoken in their voicing of the changes she had made and the compassion she'd shown for those in need of food and shelter? Another voice reminded him that her healing touch had been gentle when it should have been anything but.

But the loudest and most convincing voice of all screamed that she was a Charwyck, his avowed enemy. Gilbert excused himself his weakness; he could not be blamed for having doubts about her, for even the servants had been taken in by her self-serving show of kindness. Graeye Charwyck was not to be trusted.

Without needing to hear his footfalls in the passageway, Graeye knew the moment Balmaine left by the easing of Groan's tense body. She turned and stared at the empty doorway, then walked to it.

Tilting her head back, she looked at the mildewed wood above her head. *Never*, she thought, would she have to worry about doing herself injury on that.

Directly, Graeye went to the room containing her mother's effects and, for the last time, removed the habit. Standing in her thin chemise, she held the garment and stared at the bloodstains Balmaine had put there. It would be forever stained if she did not see to it immediately. Resolutely, she folded it and placed it back in the chest.

Laced into the brown bliaut she had worn earlier that day, she squared her shoulders and left the room. Slowly she descended the stairs, alert to the voices in the hall below.

In the shadow of the stairway, Groan standing patiently at her side, she went unnoticed as Edward's former retainers entered into the ceremony of homage, offering their oaths of fealty to Baron Balmaine.

The last to pledge himself was the handsome Sir Michael. Graeye craned her neck to better see him when he stepped to the dais. With great sadness, she watched as he knelt before the baron and placed his clasped hands within his new lord's.

"Lord, I become your man," he said, his voice strong with conviction as he spoke the words.

Balmaine answered him, and still kneeling, Sir Michael gave his oath of fealty. "Baron Balmaine, I vow to love what you love and loathe what you loathe, and never by word or deed do aught that should grieve you."

Balmaine answered him again, then raised the knight to his feet and bestowed on him a ceremonial kiss as he had with the others.

As if on cue the servants surged from out of the shadows and began to position the trestle tables for the midday meal.

In the ensuing confusion Graeye took the opportunity to lose herself among them and leave the donjon without anyone noticing. A short time later she was once again in the outer bailey. Looking about, she was disappointed to discover that Groan had left her side.

Fickle animal, she thought, with a dose of longing for the comfortable companionship he offered. Giving a doleful shrug, she began walking.

There were only two recurring thoughts in her head. One, to search out her father, and the other, to escape to the falls. She was debating the merits of each, her feet inadvertently carrying her to the postern gate and the world beyond the castle's walls, when the knight whom she had encountered earlier at the watchtower appeared at her side.

She faltered, but when he did not attempt to detain her, she continued walking. He kept pace with her. With a sidelong glance she looked at his profile and thought him only passing attractive. He had none of the dark attraction of Gilbert Bal—

Abruptly, she halted her thoughts. Among the multitude of men who surrounded her, why had she chosen the heartless baron to measure others against?

Piqued, she drew herself to a halt and turned to face the man. "What do you want?" she demanded.

His brows shot up. "The baron thought you might need an escort," he explained. "He feels obliged to offer you his protection until you are returned to the abbey."

Graeye drew a deep, steadying breath. "And when will that be—today?"

"Nay, 'tis too late now for the journey. I would guess 'twould be first thing on the morrow."

So she was given the remainder of the day to put her plan into motion. Perhaps there was still a chance for her to see it through. "Sir . . ."

"Lancelyn," he supplied.

"I do not require an escort and would ask that you allow me my privacy."

"Would that I could," he said, an apologetic smile upon his lips, "but I must follow my lord's orders."

It was on the tip of Graeye's tongue to tell him exactly what she thought of his "lord," but all her training as a novice came back to her and silenced her words before they fell from her lips.

"Then I will not see you put out, Sir Lancelyn," she said, turning back around. Head high, she retraced her steps.

She had thought the man might let her go her way,

but it soon became obvious he had no intention of allowing her out of his sight.

"Truly, is this necessary?" she asked, her irritation evident.

He drew alongside her. "Simply a precaution, my lady." He nodded his head toward the donjon. " 'Twould not be unseemly if you joined the others for dinner."

"If you are hungry, Sir Knight, do satisfy yourself," she said, "but I have no such appetite that would compel me to share a meal with your lord."

"You are working very hard at being a true Charwyck, are you not, Lady Graeye?" he tossed back at her.

Struck speechless by his unexpected words, she stumbled to a halt and stared at him. Then, lifting her skirts high, she mounted the steps two at a time and entered the hall.

Sir Lancelyn followed at a more leisurely pace.

Her rashness had been a mistake, Graeye realized immediately, for all eyes turned to watch her progress along the perimeter of the room. Though she did not intentionally seek out the baron, her startled gaze fell straightaway to his.

Brows lifted, a mocking smile upon his lips, he nodded at her.

Coloring brightly, she lowered her chin and lengthened her short stride. A great wash of relief swept her as she reached the stairs, for not only was she free of those curious stares, but Sir Lancelyn did not continue in his pursuit. It did not please her that she had afforded the dreadful man the opportunity to join the others in the meal, but she was grateful to have him trailing her no longer.

Leaving the commotion behind, Graeye went directly to the small chapel and closed herself in it. It was cool there, for the uncovered window allowed the breeze outside to stir the air within.

On her knees before the altar, she assumed the familiar position of prayer. Instead of setting herself to that most exalted task, though, she became enmeshed in the plans that would see her and her father clear of Medland before sunrise. It had to be this night. Tomorrow she would be returned to the abbey, and likely her father put to death. Aye, tomorrow would be too late for either of them.

Chapter 7

For endless hours Graeye feigned sleep upon her bench in the hall. And was miserable for it. As best she could, she kept her breathing deep and even, going so far as to mumble incoherent words when she found it necessary to shift upon the hard surface. She felt guilty for it, but there was simply no way around the deception she practiced upon the man set to keep watch over her—Sir Lancelyn.

He had positioned himself on a straw pallet not far from where she was stretched out. She resented his interference, and the man who had ordered him to it. If not for the night vigil he kept over her, she would surely have found her way to her father hours ago. Perhaps they would even be free of the castle by now. It was beyond irritating. It was infuriating.

Detecting a decided change in the man's breathing, she slowly turned her head and listened for several minutes to assure herself that he had, indeed, fallen off to sleep. Her patience wearing thin, she confirmed his state, then lifted her blanket and quietly rose from the bench.

With the exception of the wimple, she had gone to bed fully clothed, with even her shoes upon her feet so that she would not inadvertently call attention to herself in her search for them. Now, as a last-minute thought, she took up the blanket and draped it around her shoulders for the extra warmth it would provide against the cold night. Lifting her skirts to her knees, she stepped cautiously around Sir Lancelyn's sleeping form.

From beneath her bench a low-pitched moan arose that drew her to a tense halt. Breath held, her hands clenched, she waited to discover if Groan had awakened the man. Blessedly, Lancelyn's breathing did not change. Letting go a sigh of relief, she continued across the hall.

Rather than risk the main entrance, Graeye slipped down the corridor through which the servants carried the food from the kitchen in the inner bailey. As she had hoped, this door was unguarded, and she had only to lift the bar to let herself out.

Outside, the air was brisk with the threat of an early winter, lifting her hair and stirring it about her face. For a moment she wished she had thought to bring the wimple.

Grimacing, she gathered the fine strands together and pushed them into the neck of her chemise. Then, pulling the blanket over her head, she hurried to the front of the donjon. Keeping to the shadows afforded by cloud cover, she made good progress and crossed the inner drawbridge to the watchtower, whence the faint glow of a lantern lit the lower floor.

It was quiet when she finally summoned enough courage to step within. She did so with caution, her gaze sliding around the room in search of any obstacles. She saw only one guard near the stairs, only just retaining his seat upon a stool, his head slumped onto his chest.

Sinking her teeth into her bottom lip, she took a step forward and peered closely at him. In his present state he was harmless, but she knew he would prove difficult if he awoke. It took some time for her to accept the only solution to her dilemma, for it seemed such a terrible thing to do to another human being.

Repenting as she went, she walked quietly to the only other stool in the room. She allowed the blanket to fall from her shoulders as she lifted the stool. Finding it weighty enough to do the job, she stepped back to the man. She offered up a last, hasty prayer and brought it down upon his head.

With a grunt he crumpled sideways and fell to the earthen floor.

Graeye dropped the stool and knelt beside the man to assure herself he still breathed. Confirming this, she patted a thankful hand to her heart, then scrambled to her feet. She pulled the lantern from its hook and ran for the stairs, taking them as quickly as her legs would carry her.

Going directly to the room where she was certain she would find her father, she pushed back the bolt on the door. Then holding the lantern before her, she opened it and stepped within. She immediately saw Edward curled upon a straw pallet against the far wall.

Placing the lantern on the floor, Graeye crouched beside him. "Father," she called, gently shaking his shoulder.

Edward came instantly awake, shooting up from the pallet and into a sitting position in a flurry of movement. It took him a few moments to orient himself, his wild-eyed expression finally dimming as he focused on Graeye.

"What do you here, daughter?" he asked, his voice hoarse as if he had been abusing it for some time with his ravings.

"I've come to release you," she answered, sitting back on her heels. "We must leave this place ere morn comes."

He looked past her to the empty doorway. "And how did you get in here?"

"I . . ." She looked down at her hands, reluctant to

admit the horrible deed she had committed. "I rendered the guard unconscious."

"You?" He shook his head disbelievingly.

She nodded, then, seeing he was unconvinced, decided it would be wiser to explain later. "It does not matter," she said. "We must leave now ere 'tis discovered what I have done."

"Leave?" he spat with disgust. "Mayhap when I have my piece of flesh from that Balmaine bastard, but I vow not before." Grumbling, he started to rise.

"Nay, Father." Graeye reached out to grasp his filthy sleeve. "Would you be put to death before you could seek your revenge?" Truly, it was the only argument that came to mind.

Unexpectedly, he laughed. "But I will have my revenge. Aye, 'twill be done this night."

"You do not understand," she pleaded, leaning nearer. "The baron is heavily guarded. 'Twill do you no good to seek him out this night."

To her surprise and relief Edward actually seemed to put some consideration to her words. "Aye," he finally conceded, "mayhap you are right. 'Twould not do simply to slit his throat. I would see him suffer far longer than that would take—him and that murdering sister of his."

Though Graeye was opposed to such a plan, her throat tightening at the thought of such an atrocity, she knew she had gained the advantage. "Then let us be gone from here," she said, rising.

Edward struggled to his feet and lurched toward the door. However, halfway across the room he turned around, bumping into Graeye where she had followed close on his heels.

"You will remain," he said. "The king's man has assured me of an escort to the abbey for you." Then, as if noticing her clothing for the first time, his gaze raked contemptuously over the bliaut, then to her uncovered head.

Graeye was alarmed by what she saw in her father's

face. Hugging her arms tightly to her, she frantically sought a way out of the impending storm.

"And why are you dressed in this manner?" he demanded, his voice growing increasingly loud as his anger mounted.

Urgent to be away from the castle, she laid a hand upon his arm. " 'Tis of no consequence, Father," she said, her voice pleading. "I would go with you now. We can speak of it when we are safely away from here."

"Nay, I would know this instant!" he insisted, throwing his arm away so that she was left grasping air.

Graeye gave the first explanation that came to mind. "The habit became soiled," she said, purposely omitting that it was the baron's blood that had soiled it. She did not think her father had been aware of the happenings following his attack upon Gilbert Balmaine.

Though dissatisfied with her answer, Edward grunted and nodded. "You will return to the abbey on the morrow," he said decisively.

"Nay!" the word burst from her without forethought, and immediately she regretted her lack of subtlety.

"You defy me again?" he asked, daring her to contemplate such a thing.

She stepped nearer. "Father, I would better serve you at your side. I beg you, do not send me back to the abbey."

"And of what use would you be to me?" he thundered.

"I will stay with you and see to your needs. I can cook, and sew . . . and write. Together we will find another to whom you can pledge your services."

"Nay, you will take your vows and do penance for the devil that dwells within you."

She had to tell him. Knowing that she was about to unleash a storm, but that there was no other argument left to convince him to take her with him, Graeye backed away.

"You must take me with you," she said. "The abbey is no longer an option." She lowered her head and stared at the hands she twisted in her skirts. "One must be chaste to become a bride of Christ . . . and I am no longer that."

Edward did not react. He simply stared at her.

She ventured but one look at him before turning her eyes away. Seeking the door, she tried to calculate the time it would take to reach it, and the possibility of getting through it before her father—

" 'Twas that dog, Balmaine, wasn't it?" he roared. " 'Tis he who spoiled you—tell me!"

She was struck dumb by the accuracy of his guess and could only gape at him. How could he have known?

Edward moved so suddenly, she had no chance to retreat before his cruel hands grasped her shoulders. " 'Twas he, wasn't it?" He shook her. "He violated you!"

She quelled at his mistaken conclusion. "Nay," she croaked. "He did not force me."

Her words were enough to make the shaking stop. However, in the next instant she was staring into Edward's face, his nose very nearly touching hers, his breath foul upon her.

"Then you gave yourself to him," he snarled. "To our enemy."

"I did not know 'twas the baron," she said in a small voice. " 'Tis the truth. I but wanted—"

One moment she was on her feet, the next she was sprawled upon the musty straw pallet, one side of her face exploding in pain from the force of Edward's blow. Her vision had only just begun to clear when she was dragged back to her feet.

"Whore!" Edward screamed, then landed the back of his hand to the other side of her face, his heavy ring cutting her skin.

Graeye brought her arms up about her head to protect it, but Edward effortlessly knocked them aside and caught hold of her chin.

"Devil," he spat. " 'Tis the devil that lurks within your soul."

Shaking uncontrollably, she looked into his mad, reddened eyes. "I am sorry," she managed before his fist slammed into her belly. In excruciating pain and devoid of breath, she would have doubled over, but Edward shoved her back onto the pallet.

Rolling onto her side, she pulled her knees to her chest and wrapped her arms around her head, drawing in a painful, ragged breath that she might remain conscious. She was fighting a losing battle, she realized, registering that one of her hands was damp with blood. She winced at the bright, thrusting colors behind her lids. Would he continue to beat her if she lost consciousness?

Edward's thick shadow falling over her somehow worked its way into her consciousness. Blinking, she peered between her hands and saw that he stood in the center of the room, the lantern held high above his head.

"From the devil you came and to the devil you will return!" he shouted.

A wave of swirling black blinded Graeye, then it retreated. Her breathing shallow, she stared uncomprehendingly at her father, her befuddled mind resistant to his meaning. The next wave of darkness was deeper than the last, beckoning her into the comfort of unconsciousness. She fought it again and won.

At last her eyes told her what her mind could not accept—her father meant to burn her alive.

Panic burst through her, and she managed to make it onto her knees as a bellow of mad laughter swelled around the room and dropped upon her ears like killing stones. A moment later the straw pallet she was trying to raise herself from burst into flames.

Crying out, she surged back onto her heels, narrowly

avoiding the hungry licks of the fire as she pressed herself against the wall. Through the thready smoke she caught a glimpse of her father where he stood in the doorway.

"Burn!" he yelled, his pupils glowing red in the firelight. He disappeared from sight.

To fight the darkness tugging at her, Graeye closed her eyes tightly and drew a breath of smoky air into her lungs. Coughing, she opened her lids wide again and looked at the fire to the front and sides of her. The flames were not yet high, struggling with the musty fuel they had been given to feed their greedy appetite.

If she could but get to her feet ... she inched her way up the wall, then swayed forward and just barely kept herself from toppling into the flames.

Suddenly a dark shadow raced through the doorway. Groan? she wondered. Then a towering figure filled the doorway, a man so tall, he was forced to duck beneath the frame to enter. Others followed, but Graeye kept her eyes upon the impossible vision of Gilbert Balmaine, until his image colored over into lovely blues, greens, and reds that shimmered like moonlight upon a cascading veil of water.

As if from a great distance, she heard loud voices calling to her and the insistent baying of a dog. Blessedly, they melded into the thunder of water falling from an amazing height. Warm and tranquil, the water reached out and tumbled her full into its depths. Odd, but she was not frightened as it wrapped itself around her and lifted her from the pallet. Enfolding her close to its breast, it carried her along the winding currents and downward.

When it turned cold, the sudden change was enough to bring Graeye back to consciousness. Opening her eyes, she tried to lift her head to peer out at the dark night and the flux of people streaming around her, but her efforts were thwarted by a hand that pressed her face to a wonderfully solid chest. She had just accepted that it was not such a bad place to be when she realized she was being passed into another's arms.

She saw Balmaine's angry face for a moment before it was replaced by another's. "Take her to the donjon," she heard him say; then he was gone.

Trying to make sense of her situation, she stared up at Sir Lancelyn with great bewilderment and saw him grimace.

She lifted her hand and touched her face. Her breath escaped in a painful hiss as her fingers found the swelling alongside one eye and the gash on the opposite cheek.

Of course. Lowering her hand to her lap, she turned her head from the knight's probing eyes and was horrified to discover the upper floor of the watchtower ablaze, smoke billowing forth like a great, avenging storm.

Had Gilbert gone back into that? she wondered as she watched people bearing pails of water.

The tower was suddenly swept from sight as Sir Lancelyn turned to carry her away. She had just resigned herself to the beckoning arms of unconsciousness again when she was shaken by a vision of the man she had struck senseless. Was he still within? Had he been discovered and pulled to safety?

"Nay!" she shouted, trying to twist free of the arms holding her. "The guard." Throwing a hand to the knight's chest, she attempted to gain leverage over his greater strength.

Sir Lancelyn halted and looked questioningly down at her. "Guard?" he repeated.

Trying to formulate a coherent explanation, she nodded. "Aye, he lies . . . within." She struggled to tell him more, but was unable to. Her tongue felt thick and awkward, having stumbled over itself as it had formed those most inadequate words.

Still cradling her, Sir Lancelyn swung back around to face the fire. Then, with an angry exclamation, he set Graeye on her feet.

She grasped his arms to steady herself, sure that any moment she would collapse.

"Give me your vow you will stay here!" he commanded, the anger he held in check finally surfacing.

She nodded. "Aye, you've my word."

Though he knew he was taking a great risk in leaving her, the baron's wrath sure to fall upon his head should she disappear, Lancelyn could not dismiss the possibility that the guard might still be within. Prying Graeye's fingers loose from his arms, he stepped around her swaying figure and sprinted back to the watchtower.

Turning slowly around, Graeye caught sight of Sir Lancelyn just as he was swallowed by the smoke billowing out the door. A moment later she was on her hands and knees, fighting the blackness that yawned wide at her, and wondering at the insistent nudging against her side.

Struggling to a kneeling position, she lifted her head and looked into Groan's expectant eyes. When she attempted a reassuring smile for the mangy beast, she realized that the vision in her injured eye was fast narrowing. Draping an arm about the huge dog's body for support, she lightly touched the swollen flesh of her face and felt the heat rising about her eyelid. Within the hour her eye would be completely closed, she realized as she watched the growing number of people attempting to put out the fire. Unbeknown to her, tears began to flow down her cheeks.

Pressed to her side, Groan groaned loudly in acknowledgment of his mistress's distress and, lowering his head, flicked a wet tongue over her hand.

Shortly, a familiar figure closely followed by another emerged from the burning building and took shape as they moved toward Graeye. She blinked to bring them into focus, but not until they were nearly upon her did she realize one of the men was Sir Lancelyn, the unfortunate guard over his shoulder, and the other, Gilbert Balmaine.

Swaying on her knees, she stared up at that black-ened face, noting the flecks of ash caught in his hair and beard. Eyes like cutting shards of ice, he looked down at her from his great height, his hands planted upon his hips.

The guard moaned, finally breaking the eye contact that hovered between them for an agonizing eternity. Having been lowered to the ground beside Graeye, he attempted to lift his head.

Graeye reached out to him, but felt her body falling as she leaned more heavily into Groan. Only a bare defense did she put up before giving in to the drape of dark that fell over her. It was a comfort she would not long know.

Chapter 8

❧❦❧

When Graeye next looked out at the world, the light of dawn had turned the oiled linen golden. She saw the evidence of an orange-streaked sky in the muted colors that filtered through the covering and glanced off the walls.

What was she doing in the refectory? she wondered, frowning as she shifted her gaze to a flickering lamp that was suspended to the right of the window. If discovered, Mistress Hermana would think it highly improper for her to have made her bed in a room reserved exclusively for the taking of meals. It would give the woman yet another excuse to assign Graeye additional duties and forbid her the gardens. Another excuse to lay her strap across Graeye's back.

Mayhap she could sneak back to her cell, Graeye thought; then her frown deepened. Aye, she might make it, but her absence from the first morning prayers would not go unnoticed.

Thinking it might go easier for her if she was at least presentable when she came face-to-face with that woman, she started to turn onto her side to raise herself up. However, with the movement her head rushed with pain.

Dropping back, she lifted both hands from beneath the covers and touched them to her face. She found a gash over her cheekbone and a tender swelling above her left eye, which she only now realized was closed.

It was not the refectory, she realized, but the chamber that had once been her father's. That same room in which she had tended the baron's wound—was it yesternoon?

Returned to the present, she lowered her hands and expelled a breath past a throat so raw and swollen, it was nearly closed.

" 'Twas more than you bargained for, eh?" A familiar, humorless voice spoke out of the silence. Standing alongside the bed, one hand resting on a front poster, the other draped nonchalantly upon a hip, the baron stood looking down at her from that great height of his.

It was not merely the man's unexpected presence that shook Graeye—though that would have been enough—but rather his state of undress seen clearly through the one eye she leveled on him. As if unaffected by the chill that hung in the morning air, he went without benefit of an undertunic, his powerful chest bare of all but a mat of dark, curling hair and the bandages she had secured over his shoulder. Indeed, his only clothing was a pair of loose breeches riding low upon his hips, the untied laces trailing as if he had only recently donned them, and in haste. For her benefit? she wondered.

She turned her head away, wincing at the pain, but comforted by the small measure of escape she gained. Though it crossed her mind she must look a horrible mess, it was not her vainglory that suffered when those probing eyes fell upon her, but the vulnerable depths of her soul that this man seemed intent upon delving into. Well she knew she must take steps to protect herself from further hurt, and the sooner she erected the barriers that would stave off that event, the better her chances of pulling through these terrible times.

Staring sightlessly to the left, she reflected upon the baron's words. Aye, it was all more than she had bargained for.

In the space of but a few weeks a wondrous future had been placed in her lap, and then, with utmost cruelty, snatched from her grasping fingers. Desperation—and something else she dared not put a name to—had driven her to give her body to this man, then had seen her exposed. And now her father had attempted to set her afire, hoping to return her to the devil whence he thought she came. He had finally crossed that fine line of sanity and gone completely mad.

Embittered by the next thought, Graeye nearly laughed. Nay, she admitted, not even the worst day at the abbey had been so cruel to her.

Though she felt the mattress sag beneath the baron's weight as he lowered himself beside her, she turned her head farther to the side and fixed her gaze upon the door.

Open, she silently implored the inanimate object. Deliver me from this one's hate, for I cannot bear any more. But none came to rescue her from the inevitable confrontation.

Despondently, she realized she would gain little by attempting to defend herself. No matter what this man faulted her with, it would be best if she could maintain the easy comfort of silence.

When a hand appeared to cup her chin, she did not resist its urging. Instead she moved her head back around to look at Gilbert Balmaine where he sat on the edge of the bed.

Meeting those unforgettable eyes, she was staggered as she glimpsed compassion in their cool depths. Even as she sternly told her heart to find cover lest it be torn asunder by such wild imaginings, she watched those same blue depths turn caustic again.

"You have discovered your father is a cruel man, hmm?" Gilbert said. His gaze narrowed on her swollen eye, then flicked back to the other to await her confirmation. It irked him when she did not give him one.

He brushed his fingers over her jaw. "Had it not been for that mangy dog of yours waking the entire donjon with its raucous bellowing, you would have burned as your father intended," he continued, then looked again to see what her reaction might be.

She tried to pull her chin out of his grasp, but he denied her retreat, his hold firm, yet not unkind. Her mouth tightening, she chose the next-best avenue of avoidance, lowering her gaze and staring across the foot of the bed.

Determined to gain her regard, Gilbert leaned into her line of sight.

"Why did he do this to you?" he asked.

She blinked, then lifted a hand and touched a finger to his chest. "You," she mouthed, no sound issuing from her lips, but her meaning clear.

Gilbert frowned. Had she spoken true of her father's ignorance of their tryst—that the old man had not set her to seduce him? Was this the reason Charwyck had tried to end her life?

Aye, his hate for the Balmaines was that great. But that she had acted alone ... He dredged up the explanation she had offered him in the chapel, but immediately set it aside. Nay, he would not believe that she'd given herself to a stranger merely to avoid taking vows. Still, her sad, ravaged face softened his anger.

Frowning, he looked to where the tip of her small finger grazed his skin. A thousand sparks of desire emanated to all parts of his body from that one point. In spite of the warmth flooding through him, he was suddenly furious with his lack of control over that traitorous bodily function. Not even the beautiful Lady Atrice had elicited such a ready response from him.

Lust, he assured himself. Pure animal lust that had nothing to do with the deeper emotions he had felt for that other woman who was now so far out of his reach, it made him ache with longing. He had never quite recovered from her untimely death only weeks before they were to have wed.

Hauling himself back to the present to shut out the pain, Gilbert leveled his gaze upon Graeye once more.

Seeing the gathering storm upon his brow, Graeye hurriedly dropped her hand back to her side, wondering at the wisdom of her disclosure. Was it yet another mistake she had so ingenuously fallen into?

Though her eyes were stinging with the need to cleanse themselves of the tears that were gathering, she refused to cry in front of this man.

Leaning nearer to her, Gilbert rested his other palm on the mattress beside her shoulder. "I tell you now, Lady Graeye," he said in a voice gone dangerously soft, "your father's offense will not go unpunished. Not until I have seen him join his son in hell will I rest."

As she looked into his face, Graeye was stunned by the vehemence with which he spoke, but even more so by the words he chose. Was it possible his anger stemmed from the harm done her?

Absurd, she told herself. It was the damage done to the castle that angered him, and most certainly the lives that she assumed had been lost putting out the fire. Had she been standing, her shoulders would surely have sagged with that burden.

"Nothing to say?" he asked.

Slowly, so she would not disturb again the pained contents of her thoughts, she shook her head.

His gaze grew hard as flint. "You are not even slightly curious as to the destruction wrought by your actions?"

Graeye closed her one functioning eye against his accusing visage. If she was to be denied the benefit of looking away from his penetrating stare, then she would block him from her sight altogether.

Nay, she did not want to know what her poor judgment had caused—could not bear to be told she was responsible for lost lives. Mayhap later she could face it, but God protect her from having to hear the details this moment—and from this man, whom the very sight of wrenched her heart.

"Graeye," he called to her, his deep voice turning soft and insistent.

Had she heard right, or was it imagined? she wondered. The unexpected use of her given name without title—a familiarity that was highly improper considering the impasse that stood between them—brought her eye open again.

Simply seeing his face had come nearer, his warm breath fanning her lips, sent her senses spiraling to a new height that made her temporarily forget her body's discomfort. With no small amount of mortification she realized that, almost more than life itself, she wanted to feel again the security of those arms around her.

As if he sensed her reaction to him, Gilbert drew back. "There were no deaths," he informed her.

Her one eye widened. "Truly?" she croaked, then winced at the searing pain with which that one word surged from her throat.

An unreadable expression flitted across Gilbert's eyes. Nodding, he released his hold on her and stood from the bed.

So relieved was Graeye, she did not attempt to prevent the tears that sprang to her eyes.

"The watchtower is destroyed," he went on, his voice oddly emotionless. "However, the fire was contained and the walls beyond salvaged." As he turned away, he drew a weary hand over his face. "Though 'twould truly have been of little consequence had it all gone up in flame," he muttered.

"I am sorry," Graeye said, her voice so low and strained she did not think he heard her. Whether or not he had, he did not acknowledge the apology, though she thought his broad, muscled back stiffened.

"There has been no sign of your father," he said, swinging back around to face her, his fists on his hips. "I would have you tell me where he has gone."

Surprised by his request, she shook her head.

In less than two strides Gilbert was at the foot of the bed. "For the love of God, woman, you owe him no loyalty. Not only did he beat you, but the bastard tried to set you afire. Do you so easily forget that?"

Of course she had not forgotten. How could she? It was not that she wouldn't tell him, but that she couldn't. Still, she was loath to ponder what her answer would be if she did know what he was asking.

"Nay," she finally managed, then had to swallow carefully on the searing fire in her throat before she could clarify herself.

Misinterpreting her denial, Gilbert's expression went from bad to worse, turning thunderous in the space of mere seconds. "Protect him you may," he ground out, "but he will still suffer my blade ere I send him straight to hell."

Graeye hugged her arms about her. "Don't know where he is," she whispered, hoping he would hear her over the rage beating through his head.

Before he could accuse her of yet another falsehood, she thought to appeal to his logic. "Think you he would tell me when he meant to . . ." Her voice trailed off as her mind flitted ahead to the words that had nearly fallen from her mouth. It was one thing to hear another talk of what her father had tried to do, but quite a different matter for her to acknowledge it aloud. She simply could not.

Coming back around the side of the bed, Gilbert stared down at her. "Is it because you love him—your father—that you sought his release?"

"Love?" she breathed, incredulous. Aye, it was true she had wanted Edward's love, would have given hers had he allowed it, but he had not. "Nay," she whispered, meeting Gilbert's gaze. "A man like my father has no need for love. I only wanted to help him."

Was it relief she saw in Gilbert's face, softening his eyes and relaxing his mouth before, too soon, it was gone?

Shrugging off the foolish question, she turned her

thoughts to a more pressing matter. What was to become of her now? Did the baron still intend to return her to the abbey, or would he find another way to mete out punishment for the foolish thing she had done?

Though it pained her to do so, she raised her voice. Its rough, gravelly tone grated upon her ears. "You have said you will not rest until you have seen my father in hell," she began slowly. "I, too, am a Charwyck. Will you strive for my death as well?"

His eyes narrowed upon her until they were mere slits. "Had I wanted your death, Lady Graeye," he said evenly, "I would not have seen it necessary to rescue you from the fire. Though 'tis true you are a Charwyck, and more than worthy of that name, 'twill satisfy me well enough to see you returned to the abbey."

It should have been of some comfort to her that he meant her no physical harm, but Graeye found little solace in his words. Attempting to hide the pain she knew would be reflected there, she turned her face to the wall.

Silence hung uncomfortably upon the air for long, interminable minutes; then she heard Gilbert move away. Even as she began to wonder what he was doing, the door opened, and after a brief pause, closed.

So quiet was Groan upon his padded feet, Graeye was not aware of his triumphant entry into the chamber forbidden to him. His tongue lolling, he trotted directly to the bed and propped his slavering chin upon the coverlet to regard his mistress with great, soulful eyes.

Turning onto her side, Graeye laid a hand upon his head. Then, curling herself into the tightest ball she could stand, she gave over to the emotions she had held in check during her painful encounter with Gilbert Balmaine. With a sharply indrawn breath, she lost all control, her face crumpling even as she raised her hands to cover its tenderness.

Standing in the corridor, Gilbert felt his annoyance at

having allowed the beast to slip past him dissolve as he heard the unmistakable sounds from within. He was alarmed by his reaction to the mournful sobs. A woman's tears—they were a weakness he could ill afford, but neither could he deny their strong pull upon his hardened, barricaded heart.

All anger drained from him, and he stared down at his hands for a long moment as memories of his sister, Lizanne, washed warmly over him. Though seven years separated them, he had always been there to offer her solace as she had grown from a babe to a young woman. She had needed him like no other ever had—until recently. Married now, she turned to another, her husband Ranulf.

Unthinking, guided only by deeply buried instincts that found their way past the barbed walls of his soul, Gilbert reached to open the door again. Even as his hand strayed from his body, though, his mind pulled it back with the sharp reminder of Graeye's deception.

She had played him for a fool. Used him to gain her own ends without thought of any but herself. She was a Charwyck through and through.

Abruptly, his compassion stepped back from the brink of disaster. Clenching his fists, Gilbert walked away.

Chapter 9

❧❧❧

"hen I will drag her out myself!" Gilbert's wrathful voice carried down the corridor, announcing his brisk advance toward the lord's chamber long before his boots resounded upon the wooden planks.

Hearing him, Graeye glanced over her shoulder at the door before returning her attention to the activity in the bailey below. Clutching the cover about her shoulders, she leaned forward to see better out the window from which she had removed the oiled linen. The slight breeze took hold of her loose hair and swept it across her face.

Pushing it behind an ear, she watched as a continuous stream of servants crossed between the kitchen and the donjon, bearing trays laden with food that sent spirals of savory scents wafting upward. She reached with her dulled senses in an attempt to identify the various viands, but quickly lost interest in the dismal amusement she had set herself to.

Lifting her gaze, she looked to the ominous structure being raised in place of the destroyed watchtower. Though it was still far from complete, she was staggered by the efficiency with which it had been erected in so short a time.

Quite a feat. After all, it was only a sennight since the fire.

She could only wonder at what changes Medland would see come spring, when the stage would be set for complete restoration of the castle. However, it no longer pained her that she would not be there to witness it herself, for she had come to accept her fate with more grace than she could have imagined. Considering the terrible events that had plagued her since leaving the abbey, that place did not seem as unpleasant as it once had.

Blessedly, she had been left in peace to work through her emotions and allow her ravaged face time to heal. Still, these past days had been difficult.

More than the loss of the future she'd glimpsed, more than Gilbert's rejection of her, and more than her pending return to the abbey, the most difficult thing to accept had been Edward's attempt to murder her. She had fought off that terrible memory the first few days, but had finally found the strength to relive it in all its vivid detail.

Now she was grateful she had, for as painful as it had been, it had allowed her to see clearly what kind of man Edward was. He had fathered her, but that was all. He had never been a father, and never would be. He was an evil man, of the same devil he had accused her of being. True, he had gone mad, but that did not excuse him from what he had tried to do to her.

Acknowledging that had freed her of the naïveté that had nearly cost her her life. Never again, she vowed, would she leave herself open to such vulnerability.

The emotions Graeye had dealt with exclusively, but her injuries had been tended to by a healer named Lucy, a woman brought from Penforke castle—Gilbert's home—shortly after the fire. She seemed a kind enough soul, but Graeye had closed her out, answering her questions only when a nod or a shake of the head would not suffice.

Although Graeye had not seen Gilbert since the

morning after the fire, each afternoon he had sent a servant to request her presence at the midday meal. Each day she had declined. Though she knew she only prolonged the moment when he would see her returned to the abbey, she had needed the time. Now, with each successive footfall that neared her place of respite, that time was fast coming to a close.

Releasing a lengthy sigh of resignation, she grasped the edges of the cover closer, but did not turn from her place at the window.

She had just settled her gaze once again on the new watchtower, when the door to the chamber was thrown wide with nary a mannerly knock to announce her visitor.

It would have been an unnecessary courtesy, Graeye mused as she continued to stare out the window. The baron had already made his presence known by din alone.

Holding the cover with one hand, she lifted an elbow to the embrasure that she might rest her chin upon her palm, and wondered what it would take to teach manners to a man like Gilbert Balmaine. Reflecting seriously upon it, she nearly forgot that the object of her ruminations was waiting impatiently upon her.

Gilbert was not averse to notifying Graeye of his presence when she persisted in feigning ignorance of it, for his tolerance of her continued refusals to come down from this room was like a long, thin line ready to snap. He'd had enough of this game and was prepared to put an end to it.

"Lady Graeye," he said sharply, crossing the width of the room in but a few long strides and coming to stand behind her. "Methinks I should clarify myself. 'Twas not a request that you join me for dinner, but an order."

Steeling herself for the confrontation, Graeye filled her lungs with fresh air before straightening and looking over her shoulder at him. She was surprised how far she had to raise her eyes to meet his scrutiny. Had

he grown taller? she wondered with private humor.
Nay, she concluded after sweeping her gaze over him—
and ignoring the fluttering that set off within her chest.
It was but an illusion caused by his nearness.

Sighing, she turned back to the view outside and
cupped her chin in her palm once again. "I have already
eaten," she murmured, nodding toward a small table
where the tray brought earlier that morning sat.

"Aye, and very little I am told," he snapped. Reaching around her, he clamped a hand about the wrist of
the arm she was propped upon and propelled her away
from the window.

It was no easy task to keep from falling headlong
into that broad chest while holding tight to the cover,
but she managed to remain upright.

"Where are your clothes?" he demanded.

"I am wearing all that I have," she answered matter-
of-factly. She attempted to pull free, but to no avail.

His eyes flicked down over the cover, and before she
realized his intent, he had swept it away, leaving her
standing in only the thin shift that clearly outlined every detail of her body. Though she should have been
dismayed, Graeye found herself oddly indifferent to
Gilbert's attempt to humiliate her. Still, out of token
modesty, she drew her arms against her body.

"Considering there is less of you to see than you've
previously shown me, methinks your modesty is out of
place," he reminded her, his gaze raking the length of
her.

Dropping her arms back to her sides, she lifted her
chin and met his stare. "But I did not reveal myself to
you, Baron Balmaine," she said boldly.

Gilbert was taken aback by her unexpected denial,
but quickly recovered. "Truly?" he said, sarcasm evident in the single word as he stared at the defiant
sparks lighting her eyes. "And who, then, did you seduce at the waterfall?"

She looked pointedly to where he still held her wrist,
then back to his face. "He did not tell me his name,"

she said, "but he was a man who revealed nothing of the black heart that beats within your breast, Baron." Shrugging, she shook her head. "Nay, it cannot have been the likes of you."

Gilbert was set back a pace. He had heretofore glimpsed the tentative claws this small cat extended, but there had been little conviction behind the swipes she had taken. He berated himself for having left her alone so many days. She had grown cold—indifferent—and it bothered him more than he cared to admit. Perhaps, he concluded, it was too near a reminder of the long, bitter years his sister had endured, and which still haunted him.

For a moment he allowed himself transport back to that time and place when he had failed Lizanne. She had needed him desperately, and though he had fought to come to her aid, he had been struck down. The battle scars he bore, his limp, all were badges of shame he wore for that night long past.

The feel of a small hand on his chest brought him back to the present. Looking down at Graeye, he saw an unexpected concern in her eyes. "Gilbert?" she said softly.

The sound of his name on her lips chased away memories of the distant past—and memories of her treachery. Instead he remembered the softness of her womanly body and the vivid passion of their one night together. His baser needs rose to the fore, and he answered them.

Making bare note of the fear that flickered in her eyes as he swung her high into his arms, he carried her to the rumpled bed.

Not until he tumbled her to the mattress did Graeye recover sufficiently to utter an indignant protest. "Nay!" she cried, thrusting her hands to his chest as he lowered himself atop her. "Do not."

Ignoring her entreaty, he gathered her wrists and lifted them above her head. He held them with one hand as he lowered his head to capture her kiss.

Graeye knew what this man was capable of doing to her defenses. Desperate not to reveal any further weakness, she fought him with every ounce of her strength, tossing her head side to side to avoid his lips and twisting her body away from his.

It did not deter him, though, for he simply found another place to put his mouth, tasting the sensitive hollow beneath her ear.

Her pulse leaping against her determination to feel nothing for the cur, she wrenched hard to free her hands from his grasp, but his strength was too great to allow her escape. Though she continued to writhe beneath him, she feared it was only a matter of time before she succumbed to his persuasions. She could not allow that to happen. . . .

Like the brush of silk, Gilbert's hand slid up beneath her shift to curve around one small breast, his thumb lightly caressing the sensitive, straining nub there. And then his mouth was on her.

When a moan of pleasure escaped her traitorous lips, Graeye thought she would die from the humiliation of her wayward body's reaction to him. As a final act of resistance, she whipped a knee up and somehow made contact at the juncture of Gilbert's thighs.

She heard his loud groan of agony, but did not understand it until he rolled off her, a hand pressed to his injured manhood.

Naturally, it had never occurred to her this could prove the best means by which to escape the arduous attentions of a man. Seeing the pain he was in, though, she realized how effective—and simple—it had been.

Knowing that when he recovered, he would be furious with her, she scrambled to the edge of the bed. She very nearly made good her escape before he caught hold of her arm and toppled her down beside him. Without a word he forced her back into the curve of his body.

Expecting his wrath to descend upon her with a vengeance, she was prodded by her newfound sense of self-preservation to try to squirm free, but there truly was no hope of that.

When several minutes passed and nothing untoward occurred, she grew even more wary. What, exactly, did he intend to do to her? Steeling herself for his anger, she slowly turned in his hold and ventured a look at him. Immediately her dread became surprise.

His head resting on an outstretched arm, Gilbert stared back at her, his face devoid of the emotion she had been certain she would find there. In fact, he was completely expressionless, except for the one corner of his mouth that was lifted slightly higher than the other.

"And where does a novice learn to do that?" he asked.

She shook her head. "What?" she asked. Then, realizing what he meant, she forestalled the clarification hovering upon his lips.

"Though it was not my intention to do you harm," she said, " 'twas all that you deserved."

The other corner of his mouth lifting, Gilbert rolled onto his side, resting his dark head on his hand. "Aye, deserved," he conceded, not quite smiling, "and more than effective, you can be assured."

Graeye could only stare at him, wondering at what game he was playing. How did he mean to retaliate for the offense done him? When he moved away from her, it was so sudden and unexpected that it took her a moment to realize he had left the bed and now stood alongside it.

"I owe you an apology, Lady Graeye," he said as he adjusted his belt. " 'Twas quite unseemly of me to force unwanted attentions upon you."

An apology? Baffled, she raised herself to a sitting position. Though aware of her scant garments, she did not attempt to cover herself again.

"In future, though," he continued, dropping his hands to his hips in that familiar gesture of authority, "I would suggest you keep your hands to yourself and use my proper title when addressing me . . . and clothe yourself properly." He looked pointedly to where her breasts thrust themselves against the thin material of her shift.

That *she* keep her hands to herself? Anger her ally once again, Graeye squelched the impulse to cross her arms over her chest. Instead she glared at him.

At the visible stiffening of her body, Gilbert shrugged, telling himself it mattered not to him. " 'Twould be to your benefit to learn that such familiarity between a man and woman does not always go unanswered, Lady Graeye," he continued, and turned to the door.

"I will send a servant directly to see you are outfitted for dinner," he said. Just outside the doorway he paused and looked over his shoulder. "Do not keep me waiting long, or I will see you clothed myself. Is that understood?"

How could she refuse a threat such as that? Graeye forced a sickly smile. "Perfectly," she said, then stood and went to the window again. Behind her the door closed softly.

Attired in another of her mother's old garments, and having purposely forgone the familiarity and comfort of a wimple, Graeye entered the hall just as Gilbert rose from his chair, obviously to come after her as he'd promised he would. Reseating himself, he beckoned her forward and indicated the empty place to his left.

As she was ushered by the grinning young maid who had coaxed her into allowing her hair to be plaited into a single braid, Graeye suffered the curious glances that followed her progress across the unending stretch of floor. With the exception of but a few, none had ever looked upon her tainted face before, and it seemed they were quite eager to do so now.

What a sight she must present, she thought. Not only did she bear the "devil's mark," but also the remainder of bruises and cuts Edward had given her. Though her humiliation should have been great, she was curiously unmoved. Let them stare, she told herself, lifting her chin higher.

"You become more brave each day," Gilbert murmured as she seated herself.

Knowing he referred to the absence of her wimple, she let his gibe go unanswered, turning her attention instead to the trencher that had been placed before her. Typically, she would have shared it with another, so large was it, but as she had arrived in the midst of the meal, there was none to divide it with.

Ignoring Gilbert, she picked around the chunks of tender meat and fish, looking for the odd bits of vegetables she preferred. As she chewed, she glanced around her and met the stares of many people. Their curiosity amused her.

Something was missing, she shortly realized. Her gaze swept the hall once more and found that the king's men were no longer present. When had they departed Medland? she wondered as she took a sip of frothy ale.

So caught up in her straying thoughts was she, Graeye didn't notice Groan's arrival. Not until he placed his head in her lap did he gain her attention.

A genuine smile wreathing her lips, she lowered a hand and drew it lingeringly over the animal's head. Though he had been her constant companion during the first few days of her recovery, he had grown restless during the last. She had seen him only on those rare occasions when he wandered into the chamber for a quick stroke and the leavings of her meals. Searching out a worthy morsel among the many in her trencher, she slipped it directly into Groan's waiting mouth.

"Careful lest that animal grows any larger," a jesting voice said beside her.

Until that moment Graeye had been oblivious to the one seated next to her, but she instantly recognized the voice.

"Sir Michael," she acknowledged the young knight. Why he would still offer her the warmth of his smile was beyond her, but she appreciated it.

Still smiling, he leaned toward her. "I had begun to think myself invisible," he said, catching her hand to brush his lips across it.

She returned his smile with an apologetic one of her own and, as politely as possible, withdrew her hand from his grasp.

"What do you at the lord's table?" she queried, not having expected Gilbert Balmaine to look kindly upon any of Edward's former retainers.

Michael moved nearer, his lips nearly touching her ear. "It seems I have found favor with the baron," he whispered.

Uncomfortable with his proximity, she drew back and leveled her gaze upon him. "And pray tell how you accomplished such a feat."

He grinned. "The supervision of the building of the new watchtower was given over to me," he said with great pride.

He needn't have elaborated further, for having seen that worthy structure, Graeye fully understood how he had pleased Gilbert. Michael did elaborate, though, beginning an extensive narrative on the complexities involved in such a project.

Graeye listened politely, made a few comments, and when he moved too near, or his hand strayed to her leg, she scooted in the opposite direction along the bench. Groan followed her progress, grumbling with dislike as the man advanced upon his mistress.

It was not long before Graeye found herself at the edge of the bench, one leg pressed against Gilbert's chair and the other brushing Sir Michael's leg. Thoroughly irritated, she turned and looked straight into Gilbert's angry blue eyes. She realized with a start that he had likely been following their conversation for some time.

Why, then, did his anger seem to be directed exclusively at her? It was the knight who had encroached upon her space, not the other way around. By neither word nor manner had she encouraged him—quite the opposite.

Standing abruptly, Gilbert declared the meal finished and ordered all except a select handful from the hall.

Grateful to have the tedious task done with, Graeye stood before Sir Michael could offer her his arm.

"Lady Graeye," Gilbert said sharply. "I would have a word with you ere you retire to your chamber. Do regain your seat."

Turning to protest, she met his challenging stare and immediately closed her mouth. She reseated herself and watched as the others, including Sir Michael, filed out of the hall.

Sensing there was booty to be had of the remains, even Groan deserted Graeye, trotting off to join the other dogs who followed the last of the serving wenches from the hall. There was still much to do to set the great room aright, but it had been cleared sufficiently for the lord to carry on his business.

Graeye watched dispassionately as the half-dozen men instructed to remain behind, Sir Lancelyn among them, gathered across the hall to await their lord's summons. Talking among themselves so they would not appear to be listening in on Gilbert's private discussion, they turned their backs to the couple.

Knowing her moment was at hand, Graeye heaved a great sigh and twisted around so that she was face-to-face with Gilbert.

"Lady Graeye," he began, raising a booted foot to the edge of the table and pushing backward in his chair until his great weight was balanced on only the two back legs, "such behavior as I have seen displayed here today is most unbecoming of a lady." His eyes never leaving her face, he began to rub his thigh.

She had expected as much from the dreadful man, so was not overly surprised by his interpretation of what had transpired between her and Sir Michael.

"Methinks you have completely misunderstood the situation," she said. "As you obviously refer to Sir Michael's conduct, should you not take this matter up with him?"

"Aye, I will speak to him of it," he agreed, leaning farther back in his chair. "But he is hardly responsible for responding to your invitations."

Her ... Outraged, Graeye jumped to her feet and looked down at where he was perched at a rather precarious angle upon his chair. "You see only through the eyes of a man," she declared, uncaring that she had drawn the attention of the others. "And only that which you care to see. I neither encouraged Sir Michael, nor invited his attentions. In the past he has been kind to me—'tis all. I was simply returning that kindness."

Gilbert appeared unmoved. Steepling his fingers before his face, he regarded her pale visage. "Then you would not be interested in his taking you to wife?" he asked with a lift of his brows.

It was not what she had expected to hear. Her lips parting on a gasp of surprise, she sank back down upon the bench.

Why did his question dishearten her so? she wondered. Even as her mind supplied the answer, she fiercely denied it. Nay, she had absolutely no liking for this black-hearted giant. For all she cared, Gilbert Balmaine could go straight to the devil.

Secure in her resolve to distance her vulnerable emotions as far from Gilbert as possible, she turned her thoughts to Sir Michael. So he still wished to wed her. Was it because Edward was now missing, relieving him of the burden of also assuming responsibility for a man he detested? Aye, she concluded, that had to be the reason.

And what of the abbey? Had not Gilbert already made it clear he would be satisfied with nothing less than her confinement within those walls? If that was still the case, then he was simply taunting her now, using this opportunity to take his revenge upon her for the undoing of his manhood. Soon, though, he would discover his mistake in choosing this avenue as her punishment.

"I do not understand," she said calmly as she searched his eyes for the laughter he must surely harbor there. She did not find it.

" 'Twould seem the man is enamored of you and wishes you for his wife," he explained. " 'Tis my understanding he challenged Sir William for your hand and that you refused him. I am curious if you would refuse him a second time given that your only other option would be to return to the abbey."

For a long moment Graeye considered whether or not she should bother offering an explanation for choosing Sir William over Sir Michael. Though the baron certainly deserved none, she decided there was no real harm in it. "As there would have been bloodshed had I not refused Sir Michael, I agreed to wed with Sir William."

"And you were content to marry William."

Remembering her aversion to that awful man, she barely suppressed a shudder of revulsion at the thought of being his wife. "Edward chose him," she said.

"And now would you accept Sir Michael as a husband?"

After she had accepted that the abbey was, by far, a better place for her than this cruel world? Certainly not. And the sooner she left Medland, the better.

"Is it a choice you offer me, then?" she asked, thinking to play along just a bit longer.

" 'Tis one I have seriously contemplated," he answered shortly, then pressed on with his unanswered question. "Would you accept him?"

Neither had he answered her question, she thought. Sighing, she shook her head. "Nay. I would not."

Gilbert nearly lost his balance. Truly, he had expected her to throw herself at his feet in gratitude. Instead she had hurled his tentative offer back in his face. "And why not?"

"As you have said repeatedly, my place is at the abbey. Though in the past it has been my desire not to return there, I have come to accept it—welcome it, even."

"You would prefer the abbey to marriage?" he asked in disbelief.

"Aye. Besides, I fear I would not make Sir Michael a very good wife."

"What makes you think that?"

She shrugged. "I have no feelings for him."

" 'Tis not necessary that you have feelings for the man you wed," Gilbert informed her. "There is but one purpose to marriage, and well I am sure you would be able to fulfill that part of the contract." Awaiting her response, he rubbed a hand over his thickening beard.

She remained silent, her great eyes distant and unblinking.

Wondering how he might ruffle the aloof composure she had cloaked herself in, and which he found altogether too disturbing, Gilbert leaned nearer until his warm breath caressed her lips. "Is there another you would choose instead?"

Her heart beginning a frenetic beat, Graeye lowered her gaze to his mouth. Though she tried to hold back the memories of the time when it had touched hers with passion, they rushed at her, stealing her breath. She had but to lean in to feel its warmth, to know again its—

Do not! her mind vehemently protested. He only toys with you. If you give in, he will have won. Sharply pulling away from the edge she had nearly plummeted over, she tossed her head back and stared into the eyes of the man her treacherous heart beat so loudly for.

"Nay, there is no other," she lied.

A long, impregnated silence followed, broken only by the resounding thud of Gilbert's chair as he allowed it to drop down on all four legs. " 'Tis clear, then, we are in agreement as to your future, Lady Graeye."

Graeye was certain she detected irritation in his tone. "Aye, that we are," she agreed.

"You will leave at first light on the morrow," he continued. "Gather your things and have them ready to go with you." Tilting his chair back again, he motioned his men forward.

Graeye rose to her feet and stepped away, only to turn back a moment later.

"Methinks," she said, her voice low, "you should exercise more caution lest you upend yourself, Baron Balmaine. Otherwise, it could prove rather embarrassing."

As he stared at her, she smiled, then made her retreat to the haven abovestairs.

In her solitude among the generations of Charwycks long since departed, Graeye knelt before the grave of one who had borne that name through marriage only—her mother. Clutching a spray of wilting flowers to her chest, scant survivors of summer's last harvest of color, she drew her mantle about her and bowed her head.

"Long I have missed you," she whispered, loath to speak too loudly in this hallowed place. "I . . ." Tears choking her throat and stinging her eyes, she could not utter another word for fear of giving way to the sobs that rose in her chest. Drawing the back of her hand over her eyes, she flung away the moisture clinging to her lashes.

"Forgive me for failing you," she whispered, remembering her mother's strength and determination. She had been a woman who, even in the face of a man as daunting as Edward Charwyck, had not allowed him to trample her beneath his booted feet. She had always found a way around his anger and gained for herself and her unwanted daughter whatever it was she desired. Above all, she had known how to deal with opposition, something her daughter had not learned well enough so that she could gain control over her own future. But she would learn.

With a shuddering sigh Graeye laid the flowers upon

the lonely grave, then stood. Though the skirts of her bliaut had become sodden where she had knelt in the long, dew-laden grass, she paid little heed to it as she turned and walked from that secluded grave.

Nearing the freshly turned ground where Philip lay, her feet slowed. Feeling a chill, she hugged her arms tightly around herself, then turned to Philip's grave.

How long she stood there she did not know, but when she finally lifted her head, the first rays of the sun had struck the sky and turned it a glorious shade of orange.

"You mourn for him?" a derisive voice fell upon the cold air.

Startled, she swung around to face the intruder. Cloaked in a dark-green mantle that hung past his knees, leaving only a glimpse of black chausses above the tops of his boots, Gilbert stood watching her.

Indignant, she drew herself to her full height. "You intrude, sir," she said, wondering how the mere presence of this man managed to chase the chill from her limbs.

"My apologies." He offered a curt bow before walking nearer. "I would not have encroached, but your escort awaits you."

Lowering her eyes, Graeye turned her back on him and looked again to where Philip had been laid to his final rest. "There is something that has too long disturbed me," she said, "and I would have you tell me yea or nay."

Gilbert stopped beside her. "What would that be?" he asked with mounting suspicion.

She lifted her gaze to his. "Did my brother accept the cross upon his death?"

Gilbert was clearly taken aback by her question. A myriad of emotions swept over his usually composed features before his expression became stony again. He shook his head. "Nay, 'twas not a consideration. Philip died a coward."

Her anger quickening, she swung away from him, walking swiftly.

He caught up to her easily and pulled her around to face him. "Trust me in this," he said, his mouth tightening as he stared down at her. "Even had a cross been thrust upon his shoulders, he would not have accepted it."

"As you would not?" she threw back at him. "I hardly knew Philip, so I cannot pass judgment on him, but well I have come to know your black heart, Gilbert Balmaine." She swiped at the hand holding her. "Be careful lest you suffer the same fate as the man you slaughtered."

His grip tightened, his face suffusing a dark red. "I would clarify but one point, Lady Graeye," he said between clenched teeth. " 'Twas not I who laid your brother down, though I would have welcomed the opportunity to have done so."

"Think you I do not know 'twas that wicked sister of yours who dealt the final blow? That she did it to save you from Philip's blade? Nay, no matter his crimes, 'twas not my brother who was the coward, but you and your sister!"

His face came nearer. "You are wrong."

"I saw the killing wound myself!" she shouted, her belly rolling as her senses experienced again the night she had spent with her brother's corpse. "Shot through the back like an animal by a coward."

A spasm of surprise ran up Gilbert's spine. "You saw?" How could that be? Philip would have been dead near a fortnight when she was brought from the abbey. He should have been buried long before her arrival.

The sudden, bitter laughter that issued from her lips bothered him in a way he did not understand—nor cared to. "Do you think Edward would shield me from such an atrocity? He forced me to—"

Realizing she had said more than she'd intended, Graeye halted her next words. "Beware, Balmaine," she said softly. "For all the evil you may accuse Edward of, you still do not know him. Do not feel bad, though, for I did not truly know him until recently. And he is my—" She stopped, once more determined never to refer to him as "father" again.

Ignoring her warning, Gilbert pulled her chin up. "What did he force you to do?"

She shifted her gaze past his head.

"Tell me, damn you!"

She shook her head.

"I will know now."

She met his gaze. "Or what?" she prompted in a chill, wintry voice.

Taken aback by her challenge, Gilbert stared into her hard, silvery eyes a long time. "I want to understand," he finally said.

"Do you?"

God's teeth! She made him feel the lowliest cur. Pushing a hand through his unruly hair, he nodded.

She closed her eyes briefly, then met his gaze again. "Then understand this. I spent an entire night with my dead brother praying him into heaven and asking God to see justice done to those who had murdered him. So tell me again of my deceit, Baron Balmaine, but first repent of your own."

First anger, then compassion, overcame Gilbert. Deep, flaring anger for Edward Charwyck's cruelty. Then that same compassion he'd been fighting almost from the moment he'd seen her. And there was something deeper. . . .

He shook his head to clear it of the weakness it would have him succumb to. He didn't want to care for this woman. Didn't want to feel the pain she had suffered at the hands of her father. He wanted her gone from Medland before she could weave another of her witching spells upon him. Wanted her forgotten.

"You know nothing of what transpired," he said, releasing his hold on her and stepping away. "But mayhap 'tis best you think the worst of me than know the kind of man your brother truly was." He turned from her and started back toward the castle, his limp more evident than usual.

"Go back to your abbey, child," he tossed over his shoulder, his gaze sweeping her one final time before relinquishing her to the fate he had set her to.

With a heavy heart Graeye stared after him, and only when he had gone from her sight did she follow.

Chapter 10

ow long did you think to keep it from us?" the abbess asked as she lifted her hand from the younger woman's softly rounded belly.

Graeye lowered her eyes as she searched for a response, but none was fast in coming.

The abbess, Mother Celia, clasped her hands together at her waist and waited, all the while reflecting on the young woman's return to the abbey nearly five months past. Though Graeye had always been a solemn soul, there was something changed about her—a kind of sadness that came only with disillusionment of the heart.

From the day she had returned, she had been thus. When she had been urged to complete her vows of sisterhood, she had declined to do so in no uncertain terms, offering only a tersely written note from the new baron of Medland to support her stand. Subsequently, she had entered the order of the convent and kept herself conspicuously absent from all but those activities she was required to attend.

However, there was also a strength and resolve to her character that showed itself most clearly with each passing day. No longer did she seem ashamed of the mark upon her face, refusing to don a wimple even when Mistress Hermana insisted upon it. Chin high, she carried herself well among the others, paying no particular attention to the stares that followed her. Nay, she was no longer the reserved child who had left the abbey with dreams in her eyes.

The abbess let go a long, weary sigh. Though her instincts had proved correct regarding the loss of her charge's virtue, she had hardly expected this to be the result. Mildly irritated, she tapped a foot among the rushes, her gaze dropping again to Graeye's waist, which, beneath the voluminous bliaut, hinted at nothing out of the ordinary.

If not for Sister Sophia's experienced eye, it might have been weeks longer before any had known of her condition. But why had Graeye kept it to herself for so long? After all, it was not unusual for daughters of the nobility to be sent to the abbey to give birth to bastard children, thereby avoiding dishonoring their families. Even now there were four others at the convent in various stages of pregnancy.

"I was ashamed." Graeye finally found the humble words to express the hard knot of anxiety that had settled over her since she had first guessed her state three months earlier.

"Ashamed?" Mother Celia repeated. Her eyes shone with a kindness and understanding that made Graeye want to seek the comfort of her arms. "Methinks 'tis likely you have little to be ashamed of, Lady Graeye. Was this not a man's doing?"

Since she had been a novice ready to take her vows, Graeye was not surprised the abbess believed her pregnancy was the result of forced intimacy. Though it would have been easier to let her continue to believe that, Graeye could not lie to her, not even by omission.

Shaking her head, she looked away. "I fear 'twas entirely my own doing," she admitted. "I blame no one but myself."

Her declaration was met with silence. When she finally ventured a look at the other woman, she was truly surprised at the compassion Mother Celia wore upon her face.

"I would leave here if it so pleases you," Graeye offered, having already given the matter some thought.

"And where would you go, child?" the abbess asked, taking her arm.

As Graeye contemplated this question—and not for the first time since she'd discovered the new life growing inside her—the abbess led her to a bench and urged her down upon it. In turmoil she stared sightlessly at the woman's retreating back as Mother Celia walked to a sideboard across the small room. A moment later a goblet of watered wine was pressed into Graeye's hand.

"Drink it all, child," Mother Celia said, lowering herself beside Graeye. "Then we will talk of your future."

Relieved that, at last, here was someone with whom she could speak of her mounting fears, Graeye quickly drained the goblet and turned to face the older woman.

A placid smile upon her lips, Mother Celia removed the goblet from Graeye's tense fingers and set it aside. "Now," she said, "tell me of the father. Is he wed?"

Graeye was painfully aware that she did not know the answer to that question. While at Medland she had never even thought to ask about Gilbert's marital status—had assumed he was without a wife. "I do not think so," she muttered, her shame growing twofold with the confession.

"Hmm." The abbess's lips twitched. "Think you he would be willing to wed with you if he does not yet have a wife?"

This was the most remote possibility of all—absurd. Gilbert Balmaine wanted nothing to do with her, bastard child or not.

"He would not," she said, her throat tightening painfully. "Methinks he would first give himself to the . . ." Her voice trailed off as she prudently withdrew the word that had nearly fallen from her lips.

Knowingly, Mother Celia nodded. "And he knows naught of the babe?"

Graeye shook her head.

"Do you fancy yourself in love with him, child?"

Graeye's mouth opened and closed several times before any sound issued forth. "Nay!" she finally gasped. "He is the veriest of curs."

Mother Celia was quiet a long moment, reflecting back upon the note given her the day of Graeye's return. Though brief, the baron had been explicit regarding Graeye's entry into the convent. Because she had not wanted to read too much into it, Mother Celia had not understood then what she thought she did now. There was simply no reason for the man to have concerned himself with Graeye's future at the abbey, unless he'd had knowledge of her undoing—a knowledge that, she suspected, was of a personal nature.

"Do not worry," she said, patting Graeye's hands where they were tightly clenched in her lap. "You will be provided for." She stood and walked to her writing desk.

Having been excused, Graeye withdrew from the chamber and slowly made her way back to the modest room she shared with two others.

The cold, wintry months that followed Graeye's return to the abbey did little to improve Gilbert's disposition. Not only were his days filled with the management of his newly expanded estates, but also with numerous forays against the brigands that attacked his villages.

Worse, the long nights dragged by on leaden feet. When sleep finally came to him, too often his dreams were haunted by sad, pale eyes, soft lips that rarely knew a smile, and the feel of silken strands that ran through his fingers in an endless stream of burnished gold.

Most nights that he lay awake, his body burned with

a great, aching need, but he found little ease with any of the willing wenches he took into his bed. Soon he refused their invitations altogether and fell into a deeper kind of torment that made it nearly unbearable for him to live with himself. Constantly, he fought the unwanted visions of Graeye, even attempting to banish them with the fading memory of Lady Atrice, but he had no more success with that than he'd found with any of the women. It made for a restless sleep and a foul temper when the morn finally deigned to arrive.

Five months after Graeye's return to Arlecy, a messenger made his way through a frigid, pelting rain to Medland in search of Gilbert. Gilbert, however, was at Penforke. Sir Lancelyn, who had been made the castellan of Medland, bade the man pass the night at the castle and, before the sun rose the next morning, sent him on his way with a small escort to speed and ensure his safe journey. Thus the disgruntled messenger was very nearly in as foul a mood as Gilbert when he was ushered into the great hall of the donjon at Penforke.

After a brief introduction, which Gilbert cut short with an impatient wave of his hand, the man was led to await his audience on a bench against the far side of the room. Had he had not been so frightened by the size of Gilbert Balmaine, he would surely have been tempted to return the man's rude manners.

The time lengthened, and when the messenger was finally beckoned forward to deliver his message, it was found he had fallen asleep, an angry scowl upon his face.

Having spent a good deal of the morning confined with his droning steward, who had painstakingly cited each of the losses suffered from the raiding brigands, Gilbert had little tolerance for the messenger's fatigue. He divested the man of his duty by retrieving the message himself. The man slept on with nary a groan of protest.

Without regard for the elaborate wax seal that held the parchment closed, Gilbert broke it and strode back to where his steward was bent over his books. He grabbed the man's arm and held the parchment out to him.

Though he could well do it himself, Gilbert found reading and writing tedious work. Given a choice, he left it to his steward, or any other man capable of that rare talent with words. He far preferred the spoken form over the written.

Leaning back against the edge of the table, he impatiently drummed his fingers on its surface as he waited for the steward to begin reading.

" 'Tis from the abbess at Arlecy," the man informed him, squinting at the broken seal.

Gilbert stilled.

"It says, 'Baron Balmaine, there is a discreet matter of great importance that I must discuss with you regarding . . .' " He cleared his throat. ". . . Lady Graeye Charwyck. She is—' "

Before he could read any further, Gilbert snatched the parchment away. Ignoring the steward's stammered entreaty, he turned the message toward the light of a torch and held it at arm's length to read it for himself.

"She is many months with child," he read silently, then dropped his lids closed over eyes that burned with fatigue.

His heart beat a lurching rhythm in his chest as he attempted to get the surge of emotions—a mixture of outrage, disbelief, anger, suspicion, and even a spark of something he refused to put a name to—under control.

His hands trembling, he reread the message from the beginning, then paused momentarily before proceeding with the remainder. "As she was last under your guardianship, I would ask that you make haste to call at Arlecy that we might discuss this matter more fully."

Allowing the parchment to curl back on itself, Gilbert drew a hand over his face, raking his fingers through the thick growth of winter beard. Was it possible Graeye carried his child—after but one night of joining? And if she did, why had she waited so long to inform him of her condition? Was this yet another of her carefully worked deceptions?

In spite of his body's constant, treacherous yearnings for the woman, Gilbert knew he mustn't forget she was a Charwyck. Aye, it could just as easily be any other man's child she carried . . . if she carried a child at all.

In the back of his mind he acknowledged that, even without the arrival of this message, the unwanted bond between himself and Graeye would have had to be addressed sooner or later. Unfinished business stood between them, and it needed to be seen through to its completion ere he could free himself of this stranglehold she had on him. Not for the first time in the past months, he entertained the thought that if he could but have her once again, it would be enough to rid himself of her forever.

Still, if it was his child she carried . . .

His thoughts turned to the trap he had been planning to lay for the brigands two days hence. It was an opportunity he was loath to let pass, for if carried out without mishap, it would likely see Edward Charwyck, the brigands' leader, delivered into his hands.

Until that moment Gilbert had thought there was nothing he wanted more than to apprehend the man.

He was wrong.

Groaning, he crumpled the crisp parchment in his fist and called for his squire.

Chapter 11

~~~~~~~

With growing impatience Gilbert paced the room he'd been asked to wait in a very long half hour past. From time to time he stopped before the window and scanned the courtyard below, and the winter-ravaged garden that stretched far to the left. Then he resumed his pacing.

What was keeping the abbess? he wondered with deepening irritation. Though he'd given no warning of his arrival, he had been assured she would be along shortly. Considering the wintry weather, his men would have grown restless by now where they awaited him outside the walls of the abbey. Had he known the wait that lay ahead, he would have insisted upon their being brought inside as well.

Cursing beneath his breath, he dropped down upon the hard bench facing the door and began to massage the aching muscles of his leg. Since he and his men had left Penforke two days past, nearly every waking hour had been spent in the saddle. Though that by itself did not usually trouble his old injury, coupled with the cold, damp weather, it proved quite painful.

Mayhap the abbess was in the midst of none, that time of prayer taken shortly after dinner, he thought, trying to reason himself out of the foul mood he was sinking more deeply into with each passing minute.

A moment later there was a light rap on the door, then silence.

"Come," he called, and stood as the door was pushed inward.

Tall and regal as any queen, the abbess stepped inside, then closed the door behind her. "Baron Balmaine," she said, coming to stand before him. "I am Mother Celia, Abbess of Arlecy."

He had expected Graeye to accompany her, and he felt oddly disquieted by her absence. Was she in the corridor awaiting a summons? Or did she wait in one of those buildings where none but the clergy were allowed to venture?

Forcing his mind from its wandering path, he bowed, then removed the travel-weary parchment from his belt and handed it to the woman. "You wished to discuss this matter of Lady Graeye with me," he prompted.

Smiling faintly, she took the document from him and lowered herself to the bench. "Umm, yes," she said, perusing her own precise handwriting before looking back up at him. "First, though, I must apologize for having begun to question your sense of responsibility, Baron. You see, I expected you much sooner, and when you did not come ... well ..." She shrugged, gracefully lifting her hands palms up.

Lips twitching with irritation at the thinly veiled reprimand, Gilbert crossed to the window and stared down at the small procession of nuns walking across the courtyard. They kept to a line so straight and unwavering, he could have been watching a military parade.

"As I was not at Medland when your message arrived," he said, " 'twas delayed until it could be delivered to me at Penforke."

"Ahh," Mother Celia breathed. She was somewhat placated by his explanation, but she wondered at the black mood emanating from him. She had expected he would be less than pleased by her missive, but had never guessed he would feel it so deeply.

"You are here now," she said, hoping to draw him back from the window, "and we've much to discuss. Come, sit beside me." With a sweeping hand she indicated the length of vacant bench.

He did not move from his position at the window, apparently preferring the distance he had placed between them, but he did give her his full attention.

" 'Twould seem there is much to discuss," he agreed. "But where is Lady Graeye?"

The abbess nodded toward the window. "If she is not there yet, she will be shortly. Always after dinner she feeds the birds."

Gilbert glanced down into the courtyard again. For the first time he noticed the mass of birds that walked the flagged stones and flitted from ledge to ledge as they waited patiently for their promised meal. But he saw only the backs of two nuns as they passed from sight between two buildings. Shaking his head, he looked back at the abbess.

"Shortly," she said in a reassuring tone that set his hair on end.

Did she think him anxious to catch sight of Graeye? he wondered. His lips compressed tightly as he rejected such an absurd idea. Nay, it was mere curiosity as to her whereabouts that bade him search her out.

"I would have expected her to accompany you," he said, forcing as much indifference into his voice as he could manage.

"Oh, nay." The abbess shook her head vehemently, as if to impress upon him the error of his assumption. "I assure you, Lady Graeye knows naught of your coming, Baron."

"Then?"

The abbess clasped her hands and pinned him with a serene gaze. "Upon discovering Lady Graeye's condition, I took it upon myself to contact you. You are responsible, are you not?"

Drawing a deep breath, Gilbert leaned an arm against the wall alongside the window. "She has said I fathered the child she carries?" It was more a statement than a question.

What looked to be a self-satisfied smile flitted across the woman's face. "Nay, but I have guessed correctly, have I not?"

If the abbess was to be believed, and Gilbert was reluctant to extend his doubt of God to this woman, then his conclusions about Graeye's character lost much of their credibility. It unbalanced him to hear she had not laid claim to him as the father, and that she was unaware he'd been sent for.

Still, he offered a nonchalant shrug before answering Mother Celia. "There is a possibility the child is mine," he said, "but only that."

The abbess let go a deep, unexpected sigh of relief. "Then 'tis certainly yours."

Gilbert's eyes narrowed on her. "I do not know that," he said, wondering what sly trickery she was attempting to work upon him.

"Long have I known Lady Graeye—though I admit, not well. I was but a sister of the order when she first came to us ..." The abbess paused and calculated the period of time since elapsed. "Eleven years ago." She offered Gilbert a fleeting smile that lit her features and made her considerable number of years dwindle to insignificance.

Gilbert blinked, and when next he focused upon her, she looked her age again. Settling himself in for the duration, he folded his arms over his chest and nodded for her to continue.

"Graeye has always kept to herself ... a very sad child when she came to us," she said with regret. "Most of the children sent to us do visit their homes, though it may be infrequently. But it was not that way for Graeye. Not until her father sent for her last autumn did she leave Arlecy since she first arrived as a child—

and never did she receive any visitors here. 'Tis not an easy life she has had."

For an unguarded moment the walls around Gilbert's heart began to soften. He rebelled by dragging forth the crumbling memory of Graeye's deception.

"Although I have never met the man," Mother Celia continued, "I have heard much of Baron Edward Char—"

"No longer baron," Gilbert was quick to inform her.

The woman nodded. "However, this I do know. Though the blood that runs through Lady Graeye's veins is that of her father's, she is not of the same ilk."

Determined to maintain his beliefs about Graeye, Gilbert simply stared at the woman. He did wonder, though, what enlightenment she might use next to persuade him of whatever it was she aspired to.

"I had great hopes for her in your world, Baron," she said some moments later, her gaze direct. "You see, I have always known 'twas not in her heart to join the sisterhood—"

"Then why did she consent to taking the veil?" Gilbert interrupted, though he felt regret for having stepped again upon the woman's words.

The abbess let his rudeness pass without reproach. "There was no other option for her, and 'twas her father's express wish that she become a nun."

"Why?"

Mother Celia shrugged. "The mark she bears." She touched a finger alongside her own eye. "Though I know it only to be a mark of birth, there are others who would say 'tis of the devil. That was also her father's belief, and methinks he thought to appease God by offering Graeye to Him."

Turning this over in his mind, Gilbert looked out the window and down into the courtyard where a single figure had appeared. Though covered from head to foot in a long black mantle, her back to him, he knew it was Graeye. Without realizing he held his breath, he watched as she attempted to coax a reluctant bird down from its perch atop a roof. Unable to resist her offering of a large crust of bread, it was not long in coming down.

Gilbert felt not only a softening of his heart as he stared at her, but a decided crumbling of the walls that guarded it. Again his mind threw up her deceit before him, but it was useless. It would seem she had not set out to trap him into marriage as he had convinced himself, but she still had used him so that she would not be forced to take vows into sisterhood. After an internal struggle so fierce, he felt he'd taken on wounds as fearsome as the one that scarred his leg, he finally conceded to a standoff between heart and mind. But it was a confusion he could not afford—a tumultuous mixture of antagonism and yearning that he could see no way to mesh.

"How many months is she with child?" he asked, frustrated by his inability to glimpse the shape of Graeye's body beneath the layers of winter clothing.

"It approaches five months since she returned here," the abbess stated as she stood and walked toward him. "So she is at least that far along. No less, I assure you."

Gilbert's jaw worked, alternately tense and slack as he followed Graeye's progress about the courtyard. He willed her to turn around so that he could get a better view of her and see again the delicate beauty of her face. He was sorely disappointed when, a minute later, she unknowingly fulfilled his desire and turned. He could not even glimpse her hair or features, completely hidden as they were beneath the spacious hood.

"She does not belong in a cloister of nuns," the abbess murmured, having come to stand beside him. "Lady Graeye is of your world."

"Aye," he heard himself concede. "She does not belong here."

Moving nearer, the abbess captured his gaze with hers. "Then you will wed her and give her child your name?"

There was no hesitation in Gilbert's response to that ridiculous proposal. " 'Twould be impossible for me to marry her," he declared.

Frowning, Mother Celia stepped back from the baron. "I do not see the difficulty," she said, secure in the knowledge gained from her recent inquiries into his personal life. "I am told you are without a wife. Mayhap you are betrothed?"

She watched as he threw a wrathful glare down at Graeye, who once again had her back to them. "Nay," he ground out, turning the fire in his eyes upon the abbess. "Were I of a mind to wed with a Charwyck"—he fairly spat the name—"there would be naught to prevent me from doing so. But as I would never entertain such an idea, I fear 'tis not the solution you seek to this dilemma."

It was Mother Celia's keen perceptiveness that had elevated her to her position at the abbey. She used that talent now as she studied the baron. "I know naught of your dispute with the Charwycks, Baron Balmaine," she said, "but I would ask that you not visit the sins of Lady Graeye's family upon her. She is hardly responsible for any wrongs done you by their hand."

"And what of wrongs done me by her hand?" he rejoined, his anger obviously mounting.

"I know not what wrongs you speak of, Baron, nor can I guess at what Lady Graeye might have done to earn your ire. But if you condemn her, I would first have you consider your own conduct."

His head snapped back. "My conduct?" he roared.

"Aye." She nodded curtly, indifferent to his vibrant rage. In truth, she was too concerned with controlling her own emotions to worry overly much about his.

"The lady was chaste when she left the abbey, and spoiled without benefit of marriage when she was returned to us. That you would set yourself to seducing an innocent young noblewoman is beyond reproach— and then restore her to the Church with your child growing full in her belly!"

Gilbert almost choked on that, his face darkening as he met her reproachful gaze. So it was he who had done the seducing, eh?

"Then she has accused me of having seduced her," he snarled, clenching his fists so tightly, his nails dug into the toughened skin of his palms. "Truly, it doth surprise me she did not think to call it rape."

The abbess's lids fluttered momentarily before lifting again. "Nay, as I have already told you, Lady Graeye accuses you of naught, Baron Balmaine. Though I had initially thought otherwise, she made it most clear she had not been ... forced."

But she had made it clear she'd been seduced, Gilbert concluded. And it was obvious the abbess did not believe Graeye capable of any deception. Bitter laughter, accompanied by denial, very nearly made it to his lips before he forced it back down. Regardless of what lies the wench had told, he would not reveal to anyone the true circumstances surrounding her impregnation—though she certainly warranted no such consideration.

Mother Celia's voice broke into his thoughts. "I would ask that you reconsider and marry the lady Graeye."

"She is a Charwyck," Gilbert bit off, "and every bit as deceitful as her brother and father. Nay, look elsewhere, for I would not bind myself to that one."

In an instant the abbess abandoned all efforts to keep her composure intact. "Then your taking of her virtue was merely a ploy by which to have revenge upon the Charwycks?" she asked bluntly, annoyed at this man's continued obstinance.

The baron appeared taken aback by her question. "Nay," he said after a moment. "I assure you, revenge did in no way enter into it."

Mother Celia regarded him a long, thoughtful moment. Then, turning on her heel, she set herself to pacing the room. This was not going as well as she had planned....

Gilbert turned his attention back to the courtyard,

certain that simply voicing his convictions had strength-
ened his resolve to stay free of the treacherous silken
bonds the abbess would have him accept. Disappointment swept him upon discovering the place empty save
for a few remaining birds that foraged for any scrap that
may have been overlooked by the others.

Where had she gone? he wondered, his anger beginning to ease.

"Then if you will not marry her . . . ," the abbess
said.

Gilbert did not turn to face her, watchful lest Graeye
return. However, when minutes passed and she did not
reappear, he turned to consider the abbess and her res-
olute stance.

" 'Tis simple," she said with a tight smile. "You must
find another who would take her to wife."

Frowning, Gilbert crossed the room to stand over
her. She was not such a tiny thing, though, so he did
not tower above her as he did Graeye.

" 'Tis not as simple as you say," he said. "Ere she
was returned to this place, I did find a man eager to
wed with her, but she refused him." He did not tell her
that, had Graeye accepted Sir Michael, he probably
wouldn't have consented to the match. Even then,
when he had most deeply felt her deception, the
thought of any other man having her had infuriated
him.

The abbess did not appear intimidated by his nearness. Placing a finger to her lips, she pursed her mouth.
"Then 'tis apparent her heart is somewhere else, do you
not think?"

Suspicious, Gilbert stared at her.

Her eyes twinkling with what he was certain was
mischief, she reached out and patted his arm. " 'Tis a
great burden you must carry, Baron Balmaine," she
said, "but if you set yourself to discovering who Lady
Graeye has given her heart to, then there is the husband she would have. And all your problems will be
solved."

She shrugged. "And if you cannot find it in you to do that, then look for another more acceptable to her. But I warn you to be careful lest you choose a man unworthy of raising your child. And do not forget she is always welcome at Arlecy should you find it too burdensome to take responsibility for finding your child a father."

Knowing the abbess dangled bait before him, Gilbert resentfully took the hook, though he did not for one moment believe the words he spoke. "You are implying that the Lady Graeye fancies herself in love with me?"

Mother Celia laughed. "Nay, Baron, I would never think to suggest such a thing, especially now that I have met you and seen for myself the embittered man you are. It must surely be another she has given her heart to."

Though thoroughly irritated by the woman's effrontery, Gilbert did not rise to the bait a second time. She was correct, after all. He was not an amiable man. His every day was shadowed by constant reminders of the wrongs done him and his family by Philip Charwyck. Still, he was resentful of the abbess's meddling and wanted nothing more to do with it.

Swinging away, he snatched up his mantle and deftly secured it with a simple brooch. "I will be taking Lady Graeye from here," he said. "See she is ready to leave within the hour." He threw wide the door and started to step through it, but was pulled up short by the abbess's next words.

"Her sanctuary is here at Arlecy, Baron Balmaine."

He turned in the doorway and leveled his gaze upon the woman, waiting with great impatience for her to finish.

"If Lady Graeye does not wish to go with you, there is naught neither you nor I can do to remove her from this place. Hence, you may have to set yourself the task of convincing her otherwise."

In his eagerness to be gone he had not considered the possibility of Graeye choosing to remain at the abbey.

He truly did not think she would. But if she did, he knew he could not simply subdue her and carry her away. The protection afforded her by the Church took that right from him. And though he would willingly risk its wrath, he would not risk the king's.

"Come," the abbess said. "I will take you to her now."

Gilbert stepped into the corridor and allowed the abbess to precede him from the guest house. In silence she led him across the courtyard and to the gardens where she clearly expected to find Graeye, but she was nowhere to be seen.

"Wait here." Mother Celia waved to an arbor enclosed on three sides. "I will send for her."

Nodding, Gilbert stepped into the shelter, but declined a seat upon the bench. How would she receive him? he wondered, feeling his pulse quicken with the thought that any moment she would be standing before him. It was not all bad, he told himself, for at long last he had the opportunity to exorcise the lady from his every waking thought and finally find some measure of peace.

Shortly, the abbess reappeared. "She is in prayer," she said, "but I have asked Sister Sophia to send her along anyway."

"She will know the reason for her summons?"

The abbess shook her head. "Nay, I have not given any reason for asking her to meet me. 'Twill be soon enough that she knows of your presence."

Gilbert made no comment. He simply turned toward the walkway so that he could see Graeye's reaction upon discovering him in this place.

When the time dragged by and she did not appear, his impatience quickened. "She is not very punctual," he remarked, looking at the abbess, who stood beside him.

"As I have told you," she said, "this is not her world."

He scowled.

"Too," she added, "the babe has been troubling her some—"

"Something is wrong?" He pounced on that, a sudden tension falling upon him.

Mother Celia nearly laughed at his show of concern, but managed to hide her pleasure behind a twitching smile. "I do not think so," she said. " 'Tis just a malady of pregnancy that many women experience."

Carefully picking her way over the frozen ground lest she lose her footing, Graeye stopped upon hearing the abbess's voice that carried across the long, narrow strip of garden. She was with someone?

Quickening her pace, she admonished herself for having forgotten her gloves in the chapel. Though her hands had grown cold in the short time she'd been outside, she continued to hold them before her as a precaution should she slip.

As she rounded the corner, a soft, insistent fluttering in her belly reminded her of the necessity to slow her pace. Smiling, she pressed a hand to that subsiding movement and took the last steps with even greater care.

Two people were standing within the shelter of the arbor—one well-known, the other striking an unsettling chord of familiarity within Graeye. Curious as to the identity of the handsome, dark-headed visitor, she stepped nearer, searching the clean-shaven face, then the eyes that lifted to meet her gaze. Startling blue they were. . . .

Gasping in sudden recognition, she stumbled and instinctively threw out a hand to break her fall. She managed to keep her feet, though, and when she raised her head, she found Gilbert standing disconcertingly close.

It was no wonder she had not recognized him immediately, she thought, for he appeared so much younger and less ominous without his beard, even with dark shadows beneath his eyes. Aye, she had thought him attractive before, but now she was struck breathless by the handsome face revealed to her.

Though fewer than two of the baron's long-legged strides separated them, neither attempted to bridge the gap. Hence, it was Mother Celia who finally broke the stricken silence. "I believe you already know each other," she said, stepping forward. "I will leave you now to become reacquainted."

Her face serene, she took Graeye's cold hands in hers and placed a kiss upon her cheek. "Think of the child you carry," she whispered, then turned to go.

She had told him . . . of course. Graeye watched the abbess leave with mounting apprehension, and still stared after her even when the older woman was gone from sight.

Another fluttering from her baby broke her free of her stupor. Keeping her gaze carefully averted from the probing eyes she felt with every pore of her being, she slipped a hand beneath the mantle and smoothed it over the gently rounded swell.

"The child you carry." Gilbert's deep voice vibrated through the air, strumming the taut strings of Graeye's frayed emotions. "Is it mine?"

Graeye knew only a sudden need to be away from there—away from this disbelieving man who would pose such a hurtful question to her. Lifting her chin, she met his stare with one of her own, putting into it all the loathing she could summon, then turned on her heel and headed down the path the abbess had taken.

Hearing Gilbert's footsteps behind, she first thought to run, but quickly quelled that idea, knowing it was far too dangerous. There was nothing she would do to cause harm to her unborn child. Nothing. Accepting that flight was useless, she swung back around just as Gilbert reached out a hand to detain her.

He looked down at her as she peered up at him from the shadowed folds of her hood. His hand hesitated in the air before he let it drop back to his side. "Is the child mine?" he repeated.

"Nay," she said, grateful for the cover the hood afforded her. "You needn't concern yourself with my child, Baron Balmaine, for 'tis another who fathered it."

He appeared stunned by her disavowal. In silence he regarded her, searching what little he could make out of her face. "Methinks you lie, Lady Graeye," he concluded. "Aye, you will need to apply yourself more diligently to such endeavors if ever you are to become an accomplished liar." Without warning he swept her hood back to reveal her face and a swath of tawny, golden-streaked hair.

Graeye's hand shot up from the folds of her mantle to catch the hood. However, before she could take hold of the coarse material, Gilbert deftly caught her hand and enveloped her cold fingers in the warmth of his.

Quivering with an anger too long suppressed, she threw back her head and stared up at him. "Has it been so long since we last met that you would forget how deceitful I am?" she hissed between lips drawn thin. "Had I acknowledged you as the father of my child, I am most certain you would have then denied it." She leaned forward and regarded him for a long moment. "Best you be warned, Baron. Such a bent toward believing the opposite of what one is told could easily be put to advantage by those who would seek to deceive you."

Gilbert remained motionless as he examined the underlying meaning of her words and attempted to understand the emotion emanating from her. Aye, he had seen glimpses of her anger—had discovered those tiny, sharp claws of hers—but this was too much like his own embittered anger. It unsettled him to see himself mirrored in her.

When she set herself back on her heels, a forced semblance of a smile curled her lips. "Consider this, my lord. Mayhap 'twas my intention to maneuver you into accepting responsibility for this child by denying 'twas yours." Her shoulders lifted in a negligent shrug. "Or perhaps I speak the truth."

Gilbert's eyes narrowed. "I refuse to play such word games with you, Graeye—"

"Graeye?" She snatched that rare opportunity to interrupt him as he had so often done to her. "Such familiarity, my lord?"

He suddenly pulled her against him and, even as she resisted, boldly slipped a hand inside her mantle and laid it upon her belly.

She stilled at his surprisingly gentle touch, her breath stopping as those long fingers began an exploration of her pregnancy. She closed her eyes on the sudden awareness his fingertips incited, an awareness she'd thought long buried. How was it this man she had convinced herself to hate could still rouse such a response from her?

"Now tell me again this is not my child," he said.

Pulling free from her mind's desperate wanderings, she tilted her head back. "You would believe the words of one so deceitful?"

His hand still curved over her belly, he brought his face nearer hers. "Only if you confirm that which I already know to be true."

He meant to acknowledge her child as his? She searched his face, her gaze roving over features that had heretofore been hidden from her. Her eyes were drawn first to a mouth that was wider than she had thought, then up and to the side where a slight indentation was visible below one cheek. It would be a dimple if ever he smiled, she thought. And his smooth skin offered testament to having recently had a blade laid to it.

Before she could squelch the impulse, she lifted a hand and placed it alongside his jaw. Immediately the muscles leaped beneath her touch, reminding her of the inappropriateness of such a gesture. Dropping her hand, and slid it beneath her mantle, and closed her fingers around his wrist. Surprisingly he did not resist when she lifted it from her belly.

" 'Tis my child, Gilbert Balmaine," she said with rigid conviction.

His eyes narrowed. It was not the acknowledgment he had expected.

"And the father?" he persisted. Like a tightly sprung coil, he waited for the grudging admission she still owed him, and which he was determined to have.

She did not cower from his anger. "Who 'twas that scattered the seed by which my babe now grows is of little consequence, Baron. You would do best to—"

"You will be returning to Medland with me this day."

She shook her head. "Nay, I have grown content with my lot and no longer—"

Before she could gainsay him further, he swung her up into his arms and carried her from the garden.

Graeye was sensible enough not to struggle. Still, she raised her voice in fury at his arrogance. "Know you the sin you will have committed by taking me from here against my will? 'Tis my sanctuary, and you can do naught without risking the wrath of the Church and King Henry himself."

Aye, the king ... Gilbert's steps faltered at the prospect of igniting that man's fury. But he was driven by a deeper need to secure Graeye and his child for himself, so he pushed aside the consequences of the action he was about to take. Sparing Graeye no more than a glance, he stepped from the garden and onto the path leading to the courtyard, his limp becoming more pronounced as he lengthened his stride to hasten away from the abbey.

"Nay, Gilbert, do not do this," Graeye protested more loudly. "God will visit this trespass upon you tenfold."

"God!" he repeated, his eyes never wavering from the course he set. "Let Him do His worst," he muttered. "I have endured all He has hurled at me thus far. I will yet endure what is to come."

"Though you may deny Him," she said, placing a hand over his heart, "you are not godless, Gilbert. Now release me ere the damage is too far done."

At the edge of the courtyard he halted and looked down at her. "For long months I have desired to have

you in my bed—longed to feel you again as I did that
first night. You are a scourge to my very soul, Graeye
Charwyck, yet I cannot empty you from it no matter
how often I remind myself of your deceit. But I intend
to try."

Graeye was shocked by his declaration, but could
find no words that would lend themselves to a response.

"You are mine, Graeye," he asserted, "and the babe
you carry belongs to me. Now will you come willingly
or have me risk your God's wrath yet again?"

That he would lay claim to her, as well as to the
child, sent quivers of uncertain hope through her. But
what, exactly, was he saying? She searched his face for
an answer. That he would not abandon her as she had
supposed he would once she delivered his heir? Dared
she hope that what he offered was of a permanent nature rather than an expedient one?

"If I go with you," she ventured, "would you then
wed with me that the child would be made legitimate?"

He did not hesitate. "Nay, Graeye. Though I would
offer you and the child my care and protection,
'twould be impossible for me to wed you."

A great pall fell over her. "Then you already have a
wife?"

"Nay," he answered, shifting her weight, "and 'tis
not likely I ever will. I will have my heir from you . . .
and that will suffice."

Her hope came crashing down upon her. Forgetting
her earlier caution, she threw her hands against his
chest and began to kick her legs.

"Release me, you infidel!" she demanded in a voice
choked with tears. "I will not become your leman
merely to quench your thirst. Find another to beget a
child on and leave me be."

Enfolding her more tightly against his chest, Gilbert
stepped from the path and into the vacant courtyard.

Though the fight went out of Graeye, her protests
became louder. In answer to them the abbess suddenly

reappeared, placing herself squarely in Gilbert's path. "Baron Balmaine," she said reproachfully, " 'tis clear Lady Graeye has chosen to remain at Arlecy. Do be so kind as to set her to her feet."

Gilbert fell back to earth with a thud. Previous to this most recent encounter with Graeye, he would not have believed himself so foolish as to seize her from her sanctuary. Aye, it was imprudent at best, especially considering there were other avenues yet to be explored—limited though they were.

Frowning, he lowered Graeye to the uneven stones of the courtyard and stood back.

Graeye lost no time in retreat. Stepping around the abbess, she placed the woman before her like a human shield.

"Lady Graeye," Mother Celia said over her shoulder, "return to your room at once. I will speak with you on this later."

Graeye lingered a moment longer before turning and making her way back across the courtyard.

When she had disappeared from sight, the abbess stepped nearer Gilbert, her face full of displeasure. "Baron, that you would dare such a thing is simply beyond me. What could you have been thinking?" She threw her hands into the air as if asking God to deliver her from such stupidity. "Are you so completely bereft of the words that might persuade her to go with you that you must resort to forcing her? I warned you of the dire consequences of such a scheme."

He met her steely eyes. "My apologies, Abbess. I fear I acted in haste when she refused me. 'Twas indeed foolish."

Mother Celia considered him a long moment. Then, somewhat appeased, she heaved a great sigh and waved a hand for him to follow her.

Gilbert complied, and a short time later found himself standing before the guest house. Not far off was a small gathering of nuns, their eyes lowering immediately upon noticing the tall giant in their midst.

The abbess regarded the women consideringly, then led Gilbert back inside to the room they had earlier vacated.

"Now that you have seen her again, what are your intentions?" she asked, turning to face him.

He laid a hand to his chin to run his fingers through his beard, but found his face bare, having scraped away the last of the beard just that morn. "I do not know," he admitted. "I cannot take her to wife, yet neither can I give her to another. I would have her and the child with me."

"You told her this?" At his nod the abbess shook her head. "Then I understand why she would refuse such an offer, Baron. 'Tis quite unseemly what you propose." Stepping nearer, she pinned him with her direct gaze. "Tell me, do you love her?"

Gilbert was so astonished by the question, he nearly choked on his own saliva, his color deepening as he fought to control his reaction. "Love her! A Charwyck?"

Mother Celia shrugged. She no more believed his denial than she had believed Graeye's. "Then what will you do, Baron Balmaine?"

"There are other ways." He began to pace the room. After several crossings he came back to stand before her.

She did not like what she saw upon his face, the slight, triumphant smile curving his lips.

"I will petition King Henry for the charge of my child once 'tis born," he said. " 'Tis not likely he would deny me my heir."

Mother Celia was taken aback by his declaration. Aye, he might just succeed with such a petition. Having been awarded the Charwyck lands, he was obviously in the good graces of the king. "That could take a very long time," she said, attempting to dissuade him from this ruinous course of action.

He shrugged. " 'Twill still achieve me the same end."

"And what of Lady Graeye? You would take her child from her without remorse?"

His smile widened. "Nay. She will come of her own accord, and then I will have all I desire."

Mother Celia knew such a plan would likely widen the rift between these two young people, so much so that it would be impossible ever to bridge. Still, there was another way to bring them together, a way she would never have contemplated had not the baron informed her of his plans.

"There is one other possibility," she said, folding her hands before her waist as she waited to gain the baron's full attention.

He gave it to her.

Her expression turned rueful at the prospect of disclosing that which she had recently learned. "I fear I will repent for the breaking of this confidence," she began, "but I am told that, following matins, Lady Graeye is wont to slip outside the walls. She walks along the river that lies beyond."

For an interminable time the baron only stared at her.

Interpreting his silence as ignorance of what she was striving to say, she tried to clarify. "Alas," she said, " 'tis lamentable indeed, but the Church cannot extend its protection outside the walls."

He frowned with obvious suspicion. "And why would you tell me this?"

"Were I Lady Graeye, methinks I could more easily forgive you the trespass of carrying me away than that of stealing my child from me by decree of the king."

She was right, of course, Gilbert thought. Having had a fair glimpse of Graeye's temper, his means of having her and the child lost much of its appeal. He nodded. "How goes she?"

The abbess smiled. "By way of the postern gate, of course."

Chapter 12

A ngered at having been a party to what he per- ceived as trickery, Gilbert decided it was time to put into motion his other plan of petitioning the king.

For four long, wet days he and his men had hidden themselves in the woods surrounding the abbey, lying in wait for their prey to venture forth. In all that time Graeye had not left her refuge. Gilbert was certain of this, for he was not so foolish as to trust completely in the assurances offered by the abbess. Hence he'd set men to watch the comings and goings through all the gates of the walled sanctuary, lest an attempt be made to spirit Graeye away while he watched for her at the postern gate.

It was well past the hour of matins on that fourth hellish day when he and a handful of his men returned to the camp empty-handed. Heatedly barking off or- ders, his mood evident to all, he lent his shoulder to hastening their departure that they might make for London.

Sensing his fury, Gilbert's destrier shied away from him when, at long last, they were ready to ride. Reining in the flood of his emotions, Gilbert offered a soothing hand to the animal's quivering muzzle, all the while wondering with deepening irritation where his squire had wandered to. As he thought further on it, he could not remember the young man accompanying them back from the river.

When the destrier had calmed sufficiently to be mounted, he grabbed the pommel of his saddle and slid his foot into the stirrup.

"My lord, she comes!" his squire, Joseph, called as he sprinted from out of the trees to the center of the dis-assembled camp where Gilbert stood.

"She comes," he repeated.

Gilbert took hold of the younger man's shoulders. "To the river?"

"Aye, my lord, though she does not venture too far from sight of the abbey."

Though it would have been best to come upon Graeye without the hindrance of the clamor made by horses, there was no time to waste. She might return too quickly to the protection of her sanctuary.

"Good man." Gilbert slapped a hand to Joseph's back. Smiling broadly for the first time in days, he vaulted into the saddle and turned to look again at his squire. "You will ride with me," he said, then motioned to a half dozen of his men to follow.

With nary a care for the noise they made within the deep of the woods, they rode with speed toward the river. However, as they neared the clearing that lay be-yond the dense grouping of trees, and through which the river snaked, Gilbert motioned his men to spread out and proceed with more caution.

He guided his horse to the edge of the wood and peered around, but saw nothing that would indicate Graeye's presence. He glanced at the abbey beyond, thinking she might have already started back, but saw only an empty stretch of land laden with the soak of recent rainfall.

Then, to his left, he heard the beautiful trilling of a bird. It was a call he knew well. Farther up and nearer the river sat Joseph, a smile splitting his youthful face as he gestured to a place hidden from Gilbert's view.

Relief washing over him, Gilbert gave the signal, then prodded his destrier out of the covering of trees.

Though it didn't matter how noisy their approach was, for it would be impossible for Graeye to reach the abbey before they came upon her, they proceeded at barely a canter. It was a consideration based on Gilbert's worry that if they frightened her, or alerted her too soon to their presence, she might take an unnecessary risk that would harm her or the babe.

Nevertheless, Gilbert's impatience was great, for he could not remember ever wanting anything as badly.

Graeye had barely seated herself on a large rock when she heard unexpected sounds above the rush of the river. Horses! she realized, her eyes flying wide. Jumping up from the rock, she whirled about. Immediately, her gaze lit upon more than a half-dozen riders. And it was Gilbert at the head, his hair so incredibly black it could be no other.

For long days she had surrendered herself to the safety of the abbey, knowing that if she was caught outside its walls, the Church could do little to aid her. But that morn, restless and thinking to take advantage of the break in the rain, she had decided the risk was well past. And he had lain in wait all that time. . . .

She gauged the distance to the abbey and, with sinking heart, acknowledged that it was too far to traverse, especially in her condition. Nevertheless, she hauled her skirts up and hastened along the bank of the river. She had to try, for it was simply not in her to surrender so easily to this man.

Carefully picking her way over the undulating ground, she kept her eyes down to ensure a secure footing. Still the riders drew nearer, though they seemed in no hurry to intercept her. Sparing a glance over her shoulder, she saw that Gilbert's men were moving outward in an arc on either side that they might enclose her.

Futile, she realized, dragging her feet to a stop. Unless something untoward were to befall Gilbert Balmaine and all of his men—such as their horses unseating them amid the bog—she hadn't a chance of gaining the abbey. It was not even worth a token resistance.

Out of breath and warmed by the spurt of exertion, she resignedly turned and gathered her mantle around her, molding a comforting hand over her belly.

Although Gilbert rode up to her at a leisurely gait, his arrival came too soon for her liking, giving her little time to compose herself. He drew his destrier to a halt not far from where she stood and stared at her.

Though unnerved as always by his direct gaze, she stared back. "You are a more patient man than I would have expected, Gilbert Balmaine."

"And you are very stubborn," he returned.

"You expected otherwise?" At that moment she was not averse to engaging in a verbal sparring match.

"Nay," he admitted, "but I would have preferred your willingness to this."

"This," she repeated, looking beyond him to the abbey. " 'Twas the abbess, was it not? 'Twas she who betrayed me." She looked expectantly back at him.

"And what makes you think she would care to aid me?" he rejoined.

A tight smile came and went upon Graeye's face. "She brought you to the abbey, did she not?"

He shifted in his saddle. "Aye, that she did."

"Then it only follows that, in her eagerness to see me gone from Arlecy, she would stop at nothing to achieve that end."

Gilbert shook his head. "Nay, Graeye, you judge her wrongly. If 'twas not to have been this way, then 'twould have been a far less desirable way I would have laid claim to my child. Truly, she has done you no disservice. You should be grateful for her wisdom."

At that moment Graeye could see nothing good coming of such a betrayal, nor did she think it likely she ever would. Well-intentioned or not, it injured her and stole the future, albeit uncertain, that she had begun to plan for herself and her child.

Would she never be free of the domination of others? she wondered, wanting to scream at the injustice of it all. Instead she swept her eyes from Gilbert's face and looked, in turn, at each of the mounted knights on either side of her.

Aye, Gilbert Balmaine was determined to have his heir. He was convinced that the babe within her carried his blood in its veins.

Throwing her arms out to indicate the men beyond, she gave a short, harsh laugh. "Do tell. What warrants my pursuit by so many? Am I truly such a dangerous beast that all this is necessary?"

"I take no chances with that which belongs to me," he replied.

"Once again you imply, Baron, that I belong to you. I assure you, 'tis far from being the case."

"The child is mine, and I'll not have you deny me its upbringing."

"And when he is born?" she asked, sudden pain closing around her heart. "Will you then take him from my breast and cast me aside?"

"He?" Gilbert grasped at her easy use of gender. "And how know you 'tis a boy you carry?"

Though Graeye had long sensed it was a boy child growing inside her, she would not admit that to Gilbert. "I speak only in general terms. It may just as well be a girl."

He looked unconvinced, but merely held out a hand to her. "Come, Graeye," he said. "This rebellion of yours is at an end."

She took a step back. "You have not yet told me of your intentions toward me," she reminded him, refusing to be deterred.

"We will speak of it later," he said, and motioned her forward.

She shook her head. "Nay, I would speak of it now."

His gaze shooting heavenward, Gilbert threw a leg over his saddle and dismounted. "Otherwise?" he prompted as he turned to face her.

She looked more closely at the men flanking her. Her eyes lit upon the familiar visage of one positioned directly in her path to the abbey. Though he was far enough away that his features were indistinct, she realized with a start that it was Sir Michael. Disconcerted, she looked back at Gilbert.

"Otherwise I will resist you no matter the odds," she bluffed.

A corner of Gilbert's mouth turned up as he took a step toward her. "Why is it I do not believe you, Graeye?"

"Because you don't know me." She took another step backward that, unbeknown to her, had her at the edge of the bank. "Aye, 'tis simple enough for you to take me from here, but be warned, I will not make the journey to Medland easy for you."

Gilbert looked from her to the river. It was not deep, and its course was gentle, but he was unsettled by the vision of her falling into its iciness. Knowing that one more retreating step would likely land her in it, he moved no nearer. "I have already told you, Graeye, I will not marry you."

"Aye, and I have told you I will not become your leman. I will not be forced into your bed!"

Gilbert was willing to concede to her on that point. It was not in his nature to force himself upon any woman, though he could not easily forget that he had nearly done that very thing to Graeye months ago. That loss of control pained him still.

Aye, he would give her the assurances she sought. However, he would do so on his own terms, for he had no intention of holding himself from her if her resolve weakened. He would yet exorcise her from his mind and body.

"So be it," he said. "You will simply serve as mother of my child."

"I do not believe you."

His jaw worked as he fought to quell his irritation. "I give you my word, Graeye. You will suffer no unwanted attentions."

For long, silent minutes Graeye considered his vow. He was giving her what she wanted—or at least thought she wanted—but after his earlier profession of his desire for her, and his intention of having her in his bed, she was reluctant to believe him.

With a ring of steel upon steel, he drew his sword and lowered its tip to the marshy ground. Clasping a hand to the hilt that heaven might take note of what he was about to offer, he captured Graeye's stare and held it. " 'Tis my vow," he said. "I will not force myself on you."

"You would have me believe a vow you make before God, when you have made no secret of your aversion to the belief in Him?"

He resheathed his sword. " 'Tis a knightly vow I have made," he said curtly, "the ceremony of which is of less consequence than the words I have given you. However," he added, dropping his hands to his hips, "be warned now that if ever we do come together again out of mutual need, 'tis not likely I will refrain from taking what you offer—and then you are mine as much as the child you carry."

Though she was apprehensive about this last bit he had added, Graeye held her chin high. "Then I have nothing to fear from you, my lord."

"Nothing," he affirmed, taking a step toward her.

"Ergo, you leave me no choice but to accept the arrangements as such." Feeling as if she were stepping into an abyss, she walked forward and reluctantly placed her hand in his.

He hesitated, his gaze drifting down to where his fingers closed around hers. Slowly, he drew his thumb over the back of her hand.

Disturbed by the intimacy of his touch, she started

to pull away, but he tightened his grip. "Release me," she demanded in a voice that trembled betrayingly.

He did not look up, his gaze intent upon her small, fine-boned hand trapped in his, his brow creased with thought.

Graeye held her breath as she experienced anew the surging feelings she had vowed never again to allow herself. Why could she not hate him? she wondered, lamenting her body's betrayal. Why was she unable to disassociate herself from this man as she'd done her father? Had he not—

"Beautiful." His voice cut across her frantic musings. He lifted her hand and pressed his lips to the inside of her wrist.

Immediately, her pulse quickened, her eyes widening as she found herself floundering in the depths of orbs that sought to gain her soul. Knowing he felt her response against his mouth, and desperate to hold to her convictions, she tried again to pull free.

Surprisingly, Gilbert released her, though a moment later he caught hold of her thickened waist. " 'Tis past time we ride," he said gruffly. In spite of her added bulk he easily lifted her onto his horse, then mounted behind.

Though she would have liked to, Graeye did not resist when he pulled her into the firm cradle of his chest and draped his mantle around her. She was too tired to fight him anymore.

Chapter 13

"I mean no disrespect, my lord, for she is certainly welcome here, but if 'tis your child she carries, why would you not take her on to Penforke?"

Coming out of her muddled sleep, Graeye latched on to the hushed words and ran them backward and forward through her mind in an attempt to attach meaning to them. Aye, the conversation was about her, she realized. Soon, she was certain, Gilbert would answer the man's question.

She made a conscious effort to keep her breathing even and opened her eyes to narrow slits, hoping to peer out at her surroundings without alerting anyone that she had awakened.

It was the deep of night, though she knew not what hour it could be, and she lay abed in one of the smaller rooms of the donjon at Medland. This last she knew instinctively, for the room appeared much changed from what she remembered of the dank, foreboding place.

She had no difficulty recalling the circumstances that had led to her being taken from Arlecy, for it was all vividly set in her mind and rushed back at her with only the merest beckoning. However, much of the ride to Medland she could not recall, having slept through most of it.

"I do not want her at Penforke," Gilbert finally answered.

Graeye frowned. Though he had mentioned returning her to Medland, she had not thought he meant to abandon her at this place. Did he also mean to hold himself from the child when it was born?

"And when the child is born?" The other man—whose voice she now recognized as Sir Lancelyn's—asked the question for her.

Another long silence fell, and she waited it out with held breath.

"I will decide then," Gilbert said shortly.

Though the tightening skin of her belly began to itch, Graeye fought the urge to scratch.

Sir Lancelyn wisely changed the subject. "That girl you sent to serve her—Mellie, is it? She arrived two days ago. Though I have heard nothing of it myself, I am told she objects to serving Lady Graeye."

Graeye's eyes flew wide open. Was there no end to this passing of judgment against her before one even came to know her?

"She was Lizanne's maid," Gilbert said. "Though I would have it otherwise, 'tis now common knowledge what Philip Charwyck set out to do to my sister. I daresay the girl remains loyal to her former mistress and is as distrustful as I am of any others bearing that particular name."

"Think you it prudent, then, for Lady Graeye to be given into her care?"

"I will speak with Mellie and make clear my desires with regard to her handling of her new mistress. She will do as told."

"There are others, my lord, who would make a better maid."

Surprisingly, Gilbert did not rise to anger at his vassal's continued opposition to his decision. "Nay," he said, "Mellie will do fine."

"Is it loyalty you are concerned about?" the other man pressed.

"Aye, without question I have the girl's loyalty. I cannot be so certain of those who have previously served the Charwycks."

"Then you think Lady Graeye might attempt to return to the abbey?"

"I do not know what she might try, but I do know Mellie would not help her accomplish such an undertaking."

Graeye bristled. Had she not agreed to adhere to the conditions Gilbert had set forth only that morning? So long as he kept his side of the bargain, she would keep hers. And as for this Mellie, the girl would soon discover that Graeye had well and truly had the last of being trod upon. She would not allow the chit to undermine her.

She was so caught up in her indignation, Graeye failed at first to notice that Gilbert had stepped around the foot of the bed. When she did see him, she was embarrassed that he'd caught her eavesdropping. What had given her away? she wondered as she stared into his glowering face. Her breathing, she realized, for even now she was drawing quick, shallow breaths to calm her anger.

"Lady Graeye has awakened," Gilbert blandly informed Sir Lancelyn as he moved toward her.

"Then I will leave you to your privacy."

Rolling onto her back, Graeye caught sight of the other man just as he slipped through the doorway.

"You have been awake long?" Gilbert asked, drawing her attention back to him.

"Long enough."

"Then you know of my plans to maintain you here at Medland," he concluded, seating himself on the edge of the bed.

She shrugged. "Why don't you tell me more of it," she invited, knowing that her eyes sparkled with anger. "I may have missed some ere I awoke."

He ignored her thinly disguised barb. "There is not much more than what you overheard. What else would you like to know?"

"Naught," she answered. "Though mayhap there are things you would care to know."

His eyes narrowed. "Such as?"

Pushing an elbow beneath her, she began to raise herself to a sitting position. When Gilbert reached out a hand to assist her, she pushed it away.

"You should know now, Gilbert Balmaine," she said, dragging the cover over her thick chemise, which, blessedly, had not been removed with her other garments, "that I will not be bullied by anyone—most especially you and that maid you are determined to have dog my every step. And if you are of a mind to take my child from me once he is born and leave me at Medland, then I give you notice now I will use every device at my command to escape you ere the birth to ensure you never lay eyes upon the child."

At the conclusion of her tirade a muscle began to jerk in Gilbert's jaw, and his eyes hardened as he stared at her. "I have not lied to you," he said. "Though 'tis still a question as to where the child will be raised, wherever he goes, so will you."

She attempted to reach the truth of the matter beneath his expression, but found it an impossible task. "I will take your word on that," she said, "but I give you fair warning now. If you renege, you will find me all you have thus far wrongfully accused me of—and more."

"I do not doubt you for one moment, daughter of Edward Charwyck," he said dryly, then rose from the bed.

She watched him walk to the door, feeling a peculiar disappointment at his leaving. When he reached the door, he turned back to her. "I depart for Penforke at first light."

"So soon?" The words tumbled from her mouth before she could stop them.

His eyebrows arched straight up, causing her to color uncomfortably. "I had not thought 'twould be soon enough for you."

She dipped her head and pretended an interest in the pink ovals of her nails. "Aye, verily it is. 'Tis just that your haste surprises me considering all the time and effort you expended to achieve your end."

"Which is the reason I must return posthaste to Penforke. I have been gone too long, and there are matters far more deserving of my attention than endless verbal sparring with you, my lady."

Cut to the quick, Graeye could not suppress the rejoinder that came to her lips. "Then 'twould not be soon enough for you to leave this very night."

Gilbert let that pass. "I have placed you in Sir Lancelyn's care," he said. "Do not vex the man overly much. As the new lord of Medland, he is heavily burdened with the duties of keeping all in order." With that he pulled the door open and made to step through it.

At the certainty of his leaving, and not knowing when she might see him again, Graeye's anger eased. "Gilbert," she called to him.

He looked over his shoulder. "Aye, Graeye?"

"Will you visit?" Though she was not sure what, exactly, she wanted from him, she knew only a great, pressing need for him to stay.

Gilbert was in the midst of as much confusion as she. Not knowing what possessed him, though he would later question how he could have allowed himself to fall prey to her wiles once again, he pushed the door closed and walked back to the bed.

When she lifted her pale gaze to his, his restraint snapped, and suddenly he was pulling her up into his arms. Hungrily, he molded her sweet, new curves to him and sought possession of her mouth. But as he took his first taste of her, Graeye thrust her hands to his chest to push him away.

"How dare you!" she said fiercely, her eyes alight with fury. "I will not become your leman."

Dear God, what had possessed him? Gilbert thought, shocked at his complete lack of control. It was her eyes, he realized, the silent pleading that had shone from their depths. Had he been mistaken? As if burned, he released her and stepped away from the bed.

She pulled the covers to her chest. "I would ask that you leave now."

"My apologies," he said. " 'Twould seem the right decision for you to remain at Medland."

She did not answer. Instead she turned and slipped down beneath the covers.

Jaw clenched, Gilbert stared at her back a long moment, then pivoted and crossed to the door. It was the right decision, he told himself. She would give him no peace if he took her to Penforke.

Emerging from a profusion of covers, Graeye rubbed her eyes before venturing a glimpse of the world. It was the same one she had fallen asleep in yestereve, she grimly acknowledged.

She inched up onto her hands and knees, then sat back on her heels. The chill morning air struck her bare limbs and sent a shiver of discomfort shooting through her. Frowning, she looked down at her naked body, momentarily disconcerted before she remembered how she had come to be this way.

Awakening in a sweat during the night, she had thrown off the covers, but that had not proved enough. After tossing and turning for some time, she had finally discarded her chemise. Only then had she been able to return to the comfort of sleep.

Pulling the covers around her naked shoulders, she found herself pondering Gilbert's whereabouts. Had he yet left for Penforke as planned? The thought that he might have unsettled her in a way she refused to look too closely upon.

"Godspeed," she muttered, telling herself she would be glad when he was no longer around to bother her.

A sharp knock on the door halted the wanderings of her mind. Before she could call out permission to enter, the door was opened and in stepped a rather pretty young woman not much taller than herself. Over her arm she carried a fresh chemise, bliaut, and various other items of clothing.

"Ah, milady is awake," the woman said. A frown upon her puckish face, she closed the door and walked across the room. For a long moment she stared at the stain marring Graeye's face, her eyes narrowing to suspicious slits as she traced its course.

Her chin held high, Graeye endured the scrutiny with nary a blink of her eyes. "Are you quite finished?" she asked when it became obvious the woman had no other thought but to stare at her.

A self-satisfied smile revealed a row of crooked teeth. "I be Mellie," she said, puffing out her chest with much self-importance.

Truly, the belated introduction was unnecessary, for Graeye had known beyond a doubt who this impertinent woman was the moment she had come unbidden into the room.

" 'Tis the Baron Balmaine himself that has assigned me to be yer maid," Mellie went on, setting her bundle down upon the bed. "But I'll have ye know now, 'tis not a task I have any likin' for."

Graeye was grateful she had learned that much from eavesdropping upon Gilbert's conversation. Being forewarned of the maid's dislike took the sting out of it.

"And I am Lady Graeye Charwyck," she said, completing the introductions. "And I would have you know that I resent the arrangements as much, if not more, than you."

Mellie's large, round eyes grew even larger before she managed to cover her astonishment with a scornful twist of her lips. "Ye Charwycks are all the same," she declared, settling her arms across her chest.

Graeye feigned surprise. "You knew my brother?"

Mellie shook her head. "Nay, but—"

"Ah, then 'tis Edward Charwyck you are well acquainted with," Graeye interrupted, a smile brightening her face as she recalled Gilbert's penchant for stepping upon others' words.

"Nay, milady, I—"

"Then tell me how 'tis you can pass judgment on my family?" Graeye was oddly pleased at the ease with which she accomplished the rude feat a second time.

" 'Tis no longer a secret what yer brother did to my mistress, Lady Lizanne—and her brother," the maid retorted. She thrust her small, pointed chin forward for emphasis.

Graeye had no response for that, for she was still uninformed as to the exact crime that had persuaded the king to strip Edward of his lands. Briefly, she wondered how she might make the maid shine light upon that mystery. With such knowledge perhaps she would better come to understand Gilbert's hostility....

"And already I have heard tales of how Philip had done with his poor wife," Mellie continued. "Broke her neck, he did."

Graeye's eyes widened. "Broke ... ?" When she'd first arrived at Medland last autumn, she had heard the rumor that Philip had been responsible for his wife's death, but she had not known how the woman had died.

"As long as we understand each other, milady," Mellie said, stooping to scoop up Graeye's discarded chemise. Brows raised high, her lips sealed against any untoward comment, she brushed the rushes from the garment.

Graeye knew exactly what she was thinking and could not prevent the flush of color that stained her cheeks. It was on her lips to put Mellie straight on the matter when a persistent scratching at the door brought both women's heads around.

Frowning, Mellie went to the door and flung it wide. A large gray dog bounded past her and headed straight for Graeye.

"Groan!" Graeye exclaimed, scooting to the edge of the bed to take the animal's head in her lap. "So you did not forget me, my loyal friend," she cooed, allowing herself the first real smile in ages. "I have missed you."

"Out!" Mellie ordered. She stalked back toward the bed, but didn't come too close.

"Nay," Graeye said, "he may stay."

"But, milady, 'tis not seemly."

Graeye met the woman's wide-eyed stare. "He will stay," she said firmly, daring Mellie to oppose her in this.

Mellie's lips twitched. "The Baron Balmaine will not like this," she grumbled.

"I do not care a whit for what the baron does or does not like," Graeye snapped. "The dog stays."

As if in concurrence with his mistress, Groan yawned wide, ending on a loud moan that evidenced his namesake. Bristling with indignation, Mellie turned on her heel and walked back to push the door closed again. Then, muttering something beneath her breath that Graeye did not take the time to interpret, she folded the chemise and deposited it over the back of a chair.

"And when is yer babe due, milady?" the maid asked as if in passing.

Jolted by the forwardness of the inquiry, Graeye raised startled eyes to the woman.

Mellie spread her hands wide in mock apology. "Everyone knows," she said. "Baron Balmaine would have no other reason for consorting with a Charwyck, though 'tis odd he would ever have become involved with ye in the first place."

Anger was Graeye's saving grace, for it quickly replaced her hurt and embarrassment. "Where is he?" she demanded, dropping her bare feet to the prickly rushes.

Reluctantly, Groan settled back on his haunches and stared up at his mistress with eyes full of adoration.

"Gone," Mellie said, coming to stand before Graeye. Her gaze flitted briefly to where the dog had settled himself. "Left before the sun even rose this morn, he did."

Gripped with an ache that went clear through her heart, Graeye turned and pretended interest in Groan. Just as well, she thought as she stroked her hand over the animal's damp muzzle.

"They are not very fine," Mellie said, walking around Graeye to sort through the items of clothing she had brought with her, "but these will have to do ye until the cloth the baron has sent for arrives."

Graeye was surprised. "He has ordered cloth for me?"

"Aye," Mellie tossed over her shoulder. "This morn he told the steward to see it done posthaste. We will be busy, you and I, when it arrives. Ye can sew a stitch, can't ye?"

Graeye nodded. "Aye, that I can."

Mellie chuckled at some private humor. "Here now," she said, turning to face her mistress, the chemise in hand. "Lift yer arms."

Not since she was a child had Graeye had any assistance with clothing herself, and it seemed a bit late to take up the habit again. Mostly, though, it was too uncomfortable a proposition to disrobe before this woman. "I can dress myself," she said, and reached a hand from beneath the cover to take the garment.

Scowling, Mellie drew back. "And have ye tell the baron I be wantin' in my duties?"

"I assure you, he will not hear it from me." She reached again for the chemise, but the maid snatched it away before she could lay her fingers to it.

"Do not fuss so, milady," Mellie snapped. " 'Tis a duty I am not averse to providin' ye. Besides, I'll be seein' much more of ye when I tend yer bath later. Now lift yer arms—unless, of course, ye would prefer to break yer fast dressed so."

Seeing no end to this debate, Graeye released the cover. Blessedly, the chemise was dropped over her head without delay.

"Late spring, mayhap early summer," Mellie speculated, stepping back to eye Graeye's figure.

Graeye knew she referred to the arrival of the babe, since she'd obtained a clear view of her body's new shape. Instantly, her indignation flared. " 'Tis no concern of yours," she snapped, swinging around to take up the braies herself.

Mellie seemed content to let her new mistress finish clothing herself. With an exaggerated flounce she skirted the dog and went around the bed to gather up the confusion of covers there. "The lady Lizanne is also expectin' a babe," she said.

Graeye's hands paused in their task of securing the laces of the bliaut. For some odd reason she felt hurt that Gilbert had not informed her of his sister's pregnancy, especially considering his own impending state of parenthood.

She tightened the laces. "And when is it due?" she asked, hoping she surpassed Mellie's attempt at nonchalance.

"Early spring, milady." The announcement was followed by a heartfelt sigh. "Would that I could be with her durin' this difficult time."

Graeye turned to face her. "And why aren't you?"

The corners of Mellie's mouth drooped. "Alas, 'twas planned that I would go to her come a break in the weather, but the baron decided I would better serve ye, milady."

In spite of her own petulant mood, Graeye could not help but feel sorry for the maid. Beyond a doubt she was devoted to her last mistress. "Then I can understand your reluctance to serve me," she said. "My apologies that you have been forced to such a duty."

Mellie shrugged. "Have ye a wimple?" she asked, changing the subject abruptly as she eyed Graeye's face and the disarray of her hair.

Graeye stiffened. "Nay, I do not wear one."

"Hmm." Mellie peered more closely. "Properly fit 'twould likely cover that mark," she mused, not in the least put off by Graeye's deepening color. "And 'twould also save us the worry of yer hair. I am not very good with hair, ye know. The lady Lizanne hardly ever allowed me any prac—"

"I will not be needing a wimple." Graeye punctuated each word sharply.

Mellie's brows shot straight up. "As ye like, milady," she muttered.

Fighting to curb her wayward emotions, Graeye turned her back on the maid and set herself to pulling on the thick hose laid out for her. Aye, she conceded, Gilbert was right. I do have claws.

A league. That was all the ground they covered before Gilbert reined in. "Damnation!" he cursed, surprising his men. Without further word he wheeled his destrier around.

All the way back to Medland he cursed his weakness, threw profanity to the sky that would surely have seen him struck dead had God been able to hear him over the thundering of hooves.

Damn her angry eyes, her witching mouth, her dainty nose. Damn the curve of her neck, her warm thighs, her firm breasts. Damn her naïveté, her deceit. . . .

She had woven a powerful spell around him that had not lessened after her refusal of him the previous night. Nay, it had only made him want her more. Though he had tried to quench his desires with a willing maid, he had failed, and in the darkness of the first hours of morning had found himself in Graeye's chamber once again. He had been surprised to find her unclothed, the moonlight spilling in through the window allowing him a glimpse of her new curves.

It had been bold of him, but he had been unable to squelch the desire to rest his hand upon her rounded belly. She had stirred at his touch, but hadn't woken. Perched upon the edge of the bed, he had held his hand to her, marveling at the fluttering movements of his child until, too soon, dawn had arrived and ushered him from the room.

Nay, he could not leave her behind. Could not return to Penforke without her.

Having been alerted to the approach of riders, Lancelyn met Gilbert at the drawbridge.

"Say naught!" Gilbert ground out as he urged the destrier past his vassal.

With a knowing smile slashing across his face, Lancelyn kept his mouth shut and followed his liege lord back within the walls. At the donjon Gilbert hurriedly dismounted and climbed the steps to the hall.

Scraping dirt from beneath his nails, Lancelyn held Gilbert's destrier as he awaited his lord's reappearance. It was not long in coming.

"Where is she?" Gilbert demanded as he descended the steps in pairs. "By my troth, if you have allowed her to escape—"

Lancelyn looked up at him, grimacing at the wild-eyed stare, rumpled hair, and flush of color stealing up his baron's neck. "In the chapel, my lord," he said.

"Lancelyn!" Gilbert roared.

Knowing he was walking the thin line between friend and vassal, Lancelyn threw his palms up. "I but obeyed your directive, my lord."

"Then obey this," Gilbert rasped. "Wipe that foolish grin from your face." Grumbling, he strode past the man, kneading his aching leg as he returned to the outer bailey.

Not since the day he had cornered Graeye, had he been in the chapel. Swept with vivid remembrances of that confrontation, he paused before entering.

God, he had been cruel! Drawing a rough hand across his face, he tried to wipe away the memories that nicked at him rapier-sharp. They only cut deeper. If he could right some of the wrongs made that day ...

It was almost the same as that first day when he stepped inside. She was kneeling at the altar, though of course was not clothed in the stark white nun's habit.

Preferring the light to shadows, he did not close the door behind him. Why a chapel should be so morose, he did not understand. Were not the heavens said to be bright and open?

His limp prominent, he walked down the center aisle, hearing her softly spoken prayers as he neared. Latin.

Why did she not turn around? he wondered. Surely she knew she was no longer alone? Frowning, he came to stand beside her and, when she still did not acknowledge him, reluctantly lowered himself to the kneeler. His leg brushing hers, he looked down upon her bowed head and wondered at the strange words that continued to spill from her lips.

He was not usually a very patient man, but he found himself waiting on her, rather than intruding as he would have liked.

When she finally crossed herself and turned to look at him, her face mirrored surprised. Washing of all color, she swayed toward him.

Alarmed, Gilbert put an arm around her and clasped her to his side. "Graeye—"

"You came back," she whispered, staring up at him with wide, disbelieving eyes.

"Are you all right? What is wrong?"

"You came back," she repeated, her cheeks beginning to color again, a smile curving her lips.

She was fine. Sighing, he pushed a stray lock of hair from her eyes. "Aye, for you."

"For me? But why?"

"I am taking you to Penforke."

Her smile wavered, then slipped away. Blinking, she straightened from him. "I do not understand."

He wanted her smile back. Pulling her chin around, he stared into her uncertain eyes. "You belong there."

Graeye waited and prayed he would give her the words she so needed to hear—the words that had echoed in her heart and mind when she had first looked up and found him kneeling beside her. Fight it though she might, she loved him. Loved this giant who rarely had a kind word for her.

"As your wife?" she ventured.

He drew back. "I want my son born there," he said.

She felt as if she'd been struck. Of course he had not come back for her, but for the child she carried. How foolish she was to hope he would ever feel anything beyond hate for a Charwyck. Would he be able to forget their child had half that blood in his veins? Remarkably, it was not anger that surfaced at his words, though, but sorrow.

"Will you pray with me?" she asked.

He quickly stood. "Nay," he said, then turned to go. "I will await you outside."

She turned on the kneeler, following his progress down the aisle. "Gilbert," she called when he reached the doorway.

He turned to face her once again, the streaming daylight behind him making his face unreadable. "Aye?"

"I will go with you," she said, "but until you bring honor to this child, I will not share your bed."

He clenched his fists. "I have not asked you to."

"So long as you do not," she retorted.

Chapter 14

❧❧❧

It was whitewashed and clean, rising gracefully into a sky beset by the coming of night. Seated before Gilbert on his white destrier, Graeye was grateful he could not see her expression of wonder. Penforke was no Medland. Far to the contrary, it made that other castle look more a hovel than the residence of a baron.

She grimaced. How appalled Gilbert must have been at his first sight of Medland. It was a wonder he had thought to save it, rather than let it burn to the ground those many months past.

"What think you of your new home?" he asked suddenly, his mouth near her ear sending tremors of awareness up her sides.

In retaliation for his nearness, which bothered her so, she withheld the praise that might otherwise have crossed her lips. "It looks to be satisfactory," she stated, refusing to turn and look at him.

"That is all?"

His disappointment at her lack of response brought a smile to her lips. Undoubtedly, he was proud of Penforke, for it certainly was a gem, but she would not let him know that. "What else would you have me say?" she asked, shrugging.

He was silent a moment before responding. " 'Tis far more habitable than Medland," he said. "You will be more comfortable here."

"Then I was not comfortable before?"

More silence and then, unexpectedly, he laughed—a rumbling sound that rose from the depths of his chest to make itself felt against her back. "You are trifling with me, Graeye Charwyck."

Her resolve to give him naught to look at save the back of her head splintered. Twisting around, she met the devilish sparkle in his eyes. "Trifling with you?"

"Aye, the same as Lizanne. You are of a gentler temperament than my sister—though I have not seen evidence of that in some time—but you are also very like her."

It was not only the comparison with that other woman that rankled Graeye, but the sudden change in Gilbert's disposition. How was she to do battle with a man whose unexpected laughter warmed her, and whose eyes reflected something other than contempt?

"I would thank you not to compare me to the coward who put an arrow through my brother's back," she snapped, then turned to face front again.

Though she should have been pleased, Graeye found no satisfaction in Gilbert's response—a distinct stiffening that created a space between their two bodies where previously there had been none. She knew she had pushed too far, but it was too late to do anything about it. Determinedly she fixed her attention upon the looming castle.

During the long ride she had anticipated her arrival at Gilbert's home with dread, but now she found herself eager to discover what lay within those massive stone walls. When they entered the bailey, she felt none of the disappointment she had experienced upon returning to Medland. Indeed, it appeared a thriving community dwelled within these walls. So very different . . .

Reining in when they reached the donjon, Gilbert assisted her down from the horse before he turned to the dozens of castlefolk who had converged upon the courtyard to greet him—and to meet the woman he had brought with him.

Though Graeye felt a return of panic as Gilbert pulled her forward to meet the curious castlefolk, she firmly took herself in hand and forced it back down. If this was to be her home, and the place where her child would grow into adulthood, then it would bode no good for her to reveal any vulnerability to these people.

Blessedly, the introductions were brief, but sufficient; then Gilbert was passing her into Mellie's care.

"See she is made comfortable in Lizanne's chamber," he said, then stalked away before either Mellie or Graeye could protest.

Grumbling beneath her breath, Mellie led her new mistress into the donjon.

Though the many windows in the great hall were set high as added protection should an attack upon the fortress ever reach the inner bailey, there was so much light that Graeye had to stop to look better at the surroundings.

"What is it, milady?" Mellie asked. "Something is amiss?"

Graeye blinked in surprise. "Nay, naught is wrong," she said, a smile tugging at her lips.

The chamber Mellie deposited her in was not large, but it was well furnished. And though the last of the sun had set, it, too, knew more light than any at Medland ever had.

Seeking the warmth the window embrasure offered, Graeye slipped into it, drawing her knees as close to her chest as her belly would allow.

" 'Tis also where the lady Lizanne preferred to sit," Mellie said.

Graeye turned and looked at the woman. "Here?"

"Aye. Never a chair, as 'twould be fittin' fer a lady, but there."

There was no mistaking the rancor in Mellie's voice,

but Graeye chose to ignore it. "I would like a bath," she said. "Could you see to it?"

Mellie frowned. "There is not much time ere the supper hour arrives, milady. Mayhap afterward."

Graeye nearly acquiesced, then thought better of it. She would not allow the maid to dictate what she could and could not do. "Nay, I would like a bath now."

Mellie might have argued the matter further, but a persistent tap at the door heralded the arrival of the chest containing Graeye's few belongings. The tub and water for the bath arrived a short time thereafter.

Fully dressed, her hair neatly—though not artfully—arranged by Mellie, Graeye stood silent over the chest that had once belonged to her mother. Thoughtfully, her gaze shifted from the bridal habit that lay atop the lid, to the pieces of linen she held in her hand. Not once had she regretted discarding the wimple. It had been the beginning for her.

Without knocking someone entered her chamber. Mellie, she thought, but did not turn around.

"I will be ready shortly," she murmured, fingering the yellowing chin strap.

There was no answer, but a moment later she felt the undeniable presence of Gilbert at her back. Before she could react, he reached around and took the wimple from her.

"I will not have you wearing this," he said sharply.

Swinging around, she tilted her head back to look up at his set face. "I assure you," she said, reaching to regain possession of the item, "I had no intention of doing so."

He eyed her a moment, then yielded the linen. "That pleases me," he said softly.

Though he did not lay a hand on her, she felt as if he had just caressed her from head to toe. Every inch of her tingled, and as she stared up at him, she felt again that pulling spark of attraction she had first experienced at the waterfall.

Why, now, did he allow her glimpses of the man he had been then? she wondered. Why could he not continue to play the blackguard against whom she had built her defenses? Did he truly desire her so much that he was willing to set aside his dislike in order to gain her sexual favors again?

Feeling her resolve begin to weaken, she quickly turned and walked to the fireplace. " 'Tis not you I seek to please," she said as she laid the pieces of linen atop the charred remains of the fire that had warmed her as she'd bathed, "but myself."

She was truly a changed woman, Gilbert thought as he watched the wimple catch flame. Though part of him was proud of the embittered strength she had gained, another part mourned her loss of innocence. He—and Edward Charwyck—had done that to her. Just as the malevolence of Philip Charwyck had changed Lizanne overnight from a carefree, fun-loving child to an angry woman, Graeye had also changed.

Suddenly weary, Gilbert closed his eyes. It seemed that each time he touched something wonderful, it came apart in his hands. If only—

"Truly, you are not bothered by the mark I bear?" Graeye broke into his thoughts as she straightened from the hearth.

"Bothered?" He shook his head, then beckoned her forward. "Come hither and I will show you something."

Her eyes full of suspicion, she moved to stand before him. "What is it?"

He turned his back to her. "Lift my tunic."

"I will not!" She took a step back from him.

He looked over his shoulder at her. " 'Tis not seduction I have planned, Graeye," he snapped, irritated by the conclusion she had drawn.

She clasped her hands before her, distrust shining from her eyes. "Then what?" she prompted.

He was fast losing patience with her continued obstinance. "Do you lift my tunic, you shall see," he told her.

She hesitated a moment longer, then moved closer and lifted the hem of his tunic high to expose the broad expanse of his muscled back.

"To the right," he said.

Graeye did not need to be directed to the palm-sized mark just below his shoulder blade, for she had spotted it immediately. Without thought she reached up and traced its outline.

So he also bore a mark of birth, she mused, finding some of the comfort that he had sought to give her. Still, he'd been more fortunate than she to have the stain appear in such a hidden place.

Gilbert closed his eyes against the sensations roused by Graeye's touch. Just the tip of her finger against his skin was enough to take him back in time to when they had made love beneath the stars. Almost he could feel again the moist warmth of her skin against his, and the hunger of her untried mouth.

Knowing that if he did not pull back now he would lose control and find himself the recipient of her indignation, he stepped away from her. "You see, I, too, bear a mark," he said, turning to face her. "And that is all 'tis."

She simply looked at him without speaking.

"Think you I am a spawn of the devil?" he prompted.

His words brought Graeye fully back to the present, and with a spark of devilment she replied, "Mayhap not a direct descendant . . ." A look of surprise flashed across his face, and she let loose a teasing smile.

It was Gilbert's undoing. A smile tugging at his own lips, he held out his arm to her. "Supper awaits," he said.

Feeling as if some bridge had just been crossed, though she knew she dared not harbor such false hope, Graeye took his arm.

• • •

Surprisingly, it was not the curiosity of the castlefolk that made the meal an ordeal for Graeye, but the unreadable stares from Sir William and Sir Michael. Unreadable, aye, but exuding a menace Graeye found utterly disturbing.

She was no fool; she understood why each man should be angered by her presence. Sir William because of his natural dislike for her, and Sir Michael because thrice she had refused him. The young man's pride must be sorely wounded to see her now seated next to his baron and burgeoning with that man's child. That Gilbert would place trust in either of them, most especially Sir William, made her wonder at his wisdom.

In spite of her unease she held herself proudly erect throughout the meal, conversed with Gilbert when he addressed her, and managed to consume a healthy serving of the wonderfully prepared viands.

Though Gilbert's brow drew thunderous at her question, she finally asked about the two Charwyck knights he had taken into his service. Immediately, the unspoken truce between them found itself on shaky ground. Gilbert grudgingly informed her that Sir Michael had become a member of his household knights, and that Sir William had been allowed to maintain his position as castellan of Sulle.

Curious as to the reason William was at Penforke, Graeye pressed to discover more, but Gilbert turned tight-lipped and distant.

Contenting herself with what he had allowed her, she retired to her chamber shortly thereafter and found serenity in the sleep that soon claimed her.

Chapter 15

Curses. Loud, obnoxious words that wound their way up the stairs and slipped beneath Graeye's door awoke her some hours later.

Taking up the robe Mellie had left for her at the foot of the bed, Graeye ventured out into the corridor. There the voices raised in anger grew louder, and as she traversed the shadowed stairs, she heard the sounds of a struggle.

She hurried into the hall and halted at the sight of several knights crowded around something on the floor. "What has happened?" she asked as she squeezed between two of them. Though none bothered to answer her, she saw Gilbert pulling Sir Michael from atop William.

"I will fight my own battles," he ground out as he pushed the young knight behind him that he might confront William himself. So furious was he, he did not notice Graeye's presence.

She winced at the sight William presented as he struggled to his feet, his bloodied mouth having given up several teeth to Michael's fist.

"You bastard," the man spat, spraying Gilbert with blood. "I will see you dead for this!"

"Then come now and let us put a quick end to it," Gilbert beckoned, nodding to the sword that hung at William's side as he drew his own.

Though William's pride had him reaching for his hilt, something else stayed his hand. Smiling, he shook his head. "Nay, there will come another time, Baron Balmaine. You and I will meet again."

"Now is as good as any."

William continued to smile his bloody smile. "Soon," he said, then turned his back on Gilbert and looked at the knights before him. "Step aside," he growled.

The men glanced questioningly at Gilbert. To Graeye's amazement he nodded for them to allow William to pass.

Without looking back the knight exited the hall.

"Gilbert," Graeye called to him. Completely unaware of the startled looks she received from those who had not yet noticed her presence—most especially, Sir Michael—she stepped forward.

Surprised by her appearance, Gilbert momentarily forgot what he'd been about to do. It did not help matters to realize what a becoming picture Graeye presented with her swath of golden hair thoroughly tousled from a restless sleep. Truly, she looked as if she'd just come from the arms of a lover.

So disturbing was this last thought, it shook Gilbert free of the spell he had fallen under. He ignored the questioning hand Graeye laid on his arm and searched out the two knights he'd chosen earlier to follow William Rotwyld. Catching their expectant gazes, he nodded to them.

Wordlessly, they hurried after their prey.

The signal was not lost on Graeye. Glancing over her shoulder, she watched as the knights departed. "What transpires, my lord?" she asked.

Tight-lipped, Gilbert resheathed his sword before looking at her. "You should be abed," he said as he grasped her upper arm and led her away from the others.

"Aye, and I was," she retorted. " 'Twas all the commotion that awoke me."

"Then you should have stayed in your chamber," he said, pulling her up the stairs. " 'Tis unseemly for you to expose yourself to my men in this manner of dress."

At the landing she pulled her arm free of his grip before he could usher her down the passageway. "And what is wrong with it?" she asked, her indignation evident as she swept her hand downward to indicate the fullness of the robe.

Gilbert frowned. Aye, she was adequately covered, but that damnable hair falling about her shoulders and the flush upon her cheeks was simply too much.

"Graeye," he groaned, rubbing both his hands over the back of his neck so he would not be tempted to touch her. "Do you not know how beautiful you are? I would wager that at this moment every one of those men is wondering what it would be like to have you in his bed."

Graeye was startled by his words, his tortured voice, and her walled heart thrust itself against its barriers. Though she knew she should keep her distance, she moved closer until there was but a hand's width separating them. "Are you also wondering, my lord?" she asked.

Good God, Gilbert thought, was she toying with him? He looked into her upturned face. Didn't she realize how near he was to breaking his vow and carrying her off to his chamber? Nay, he would not give her the opportunity to punish him further. It was she who would have to seek the first intimacy if they were ever to come together again.

"Nay," he finally answered, his breathing ragged, "but I am remembering."

She didn't answer for a moment, and the look in her eyes made him think she was remembering too. Then she stepped away and changed the subject. "Why has Sir William gone?"

Gilbert was relieved she had abandoned the game

she'd been playing with him, but he was not pleased by her question. Still, he would have to tell her, for it would soon be common knowledge what had taken place that night.

"He has been divested of the lands he held vassalage over," Gilbert said matter-of-factly. Then, as if that explained everything, he turned and headed down the passageway.

Graeye caught up with him just as he reached her doorway. "Why?" she persisted.

He motioned her inside her chamber. " 'Tis time you were abed."

She didn't move. "You are not going to tell me why Sir William fell into disfavor with you?"

Though he did not wish to, Gilbert suspected he would not be rid of her if he did not tell her—and would not be rid of the desire pounding at his insides. "For crimes committed against the people of Sulle, and moneys stolen from its coffers, I have seen fit to wrest the lordship from him."

Graeye was not surprised, but she could not help but wonder why Gilbert had given the man a chance in the first place. Then she remembered the knights who had been sent to follow William. Suspicion leaping upon her, she narrowed her gaze on Gilbert's face.

"He will go to Edward, won't he?" she said. Though his expression gave nothing away, he did not respond, and she had her answer. This was how he meant to uncover Edward's whereabouts.

" 'Tis what you had planned all along, isn't it?" she prodded. "You are not such a fool to place trust in a man like William."

"You disapprove?"

In turmoil over how she should answer him, she broke eye contact and stared down at her protruding belly. Why could he not leave well enough alone? What good could possibly come of seeking revenge against a man for past wrongs? It was done.

"Edward is an old man," she began. "The revenge

you seek grows old as well. Why not leave him be? He is no threat to—"

"There you are wrong," Gilbert interrupted, his words harsh. "Edward Charwyck still plagues me. He and the brigands he has gathered about him attack my villages, murder my people, and steal their goods. Had he but disappeared, I would have left him to his misery, but he gives me no choice."

To steady herself against the onslaught of his words, Graeye reached out a hand to the door frame. She had known nothing of the raids against the villages— nothing of the deaths or thievery. How naive she had been to believe Edward would simply let matters be. Had he not sworn vengeance against Gilbert?

"Ah, Gilbert, I am sorry," she lamented, now wishing she had not pursued the matter. "I did not know."

"You could not have," Gilbert said as he lifted her chin to study the sadness in her eyes. "But do not think on it anymore. There is naught you can do."

She nodded.

Sensing her defenses had faltered, he unashamedly took advantage of the opportunity and pressed a brief, gentle kiss to her mouth. Though he gave her little time to respond before pulling back, he detected no resistance. No matter, he told himself. It would likely return on the morrow.

"I must needs return to the hall," he said, stepping away. "Good eve."

Graeye watched him go, then turned back into the loneliness of her room.

The trap was not as easily laid as Gilbert had hoped it might be. Though William had, indeed, led his knights to Edward's camp in the western reaches of the barony, by the time Gilbert arrived with his army to do battle, there were only the barest traces that anyone had ever been there.

Frustrated and angry, he returned to Penforke

empty-handed and suspicious. For days he brooded and pondered the question uppermost in his mind. Now that William was gone, could there be another among his men who carried word to Edward, always keeping the old man just out of reach?

It crossed his mind that Sir Michael might have maintained loyalty for his old baron, but he quickly rejected the idea. Numerous times, and in numerous ways, the young knight had proved himself loyal to his new lord. Had he not attacked Sir William when that man had hurled insults and curses at Gilbert?

Who, then?

Chapter 16

One day fell into another, and soon the season of spring was fully upon the inhabitants of Penforke.

On her knees in the rich earth of the flower garden she had prodded back to life after a cold winter, Graeye attempted to salvage the cluster of fragrant woodruff Groan had seen fit to make a bed of. It seemed a hopeless cause, for the small white flowers were well and truly crushed, but she was determined to save them.

With the return of the young girl Graeye had sent for a pail of water, Groan also reappeared, his head hanging low as he ambled toward his mistress.

Graeye nearly gave in to his sorrowful eyes, but knew it was too soon to forgive him his trespass. This was not the first time he had done damage to her flowers.

"Nay, back with you," she scolded, trying to sound firm in the face of a weakening resolve. When he simply stared at her, she shook her head and waved him away.

Heaving a lengthy sigh, Groan turned and headed back toward the donjon.

"I brought the water ye asked for, milady," the girl said as she set the pail alongside Graeye.

Pulling her gaze from Groan, Graeye smiled up at her. "Thank you, Gwen."

" 'Twas nothin', milady." The girl blushed, then extended a hand that held a small, brightly polished apple. "For the babe," she mumbled.

Reflexively, Graeye laid a hand to her belly, which had grown two months larger since she had first come to Penforke. " 'Twas kind of you," she said, reaching to take the fruit.

She had been surprised that it had proved less difficult for her to gain acceptance at her new home than at Medland—in spite of the fact that she appeared to all to be Gilbert's leman. Or perhaps because of it . . .

The castlefolk's curiosity satisfied, they no longer made her uncomfortable with their seeking stares. Instead they treated her as if she were the lady of the castle. And Gilbert did not dissuade them from the notion, though neither did he speak of wedding her to make it fact, nor to assure his child's legitimacy.

Still, things were better between them since that night he had informed her of Edward's undertaking to destroy all that the Balmaines possessed.

Though the attraction was always there—it could not be denied—Gilbert had not broken his vow, and Graeye had not given in to her unruly emotions. An innocent touch . . . an accidental brushing against each other . . . an unguarded smile. That was all.

"Milady." Gwen broke into Graeye's thoughts. "I was wondering if this evening ye might show me again that fancy stitch ye put round the neck of the baron's red tunic."

It was Graeye's turn to blush. She had not meant to have anything to do with the stitching of Gilbert's clothes, for she thought it too intimate a task. However, the young girl's clumsiness with the needle had prompted her to assist in the adornment of that one garment. And Gilbert's coming upon them as Graeye had bent her head to the task had taken her completely unawares. His discovery would not have been entirely bad had he not seemed so pleased by the gesture. Unnerved, she had nearly thrown the tunic at him.

"Aye, Gwen," she agreed, "I will show you again." But on one of her own garments this time.

Pleased, Gwen swung about and hurried back down the path. However, at the door to the donjon, she turned to Graeye again. "I nearly forgot," she bubbled.

The apple halfway to her mouth, Graeye paused. "Yes?"

"The baron was looking for ye a short while ago. I told him ye were here in the garden."

"Did he say what he wanted?"

"Nay, but he was smiling, milady."

Smiling? What good news had been borne him, then? Had he once again discovered Edward's whereabouts? Graeye frowned at the remembrance of his failure to capture the old man two months past. The week that had followed had been difficult for all.

She had been shaken as she glimpsed again the wrathful man who had come to take possession of Medland. But it wasn't fear that had unsettled her—it was surprise. For the first time since he had forced her from the abbey, she had come to realize and appreciate the changes the months of separation had wrought in him. Her anger had made her blind to the softening of his disposition. As ruthless as she knew him capable of being, he had been amazingly tolerant of her defiance and scorn.

When the object of her thoughts suddenly appeared before her, Graeye started so violently, she nearly upset the pail of water.

"It appears a waste of time," Gilbert said, grimacing at the wilted plant that lay propped in her lap.

"What . . . oh!" Hurriedly, she began packing the soil around the base of the woodruff. "Methinks it will come back."

"You have too much faith," he grumbled as he lowered himself to his haunches.

"Or you have too little," she tossed back, reaching for the pail of water.

Gilbert took it from her. "Perhaps."

Surprised by his yielding, she turned questioning eyes upon him, but he only smiled. "You behave as if you've a secret you wish to tell someone," she ventured. "Do you wish to tell me?"

His smile grew teasing. "How much?" he asked, indicating the water with a nod of his head.

What a peculiar mood he was in, she thought. "Pour and I'll tell you when to stop.

"That is enough," she said a moment later. "Now, what—" The sudden jab to her ribs stole her breath and promptly set her back on her rear end.

Tossing the pail aside, Gilbert lowered himself to his knees and took hold of her arms. "What is wrong?" he asked, his face a mirror of concern as he pulled her toward him.

Recovering, Graeye laughed and patted a hand to her belly. "Your child is simply making himself more comfortable."

His brows knit, Gilbert looked down at her fullness. Then he smiled again. On impulse he placed his hands on either side of her belly, then dipped his head and laid his ear against it.

Graeye was too shocked to do anything but stare at the top of his dark head.

He did not have long to wait to feel the next movement, though it was less intense than the last. "Ah," he breathed, lifting his head. "He is strong—and impatient."

"Like his father," she said softly, her heart growing heavy in her chest.

Thinking to content himself with a brief taste of her lips, Gilbert angled his head and pressed his mouth to hers. But she gave back to him, opening like a flower beneath his coaxing. Encouraged, he took all she of-

fered, sliding his hands up the sides of her breasts as he
swept the insides of her mouth with his tongue.

Graeye cradled his face between her palms, ignoring
the warning voices in her head, which truly were mere
whispers. Though she had fought it nearly every day
these last months, she wanted this. She wanted to know
again the man from the waterfall. She wanted to wipe
away all the pain—

"Apologies, my lord," a voice intruded, effectively
pulling them apart. "I had thought you would be
alone."

Hearts beating a wild pattern, Graeye and Gilbert
looked to where Sir Michael stood a short distance
away, his eyes cast down.

Looking as if he wanted to throttle the man for his
ill timing, Gilbert rose, assisting Graeye to her feet
with a hand beneath her elbow.

Though she was embarrassed to have been caught in
such circumstances, Graeye saw the interruption as di-
vine intervention. Dear God, why had she allowed the
intimacy? she chastised herself. All that lay in that direction was Gilbert's bed. And she would not be his
leman!

"What is it you want?" Gilbert asked sharply, stepping forward to put Graeye behind him.

Grateful for the consideration that freed her from
having to meet the young knight's eyes, for he made
her feel terribly uncomfortable, she began to pick at the
dirt and leaves strewn across her skirts.

"A man comes—a villager," Michael answered. "He
says he knows of Charwyck's whereabouts."

Graeye's hands stilled as she awaited Gilbert's response.

At last, Gilbert silently rejoiced, an intrusion he
could forgive. Eager to know more, he walked over to
Michael and laid a hand on his shoulder. "Where is
he?"

"The inner bailey, my lord."

Though his first thought was to go directly to the

man, Gilbert needed a few more minutes with Graeye. "Take him to the kitchens and see he is given something to eat," he said. "I will be along shortly."

"Aye, my lord." Michael strode back down the path.

When he was out of sight, Gilbert turned to Graeye. Her posture—her hands clasped before her, her chin tilted up—told him the opportunity had passed to crumble her defenses. Obviously, she regretted what had occurred and would not welcome any more advances. Still, he wanted to touch her again.

"You—you have not told me your secret," she reminded him, sidestepping the hand he reached to her.

His arm dropped back to his side. "Secret?"

She nodded. "You did not come out here to assist me in saving a doomed plant, did you?"

Although he was disappointed by her withdrawal, Gilbert smiled at the remembrance of the news he had received a short while ago. He should go to Lizanne, he knew. He had promised her he would visit again when the child was born. But that was before Graeye . . . before the child growing in her belly. He could not leave her now, nor could he risk leaving the land while Edward Charwyck was still somewhere out there.

"My sister, Lizanne, has been delivered of a girl child," he said.

Graeye experienced a moment of joy before she reminded herself of the wrongs the woman had done her brother. "I see," she said, shifting her gaze to the colorful variety of flowers surrounding her.

"You are not pleased for her?"

"Should I be?" She fingered the hard bud of a rose. "She is, after all, responsible for Philip's death."

Gilbert crossed his arms over his chest. "I have told you, Graeye—the only one responsible for your brother's death was he himself."

This was the most frustrating of all barriers Graeye had to contend with. In all of Penforke there was no one who would speak of the terrible thing Philip had done to earn his death—not the castlefolk, not the knights, not Gilbert. Sighing, she met his gaze. "Until you offer me evidence otherwise, I have no choice but to believe what Edward told me."

Gilbert wanted to argue that, but thought better of it. "You are not ready to know the truth," he said.

Her temper flared. "And when do you think I will be ready—when I am an old woman?"

"When you trust me enough to know I would not lie to you," he replied, suddenly wishing himself away from this place and confrontation.

Unwittingly, Graeye accommodated him, lifting her skirts to step past him. "As you have not seen fit to offer me the same consideration, that could be a very long time," she flung over her shoulder as she made for the donjon.

Raking a hand through his hair, Gilbert let go a long sigh. "Fortunately, I am learning patience," he muttered.

Anticipating that Gilbert and his men would be leaving at first light to go in pursuit of Edward, Graeye arose from a restless night's sleep and hurried about the castle awakening those who were still asleep, despite the clamorous preparations being made for the departure. She set the kitchen servants the task of making the morning meal, though it was still hours before it would normally be served, and the others she directed to ready the hall.

As had become customary for her, she worked alongside those in the kitchen. Normally bread, cold meat, and ale made up the first meal of the day, but she decided that roasted venison, a variety of cheeses, fruits, and hot bread should be served instead. The servants did not question her, though they were clearly disconcerted by the effort required to serve such a sumptuous morning meal.

While the hot viands were being arranged on platters, Graeye hurried back to the hall. A healthy fire burned in the hearth, and numerous torches were lit about the room. The benches that had so recently served as beds had been pulled away from the walls, and the tables set and readied for the morning repast. Even the rushes had been turned and respread.

Pleased with the transformation, she called for ale to be poured, then crossed to the great double doors. It was time to announce the meal.

Stepping outside to a sky that was nearly as dark as it had been an hour past, Graeye paused to indulge in the cool air that struck her warm skin. Until that moment, she had not realized how heated she had become working in the kitchens.

Pushing a damp lock of hair out of her eyes, she looked out across the inner bailey. Here and beyond, there was the hustle and bustle of activity. By the light of torches, horses were being groomed and outfitted, weapons and armor cleaned and polished, and soldiers spoke excitedly of the raid upon Edward's camp.

Shortly, Graeye's searching gaze lit upon Gilbert where he stood alongside his destrier. Tall and broad as he was, it was not difficult to pick him out from the rest of the crowd.

As soon as she saw him, she realized he had been staring at her. Agitated that his entire attention was focused on her, even though several men around him sought to gain his regard, she swallowed hard.

Then, with the fervent wish she had taken more care with her appearance, she removed the cloth she had tied around her waist and smoothed her hair as a lopsided grin transformed the serious planes of Gilbert's face.

Her heart lurched. Since their confrontation in the garden the previous morning, she had not spoken a word to him. It had suited her fine, or so she thought. Now she realized how petty it had been, and wished she had not snubbed him when he had attempted to engage her in conversation later in the evening. However, it had seemed her only defense against the kindness he was showing her too much of lately. If not for her continued obstinance, they would certainly be lovers again, and she did not want that. Did she?

She watched as he disengaged himself from his men, crossed the bailey, and mounted the steps to the donjon.

"I had hoped not to awaken you," he said, coming to stand before her.

Uncomfortable with his intense regard, which boded no good, she looked away. "You did not. I purposely rose early to ensure the men were well fed before departing."

" 'Twas not necessary. Ale and a crust of bread would have sufficed."

Much against her will, she met his steady, probing gaze and saw the desire he made no attempt to conceal. "Sufficed, but that is all," she said, grateful they were not alone. " 'Twould not be fitting for them to ride into battle and have their bellies gnawing with hunger."

Gilbert stepped closer. "Do you also worry about my hunger?" he asked softly.

Knowing he was only playing a word game with her did little to prevent unwanted feelings from surfacing. She vowed she would not succumb to him as she had yesterday, and tossed her head back and propped her hands on her hips. "I worry only of the hunger in your belly," she said.

He stared into her eyes. Then, giving her no time to protest, he took her arm and pulled her into the shadows. "Which is where this hunger starts," he said as he forced her back against the wall with the length of his body, his hands on either side of her.

Graeye stiffened, trying hard to ignore the press of his man's flesh against her swollen abdomen. "Let me go."

"You also hunger for it, Graeye. Do not lie." His voice was low as his hips began to move against her.

She tried to push him away, to deny the feelings he

roused, but he was like a rock. "Gilbert, there are others about," she protested, feeling suddenly breathless.

"If that is your only concern, be assured they cannot see." Cupping her chin, he lifted her face to his and touched his lips to her temple, then to her ear.

Desperate to end his seduction before she surrendered to her body's yearnings, she ducked beneath his arm. However, he caught hold of her and pulled her back.

"How long do you think to punish me, Graeye?" he asked, pressing his forehead to hers. "How long will you deny what is between us?"

"Forever," she breathed.

"Forever," he repeated bitterly. "Unless, of course, I agree to marry you."

She nodded. " 'Twas the bargain we made. I will not become your leman."

"Then you would have me seek my pleasure elsewhere?"

The thought of him lying with another woman pained her deeply, as it did each time she pondered the possibility. "Have you not already?" she asked.

He drew a deep breath, then released her and walked from the shadows. His back to her, he looked out across the bailey. "I have not," he said, then added, "yet."

One moment relieved and the next distressed, Graeye stared at his back. She did not want him to seek another, yet could not give him that which would prevent him from doing so. She wanted more. She wanted commitment, and for their child to be legitimate. But there seemed no use in pursuing the matter further.

Sighing, she stepped into the light. "Gather your men, for the meal is about to be served," she said, then turned to go back inside.

"Why do you act the lady of the castle when I have denied you the title?" he asked, keeping his back to her.

Her heart sank. Would he take this from her? It was really all she had to show she was the mother of his future heir. "You do not wish me to?" she asked as she stepped before him.

Dragging his eyes from the busy scene, he looked down at her. "It seems much work for so little reward," he replied. "Especially now that you are so heavy with child."

Unconsciously, she smoothed her hand over her abdomen. "There is naught else for me to do," she said. "Besides, 'tis my destiny."

"Your destiny?"

A faint smile touched her lips. "I may never be your wife, Gilbert Balmaine, but I will always be your child's mother." With that she returned to the hall.

Chapter 17

✦❧❦❧✦

Something had gone terribly awry. And not for the first time, Gilbert reminded himself as great, roiling anger boiled through him, striving to break past his hard-faced exterior.

Two of the three men he had set to watch the village were dead—gutted like pigs at a slaughter—and the third had sustained wounds that, at the very least, would see him crippled for life. Though his injuries were far worse than Gilbert's had been those many years ago, Gilbert knew well the long suffering that lay ahead for his loyal retainer . . . providing he lived. For a fighting man it was a fate worse than death.

"Charwyck!" Gilbert spat. He urged his destrier forward, glaring at the devastation before him with smoke-reddened eyes. In respectful silence his men followed him through the center of the deserted village, where fires still burned and thick smoke choked the air. There Gilbert dismounted and motioned for half a dozen of those nearest him to follow.

Mantles drawn over the lower halves of their faces to preserve some purity of air, they spread out in search of the wounded. In spite of the intense discomfort, the men were thorough in that endeavor, but soon discovered there were only casualties—two who needed but the blessings of a priest to aid them in that most exalted journey the church promised awaited all God-fearing men.

It appeared all the other peasants had made good their escape to the surrounding woods. As none had come forth when the knights arrived it was likely they were even now making for the protection of the castle's walls.

Still, it was difficult for Gilbert to be grateful for such a small loss of human life. These were his people, and it had been his responsibility to keep them free from harm. That he had failed grieved him deeply, but worse, it fanned the fires of his vengeance.

The only thing that kept him from losing control as he watched the village complete its descent to the ground, was his determination to discover who had betrayed him and see that one suffer for the misdeed. Now, more than ever, he was convinced there was another traitor among his men.

Methodically, Gilbert analyzed the events that had led to this terrible injustice. When word of the discovery of Charwyck's camp had come yestermorn, he had grown restless with the desire to finally get his hands on the old man. But, ever cautious, he had sent men to verify the information the villager had brought him, even though he'd had no real reason to distrust the man. Upon confirmation he had wasted no time in gathering together his army, leaving only a handful of men at each village to continue the watch he had set them months earlier.

Somehow, though, Charwyck had been given fair warning of their coming. The remains of his camp had revealed an almost leisurely departure. But the old man had left Gilbert a message—stringing up the soldier who had remained to watch the camp until Gilbert arrived. The sight of the man hanging from a tree in the middle of the clearing had torn a roar of fury from Gilbert's throat. Other than cutting down the unfortunate soldier, no time had been wasted in pursuing the brigands.

Though Gilbert had left the castle well enough provided for, the vulnerability of the villages had spurred him and his men on. In a blur they had progressed through the countryside, passing villages mercifully untouched by Charwyck's evil hand.

Gilbert had just begun to think himself fortunate to have suffered no more ill consequences when, from a distance, great plumes of smoke rising above the treetops had turned him north.

They had come too late.

Gilbert's fists clenched, his knuckles whitening as he turned to look at the men who awaited his next orders. With an eye toward exposing the traitor, he looked at each in turn, thoroughly assessing them. Most had been in his household for years, and never before had he been given any just cause to question their loyalty. He was almost ashamed that he would now, but this tragedy was no mere happenstance.

As the man was partially hidden by the bulk of another knight's horse, Gilbert almost overlooked Sir Michael. Though he again started to dismiss the possibility of the young knight's treachery, something niggled at the back of his mind. Beckoning it forward, he recalled Sir Lancelyn's remark made to him two months earlier.

On the morning he had made ready to depart from Medland, fully believing he could leave Graeye behind, his vassal had approached him and warned of Sir Michael's reaction to the news that Graeye carried Gilbert's child.

Gilbert had not bothered to learn the specifics, for at the time he had been far too annoyed by the idle talk that had led to such a conclusion, accurate though it was. Now, he realized, he should have paid more heed to the warning.

Aye, he concluded, seeking to catch Sir Michael's elusive gaze, the man certainly had motive for betraying him to Charwyck. Had he not made clear his desire to have Graeye for himself? And to discover that his new baron had already laid claim to her, and worse, gotten her with child, would certainly have given him reason to seek revenge.

Mercilessly berating himself for having been so blind, Gilbert swung himself into the saddle.

"Sir Michael," he called, "come forth."

The knight sat straighter in his saddle, his gaze falling upon Gilbert's unsmiling face before skittering away.

The others were quick to sense something was amiss, their heads swiveling to stare at the knight. Even as Sir Michael hastened to turn his horse about, the men efficiently closed ranks around him, leaving him only the path ahead, toward the baron.

"Come forth, man," Gilbert repeated, his voice a snarl of anger. "I must speak with you on a matter of grave importance."

Obviously in a quandary as to how he might save himself, Michael remained unmoving in his saddle. His gaze, though, strayed far beyond Gilbert to where uneasy refuge lay among the trees.

"What know you of this, Sir Michael?" Gilbert taunted, throwing his arm out to encompass the devastation. "Mayhap you can enlighten me as to how Charwyck knew of our coming, hmm?" He guided his horse nearer, readying himself for the moment when the knight would break free in an attempt to charge past him.

"Did he promise you the Lady Graeye in return for that information?"

Michael allowed him to come no closer. Driving his heels into his destrier's sides, he spurred the animal forward, setting himself a course to the right of Gilbert.

Gilbert wheeled his own horse around and urged the animal into the other's path, forcing Michael to take the less desirable course to the left, through the obstacle-strewn village. However, determined he would not get that far, Gilbert gave chase.

As he drew alongside Michael, Gilbert surrendered the reins to guide his mount with only the pressure of his legs. Then, with a bellow of rage, he launched himself sideways and collided with the other man, sending them both flying through the air.

"You stole her from me!" Michael screamed the moment before they slammed to the ground.

Gilbert took the brunt of the fall, Michael atop him. Ignoring the lancing pain shooting through his injured leg, he threw his greater weight sideways, pulling the other man beneath him.

"You bastard," Michael spat in his face, struggling for the dagger belted at his side. "You had your pleasure with her and then tossed her aside like a common trollop. She was mine—never yours."

"You know naught!" Gilbert snarled, seizing the weapon Michael sought and pitching it behind him.

"There you are mistaken, Baron." Michael laughed, his lips peeled back in a grotesque sneer. "I know Charwyck will see you dead and that bastard whelp of yours sliced from his daughter's belly ere he'll rest."

The threat against Graeye and his unborn child closed a fierce hand around Gilbert's heart. "How long?" he demanded, grabbing hold of the neck of Michael's tunic. "Have you betrayed me to Charwyck since the beginning—since you gave me your oath of fealty?"

Eyes cold and hard, Michael stared up at him. "Nay. 'Twas only when I discovered you had taken Graeye for yourself that I betrayed you."

"Your attack on William—"

" 'Twas convincing, wasn't it?" He chuckled. "You are a fool, Balmaine."

Raging, Gilbert propelled himself backward, dragging Michael upright. "Will you die a knight—or a coward?" he ground out, thrusting the man away.

As Michael struggled to regain his balance, Gilbert

withdrew his sword so swiftly, its arcing descent made the air sing a shrill song of death. "Draw your weapon," he ordered, "ere I disembowel you where you stand and save myself the ceremony of chivalry."

Michael's eyes flickered past him to where the others sat silently astride their mounts, their faces hardened against the one who had betrayed their lord. All was lost, he knew. For that one taste of revenge he had forsaken all.

" 'Twill not be necessary," he said, looking back at the baron. Drawing himself fully upright, he unsheathed his sword and angled it to the ground. He stared down its glowing length for some moments before raising the tip heavenward.

All watched as he placed the flat of the blade to his lips and lifted his eyes for a moment of prayer. Then, before Gilbert fully understood his intent, the knight turned the sword on himself, grasping its sharp edges with both hands and plunging it into his vitals.

Still standing, blood running from the mortal wound and puddling at his feet, Michael threw back his head and met Gilbert's disbelieving stare.

"All for a woman," he choked. "One you don't even want." With a desperate gurgle he slumped to the ground and drew his last, wheezing breath before death snatched it from his shuddering body.

Lowering his sword, Gilbert crossed the short distance to where the knight lay and knelt beside him. He stared into the glazed, sightless eyes that were fixed on the blue sky above.

"Again you are wrong my poor, misguided enemy," he murmured, drawing the lids down over those tormented eyes. "I do want her."

Graeye meant to close her tired eyes only a moment—to give them a rest from the stitching that, with just a bit more effort, would see the fine chemise finished ere it was time to withdraw to her chamber for the night. Leaning her head back against the chair, she was only vaguely aware of her hand losing its grip on the material, and did not even notice when it stole from her fingers, slithering off her lap and onto the floor.

The warmth of the hearth wooed her ever deeper into sleep, something she'd had too little of lately. Giving completely over to it, she curved a hand over her belly and went blissfully adrift.

It was how Gilbert found her less than an hour later, that great mangy dog of hers stretched out alongside the large chair that swallowed her small frame. At his approach the animal raised its head from its paws and eyed him with suspicion, a low rumble of warning bubbling from deep in his throat.

Scowling at the beast, Gilbert walked around the back of Graeye's chair. The dog continued to glare at him, its muzzle quivering. If Gilbert hadn't been certain an altercation would likely ensue that would awaken Graeye, he would have dragged the animal from the hall, but it was simply not worth the chance. Shaking his head, he broke the eye contact and turned his attention upon the one he had come to see.

A fierce possessiveness stole over him as he stared down at Graeye's sleeping form, his eyes missing nothing—the bloom of color that enhanced the loveliness of her face, the lustrous sweep of her tawny hair where it fell over her shoulder, the burgeoning evidence of her motherhood and the way her hand rested thereon. In the sweet innocence of her sleep she was even more beautiful than he remembered.

Though it had been less than a sennight since he had left her to pursue Charwyck following the burning of the village, he felt it had been much longer.

And still the old man had managed to elude him. Gilbert had finally concluded that the brigands had left his property, for there had been no more raids nor a single sighting since.

Feeling his anger begin to mount, he shook it off, refocusing on the woman before him and forgetting that she was of any relation to the man he burned to put his blade through. Impulsively, he lifted a tress of that silken hair, touching it to his lips before letting it slide through his fingers.

Sir Lancelyn, who had accompanied Gilbert in the search for Charwyck, entered the hall, and Gilbert waved him away. Immediately, the man retreated, leaving the baron and his lady to their privacy.

His back to the fire, Gilbert kneaded his pained leg as he continued to watch Graeye sleep. Her lids flickered from time to time as if she might awaken, but with a soft sigh and a caress to her abdomen, she resumed her deep breathing.

It was the child disturbing her, he realized. Though he was sorely tempted to lay a hand to her that he might feel its movements for himself, he suppressed the urge for fear of awakening her. In anticipation of a long wait, he spread his legs wide and clasped his hands behind his back.

It was not the baby that awoke Graeye, but an unsettling sensation that persisted in disturbing her dream. Opening her eyes, she focused on the silhouetted form that stood over her and slowly assumed the shape of Gilbert.

Nay, she corrected herself, a smile twitching at the corners of her mouth, it was still the dream she was in. Sighing, she lowered her lids and allowed the darkness to enfold her once again in its comforting embrace.

"Graeye." His voice intruded upon her languid, downward spiral.

A frown creasing her brow, she opened her eyes again and stared at the figure that was now leaning over her. "Gilbert?" she said.

Was it truly he come home to Penforke? she wondered as she battled her drowsiness. Or was this merely a continuation of her dream? Blinking, she peered closer and saw the vivid hue of his eyes that no dream could have reproduced so accurately. Though she felt a momentary thrill, she quickly suppressed it.

"Aye," he confirmed, leaning nearer to slip an arm behind her back and one beneath her legs. " 'Tis time you were in bed."

Having witnessed the brief exchange with perked ears, Groan instantly sprang to life, thrusting his great head between his mistress and the man who meant to carry her away. Showing his sharp teeth, he let go a deep growl.

Before Gilbert could take matters into his own hands, Graeye reached out and laid a hand on the animal's head. " 'Tis all right," she murmured. "Go lie down."

Though he did so with great reluctance, Groan backed away and settled himself near the hearth.

Gilbert lifted Graeye high against his chest, gritting his teeth in blackening irritation at the animal's overprotectiveness. Though it still took little effort to bear her, he immediately noticed the difference in her weight, for she had not allowed him to come so near during the past months. She yawned, nestling her head against his shoulder and sliding a hand up around his neck as he carried her toward the stairs.

Gilbert was as surprised as Mellie when the two of them came face-to-face on the landing above.

"Milord!" she squealed, jumping back in surprise. "I—I was not told of your coming."

One eyebrow arched, Gilbert took in her rumpled garments, tousled hair, and the telltale bloom of color on her lips. " 'Tis obvious," he said derisively. "And what has kept you from tending to your mistress's needs?"

"Mellie, is that you?" Graeye asked before the maid could answer. Though still not fully alert, her exhaustion holding her back from too quickly gaining that advantage, she was more than aware of Gilbert's mood. Raising her head, she searched out the dimly lit corridor for the girl.

"Aye, milady." Nervously, Mellie smoothed her hands over her skirts.

Graeye was not uninformed as to Mellie's frequent

trysts with a particular knight. In fact, viewing it as an avenue by which she could gain privacy for herself, she encouraged it by merely ignoring it. Though they never spoke about the trysts, the two women had come to a kind of understanding. "Are you feeling better?" she asked.

"What? Oh . . . some." Mellie was slow to catch hold to the line her mistress was throwing her.

"Hmm," Graeye murmured, settling her cheek back to Gilbert's chest. "See that you get plenty of rest tonight."

Gilbert saw through the ruse, but kept his mouth closed as he edged past Mellie and made for Graeye's chamber. There would, after all, be plenty of time to reprimand the girl.

To his surprise the room was in readiness, but only tolerably so. A fire burned uncertainly in the brazier, barely keeping the chill from the room. Around the perimeter several candles had been lit, but not nearly enough. On a table beside the bed sat a basin of water, though it was missing a hand towel and looked to have grown cool. And the bedclothes were turned back from a bed that had been poorly made.

Nay, he would not go easy on Mellie, he decided. In fact, were he not so bone-weary, he would seek her out as soon as Graeye was settled. Shouldering the door closed against intruders—most especially that drooling beast—he crossed to the bed and sat Graeye upon the cool mattress.

Rubbing her eyes, Graeye rid herself of the last of her sleep, then dropped her hands into her lap. "Did you find him?" she asked, raising her gaze to Gilbert's.

He looked tired, she thought. An unwanted pang of compassion struck her as she took in the dark circles beneath his reddened eyes and the several days' growth of beard shadowing his jaw.

"Nay," he answered. Turning, he went to stoke the fire. "He has disappeared completely."

Eyes narrowed, Graeye watched his movements. His

limp was worse than she'd ever seen it. "Think you he will return?"

Gilbert looked up. "Aye."

She dropped her gaze. Since word had first come of the discovery of Edward's camp, she had lived with a mixture of fear, dread, and relief. Following the burning of the village, Gilbert had returned only briefly to gather supplies to pursue the brigands. So briefly, in fact, that she had not had the chance to speak with him before he and his men had set off. This past week had been difficult.

Going to the washbasin, she plunged her hands into the tepid water and splashed handfuls of it over her face. Then, finding no towel, she stood indecisive a moment before settling upon her bliaut to wipe away the moisture. Even as she lifted its skirt, Gilbert's hand came around her and dangled a piece of linen before her. It was the covering from the small table across the room, she realized.

"Thank you," she murmured, stealing a quick glance at him as she wiped her hands and face.

He turned her around to face him. "I have missed you," he said, staring into her startled eyes.

"Me?" Blinking, she swallowed hard on the sudden ball of nervousness constricting her throat.

"Aye." He slid his hands down her arms, then inward to the laces of her bliaut.

Realizing his intent, she jumped away, placing the bed between them. "You forget yourself, my lord!" she protested, fumbling to draw the laces tight again.

"Come, Graeye," he coaxed. He extended a hand to her, though he did not move closer. "I only meant to help you prepare for bed."

"I do not think so," she said.

Wearily, he pushed a hand through his thick hair. "I will be sleeping in here tonight," he said, then reached to unfasten his sword.

Outraged by his audacity, and alarmed by the speed with which he was disrobing, Graeye gaped at him.

"What of your vow?" she demanded, even as the sight of his powerful chest warmed her as no fire possibly could. "Would—would you be so bold as to dismiss it with nary a prick of your conscience?"

He sat on the edge of the bed and began tugging off his boots. "Nay," he said, dropping one boot, then the other, to the floor before standing again. "I will abide by my vow not to force myself upon you."

"Then what do you think you are doing?" she squawked as he loosened his chausses.

At the first sight of those tapered hips, she whirled around and presented him with her back. Still, it was not simple modesty that bade her take such an action, but the need to hide her response from him.

Tossing the chausses over a bedpost, Gilbert sighed. "I am making ready for bed," he answered, then turned to use the washbasin.

"Your solar is down the corridor."

"Which I have yielded to Sir Royce."

Sir Royce? The king's man who had secured Medland for Gilbert all those months past? Stealing a glance over her shoulder, her eyes lit upon Gilbert's bare buttocks. Flushing, she looked away. "I—I did not know he had arrived. You've business with him?"

"Nay, he is only passing through. We met up with his party this afternoon."

She twisted her hands in her skirts. "He will be staying long?"

"Nay, just this night."

Then she could avoid him. Though she had adjusted well to Gilbert's people, the thought of meeting the king's man again unsettled her.

"You could sleep in the hall," she suggested.

"Aye, but you are here."

Silence followed, though the air was fraught with the tension of Graeye's futile search for a rejoinder.

Indifferent to his nudity, Gilbert moved about the room and snuffed all but one of the candles before returning to the bed. Grimacing at Graeye's stiff back, he lowered himself to the mattress and drew the covers over his naked loins. Then, a hand behind his head, he stared at her rigidly held figure. How curious, he mused, that from behind she displayed no signs of pregnancy.

Reaching over, he turned the covers back. "Come to bed, Graeye. You need not fear I'll go back on my word."

Graeye was not convinced, especially as she was as distrustful of her own desires as she was of his. Biting her lip, she glanced over her shoulder and was relieved to find his eyes closed, his head angled away from her.

Aye, he would keep his vow not to force himself upon her. But what if he touched her again as he had in the garden?

Stubborn to the end in spite of her exhaustion, she held out until she heard his breathing turn deep. Then, letting the tension drain from her, she loosed her bliaut and drew it off.

A short time later, clad only in her chemise, she walked around the bed to where the last candle burned. Hesitating, she looked down at Gilbert's face and, for the first time, noticed how very long his lashes were where they rested upon his cheeks. As her gaze lingered over his features, it struck her she had never before observed him during sleep. And yet she had been so intimate with him as to create this child growing inside her.

If only things had been different, she lamented. If only she had grown up with the love of both parents and been allowed to choose which path her destiny would take. And how differently would Gilbert have perceived her had this all-consuming vengeance he harbored never been born? Would there have been a chance for them to make a life together? Could he have grown to love her as she loved him?

Tears pricking the backs of her eyes, she determinedly redirected her attention. Licking her thumb and forefinger, she pinched the wick of the candle, then turned to pick her way back around the bed, where she imagined she would cling to the edge throughout the long night.

"Ow," she breathed when her foot came down on the rough sole of a boot he had left beside the bed. Wrinkling her nose, she made her next step more cautious than the last.

An outflung arm arrested her progress as she crept past Gilbert.

"You are supposed to be asleep!" she exclaimed, recoiling from the hand that sought to catch hold of her.

"I was," he gruffly replied, seizing her about her thickened waist and drawing her to the bed. " 'Tis your game to play at being asleep, not mine."

Unwilling to put up a pointless struggle against his greater strength, Graeye allowed herself to be drawn down upon the bed. Her mind, meanwhile, rushed with imaginings of what his intentions were now that he had her cornered.

"Do you prefer to lie on your side or your back?" he asked, pulling her nearer.

She was bewildered by the unexpected question. "My . . . side," she whispered.

Obligingly, he pulled her into the curve of his body, his hard warmth pressed along her back. After dragging the covers up, he slid an arm around her and settled it in the narrow valley below her breasts and above her belly.

Though she tried, Graeye simply could not relax while he held her, her thoughts turning to an awareness of each place their bodies met. She distinctly discerned the swells of his broad chest where they pressed against her back, and felt the steady thud of his heart. Lower, his loins nestled her buttocks. A shudder swept through her.

Gilbert's solution to what he perceived to be a chill was to press her even nearer, though there truly had been no space separating them before.

"Relax," he said. "I do not bite."

"I did not think you would," she said, uncomfortable with his ability to read her so easily.

"Hummph," he grunted with obvious disbelief. Sliding his hand to her abdomen, he rested it there.

It was a long night that followed.

Chapter 18

"And how does Sir Michael?" Sir Royce asked Gilbert between bites, his voice raised loudly as he tried to make himself heard over the din of hungry, talkative men. "I notice him to be absent from the hall. He is still in your service, is he not?"

As the king's man lifted another morsel to his mouth, he found himself staring into eyes suddenly cold and stony. A weighty silence descended upon the hall as his question went conspicuously unanswered.

His meat dagger suspended in midair, Gilbert looked from Sir Royce to his men. The abrupt termination of their conversations had left this terrible, expectant silence that he alone would have to deal with. Scowling, he watched as many gazes flickered from him to the lady beside him, whom he'd ushered into the hall much against her will a half hour earlier.

A moment later Gilbert, too, turned his regard upon Graeye.

Looking as if she had completely disassociated herself from any and all, she sat quietly seething, one hand gripping the stem of her chalice, the other stroking the handle of her meat dagger. As if entirely unaware of the attention turned upon her, she continued to stare at the trencher that had been set between her and Gilbert.

Other than her protests against dining with the king's men, which had proved an embarrassment for Gilbert when they had descended to the hall, she had refused to say anything more since he had settled her beside him. She would not even look up.

Gilbert had not understood her aversion to dining with them, for she regularly took her meals in the hall. And it was not as if she had awoken in a poor mood, for her disposition upon wakening that morning and finding him still in her bed had been pleasantly peaceable. In fact, when he had begun to knead his aching leg, she had even offered to do it for him. Naturally, he had declined.

However, she had turned indignant when he had suggested she join him in welcoming their guests. She had told him in no uncertain terms that she had no intention of accompanying him to the hall, and that he should go along without her.

Not understanding, he had insisted—to the point that when she had turned her back to him, he had seen her dressed himself. And it had been no mean feat, either, for she had opposed him all the way, going on about the humiliation she was sure to suffer in the presence of Sir Royce.

Too late Gilbert had seen the error of having forced her compliance. The curious, furtive glances the king's men had bestowed upon her as they entered the hall had finally convinced him of what Graeye had tried to convey. Though she'd adjusted well to the curiosity of Penforke's castlefolk, this was different.

Not only was she was an unwed noblewoman grown heavy with a misbegotten child, she was publicly seated beside the man who had fathered it—a man who had no intention of righting the situation by wedding her.

Not for the first time since discovering this, Gilbert wished he had allowed her to remain abovestairs, especially now that Royce had introduced this latest topic, which he was not about to discuss during a meal.

Sighing heavily, he turned his attention back to the king's man. "Let us speak of it later," he said, his tone conveying more than his words.

Instantly, the meal resumed its previous course, the noise of a hundred conversations converging upon the air at once.

"My lord," Graeye said to him. She lifted her gaze from the trencher to scan the occupants of the other tables. Only a handful looked their way.

Carrying a tasty morsel to his mouth, Gilbert leaned nearer to hear her.

"Why *is* Sir Michael not among your men?" she asked. "Has he displeased you?" Frowning, she turned her lovely pale eyes upon him.

So she had not been ignorant of the happenings around her, Gilbert concluded, not liking the tight corner she was backing him into. It was simply not the time or place to be drawn into this particular conversation, and he thoroughly intended to avoid it at all costs. There would be time later, in private, when he could tell her of the young knight's death.

As nonchalantly as possible, he speared a small piece of meat and offered it to her.

"Nay," she declined, shaking her head. "I am not hungry."

"But you would have eaten had I allowed Mellie to carry a tray up to you," he said, his brows lifting as he dared her to deny what she had spent much breath trying to convince him to grant her.

"Which is what I would have preferred!" she snapped. Then, remembering they were not alone, she looked around to see if she'd called undue attention to their exchange. None seemed overly interested.

"Give up this pouting, Graeye," he chided, speaking just above a whisper, "and eat, that our child will grow strong and healthy ere he ventures out into this cruel world."

Her lids flickered as she considered his words, then she abruptly thrust her chin forward. "Know you what they are thinking?"

"I know exactly what they are thinking," he replied softly, lowering his face nearer to hers. "They are envious—the lot of them."

Openmouthed, Graeye stared into his blue eyes that sparkled with the barest hint of laughter. "Aye, envious," she returned in a hushed voice replete with antagonism. "Envious they do not have a whore to warm their beds as you do."

It was the wrong thing to say, for immediately Gilbert's eyes lost all evidence of humor, turning hard and barren as their color deepened to near black. She recoiled inwardly at the change her words had wrought, knowing she had pushed him too far. Breath held, she waited to discover what reprisal he would seek against her.

For long moments he stared at her, his face an impenetrable mask. Then, as if he did not trust himself to speak, he pressed his lips tightly together and thrust his dagger forward that she might take the meat from it.

She acquiesced, lifting a hand to pluck the morsel from the tip. However, Gilbert was not content with her small concession.

"Nay," he said, his harsh voice stopping her hand where it hovered above the meat. "With your teeth."

Her anger flared again. "You are perverse!" she whispered.

"Aye, and do you not forget it."

In her present mood Graeye would have liked nothing better than to let her anger have free rein, but she wisely fought it down. Taking a deep breath, she parted her lips and leaned toward him.

There was none of the vexing triumph on Gilbert's face that she would have expected when he delivered the meat to her mouth. Instead, expressionless, he turned back to the trencher and fished out another piece for her.

Fuming, Graeye took her time chewing.

Gilbert seemed content to wait her out, and when she finally swallowed, the dagger was there again.

"I can feed myself," she protested.

"Aye, but our child cannot," he said, pushing the meat nearer.

Sighing, she took the morsel, fully expecting him to return with another at any moment. However, he seemed to feel he had proved his point. Pressing her meat dagger into her hand, he returned to his own nourishment.

"And do not feed any to that beast of yours!" he bit off, his eyes lighting momentarily upon Groan's head where it rested on her knee.

Lest he take any hesitation as defiance, Graeye reluctantly complied, searching out the scant vegetables that she preferred over any meat. She was surprised to discover how hungry she truly was once she started eating.

She decided to give it some time before reintroducing the question Gilbert had yet to answer, and it wasn't until the trencher was nearly empty that she finally braved it again.

"My lord," she began, running the tip of her tongue over her lips, "you did not answer my question about Sir Michael."

He eyed her over the trencher, his mouth tightening. "I did not forget," he said succinctly. " 'Twill wait."

He was hiding something from her, she knew, for what was the harm in telling her of one man's whereabouts? Still, she resigned herself to biding her time. She was not up to braving the beast twice in one morning. Nay, not even twice in one day.

"He is dead," Gilbert informed Sir Royce as he leaned back in his chair.

As if struck with a fist rather than those dispassionate words, Royce recoiled. "Dead?" he repeated with disbelief. "But how?"

Gilbert met his wide-eyed stare. "By his own sword he took his life. But had he not done it himself, I would gladly have seen the same end to him."

Coming out of his stupor, Royce turned the possibilities over in his mind. "Ah," he said a short time later. " 'Tis the same as Sir William, is it not? He betrayed you—to Charwyck."

Having assumed his favored position of tilting his chair backward, Gilbert stared out at the hall, which was empty of all but the two of them. "Aye," he growled. "And his betrayal cost the lives of two villagers and three of my best men, and the ruination of an entire village."

"But I understood you to have set men to watch the villages to ensure against further raiding," Royce said.

"I did, but when I received confirmation of Charwyck's place of encampment, I left only a token watch at each village and took the greater number of men to ride with me." He drew a hand down his face before continuing. "Charwyck was warned of our coming ere we ever reached him."

Royce shook his head. "So Sir Michael carried word to him of your intent to raid his camp."

" 'Tis assuredly what happened."

"And 'twas because of Lady Graeye he betrayed you?"

Sighing, Gilbert settled his chair back on its four legs. "Aye, he wanted her."

Pressed against the wall near the bottom of the stairway, Graeye squeezed her eyes closed, but could not block out the offense that had just been laid at her door. Men had died because of her, villagers left homeless—all in the name of the vengeance Edward was set upon extracting, and Sir Michael's betrayal.

She knew it was wrong of her to eavesdrop on their conversation, but she had come unsuspectingly upon it, and Gilbert's words "He is dead" had precluded any thought of withdrawing or revealing herself. Now she understood his reluctance to speak of Sir Michael during the meal—it was not idle conversation, after all.

"Then Charwyck knows of the child she carries," Royce concluded. "And if not from Rotwyld, then from Sir Michael."

"Aye, he knows, and knowing that 'tis my child she carries, 'tis likely he will try again to harm her." Abruptly, Gilbert pushed to his feet and began pacing the room.

"Sir Michael took much satisfaction in describing to me exactly what Charwyck intends to do," he said as he passed Royce a third time.

The knight could well imagine what that might be, but emotionally removed from the situation as he was, he saw more clearly the truth of the matter. "Unless Charwyck has gone completely mad, 'tis not Lady Graeye's life I would fear for, but rather the safekeeping of your child—and then, of course, your own life."

Gilbert ceased his pacing and turned back around. "What speak you of?"

Dropping his elbows to the table, Royce clasped his hands and leaned forward. "I speak of your heir. The old man wanted an heir for his properties—'twas his only reason for bringing Lady Graeye from Arlecy. Now he has a grandchild soon to enter this world who will be more valuable by far than any made from the union of his daughter with Sir William. If he could but lay his hands on this child and see to your swift demise, then he would have your properties and those he lost to you."

His mind working throughout Royce's explanation, Gilbert nodded. "Aye, you are right, 'tis exactly what he would aspire to—providing he has yet any wits about him."

"What will you do then?"

What he had set out to do from the beginning, Gilbert thought. Nay, that was not exactly true. It was not until the old man had attempted to burn Graeye alive that he had acquired a real thirst for Edward's blood.

"He will suffer the same fate as Philip," he said harshly. "And then I will be free of the curse of the Charwycks."

"Do you so soon forget that Lady Graeye is also a Charwyck?"

The reminder jolted Gilbert and left him speechless.

Beside Graeye, Mellie tugged on her arm. "Milady," she whispered with great urgency. "We should return to yer chamber."

Graeye glanced over her shoulder. Until that moment she had completely forgotten the other woman's presence. It was a shock to find herself staring into that puckish face. Shifting her burden of soiled linens to the opposite arm, Mellie motioned Graeye to follow her back up the stairs.

Having no desire to linger long enough to hear Gilbert's answer, for it was obvious what that would be, Graeye conceded. Hitching up her skirts, she accepted the hand Mellie fit beneath her elbow, and together both women stepped lightly up the stairs. They didn't speak until they reached Graeye's chamber.

"Ye needn't worry I'll be runnin' to the baron with news that we overheard his conversation, milady," Mellie said as she pushed open the door and stepped back that Graeye might precede her.

Graeye walked inside and went to stand before the window. "I am most grateful for that consideration, Mellie," she said. And she truly was, for she did not think she could stand more of Gilbert's anger. He would surely consider it further deceit to learn she had listened in on his conversation with Sir Royce.

"Like for like," Mellie answered.

Her brow furrowed, Graeye looked over her shoulder.

The maid shrugged. "Ye did me a good turn yester-eve," she explained, "and I would but repay in kind. Of course, I'll no longer be beholden to ye fer it."

"Of course not," Graeye said, offering a weak smile of appreciation.

Much to her surprise Mellie returned the gesture. Then, shifting her burden once again, she swung about and flounced out of the room.

Though Mellie still tried very hard not to like her, Graeye mused, the girl had lost much of her initial hostility. She was almost friendly at times.

That thought only momentarily dispelled her anguish at what she'd overheard. Holding tight to the emotions that threatened to overflow, Graeye turned back to the window.

There was more she needed to know, Graeye decided later that day, and only one person who could tell her. But how was she to convince Gilbert she was ready for the truth about Philip?

As the last of the king's men disappeared from sight over a distant rise, she shifted her gaze to the bailey below and caught sight of Gilbert as he strode toward the donjon. Should she go to him? she wondered. Or would he come to her?

Her quandary was resolved a few minutes later when Gilbert entered her chamber.

"I had thought you would be resting," he said as he closed the door behind him.

Knowing her moment was at hand, yet uncertain as to how she should broach the subject, Graeye did not turn from the window. "I am not tired," she said, hugging her arms more tightly around her and leaning farther out to let the cool breeze snatch tendrils of hair about her face.

Laying his hands to her shoulders, Gilbert gently pulled her back and turned her to face him.

Instantly, she averted her gaze for fear he might read the guilt there, assuming he did not yet know of it. Dared she hope Mellie had kept her word? It would seem so, otherwise she was certain she would have known of his displeasure before he even entered the room.

Pulling away from him, she lifted her loosened hair over her shoulder and set herself to braiding it.

"I prefer it unbound," he said, taking the one step that brought him to her again.

Too overwrought to comprehend his words, she continued plaiting.

"Graeye." He closed a hand over hers to halt the jerky movements that betrayed her anxiety.

With no choice but to give him the attention he sought, she took a deep breath and peered up at him from beneath her lashes. "Aye, my lord?"

"You are still angry with me?"

Though she knew he referred to their argument in the hall, at that moment she could not think what had precipitated it. Frowning, she searched backward and laid her finger to it a moment later.

It had all started because of her resentment at being forced to dine at his side as if she were the wife he refused to make her. It all seemed so trivial now that she carried the burden of those men's deaths upon her shoulders.

"Angry?" She shook her head. "Nay, no more. I behaved poorly and am repentant for the embarrassment I caused you."

Gilbert's brows shot up. He had expected her to continue with where they had left off during the meal. Why was she deigning to leave the subject be? he wondered, his guard going up.

"What are you about, Graeye?" he asked. His lips thinned as he searched her face and the reddened eyes she tried to conceal beneath her spiky lashes. "And why have you been crying?"

"Forgive me, Gilbert," she said. " 'Tis the pregnancy that makes my moods flighty."

Aye, he had heard pregnant women were ofttimes unpredictable. It was how his father had explained away his mother's moodiness when she'd carried

Lizanne. Still, his instincts insisted there was more to Graeye's peculiar behavior than merely her impending motherhood. Her anger was almost preferable to this.

Albeit skeptical, he nodded his grudging acceptance of her explanation and drew her to the bed.

"I would apologize for obliging you to attend the meal with me," he said, urging her down beside him. "I did not realize 'twould cause you such discomfort."

She stared at her hands, not answering.

"Well?" he murmured.

She chanced a look at him. "Truly, Gilbert, you need not apologize. 'Tis done. The worst is over with and . . ." She looked away. "In the future I will have no such qualms dining at your side."

He was quiet a long moment, wondering if he was reading more into her demeanor than was truly there. Nay, something was wrong. The woman he had lived with these past months would not so easily let go of the quarrel they had begun only hours ago. But he would leave it be, for he had yet to answer the question she had put to him earlier. And answer it he must, for she would eventually hear of it from others.

"I owe you an explanation regarding Sir Michael—"

"Nay!" she blurted out, shaking her head. "It does not matter. 'Tis of no consequence . . . truly."

Gilbert was surprised by the vehemence of her words. What an enigma she had become. "He is dead," he said quietly.

She threaded her fingers together over her belly, her gaze intent upon their awkward meshing. "I had guessed as much."

He lifted her chin, forcing her to look into his eyes. "And how came you by that conclusion?"

She shrugged. " 'Tis obvious ill fortune befell him. Otherwise you would not have been so reluctant to discuss the matter."

He wondered at her reasoning. He was more inclined to believe she'd either eavesdropped on his conversation with Royce, or someone else had and carried the news to her. Mellie? Nay, he did not think so.

"You are saddened?" he asked.

"Of course." Tears filled her eyes.

Tears! Gilbert pulled her against his side, stroking a hand over her hair as she spilled silent grief upon his tunic. He did not understand how she could cry over a man whom she had professed to have no feelings for.

"Mayhap you loved Sir Michael after all?" he asked when she calmed. That possibility did not sit well with him, but he had to ask.

She tilted her head back. "Loved him? Nay, Gilbert, I have told you before that I did not love Sir Michael. That has not changed."

His relief was immeasurable, but quickly forgotten as he realized she had not asked the cause of Michael's death. It only served to strengthen his belief that she'd been privy to the information beforehand.

"Graeye—"

"Gilbert," she interrupted, "I need to know of Philip's crimes. Won't you tell me?"

He stiffened, dropping his arm from around her. "You tread where you ought not to," he warned, his voice chill.

"I need to know," she pleaded, edging nearer and placing an entreating hand upon his arm. " 'Tis your child I carry, Gilbert Balmaine, yet I know nothing of you—and little of my own family. I would simply know the truth of it."

"And would you accept as truth what I reveal?"

She nodded. "Aye, Gilbert, methinks I am ready now to know and accept it."

Standing from the bed, he walked over to the hearth, his back to her. "Know you that your brother was betrothed to my sister, Lizanne?"

"Aye, Edward told me."

"She adored your brother—fancied herself in love with him, though 'twas only his looks and her youth that led her to believe herself to be in that absurd state.

Near five years ago, when she was but turned fourteen, at the behest of my father I took her from Penforke to be wed with Philip."

He fell silent, and Graeye could only guess at the emotions rising in him as she saw his muscles bunch and tauten beneath his tunic.

"Though 'twas during the time of Stephen's reign when lawlessness abounded," he continued, "I was too self-assured to believe the short ride warranted a sizable escort. You see, I had not counted on the delay caused by such a cumbersome baggage train, and when night suddenly fell upon us, we were forced to erect a camp."

Again he paused, leading Graeye to believe something terrible had befallen their camp. In the next moment he confirmed it.

"We had only bedded down for the night when we were set upon," he said. "All my men were slaughtered and Lizanne was ..."

She heard him draw a deep breath, but no words followed. "Violated?" she asked delicately.

"Nay, though nearly," he growled. "And then that bastard brother of yours refused to honor the marriage contract on grounds she was no longer chaste."

His anger was mounting, Graeye realized, and sought to distract him from the subject of his sister. "What of you, Gilbert?" she asked. "Did you manage to escape?"

With an invective he swung away from the hearth and advanced on her. "Think you I am a coward?" he roared.

Alarmed by the force of the anger she had ingenuously sparked, Graeye eased herself farther back on the mattress and drew her knees up. It was a tangible thing that stood between them, an anger so deep, she felt she would have to physically push it aside to reach the man beyond it—were she strong enough.

"Nay, Gilbert. Pray do not put words in my mouth,

or thoughts into my head. I did not mean to imply such a thing. You know I would not do that."

"Do I?" he rasped, coming to stand only a few feet from her. "Did you not accuse me of being a coward before?"

Had she? She had to search through each of their encounters to discover the one he referred to. She remembered it with dread, for she had, indeed, accused him of such a failing in the graveyard the morning he had sent her from Medland.

"Aye, you are right," she admitted, "and I am more than sorry for having done so. But I was angry at the time and only sought to hurt you as you were hurting me."

He did not respond.

"Come sit beside me," she urged.

He moved closer, but ignored her invitation. "I fought them ... I wounded some ... I killed some." He placed his hands on the mattress and leaned near her. "And then they left me for dead ... a cripple."

"Nay, not a cripple," she protested.

Catching her hand, he placed it on his thigh where the thick ridge of the scar could be felt through his leggings. "A cripple," he repeated as he drew her hand downward.

Though she had to go onto her knees and lean precariously over the edge of the bed, Graeye did not resist. She allowed him to guide her hand lower and around the side of his calf where the scar finally melded with the smoother skin below.

"So many promises to keep and I failed," he said. "As if 'twas only yesterday, I still remember Lizanne's scream. Do you know how it feels to live for years with such a reminder of your failings?"

Graeye shook her head, unable to bring herself to look back at him.

"Would you like to know who ordered the raid upon our camp?" His voice, filled with raw pain, grated in her ear.

Lifting her head, she stared at him through the veil of hair that had fallen over her face. He was like a caged animal, she thought. Or rather, like one caught in a hunter's trap—oddly resigned to its fate, yet ready to hurl itself at the offender if given the chance. She put a hand to her throat as she fought to calm her racing heart.

"Not even a guess?" he prodded, his mouth a cruel slash across his handsome face.

She knew what he wanted to hear, and didn't disappoint him. "Philip?" she mouthed, no sound emitting from her lips.

His brows raised. "What?"

She summoned every last bit of courage. "Was it Philip?"

He smiled, a bitter smile that only served to frighten her more. "How very perceptive." He articulated each word carefully before assisting her back to a sitting position.

"Why?" she asked. "Why would he do such a thing?"

"You have much to learn about the blood that runs through your veins, Graeye Charwyck. 'Twas not simply that Lizanne was not beautiful enough for him, but mostly that her dowry was deemed insufficient when the opportunity arose for him to wed a wealthy widow. So he thought to be rid of my sister without suffering the consequences of a broken betrothal. He ordered our deaths."

Shaking her head, Graeye lowered her eyes. It was not that she didn't believe Gilbert, but that she didn't want to. Aye, her memories of Philip were alive with the cruelties he had visited upon her, but what Gilbert was accusing her brother of was the purest form of evil she had ever imagined.

"So you are not ready to accept the truth after all," Gilbert concluded, contempt darkening his words.

"I had not thought the truth would be so terrible," she admitted, forcing her gaze back to his. " 'Tis difficult to accept how such evil could be in a man's soul. It frightens me."

Her reluctant, albeit undeclared, acceptance of the truth calmed him—somewhat. "Did you learn nothing from your father's attempt to murder you?"

That was not something she was likely ever to forget. But the old man had been half-mad over losing everything dear to him—and all to a man he believed responsible for the death of his precious son. What was Philip's excuse for the evil in his heart?

"When—when did you discover 'twas Philip who was responsible for the attack?" she asked.

Straightening, his fists on his hips, Gilbert stared down at her. "Last summer," he said, "when he decided he would have Lizanne after all—even after she was already wed to another."

His hand strayed downward to knead the injured muscles of his leg. "He stole her when she was returning from a village on her husband's property," he continued. "The bastard beat her and then tried to force himself upon her. He would have had her, too, if her husband and I had not discovered his encampment."

Graeye felt as if he was leaving something out, but did not press him on it.

"Your brother was bested in a fair duel, Graeye—and not one between me and him, as you think. Though 'twas Philip's blood that I craved to dress my blade, I fought another . . . and killed him. 'Twas Lizanne's husband who fought your brother, and when he bested him, the coward yielded. The coward yielded."

He saw the question in her eyes and shook his head. "Unlike Philip, Ranulf Wardieu, my sister's husband, is an honorable man. 'Twas only when your brother turned on him and attempted to put a knife through Ranulf's heart that he earned the arrow through his back."

"Your sister," Graeye said.

"Aye. 'Twas more than justified."

She nodded. Now she understood—and believed. "I

am sorry. I did not know. 'Tis no wonder you hate me as you do."

At her words Gilbert's eyes lost most of their hardness.

"I do not hate you, Graeye," he said, leaning forward to lift a handful of her hair from her lap. "If I did, 'twould not matter that you carry my child." He rubbed the silken tresses between his fingers, seemingly entranced by the play of light over the strands.

Hope bloomed inside Graeye. Was it possible he might one day come to care enough for her that they could put aside their differences and raise their child in harmony?

He must have seen it in her eyes, for he straightened abruptly, letting her hair slip through his fingers. "But I will not wed you," he said. He walked to the door.

Desperately wishing to feel the comfort of his arms around her again, but fearing his rejection, Graeye squelched the impulse to go to him. A moment later he was gone.

Anguish in her heart, she lay back on the bed and stared up at the ceiling.

Now she clearly understood what had driven Gilbert's anger when he had come to Medland and discovered her identity—why he had believed she had deliberately seduced him. And why he would not marry her, even to give their child his name.

She had not thought she would ever forgive him for all the wrongs he had done her, but now found she had no choice. For too long she had fought him, and for all the wrong reasons. His anger was his due, even if she was innocent of all he had accused her of.

If it took her until the end of their time together, she would right the wrongs done him and his family and prove to him she could be trusted. Noblewoman or not, if he wanted her as his leman, she would no longer hold herself from him. Though that surrender pained her, she acknowledged the losing battle she had been waging against him. It would have come to the same thing in the end, she reasoned, for long she had desired to feel again the caress of his hands.

Above all, she wanted peace between them, and she would have it. Though there was little comfort in the vow she made herself, Graeye found strength in it.

Chapter 19

She had seduced him once before, so there was no reason she could not do it again, Graeye tried to convince herself, though without much luck. Gilbert was not proving as willing as he had been on that night long past. Indeed, it was all she could do to gain a moment alone with him, and then he was too soon gone.

For two days she had attempted to get near enough to stir the desire he had professed having for her. And for as many days he had evaded her. No longer did he seem interested in seeking her out. Instead he brooded when they were forced together for meals, and kept his conversations with her short and detached.

But today was a new day, Graeye told herself as she watched Gilbert leave the smithy, where new weapons were being forged for the coming battle with Edward. When he entered the stables alone, she knew she'd found her opportunity.

Squaring her shoulders, she skirted the corral and entered the building that smelled of horses and fresh-cut hay. In the doorway she peered to the left and right, wondering which stall Gilbert had disappeared into. She had just determined to go left when a whinny brought her head around. Triumphant, she changed directions, coming upon Gilbert just as he began to brush his destrier's coat.

Her breath caught at the sight of him, her eyes widening as something inside her stirred to life. He'd removed his tunic, and his bare back glistened with the warmth of the smithy, the thick muscles rolling beneath his skin as he applied himself to his task.

Thinking her presence unnoticed, she hesitated a moment longer to allow her gaze to stray lower, past a tapered waist, to the cream-colored breeches riding upon his hips.

Finding herself uncomfortably warm, she swallowed hard and forced her eyes to the back of his head. "Are there not grooms to do that?"

He must have heard her approach—known she watched him—for he showed no sign of surprise at her voice. "There are," he answered indifferently. Without turning to look at her he drew the brush over the animal's flank.

Refusing to be put off, Graeye stepped into the stall and began to pick her way across the hay-strewn floor.

"Come no nearer," Gilbert ordered before she had taken more than a few steps.

"But—"

"No nearer!" he repeated. "I would not have you trampled beneath this animal's hooves."

For the first time she turned her attention upon the horse and saw what Gilbert already knew. The highstrung destrier was agitated by her presence, its limbs tense and its great eyes rolling. Snorting a warning, it tossed its head and began to paw at the ground.

"Step back," Gilbert demanded, glancing over his shoulder at her. If he was startled by her appearance, which she'd spent an inordinate amount of time on, it did not show.

Frowning, she stepped back to the stall entrance. All was not going as planned. She finally had caught him alone, and she could not get near enough to him to catch his interest.

"What is so important it cannot keep?" he asked.

"You have been avoiding me."

Though he spared her a glance—and only that—he did not pause in his labors. "Aye," he admitted, "for good reason."

She was surprised he would acknowledge it. "What reason is that?"

He kept her waiting a long time on his answer, moving about the destrier as if she had not even asked the question.

"'Twas I who was not yet ready to speak of Philip," he finally said as he applied himself to the tangled mane. "The memories are still too vivid. Speaking them aloud made them come alive again."

Wanting desperately to ease the torment behind his reserve, she took a faltering step forward. "Gilbert—"

"Stay where you are," he ordered, glaring across at her. "If you do not have a care for yourself, then have a care for the babe."

He was right of course, but acknowledging it did little to assuage the hurt his angry words wrought. "Gilbert," she implored, "if I cannot come in, won't you come out? I do not wish to talk to your back."

"There is naught to talk about," he said, though he did cease with the grooming to level his unmoving stare upon her.

Graeye fought the angry fire his nonchalant words fanned to life, but she could not check the retort that sprang to her lips. "You are a stubborn man, Gilbert Balmaine. I come to make peace with you and you scorn me. Are we to live together in constant turmoil?"

It was all she could do to stand her ground and not turn and flee to the comfort of her chamber. It would be too easy to do, yet it would solve nothing.

Sighing harshly, Gilbert set aside the brush and strode over to her. Placing a hand on either side of the stall entrance, he looked down at her. "Is it peace you desire, Graeye, or merely another truce?"

With him towering so far above her, the heat from his body enveloping her, it was difficult to think straight. Drawing a broken breath, Graeye gave in to the desire to touch him. She leaned toward him and placed her palms on his chest. "'Tis peace I seek," she whispered.

As if she had scalded him, he swept both her wrists together and lifted her hands from him. "I have warned you before," he bit off. "Do not touch me unless you are willing to suffer the consequences."

A slight, uncertain smile curving her lips, she stared up at him. "I am willing. 'Tis verily the reason I have come to you."

The anger upon his face dissolved into disbelief. "Is it a game you are playing?"

To prove otherwise, she attempted to free her hands from his grasp, but he would not release her. Having accepted that if there ever was to be a future for them, she must yield first, she boldly stepped nearer.

"Ah, Gilbert," she sighed. "I am well and truly done fighting you."

The declaration only served to intensify Gilbert's disbelief. What did she mean she was done fighting him? That she would no longer argue with him? That she would set aside her belligerence? That she would come willingly to him that they might both find pleasure in each other's body?

As if she'd read his thoughts, Graeye leaned nearer until her breath was on his, her belly pressed to his hips. "There will be peace between us," she said as she raised herself to her toes, offering her mouth in silent invitation.

Astounded by her acquiescence, Gilbert did not immediately take what she offered, what he had so long desired. Instead he searched her face—her pert nose, the warm flush along her cheekbones, the delicate bow of her softly parted lips, and the limpid eyes she opened wide to him when he remained unmoving.

"Let it be again as it was on that first night," Graeye implored, suddenly fearful of his rejection.

Suddenly, she was in his arms, his mouth merciless, his hands urgent upon her body. Though she heard the warning voices, heard their faint cries when she touched her tongue to his, she could not turn back. This was what she wanted.

"Would you have me stop?" he rasped against her mouth.

She shook her head, the single word she spoke lost amid the kiss that brought their mouths together again. Drawing a hand over the stubble shadowing his jaw, she pushed her fingers into his thick hair to hold more tightly to him.

He accepted what she offered—and demanded more. Hungrily, his mouth plied hers with fervent kisses, drinking from her as a man who had not quenched his thirst in a very long time. Without breaking the contact he pulled her against the wall of the stall and locked her between his thighs. Groping for the laces of her bliaut, he loosed them, then slid his hands inside only to encounter the chemise. Rumbling an invective into her mouth, he began to drag her skirts up.

A sound somewhere in the stables broke through Graeye's hazy consciousness. "Gilbert," she gasped, "we should return to the donjon. Someone might come upon us."

Breathing heavily, he lifted his head. "None would dare interrupt," he said, and closed his hand over her warm thigh.

Nay, but they might see their lovemaking, she thought. "I ...," she began, then trailed off at the thought of losing Gilbert to reasoning. Shaking her head, she slid her hands up his chest and around his neck.

Though he did not think he could wait, Gilbert saw the distress in her eyes the moment before she shut-

tered it with a coaxing smile. He reluctantly stepped
away from her, and held out his hand. "Come," he said,
"we will find privacy abovestairs."

Abovestairs? Graeye looked up and only then realized that a loft lay overhead. It would not offer the solitude of her chamber, but it was preferable to the stall.
Smiling, she placed her hand in his and allowed him to
lead her up the stairs.

In a corner radiant with sunlight, Gilbert gently laid
her down on the hay. Having regained a measure of
control over his desire, he leaned over her and leisurely
savored her brilliant hair where it was spread out beneath her.

"Never have I wanted a woman more than I want
you, Graeye," he said gruffly as he brushed the hair
back from her brow.

She could find no words to answer him. That he still
wanted her was enough. Her heart pounding wildly,
she slid her hands up over his chest, her restless fingers
probing the powerful undulations she found there.

Pushing up her skirts, Gilbert pressed a knee between her willing thighs. When she parted, drawing her
knees up to accommodate him, he groaned aloud.
Sweeping aside her undergarments, he ran his hands
over her belly, then up her sides. Tiny moans of pleasure broke from her throat when he caressed the sensitive nubs of her heavy breasts.

Arching over her, he took her cries into his mouth.
Had she not been so small and he so large, it would
have been a difficult task given the protrusion of her
belly, but there was just enough space that she would
feel no discomfort.

His mouth maintaining its possession of hers, he
pressed his hips to her center of heat. When she arched
upward, moving against his straining manhood, he
thought he might go mad with wanting her. With the
last of his restraint slipping away, he slid a hand between her quivering limbs to find her moisture.

At his touch Graeye tossed her head back and arched

higher, thinking to assuage the deep ache she had first experienced all those months past. But still he held himself from her.

As he loosened his breeches, Gilbert watched the play of rapture over her flushed face. He was surprised that he had once entertained thoughts of her being a fairy, for now he saw that she was wholly a woman. Freed from his breeches, he pressed his length to her, but did not enter. In a moment, he promised himself. He did not want it to be over too soon.

"Gilbert!" His name broke from her lips as her flesh met his. Her breathing shallow and rapid, she opened her eyes and looked questioningly at him. "Do not cease now," she beseeched.

Reveling in the sweet huskiness of the voice he had been deprived of during their first joining, Gilbert tried to make sense of the words she spoke. Cease? Not even if she begged otherwise could he do that.

"Please, Gilbert," she pleaded as she reached urgent hands to his hips.

The control he sought still eluding him, he lowered his head and pressed his lips to her belly, then moved them up her body and captured her mouth again.

Graeye rubbed her torso against his, her breath coming in short gasps between the impassioned strokes of his mouth. Tilting her head back, she offered him her throat. She clasped him tighter as he laid his lips to it— kissing, sucking, and nipping her heated flesh.

When she was thrashing beneath him, her hands sliding between them to seek his manhood, Gilbert knew he could hold out no longer. Raising himself up, he easily found her moisture. His breathing ragged, his teeth clenched against the yearning to plunge himself fully into her warmth, he slowly fit himself inside her.

Though she welcomed him, her discomfort was evident in the stiffening of her spine. He held himself unmoving, allowing her to become used to him, moisture beading on his brow with the effort to refrain from taking her too quickly.

Slowly, she relaxed, her hands sliding down his back to grip his buttocks.

Gilbert needed no more encouragement. Still, he had enough wits about him to proceed slowly. Though she had already given him her virginity, she was nearly as untried as an innocent, and this time he was determined she would reach the same pinnacle he aspired to.

Exercising control over his baser needs, he withdrew partway before sinking more deeply into her. He paused again, his eyes searching her face.

She met his stare. "Show me," she whispered, then turning her head, gently sank her teeth into his shoulder.

He surged fully into her, his thrusts quickening as she responded with tentative movements that strove to match the rhythm of his. Though he was fast losing all sense of reality, still uppermost in his mind was the need to see her satisfied before he found fulfillment himself. But when he heard Graeye's moan of pleasure, the sweet sound drove him further from his objective.

He was losing control again, he acknowledged before the thought began its slide back into his subconscious. Aye, it was not as if he could not take his ease of her now and pleasure her later, he reasoned. It had just been so long.... Groaning aloud his pending satisfaction, he thrust faster, wresting the rhythm from Graeye as he pulled her buttocks up to meet him.

"Take me with you," he heard her pleading voice even as he approached the edge of oblivion that offered the possibility of freedom from the stranglehold this woman had upon his desires. As nothing else could have done, her voice pulled him back from the brink.

"Aye, love," he said, wondering at the ease with which the endearment fell from his lips before setting himself to her pleasure. Like no other woman before, though there had not been so many during these past years, she responded wonderfully to his every touch and caress.

Carefully, he nurtured the heightened stirrings of her

body, pausing only when it became too agonizing to deny his own needs, then resuming once he regained control. Though her release was not long in coming, it seemed ages.

He felt her tightening, felt a sudden stillness within her the moment before she convulsed amid cries of pleasure. His breath coming in sharp rasps, he stared at her lovely face, imprinting the rapture he found there forever upon his mind.

Her body softened beneath his, her features relaxing. At that moment Gilbert unleashed the storm that had been raging inside him. One moment he was straining over her, seeking that same place she had found, and the next he was rolling away. Holding tight to her, he took her with him as he fell back upon the hay.

Feeling as if there were not a bone left in her body, Graeye lay pleasantly satiated against him, her head tucked beneath his chin. Though she had known there was something beyond what she had felt that first time with this man, it was more than she had ever imagined. He had taken her to that elusive place, and she had not found it wanting. It was some time before either spoke, but when Gilbert finally did, his voice was gruff, his words terse.

"Never again refer to yourself as 'whore,'" he said. "My men will respect you as if you were my wife. Do you understand?"

She nodded, for he spoke true. Although most believed she'd been Gilbert's leman since her arrival at Penforke, none had shown her anything but deference.

"Gilbert, will you ever find it in you to forgive me the wrongs my family has done yours?" she asked as she ran her fingers lightly over his chest.

Her unexpected question jolted him—and the pain behind her words. "I do not blame you," he said truthfully.

"Aye, you do," she countered. "Naught has changed. I am still a Charwyck, and you hate—"

"Nay, I have told you, I do not hate you, Graeye."

If only she could believe him. "Then you are a fool," she replied, tilting her head back to study his face.

"And not for the first time," he said, and smiled. The dimple that she had suspected would be there if ever he genuinely smiled appeared.

She was captivated, unable to squelch the impulse to touch it with the tip of her finger. He stiffened momentarily, then smiled wider.

Her hand resting alongside his jaw, she met his gaze and thought she saw there what was also in her heart. She was stunned. Was it possible he loved her, but could not bring himself to admit such a thing—as she could not? Nay, she concluded, it had to be something else. Contentment, perhaps.

Chapter 20

❧❧❧

raeye awoke in Gilbert's bed the following morning. She knew it without opening her eyes. Would have known even had his body not been curled around hers, his arm encircling her thick waist. The long night of love they had shared could not be easily wiped from her mind. Too, it had only been a few hours since sleep had finally taken her.

She looked around the bright, sun-streaked room—evidence that late morning was upon them—and her gaze rested on a delicately worked wall hanging. She had noticed it yestereve, so out of place was it. Truly, it was the only thing in the lord's solar worth taking note of.

Not once since she had been at Penforke had she entered Gilbert's private chamber. Until yestereve she had not been fool enough to do so.

The only unexplored room, it had come as a surprise. Unlike the rest of the donjon, it was sparsely outfitted, its furnishings shabby and aged. Mostly, though, it was a cold place, no warmth to be found anywhere except in that beautiful wall hanging, which depicted each of the four seasons.

As she would be sharing this room with Gilbert

henceforth, would he mind if she made changes? she wondered. It was simply too dreary to contemplate spending much time in otherwise.

His hand caressing her belly pulled her back to his presence.

" 'Tis good you are such a large man, Gilbert Balmaine," she murmured, thrilling at the sensations his fingers kindled over her taut skin. " 'Twould not be so easy for you to fit your arm round my waist were you not."

Deep, sleepy laughter rumbled in his chest as he nuzzled the back of her neck. " 'Tis better you are such a small woman."

Her brows knit as she remembered what Lucy, the healer, had said to her several weeks past. Though she had tried not to think too much about it, Lucy's words frightened her. "Lucy says my labor will be difficult," she said. "I am too narrow."

Gilbert grew still. It had not occurred to him the effects of birthing on one so small. Foolish! he chastised himself. Had not his own mother, a woman not much larger than Graeye, died after giving birth to Lizanne?

Squeezing his eyes closed, he hugged Graeye tighter. The thought that he might lose her tore at him in a way that defied close scrutiny. The only thing he knew for certain was he could not lose her. The light she had brought to his life still had many shadows to chase away.

The admission surprised him. It went beyond desire, beyond what he had felt for the woman he had once been betrothed to. And he had fancied himself in love with Atrice. What, then, did he feel for Graeye?

"Are you still awake?" she asked, easing onto her back.

He loosened his hold. "Aye," he said, pushing himself up on an elbow to look down at her. Reaching forward, he brushed the hair from her silvery eyes. "Do you not worry. Lucy is a skilled healer and has delivered many children. You will be fine."

She frowned. "The baby—"

"Will come into this world hale and screaming," he assured her, grinning lopsidedly.

She looked unconvinced. "Gilbert, if anything should happen to m—"

Swooping down, he seized her lips, capturing her words as he urgently drew the honey from her. "Now," he said, when she had succumbed completely to his persuasions, "we must needs be rising." Smiling, he rolled away and stood from the bed.

Disappointed that they had not made love again, Graeye pulled the covers up to her chin and watched as he moved about the room.

"Do you hurry," he said, glancing up from knotting his breeches. "I will have cook pack us some food and we will go for a ride. Would that please you?"

She struggled upright. Not since her arrival at Penforke had she been outside the castle walls. "Truly?" An expectant smile wreathed her face.

At his nod she swung her legs over the side of the bed and dropped to the rushes. Then, chattering her excitement, she hurried to the chest that had been moved to the solar yestereve.

Seeing her fully naked in the light of day, burgeoning with the evidence of his child, Gilbert nearly withdrew the invitation. Though not unwieldy, she was past her seventh month of pregnancy. Was it safe?

He shook his head. Whatever had possessed him to offer? The answer came immediately to him. He had wanted to please her.

They would not go far, he decided, knowing how great her disappointment would be were he to renege. Just to the stream. And they would take an escort, for he still did not trust his lands to be free of Charwyck's brigands.

Gilbert had chosen a lovely spot, Graeye thought with pleasure. The winding stream, though deep enough only to dip one's feet in, ran clean and sparkling beneath a sun risen to the top of the sky.

In some ways it reminded her of the river at the abbey. In others, of the falls where she and Gilbert had first met. That last remembrance sent a flush of color over her face and set her palms to tingling.

Dismounting first, Gilbert held up his arms to lift her down. With a hesitant smile she came into them.

"Still like a feather," he said as he set her to her feet.

She made a face. "Surely you jest, my lord."

"Mayhap a little." He dropped a kiss upon her brow, then took her hand and led her to a grassy mound beneath a tree. Spreading his mantle, he urged her down beside him.

"I am ravenous," he said, eyeing the sack she held. She laughed. "Of that I am certain." Settling her back to the tree, she picked loose the string holding the sack closed and peeled the cloth away to reveal a fine selection of bread, cheese, and fruit.

"Would that your men could join us," she said, glancing at the knights he had posted about the periphery of the clearing. "There is so much here."

The square of cheese Gilbert carried to his mouth paused midair. "I had hoped you preferred my company to theirs."

She had not intended to imply otherwise. Peering up at him from beneath her lashes, she glimpsed vulnerability in his face before he masked it with a lift of his eyebrows.

"Aye," she said, "That I do. It just seems such a waste—"

"Do you not worry," he said. "I will eat whatever you cannot. Now, feed my son."

"Or daughter," she could not resist saying, though she was as certain as he that it was a boy child he had planted in her womb.

Conceding with a careless shrug, Gilbert popped the cheese into his mouth and followed it with a swallow of wine from the skin at his belt.

The silence hung easily over them for some time before Graeye finally asked the question uppermost in her mind. "You will be disappointed if 'tis not a son?"

Slicing a wedge from an apple, Gilbert held it out to her, obviously in no hurry to answer. She accepted it, but did not eat it.

"Though I would like a son," he said, turning his dagger to catch the glint of the sun, "if you give me a daughter, I will love her the same."

Love? His admission shocked Graeye so completely, she felt faint for a moment.

"And if 'tis a girl," he continued, "mayhap the second will be a boy."

"The second?" she repeated, turning disbelieving eyes upon him. "Think you I would bear you another bastard child?" Her voice rose with indignation.

He moved closer, his thigh brushing hers. He caught the lock of hair that had escaped its braid and tucked it behind her ear. "You think I would let you out of my bed now that I finally have you in it, Graeye Charwyck?"

Nay, he would not, she knew. And worse, she did not think she could leave it. She looked away from those disturbing eyes and stared down at the yellowing slice of fruit. "Will you ever wed?" she asked in a small voice.

She felt him stiffen.

The fire so recently doused returned. "I did not mean to me, Gilbert Balmaine! Nay, I speak of another—one who would bear you legitimate heirs. Who would see my child cast aside in favor of hers."

Remorse flashing across his face, he cupped her chin and lowered his mouth to hers, gentling her temper with his kiss.

She hesitated only briefly before leaning into him, feeling his arm go around her as she desperately met each thrust of his tongue. She wanted to believe this was his answer and that it was what her heart needed to hear—though he would not marry her, neither would he wed another. But why couldn't he simply say it? Because he would be lying?

She pulled out of his embrace. " 'Twill not do," she said firmly. "I will have my answer."

His breathing ragged, Gilbert plowed a hand through his thick hair. "Nay, I will not wed," he said, meeting her gaze. "Be you assured none other but you will share my bed."

Though it was the assurance she had been seeking, what she had gained seemed terribly shallow. She was still his leman. And if he did not too soon grow tired of her, would remain just that. But what more could she ask? Legitimate or no, her child would be his heir. And he had said he would love it. Love . . .

She closed her eyes and held to the love she felt for this man who would never allow himself to forget her deceit. Who could not overlook that she was tainted with the same blood that had run through her half brother—Edward Charwyck's blood. How sad that she loved a man bent on pursuing a vendetta that excluded all matters of the heart.

"Graeye, are you well?" he asked, his voiced edged with genuine concern.

Her lids fluttered up. Though she tried to hide her pain, she doubted she was successful. "Have you ever been in love?" she asked.

With a harsh sigh he put an arm around her and pulled her back against his chest. She did not resist, simply settled herself against him as if it was where she had desired to be all along.

"Love. 'Tis a fanciful notion," he said, "and years ago I did think myself in love."

Graeye felt a jealousy she knew she had no right to feel. "Who was she?"

He pressed his lips to the crown of her head and spoke into her hair. "My betrothed, Lady Atrice—a beautiful woman inside and out."

"What happened?"

"Shortly before we were to be wed, she fell from her horse. She lingered a few days, then died."

Graeye's jealousy faded as quickly as it had risen. In its place came a great sadness—not only for the young woman who had died, but also for herself. Here was yet another obstacle between her and Gilbert. To do battle with the hate he harbored against her family was one thing, to compete with the memory of one he had loved and lost, quite another.

Not until Gilbert pronounced it time to return to the castle did either speak again.

"Will you bring me tomorrow?" Graeye asked as he lifted her onto the saddle.

He shielded his eyes against the sun and met her imploring gaze. "So soon?"

"Or the day after."

Laying his hand on her leg, he smiled up at her. "I will bring you every day if it so pleases you."

She smiled. " 'Twould please me immensely."

Chapter 21

❧

It was no simple task to enter the great fortress of Chesne, home to Lizanne and Ranulf Wardieu. Though he came with the peasants, the porter at the gate subjected him to much scrutiny before finally allowing him within, and only then after thoroughly searching him to ensure he carried no weapon.

It was a humiliation Edward Charwyck intended to repay on the first unfortunate soul who crossed his path.

Toting his basket of bread to be baked in the lord's oven, he followed the others across the outer bailey. Since he appeared to be but an old peasant man outfitted in rags, none paid him any notice when, after leaving his bread at the ovens, he slipped behind the granary to study the comings and goings of the castlefolk. There would be a pattern, he knew, if he could but find it.

Sometime later a large man with pale-blond hair crossed the inner drawbridge, making for the stables with his knights in tow. Edward knew he was the lord of the castle, Ranulf Wardieu.

It was not easy to contain the impulse his mad mind urged him to, but the piece of sanity he had left reminded him he was without weapon and would be heavily outnumbered even had the man come alone.

Were all spawns of the devil fair of hair? he wondered, thinking of the one carrying Balmaine's bastard whelp. Nay, Balmaine and his sister were dark. How could one be certain, then? Not all carried the mark of the devil clear upon their faces as his daughter did.

Slurping the excess of spittle from his sagging cheeks, he pressed himself deeper into the shadows and waited to discover whether or not Wardieu was going to make it easy for him. Within minutes he had his answer.

"So 'tis to be easy, hmm?" he muttered when the falcons were brought from the mews. A wicked smile curved his mouth as the hunting party mounted their horses.

By the time they rode out beneath the portcullis, the old man was trembling so with excitement, he feared his heart might burst. Rubbing a hand to his chest, he stepped from the shadows, his empty basket concealed beneath the patch-cloth mantle hanging lopsided from his shoulders.

He entered the donjon via the kitchen. When a serving wench asked him why he was there, he knocked her unconscious—perhaps even killed her—and hid her in the pantry.

"Meddling bitch," he muttered, then peered around the corner at the enormous hall that put the one at Medland to shame. There were a few servants about, but none noticed him as he crept along the walls to the stairway.

At the landing above he heard the women's laughter before he came upon them. He skulked down the corridor, pausing outside the room the voices emanated from.

The door stood open a hand's width, giving him a view of the backs of two women bent over an embroidery frame—one dark-headed, the other fair like the lord of this place. There were others there, too, but he could not see them.

"Nay, daughter, 'tis too large a stitch you make," the pale-headed one laughingly admonished.

There came a heavy, frustrated sigh. Unladylike. "Give me a sword, a bow, a sling, but pray do not give me a needle!"

Youthful laughter from those he could not see followed the heartfelt declaration.

"And who will teach Gillian the ways of a lady if 'tis not you, Lizanne?"

Edward's heart lurched as he experienced again the impulse to slay his enemy. He thought of the knife he had taken from the kitchen, but once more his tentative grasp on sanity prevailed. Aye, in good time he would have her flesh, but not this day.

"Ah, Lady Zara, 'tis a waste of time," Philip's murderer said.

Edward pressed himself back against the wall, his gaze darting along the corridor as he wondered behind which door the child lay.

The woman chuckled. "You have already told Ranulf of your gift. What will my son think when you do not deliver it, hmm?"

"Much better of me if he does not feel obliged to wear it. Just look at this—'tis more like a pig than a horse!"

"You must needs only make its legs longer."

A shriek. "Then 'twill look like a pig with long legs!" The sound of a stool scraping across the floor had Edward gripping the knife handle. Mayhap he would have her flesh this day, after all.

"And where do you think you are going? You promised me an hour—a full hour, Lizanne!"

The feet approaching the door faltered. "It has been at least that long."

"Nay, it has been less than half that."

A groan. "You would hold me to it?"

"Aye, that I would."

"But Gillian—"

"Is sleeping. Now, sit down, Lizanne."

A long silence followed before the woman won her daughter-in-law's grudging capitulation.

Regaining his breath, Edward slipped past the room and headed for the door at the farthest end of the corridor. It would be the lord's solar, and if he guessed correctly, there he would find that which he sought.

Easing the door open, he pressed his face to the crack and swept the room with eyes grown greedy and reckless. Though taken aback by the presence of a maid seated alongside the sleeping infant, he was not disappointed.

The girl was humming to herself, holding a small garment close to her face as she pushed a needle through its bodice.

Subduing the half-sighted maid was simple. However, preventing the child from awakening when he lifted its small body and placed it in the basket proved trying.

Wedging a sheet around the fitful baby, Edward stared at the abundance of flaxen hair covering its head. Aye, though it was a girl child, worthless in his estimation, they would still come for it. And when they did, he would be waiting to exact his revenge, gaining for himself the child he really wanted—the Balmaine heir.

Turning to the bound maid who squinted up at him and mumbled something behind the gag he'd shoved into her mouth, he placed the knife against her cheek.

Her eyes grew round, her body shaking with fear.

"Tell them this," he rasped, leaning near her so she could better see him. "The child's life for Philip's." Then, in one swift motion, he cut a half circle in her flesh.

She screamed her pain against the gag, but it was too choked for any but Edward to hear. Smiling, he tossed the bloodied knife upon the sheet alongside the child, then concealed the basket beneath his mantle.

Whether or not he made it outside the castle's walls to where his men awaited hardly mattered now. The child and the knife it shared its bed with ensured he would have his revenge, be it this day or a fortnight hence.

Lizanne did not walk from the sewing room. She ran. Her eyes crossed, her fingers stiff, her rear end sore from sitting too long on that damnable stool, she hurried down the corridor.

At that moment she wanted only two—nay, three—things. To find a comfortable chair. To place Gillian to her heavy breasts. And to discover a way out of the commitment she had made to take up the needle.

At the door to the solar she paused, straightened her bliaut, and took a deep, calming breath. Then, not wanting to disturb Gillian if she was still sleeping, she quietly entered the chamber.

Her expectant smile was wiped away at the sight of the young maid lying among the rushes, struggling to free herself from ropes that bound her hands and feet.

It came to Lizanne at once.

"My baby!" she cried, rushing forward to stare down into the empty cradle. Frantically, she pushed aside the covers, searching for the tiny body that had long been gone.

Her scream brought all within earshot running.

Lady Zara was the first to make it to her side. "Dear God," she exclaimed, beginning a search of the empty cradle herself.

Shaking free of the paralyzing fear, Lizanne grabbed Zara by the shoulders. "Ranulf," she gasped. "Send for Ranulf." Pushing her mother-in-law toward the door, she caught sight of the steward standing there.

"Seal all entrances to the castle," she ordered. "Allow none within or without until my husband returns." Nodding, the man turned and ran.

Lizanne dropped to her knees beside the maid and pulled the girl's head onto her lap. Wincing at the sight of her poor, ravaged face, she removed the gag with hands that trembled violently. "Marian, where is my baby?"

The girl mouthed words, but no sound came out. Drawing a wheezing breath, she swallowed hard and tried again. "H-he took ... her, milady," she cried, her voice reflecting the pain of her injury.

"Who? Who took her?"

Marian shook her head. "Do not know. Old man. He said—"

"Yes?"

She coughed. "The babe's life for ... Philip's?"

Lizanne's eyes widened, her mouth going slack as the implications fell around her like a pelting rainstorm.

Dear God, no. It could not be.

Her gaze flickered to the cut on Marian's face. Though there was too much blood to be certain, she knew. Whimpering, she lifted the skirt of her bliaut and, as gently as possible, wiped the crimson away.

"Charwyck," she choked, her eyes tracing the crude *C* she'd revealed. With a broken sob she covered her face with her hands and began to pray as she'd never done before.

It seemed the world would end before Ranulf returned from his hunting. In fact, it was less than a half hour before he flung himself from his horse and sprinted up the steps to the hall.

Immediately, Lizanne was in his arms, letting loose the flood of tears she had been trying so hard to keep in check.

"Gone," she wept as Ranulf held her. "He has taken my baby."

Knowing every second that passed took Gillian farther away, Ranulf pulled back and lifted her chin. "Who, Lizanne? Who has taken her?"

She muttered something unintelligible and began to sob louder. "Strength," he said, giving her a shake when she crumpled against him. "Where is your strength, warrior wife?" He shook her again, and this time she met his gaze.

"Charwyck," she spat, dashing her tears away with the back of her hand. "'Tis he who has taken our Gillian."

Only once before, when he had believed Lizanne lost to him, had Ranulf felt such pain and rage. Roaring it aloud for all to hear, he pulled her to where his mother stood beside the maid who had cared for the babe.

"Everything," he demanded, slamming a fist on the table the girl was slumped over. "You will tell me everything—and be quick about it!"

He allowed himself only a moment of regret when Marian lifted her face to reveal the cruelty of Edward Charwyck. He could afford no more, though his compassion for her plight shone in his eyes.

The maid had cried herself out completely, so she was better able to relate to Ranulf the events that had led to the taking of the babe.

"A basket," Ranulf echoed. "And how came he into the donjon?" he asked no one in particular.

"Through the kitchen entrance," Lizanne said.

"And none tried to stop him?" He could not believe the man had slipped within the walls undetected.

"Aye, but she is dead," Lizanne said. They had found the serving wench's body in the pantry.

Ranulf bellowed again and smote a fist into his palm. Blood. He wanted the blood of the old man as much as he'd wanted the blood of the son. And he would have it. Every last drop. His face a cold mask of rage, he turned to look at Walter, his trusted friend, who stood beside Lady Zara. "We ride now," he said.

The vassal stepped away from his wife and came to stand before his lord. "All is in readiness, my lord," he said. "The horses are saddled and mounted, provisions gathered, and the dogs eager to catch the scent."

Delegating emotion to the confines of his heart so that his judgment would not be clouded—truly an impossible task—Ranulf turned to Lizanne. "We will need a fresh scent," he said, his angry red coloring receding as his warrior's logic gained the upper hand.

"The sheets," she exclaimed, coming to life. "And I must change." As she swung toward the stairs, she fervently wished herself already in man's clothing.

Ranulf caught hold of her and pulled her back around. "Nay, you will stay." He spoke firmly, though his voice still trembled with anger. "We will find her. 'Tis my vow to you."

"I will not stay! 'Tis my child! I did not labor to give her life only to abandon her now." Wrenching her arm free, she swung away. "If you leave without me, husband," she called over her shoulder, "I will follow. You know I will."

Aye, she would do just that. Frowning darkly, Ranulf watched her mount the stairs and disappear from sight. Of course he could set a man—nay, a good half-dozen men—to ensure she did not follow, but woe be to those who found themselves such a duty. And still, she would likely escape them. Damnation, but she was no tamer than the day she had forced him into a sword fight with her!

Turning to Walter, Ranulf threw his arms into the air. "Have my wife's horse saddled."

"If she goes, I go too!" Lady Zara exclaimed. Not waiting for the dissent that was sure to follow, she lifted her skirts and sprinted across the hall like a spirited mare.

Both men turned and stared at the tiny woman who was too much like Lizanne to waste any breath upon.

Chapter 22

❧❧❧

Still Gilbert would not attend mass with her. Would he ever? Graeye wondered as she crossed the bailey, Groan tight on her heels. In these past weeks since she had come to his bed, she had sensed a weakening of his resolve to distance himself from God. Indeed, he had hesitated a long time before refusing her that morning.

Whether it was tomorrow or when their babe was born—only a few weeks hence—she was determined to have him on his knees beside her in the chapel. Only then, she was convinced, would the wounds of his tragic past heal. Then maybe he could love....

"'Tis the stars you wish for, Graeye Charwyck," she chided herself as she slowly mounted the steps to the donjon. With each passing day the child grew more and more heavy, claiming every stretch of space inside her body until Graeye thought she might burst.

Ah, this one was not going to be small, she mused. Nay, it would be more of Gilbert than her.

Refusing to allow her mind to drift down the disturbing path to the difficult birthing that lay ahead, she stepped into the hall. Instantly, Groan sprinted across the rushes to growl a threat to the stranger there. A quelling reprimand from Gilbert sent him beneath a bench. Though relations had improved between the two males, it was still far from friendly.

As it took her eyes a moment to accustom themselves to the indoors, Graeye heard the voices before she saw the men at the far end of the hall. Upon the raised dais sat Gilbert, Sir Lancelyn on his left.

"Graeye," Gilbert called, rising to cross to her side. "We've a guest."

A twinge of discomfort came over her before she pushed it aside. It mattered not what this man, or any other, thought of her. What mattered was that Gilbert would claim this child as his own. Thrusting her chin high, she took the arm he proferred and walked beside him to the dais.

"Sir Lancelyn." She acknowledged the man with an awkward curtsy.

On his feet the vassal bent over her hand. "My lady, you grow more beautiful each time I chance to cross your path."

She blinked. Such flowery prose? For whose benefit? Looking up at Gilbert, whose eyes mirrored displeasure at the man's words, she knew it had not been for him. For her, then? But she had thought Sir Lancelyn rather cool toward her. . . .

It was courtesy only, she concluded, finding no other place to hang this curiosity.

Gilbert did not deny his jealousy at having another man appreciate that which was his, and which he would share with no other. Nay, he was past that. He was damned jealous, his insides tightly sprung with resentment. What he would be like if a man ever ventured beyond the chivalrous courtesies with Graeye, he could not begin to imagine, but God preserve the soul of one who dared such a thing.

Graeye disrupted the tension that had built around the three of them. "You have business at Penforke?" she asked Lancelyn.

His gaze flickered to Gilbert; then he wisely stepped back and leaned against the edge of the table. "Aye."

"You will be staying long?"

"Nay, I cannot," he said, his gaze going twice more to Gilbert before settling upon her. "I must needs return to Medland ere night falls."

Then he would have to ride like the winter wind to achieve that end, Graeye mused. "And how does Medland fair?"

"All is well, my lady. The people are content, the crops sowed, and soon the donjon will be taken down that a stone tower can be erected in its place."

All that? It was difficult to comprehend such changes in so short a time. Lancelyn was, indeed, the laudable man Gilbert claimed him to be.

A hand to her arm, Gilbert pulled Graeye away, seeking the privacy of the stair's shadows. "'Twill not be possible to take our ride today," he said, his irritation slipping as he looked upon her rosy-cheeked face. "Methinks it likely to be hours ere I have finished with Sir Lancelyn."

"Is there something wrong?"

"There is naught for you to concern yourself over."

She did not think she should believe him, but saw nothing in his expression to dissuade her from the sense of security she'd had since coming to Penforke.

"Very well," she said, though she was greatly disappointed at not being able to take advantage of the lovely day. Since that first time Gilbert had taken her to the stream, they had returned each day the weather allowed. And the last three had been wet and overcast. She sighed. Mayhap tomorrow would dawn as beautifully as this day.

He dropped a kiss upon her lips, and urged her up the stairs. "Tomorrow," he promised, beginning to turn away.

She smiled at him, then began the long trek up the stairs. She got only as far as the second step before she was swept from her feet and settled against Gilbert's

chest. He quickly carried her up the stairs and set her
to the landing at the top.

"Chivalrous, my lord," she teased. "Mayhap I should
ask Sir Lancelyn to visit more often." She jumped away
before his hand could land on her backside.

"Methinks I should have rescued you sooner from
Lizanne's chamber," he grumbled. "Your tongue grows
more like hers every day."

It was the first Graeye had heard of it and, considering what she knew of his sister from Mellie, the
comparison surprised her. Still, it did not offend her,
for she'd found much to admire in the fearless woman
Mellie had told her about. Mellie had not gone into
much detail but she had explained to Graeye that a
year earlier, when Gilbert was at court, a vengeful
baron had laid seize to Penforke, demanding satisfaction for some wrong he claimed Lizanne had done
him. Rather than risking the safety of the castle's inhabitants, Lizanne had given herself over to the baron.
Curiously, Lizanne had later wed that same man. One
day, Graeye hoped to have the full story on what had
transpired.

She wrinkled her nose at Gilbert, then walked down
the corridor to the solar. Directly, she went to the window embrasure and settled herself there that she might
gain some sun upon her face. It felt wonderful, though
it could not compare with the excursions to the stream.
Resting her hands upon her belly, she peered down at
the activity of the inner bailey.

Though she paid no heed to the knights and men-at-
arms, she missed nothing of the villagers who had come
earlier that morning, as they did nearly every day, to
perform various duties for their lord. Focusing upon a
large peasant woman draped in a worn mantle, an idea
came to her.

Excitement rushed through her. An adventure—not
unlike those Gilbert's sister had undertaken, though on
a smaller scale, of course. Dared she?

She nibbled her lip. With the leaving of Edward from

the lands, had not Gilbert pronounced the demesne safe? Aye. In fact, the last few times they had gone to the stream, he had not brought along an escort.

Her smile faltered as the next obstacle dropped into her path. Where could she obtain peasant's clothes that would make her less conspicuous to the guards? If she could but solve that dilemma, it was likely she would succeed. Although each person who came within the castle's walls was thoroughly scrutinized, merely a count was taken when they left to ensure none stayed behind.

One of her mother's old bliauts, she thought. Mayhap, if she left the laces loose, she might yet fit into it. And with a little soil the coarse black mantle given to her at the abbey would complete the disguise. Both were in the chest.

But how was she to get past Gilbert? She could not pass unseen through the hall. . . . The frown on her brow dissolved. The hidden stairway. Gilbert had shown it to her a fortnight past. Aye, if she took a torch, she would be able to negotiate it fine. And mayhap even return by it without any being the wiser as to her little jaunt.

Beaming, she hastened from the window and went to the chest. Easing herself to her knees, she sorted through the clothes there, finding the old bliaut first. Laying it aside, she dug deeper and, moments later, pulled out the bridal habit she had long ago buried. She paused over it, running her hands down the fine material as she recalled the last time she had worn it—the day Gilbert had come to Medland. How different he now was from that wrathful man who had cornered her in the chapel. Different, but still cynical.

Sighing, she laid the habit aside. Mayhap its material could be used to fashion a baptismal gown for the babe.

The mantle she located next was of rough, inferior wool. It had been given to her upon her return to the abbey. Though perhaps too warm for the day, it would be necessary to conceal her shape and face. Laying it alongside the bliaut, she began to loosen her laces.

A tap on the door interrupted her. Quickly, she dropped the lid of the chest and sat herself squarely down upon it.

"Come," she called.

"You are not feeling well, milady?" Mellie inquired, closing the door behind her.

"Tired."

"Ahh," the maid knowingly sighed, coming to stand before her mistress. "The babe." Her gaze flickered to where the garments lay alongside the chest. She frowned, but said nothing.

Nervously, Graeye laid a hand to her belly. "Aye, he never stops moving."

Mellie smiled. "I'll help ye to bed," she said, putting her arm beneath Graeye's elbow. "Rest will do ye and the babe good."

"I—I am suddenly quite hungry," Graeye said as she allowed Mellie to assist her in rising. "Mayhap you could fetch me some bread and cheese?"

Letting go her arm, Mellie peeled back the covers and motioned her forward. "Ye'd like a tankard of mead with that?"

Graeye started to decline, but on second thought nodded. "Aye, that sounds fine," she said, lowering herself to the mattress.

"Then I will fetch it now." Turning, she went quickly to the door. "Anything else, milady?" she asked, peering over her shoulder.

"Mayhap some fruit ..."

Nodding, Mellie slipped out into the corridor.

Graeye pulled the mantle around her, slumping within the folds of the hood to hide herself from the castlefolk she passed. If any gave her notice, she did not know, for she kept her head down.

Keeping to the shadows as much as possible, she

crossed the bailey without mishap and ensconced herself within the narrow alley that ran the back of the smithy. Only then did she peer out from the folds of her hood to spy the gatehouse.

The portcullis was raised, its two guards standing before the gaping portal exchanging boasts of one kind or another. Still, they were alert.

Deciding she would wait until she saw another pass from the castle unhindered, she settled herself back against the wall, shifting the sack containing the food Mellie had brought her to the opposite hand.

A moment later something cold and wet against her palm nearly had her screaming aloud. A hand to her mouth, she stumbled backward, her eyes lighting upon the large dog who stood gazing up at her with great, questioning eyes.

"Groan!" she gasped.

In reply he wagged his tail and groaned.

Graeye could not risk being seen with him, for surely he would give her away. "Nay, Groan," she scolded, wagging a finger at him. "Go back."

He looked behind to where she indicated, then at her, his great tongue lolling.

Exasperated, Graeye stomped her foot. "Bad dog," she said. "Go!"

He groaned louder, setting her nerves on end. Then, with another groan, he squeezed himself around in that narrow space and ambled away. At the entrance he turned and looked back at her expectantly but, when she waved him away again, went with his tail between his legs.

Stepping forward a minute later, Graeye cautiously peeked around the building to assure herself he was not lurking anywhere near. She was surprised, for he had disappeared so completely, she could not be certain he had ever really come.

Seeing a peasant approach the gatehouse, she held her breath, waiting to see if the man would be allowed to pass without search. He was.

Excitement stirred her insides. Assuring herself the hood hid her features, the mantle her cumbersome body, she stepped forward. Just then the baby kicked, striking her side with enough force to snatch her breath. She had only just recovered when it threw another limb out to meet the other side.

Moaning, she slipped back into the shadows and ran a soothing hand over her belly. "A few more weeks," she whispered. The anxious child calmed a short time later.

Clutching her sack, Graeye once more stepped from the building and made her way to the gatehouse. Luck stayed with her, and she crossed the drawbridge a minute later.

Smiling broadly at having succeeded in her venture, she set her course across the wide, open grassland. Beyond, through the trees, lay the stream.

As she approached the cover of woods, the gathering thunder of hooves halted her progress. Swinging around, she shielded her eyes against the sun's glare and picked out the large group of riders descending upon the castle.

Who were they? she wondered, experiencing her first misgivings since leaving the castle. Over her shoulder she saw that the portcullis had been lowered. Enemies? Dear God, had she made a mistake in leaving the safety of the walls?

She looked again at the riders and found them fast gaining ground. Fear gripped her as she realized she stood in their path. As fast as her feet could carry her, she made for the shelter of trees.

Still they came upon her, veering away to avoid trampling her beneath their horses' hooves.

In her haste, Graeye stumbled and landed on her fours, both surprised and terrified when a shout brought the riders to a halt. Gaining her feet, the hood fallen from her head, she turned to stare at them. Her searching gaze caught and held that of a man with hair so pale, it looked to be white. And he was near as large as Gilbert.

Breaking from the group, a dark-headed man who moved with fluid ease upon his horse's back rode toward her.

Graeye quickly realized her mistake when, a moment later, she found herself staring up at a woman clothed as a man, a thick braid hanging over her shoulder. She was lovely, though fatigue had taken its toll on her.

"You are well?" the woman asked, the concern upon her face genuine, unwavering even when her eyes lit upon the stain marring Graeye's face.

"Aye," she answered. "No harm has been done."

The woman's gaze swept her once more, then, nodding, she urged her horse back around.

Immense relief washed over Graeye when the riders continued on to the castle. Slipping behind a tree, she waited to see how they would be received. It was not long before the portcullis was raised and they were allowed within.

All was well, then. Friend, not foe.

"Lizanne." Smiling, Gilbert held his arms up to receive her down from her mount.

She had no smiles for him, though, nor warm words for the brother she had not seen in well over nine months. Her mouth set in a grim line, she allowed him to assist her down.

"Something is wrong?" he asked, turning questioning eyes from her to Ranulf.

"Charwyck." The name was spat from her lips.

Immediately, Gilbert's hands fell from her waist, clenching into fists at his sides. "What speak you of?"

"He has stolen my child," she burst out, her eyes brimming with tears.

Stepping forward, Ranulf gathered her against his side. "We must speak, Gilbert," he said, then turned to mount the steps to the donjon.

Gilbert fought down the explosion of anger tearing at his insides. He must not give in to it, as it would only distress Lizanne more. Tight-lipped, he exchanged a knowing glance with Sir Lancelyn, then motioned for the man to follow.

In the hall serving wenches scurried to laden the tables with refreshments for the weary travelers. With one sharp word Gilbert sent them back to the kitchens. When Mellie appeared, her hands flapping with excitement at Lizanne's return, her mouth tumbling words he found too annoying to tolerate, he sent her away too.

When the hall was clear of prying eyes and ears, Gilbert leaned toward Ranulf. "Tell me," he prompted.

Ranulf finished the tankard of ale his parched throat had demanded. "Four days past, in the clear light of day, Gillian was taken from Chesne. 'Tis certain Charwyck who stole her."

"How know you this?"

It was Lizanne who answered. "'Twas an old man. He told the maid it was Gillian's life for Philip's. Then he cut a *C* into the girl's face."

Gilbert drew a sharp breath and pounded his fist on the table. "Damnation!" he exploded. "Will we never be free of the devil?"

Ranulf stayed Gilbert's temper with a hand to his arm. "The dogs picked up Gillian's scent," he said. "We followed it for two days, but lost it on the third. As Charwyck was heading south, we continued on here. Have you—"

"Aye." Gilbert tossed back into his chair, going onto the rear two legs and nearly upending himself. Angrily, he kneaded his thigh. "Sir Lancelyn brought news this morn of Charwyck's return. The man's brigands pillaged a village near Medland yesterday."

With a nod Lancelyn confirmed this.

"Then he is near," Ranulf said, rising abruptly. "We will find him."

Lizanne rose—nay, stumbled—to her feet. Clearly,

she was exhausted, her shadowed eyes haunted, her face drawn with worry.

Beginning to think logically again, Gilbert shook his head. "'Twill do no good to rush out without direction," he said. "We must plan if we are to succeed in recovering Gillian unharmed. Methinks the babe is but a pawn to lure us, the ones Charwyck believes responsible for Philip's death, to his lair."

Though reluctant, Ranulf and Lizanne resumed their seats.

"We do have an advantage—an unexpected one," Gilbert said as he leaned forward. "The villagers felled one of Charwyck's men during the raid. Though the man is wounded, methinks he will talk before long."

"Where is he?" Ranulf demanded.

"Later," Gilbert said, though he, too, was anxious to discover the man's secrets. "He must be tended to first. His wounds are severe."

Gritting his teeth, Ranulf nodded. "How many men can you spare?"

"As many as it takes."

The beginnings of a plan taking shape, it was only a short time later when the two men and Lizanne rose from the table. They traversed the hall, only to be brought up short by Mellie before they reached the doors.

"Milord," she called, skidding over the rushes in her haste to reach Gilbert. "'Tis Lady Graeye. I cannot find her."

With a deep sense of foreboding Gilbert met the girl's anxious gaze. "She is not in the solar?"

"Nay, milord, though I left her there but an hour past. She said she was tired—needed to rest."

"You have *that* woman under your roof?" Lizanne exclaimed, swinging around to glare at her brother. "You said you would keep her at Medland. Why is she here?"

"Circumstances change," Gilbert growled, then

turned his attention back to Mellie. "Mayhap she is in the gardens?"

The maid blinked. "I—I do not know, milord."

Gilbert turned to Sir Lancelyn. "Send word to search the castle. She must be somewhere near. None would dare have allowed her to leave."

"Milord." Mellie tugged on his sleeve. "There is the matter of her habit."

He looked back at her. "Her habit?"

"Aye, that she had in her chest. This morn she had it and one of her mother's old bliauts laid out. The habit is still there, but the bliaut is missing—and the mantle she brought with her from the abbey."

"Show me."

Frowning, Lizanne watched her brother disappear up the stairs.

In the solar Gilbert angrily swept aside the white garment. Had Graeye left him? Returned to the abbey? Or worse, to her father?

"'Tis as I said, milord, the other garments are gone," Mellie said from beside the bed, wringing her hands. "Methinks 'tis what she wore to escape unnoticed."

"Why would she want to escape?" he barked. "Dear God, she will soon give birth to my son!"

Mellie cursed the loyalty for the baron's leman that she had unwittingly allowed to creep upon her. If only she had told him of the conversation she and her mistress had been privy to.

"Milord, do you beat me," she ventured, though she knew he was not of that bent, "I will understand and take my punishment as you see fit."

He swung around and glared at her. "What are you babbling about?"

Slowly, she came forward. "'Tis your conversation with the king's man, Sir Royce. Milady and I chanced to overhear your talk of Sir Michael's death—though we did not purposely set ourselves to eavesdropping. Nay, milord, we did not." She ventured a glance at his thunderous face, then looked quickly away. "Lady

Graeye was very disturbed by it—methinks blamed herself for the knight's death and the loss of the village."

Gilbert swung away. It would certainly explain Graeye's odd behavior that day. Still, he could not believe she had left him. She had seemed content enough.

Nay, he harshly corrected himself. She had not been content as his leman. She had simply accepted the role when there was naught else she could do.

How his leg pained him, alternately throbbing and burning as he paced the room, seeking answers to questions he had not thought he would have to ask. Mayhap she would still be found. . . .

Abruptly, he abandoned his pacing. The chapel. Would his men think to look there? Renewed hope surging through him, he left the solar and descended to the hall.

He did not get far before Lizanne took hold of his arm. "Gilbert, there was a peasant woman we passed on the approach to Penforke. Methinks now it may have been this Graeye Charwyck in disguise."

Gilbert's brow creased. "What makes you think that?"

"She was alone, empty-handed, and—"

"What did she look like?"

"Fair. Pretty . . ." She shook her head.

"How was she clothed?"

"A black mantle, and methinks 'twas a brown gown beneath. Also, there was a stain upon her face—"

"God's teeth!" Gilbert exploded. "'Twas her."

"Then she is taking word to her father," Lizanne concluded. "Likely she has been doing so for some time now, Gilbert. She has betrayed you."

Gilbert could not believe that. All was not as it seemed. "What direction did she take?" he asked.

"To the east—into the woods."

His relief radiated through him like summer's first heat. She had gone only for the outing he had promised her. Aye, she had been restless these last days, and disappointed when he'd canceled the excursion to meet with Lancelyn.

"Nay, she has not betrayed me." He spoke with conviction.

Lizanne laid a hand on his shoulder. "She is a Charwyck, Gilbert. Do not let her make you a fool."

"You are wrong," he said, his face drawn into hard, unmoving lines, his voice as cold as a winter's frost.

Dawning realization struck Lizanne squarely between the eyes. "For God's sake, Gilbert, you do not love the woman, do you? She is Philip's sister, after all!"

Seeing the anguish in Lizanne's desperate, imploring eyes, Gilbert's anger eased. As no other possibly could, he understood the suffering that prompted her words. Lightly, he touched her face. "In name only is she a Charwyck," he said, accepting the words even as he spoke them. "And even that will no longer be."

Lizanne blinked, her eyebrows slowly gathering together. "You cannot mean you would wed her?"

He nodded, then kissed her cheek. "'Tis much the same as when I learned you had wed Ranulf, little sister," he reminded her. "But you chose well, as I have."

Lizanne only shook her head and dropped her hand from his arm.

"Come," Gilbert said, motioning the men to follow. "We ride to the stream." With the possible danger Graeye had placed herself in, he was taking no chances of going unescorted. He would be prepared if Edward Charwyck reached her ahead of him.

Partially obscured by the leafy trees, its long journey half-completed, the sun settled itself to the top of the sky.

Graeye sighed. Though she knew she should be making her way back, she simply could not bring herself to leave. Not yet. Especially considering the amount of effort that had been required to slip away.

And no matter Gilbert's wrath. Were he to have discovered her missing, it would be worth the freedom she had gained even for this short period of time. A small price, she concluded.

Idly, she picked at her meal, listening to the water's song as it flowed past. She missed Gilbert—so wished he was with her. It was not quite the same.

Blushing, she remembered how he'd made love to her beside the stream just a week earlier. It had been wonderful—nay, splendid. Closing her eyes, she allowed the memory to revisit her in all its detail.

The brilliance of his impassioned eyes. The sun at his back forming a halo around him. The meeting of their bodies . . .

A sudden thundering of hooves intruded upon her memories. It would be Gilbert, and he would be angry, she told herself, then immediately questioned her conclusion. Why would he come with so many? Mayhap it was Edward and his brigands. . . .

Thinking to seek cover, Graeye pushed to her feet and made for the nearest refuge of heavy foliage. But it was too late. The numerous riders reached the clearing before she was halfway to her destination.

Her heart pounding furiously, her hand curved around her belly, she swung around to confront them. Mercifully, her eyes fell first on Gilbert, who rode before the others.

Her shoulders sagging with relief, a smile curling her lips, she hurried forward to meet him. "Gilbert, you frightened me," she said, hoping he would not be too angry with her for stealing away from the castle.

Tossing aside the reins, Gilbert dismounted and pulled her into his arms. He savored the feel of her, sending up a prayer of thanks that surprised him as he silently conveyed the message to a God he had not believed in for so long.

Then, with firm resolve, he put her at arm's length. Though it was difficult to speak angrily when he was so relieved at finding her unharmed, he knew he must impress upon her the seriousness of her act.

"'Twas foolish, Graeye," he rebuked her. "Have you nary a care for the safety of yourself, or our child?"

It was less than she deserved, Graeye reminded herself as she pushed down an indignant retort.

"Aye, 'twas foolish," she agreed, her smile apologetic. "And rather pointless without your company. But now that you are here ... "

Gilbert would have liked nothing better than to linger in this place with her, but there were more pressing matters to be dealt with. "We must return to the castle," he said as he turned her around.

"Ah, the visitors," she said, and was surprised when her eyes lit upon two of those who had nearly trampled her beneath their horses. Though the pale-headed man's face showed nothing of his emotions, the woman alongside him clearly expressed hers—anger.

"Aye," Gilbert said as he lifted her onto his horse.

"Who—" Graeye began.

"Introductions can wait until we are returned," he said, catching her uneasy stare toward Lizanne.

Something was wrong, Graeye realized. Terribly wrong.

She was not overly surprised when Gilbert introduced her to his sister a short time later when they gathered in the hall. On the ride back she had guessed as much, not only from the woman's resemblance to her brother, but from the enmity she exuded. It was the same emotion Gilbert had subjected her to that first day at Medland. To be confronted by such an obstacle after having so recently overcome one of similar proportions greatly burdened her.

"Lady Lizanne," Graeye acknowledged with a shallow curtsy.

The woman stared at her a long moment, then spun on her heel and walked away.

Hurt, but refusing to suffer the same punishment twice in a lifetime, Graeye left Gilbert's side and followed. Near the stairs she caught up with Lizanne and placed herself before her.

"I understand your hatred for the Charwycks," she said with a lift of her chin, "but do not pass judgment on me ere you have come to know me."

Taken aback, her green eyes wide and flashing, Lizanne looked down upon the smaller woman. "I want my child back," she finally responded in a wintry voice.

Child? Confused, Graeye looked to Gilbert, who was striding quickly toward her. Someone had taken Lizanne's baby? But who— Of a sudden it came to her, a cry of anguish stealing from her lips as she realized it was the work of the man who had fathered her.

"Nay!" she gasped, shaking her head. It was all a nightmare. It could not be so ... but it was. Turning, she fled up the stairs to the solar, throwing the door closed and pushing the bolt into place a moment before Gilbert reached it.

"Open the door, Graeye," he called.

Her forehead pressed to it, she shook her head. "Pray, leave me be," she pleaded.

A lengthy silence followed; then Gilbert's voice filtered through, deep and patient. "Graeye, it is not your fault. No one blames you."

She almost laughed. "Do they not?" she asked disbelievingly, her heart turning embittered at this new trial God had set upon her.

"Lizanne will come around," he said. "She is frightened, 'tis all."

Nay, that was not all, but it seemed useless to argue the matter further. "Please, Gilbert," she implored, "I need to be alone."

She heard his harsh sigh. "Very well. I will give you the time you need, but do not think to lock this door against me once night falls."

She did not answer him and, a moment later, heard him walk away. Relieved that he had given in so easily, she crossed to the large chair set before the cold hearth and eased herself down into it.

Knowing it would be too easy to lose herself in the anguish that beckoned, she cast it aside. She would not cry for the lost child, for no help could come of it. Nay, she would search for a solution.

"And how am I to right this wrong, Lord?" she asked some time later when the dilemma loomed as threatening as before. As if in answer, she heard again the conversation between Gilbert and Sir Royce. Edward still wanted his heir—the child she carried.

Pained by the answer she had sought, Graeye hugged her arms around her belly. "No harm will befall you," she vowed in an attempt to convince herself of the plan taking shape in her mind. "And Lizanne will have her child back."

Chapter 23

The conversation ceased when Graeye stepped into the hall. Seated on benches around a trestle table, the half-dozen occupants looked up and watched her approach.

Gilbert strode toward her, meeting her halfway. Taking her hands in his, he searched her face. "You look tired," he said. "Did you get no sleep?"

"I could not," she answered, touched by the compassion shining from his eyes.

He nodded, then, remembering she had not come down for either the dinner or supper meals, beckoned to the servant who stood at the sideboard. "See if you can find the Lady Graeye something to eat," he ordered.

Bobbing his head, the man hurried from the hall.

"You are making plans to go after Edward, are you not?" Graeye asked as she looked beyond Gilbert to the others. Among them were Lizanne, her husband, and Sir Lancelyn. The other two—an older man and woman—she did not recognize, though she suspected the woman to be a relation of Ranulf's, for her hair was nearly as fair as his.

"We must," Gilbert answered, wishing there was some way to shield Graeye from the inevitable.

She looked back at him. "I know," she said. "May I join you?"

He had thought he could send her back to the solar with a tray of viands, but the determination on her face told him otherwise. "We are nearly finished," he said in an attempt to dissuade her.

She leveled her gaze on him. "Do you not trust me?"

His hesitation was not meant to confirm any misgivings he had about her, but, rather, was a result of his consideration of Lizanne's distrust.

"Aye, I trust you," he said gruffly, "but I do not think 'tis necessary that you—"

"Please, Gilbert."

"Very well." His reluctance obvious, he led her to the table and seated her beside him.

She was unwelcome, Graeye knew, but braved the air of discontent that rose around her. Although no words were spoken against her, she couldn't help but notice the glares Gilbert received from all but Lancelyn and Ranulf.

Stiltedly, the conversation resumed, and as Graeye picked at the food delivered to her by the servant, she listened intently. There was much she did not understand, having come too late upon their meeting, but when talk turned to the course their search would take, she knew this was information she might make use of.

"Then, as 'twould seem he is headed north," Gilbert said as he unrolled a map of the barony and weighted its corners with half-empty tankards, "'tis the direction we must go." He paused to study the map, then jabbed a finger to a wooded area. "According to Charwyck's man, the encampments have been here, here, and here. Do you see the pattern?"

Charwyck's man? Graeye's brow furrowed. "Who speak you of?" she asked.

Mild annoyance flitted across Gilbert's face. "One of

Edward's brigands," he explained. "The man was wounded in a recent raid upon a village and captured."

She would have liked to ask more, but knew further questions would be unwelcome. Nodding, she looked back at the map. Where was the man being held? she wondered. Was this the reason for Lancelyn's visit that morn?

"Aye, a pattern," Ranulf agreed, "providing this man speaks the truth."

"Which is why we must split into two parties," Gilbert answered. "You will lead your men in this direction"—he pointed to the northwest portion of the map—"and I will lead mine northeast. If we do not discover Charwyck's whereabouts, we will meet here, at Cressing Bridge."

"And from there?" Lizanne asked, her eyes intent upon Gilbert.

"From there," he said, rolling the map back into a tight coil, "we move south."

"Then we ride at dawn," Ranulf said, rising from the bench.

There was a murmur of agreement as the others rose and moved toward the stairs.

"Come," Gilbert said, his hand beneath Graeye's elbow, assisting her upright.

"You will be gone long?" she asked as they mounted the stairs.

"A few days, perhaps more. It depends on the chase Charwyck leads us." Upon entering the solar he turned her around to face him. "But this time I will not come back empty-handed, Graeye. Do you understand what that means?"

"Aye, I do," she answered without hesitation. "Edward must be stopped."

Gilbert's relief was visible, his shoulders easing beneath his tunic. "Will you wish me well?"

His question startled her, for she had not thought him still suspicious of her. Had she misinterpreted these past weeks they had spent together?

"Do you not know me yet?" she asked. "Have you not guessed at the feelings I have for you?"

He went very still, his eyebrows gathering as he stared at her expectant face. "Tell me of these feelings," he urged.

She opened her mouth to voice them, but thinking better of it, shook her head. A confession of the love she had for him would only leave her vulnerable. And what if he did not believe her?

"It does not matter," she said, walking over to the bed, where she began to disrobe.

Gilbert came up behind her, his hands on her shoulders stopping her from drawing the bliaut over her head. "I plan to wed you," he said near her ear.

Stunned by his declaration and uncertain she had heard right, she spun around in his arms. "W-what?" she breathed, her eyes searching his face.

He smiled. "When I return, I intend to make you my wife."

Feeling weak, she gripped his arms. "Why? You said—"

"I know, and I believed it true." He sighed heavily. "But you are to be the mother of my child, and 'tis unseemly that my son should bear the name of bastard."

Legitimacy. Though it was what she had wanted, Graeye could not hide her disappointment. Did he feel naught for her? Nothing akin to what she had believed to have glimpsed in his eyes? "That is all?" she asked.

"What else would you have me say?"

With a defeated smile she pulled out of his hold and turned away. "I had hoped you might have some feelings for me," she said as she tossed back the bedclothes and began to remove her garments.

"Those same ones you profess to have for me?"

"Aye."

"But you have not yet told me what they are."

Laying the bliaut and chemise aside, Graeye boosted her awkward body up onto the mattress and pulled the covers to her chin.

"Would you believe me," she began, looking at him as he stood alongside the bed, his hands on his hips, "were I to tell you 'tis love I feel for you?"

He hesitated, then lowered himself to the mattress. Leaning over her, his eyes that brilliant blue, he pushed a stray lock of hair behind her ear. "Should I?" he asked, his voice deep and husky.

The most difficult part done with, her pride laid out before him, Graeye nodded. "I know no other name for it."

He brushed his mouth over hers. "I believe you," he murmured.

But he would not make such a declaration himself, Graeye knew. Whatever it was he felt for her, be it love or simple affection, never would he make himself vulnerable to her as she had just done.

Telling herself it was enough, though her heart did not believe it, she gave over to the sensations his mouth stirred, and opened her body to his.

The dawn came too soon and took Gilbert with it.

From her chamber Graeye watched the riders dissolve into the landscape. Though they went as one group, soon, she knew, they would split in two and take different directions.

Earlier, when she had looked out upon the bailey, she had been surprised to see the lady Lizanne among those preparing to leave. She should not have been, considering the notoriety surrounding the woman. Lizanne was strong, unafraid of what awaited her.

The acknowledgment had deepened Graeye's conviction to recover the child Edward had stolen from Lizanne. It was not that she didn't trust Gilbert to bring Edward to justice, but that she feared for the safety of the babe caught up in the battle that would likely ensue.

If all went as she planned, Edward, thinking to have gained what he sought—the Balmaine heir—would let down his guard. And when he did, she would have the chance to steal away with Lizanne's child.

She dressed quickly and went in search of Lucy, knowing that the healer would have access to the prisoner Gilbert had spoken of the night before. In a small room off the cavernous cellar, she found the woman preparing one of the many unguents she used in her healing.

"Good morn, Lucy," Graeye greeted her, coming alongside the table the woman worked at.

Surprised by her appearance, Lucy paused in her labors and looked at Graeye. "What are ye doing here, child?" she asked.

"With Lord Gilbert gone there will be naught for me to do these next days," she explained, hoping the woman would not notice how nervous she was. "I had thought, perhaps, to use the time wisely and learn of your herbs and medicines."

Frowning, Lucy turned her attention back to the preparation. "Lord Gilbert said naught to me of it," she mumbled as she picked up a pestle and began to mash the contents of the mortar.

Graeye placed her elbows on the table and leaned forward to see better. "He does not know of my interest," she said, wrinkling her nose at the unpleasant odor produced by the combining of strong herbs.

The woman finished with her preparation before giving Graeye an answer. "I suppose there can be no harm in it," she said as she spooned the unguent into a small pot. "If ye like, ye may assist me. However," she added, her eyes going to Graeye's belly, "if the babe starts troubling ye, I want yer promise ye will tell me."

"Of course," Graeye agreed.

The next hours were filled with treating all manner of ailments the castlefolk suffered from, and it wasn't until after the noon meal that Lucy paid a visit to the prisoner who was locked in the lower room of a tower.

"Ye needn't worry about this one," Lucy reassured Graeye as she fit the key in the lock and pushed the door open. "Angry he may be, but never again will he carry a sword for that devil Char—" Abruptly, her words ceased. "I am sorry, milady," she apologized. "I forgot."

"I am most grateful you did," Graeye said, smiling. It was good the castlefolk no longer drew parallels between Edward and herself. And soon, if all went as planned, none would be able to.

As soon as they entered the room she understood the reason for Lucy's nonchalance toward the prisoner. The man lay on a pallet in the center of the room, the rough blanket covering him unable to hide that one leg had been removed to preserve his life.

It was nearly enough to send Graeye from that place, but with firm resolve, she followed Lucy to the pallet.

At first, his hair dirty and grown far too long, his jaw heavy with beard, the man seemed as unfamiliar to her as any stranger. When he lifted his lids and peered at her, though, she recognized him. Though she could not recall his name, she knew him to be one of Edward's senior knights, a man second only to William.

"Is it you, Lady Graeye?" he asked, his delirium evident in the thick slur of his words.

"'Tis I," she acknowledged.

Nodding, the man turned his head and stared at the far wall.

On her knees beside him Lucy raised questioning eyes to Graeye. "Ye know him?"

"He looks familiar," Graeye answered evasively as she bent down beside the woman.

Clearly, Lucy was experiencing some misgivings over having brought Graeye with her, but she said nothing more. Returning her attention to the man, she turned the blanket back and leaned nearer to examine the bandaged stump that remained of his leg.

How, Graeye wondered, was she to gain a few minutes alone with him? She could not ask him the questions she needed answered in Lucy's presence.

However, when her gaze fell to the sack containing the woman's medicines, she found the answer.

While Lucy removed the bandages, Graeye carefully withdrew the one pot the healer used on open wounds and pushed it beneath the straw of the pallet.

"Hand me the brown pot," Lucy directed, holding the wad of bandages to the wound as the blood began to flow again.

Graeye made a pretense of searching the sack. "I cannot find it," she said a moment later. "'Tis gone."

"Nonsense," Lucy retorted. "Here, hold this and I will look myself."

Swallowing the anxiety that rose at the prospect of getting so close to the man's horrible wound, Graeye came around the pallet and relieved Lucy of the task.

"Ah, where could I have left it?" Lucy cried a few seconds later.

"Mayhap 'twas left at the armorer's," Graeye suggested. "'Twas last used on that man."

Springing to her feet, Lucy hurried to the door. "Do not get too near him," she called over her shoulder, then disappeared.

Knowing she had not much time before the woman returned, Graeye bent over the man. "Sir Knight," she said, "I must speak with you ere the healer returns."

It seemed a great expenditure of energy, but he turned his head to look at her. "I am going to die," he said. "Soon."

"Nay." Graeye shook her head. "Lucy is a great healer. You will not end your days here."

He closed his eyes. "You forget. A man must also want to live in order to be healed."

And he did not, Graeye realized. Of course. What man of the sword could live out his days after losing a leg? "I will pray for you," she said, hoping it would offer some solace.

He opened his eyes. "Save your prayers, lady," he said, then began to close his eyes again.

Graeye grasped his shoulder. "Sir Knight, is it true Edward is headed north?"

The man's lids narrowed on her, but closed no farther. "'Tis what I told your lover."

She ignored the gibe. "But was it true?"

"Why do you wish to know?"

The lie. She had to make it convincing. "I would go to my father." Never had she thought to refer to Edward as "father" again, but the situation demanded it. "He wants the Balmaine heir, does he not?"

The man nodded.

"'Tis revenge I seek against the baron," she continued. "He has mistreated me and forced me to become his leman. I would deliver the child into my father's hands. Then all that Balmaine has taken from us will be ours again—and more." Would he be convinced?

The knight mumbled something she could not understand; then his eyes flickered closed.

Sinking back onto her heels, Graeye let go a defeated sigh. She had not convinced him. How was she to find Edward if—

"Long I served your father," the knight said suddenly, "and well I know how his mind works—even as mad as he is. Aye, 'tis true he was headed north, but he will not go there now."

Anxious, Graeye leaned near him again, but he did not open his eyes. "Why?" she asked. "And where will he go?"

"Though he knows not whether I lived or died, he would not chance my knowledge of his plans. Nay, he will turn south now."

"Toward Penforke?"

"Aye, but not too near—not yet."

"Where?" She was growing impatient. Any moment Lucy could return, and she would never know this man's secrets.

"Dewhercy," the man breathed. "'Tis where he will do battle with . . . Balmaine."

Dewhercy? Where had she heard that name before?

She was certain it had been Gilbert who had spoken of it. . . . Ah, she hit upon it. Dewhercy was the lake the rivers emptied into. He had promised to take her there after the babe was born.

Catching sound of Lucy's approach, Graeye quickly retrieved the medicine pot and rolled it across the floor. When the woman entered, anxiously wringing her hands, Graeye pointed to it.

"There," she said, still holding the bandages to the wound. "I spotted it a moment ago. It must have fallen from the sack."

Mumbling prayers of thanks, Lucy retrieved it and hurried back to the pallet. Shooing Graeye aside, she made quick work of applying the unguent.

"I must needs return to my chamber and rest," Graeye said, moving to the door. "Mayhap I can assist you again on the morrow?"

"Aye, if you are up to it," Lucy tossed over her shoulder. "We shall see."

As the sun fell beyond its zenith the next day, Graeye reflected on the events of the previous night.

If not for Mellie's help, which had been gained at the cost of much pleading and reasoning, she might not have ever found a way out of the castle. Fortunately, the servant's loyalty still lay with her former mistress, Lizanne.

Although Graeye had given few details of her plan to rescue the child Edward had abducted, she had finally convinced Mellie of the worthiness of her scheme. In fact, the woman had added to it, which was the reason Graeye traveled by horse, rather than on foot.

She'd encountered her greatest obstacle when Mellie had set herself to distracting the guard at the postern gate long enough for Graeye to slip through. Though she was a becoming wench, the man had been resistant to her wiles, and it had taken much fine ale to finally bring him around.

As promised, the horse had been tethered at the edge of the woods, a gentle old nag that looked to pose no threat. The difficulty had come in mounting the animal, for Graeye had not reckoned with the encumbrance of her pregnancy. Always Gilbert had lifted her astride. But she had made it, and now found herself many miles from Penforke as she followed the river's course south.

It could not be much farther to Dewhercy, she assured herself. Mellie had said a swift horse could easily deliver one to that place in a few hours. However, the nag was not swift, and Graeye's pregnancy made her averse to pushing the animal. Thus she had guessed it likely to take three times the servant's estimation.

Though she was all too aware of the struggle that faced her to remount the nag, Graeye finally gave in to her thirst and reined the animal in. She had taken only her first handful of water from the river when a noise, not of nature, caught her attention. Straightening, she looked around her, but was unable to locate the source. Even as she resolved it to have been of her imagination, it came again.

She raised her hand to shield her eyes from the sun's glare and searched out the wooded area. It would be one of Edward's brigands, she was certain. It had to be.

A moment later she was proved correct, though she would have wished it to be any other man than the one who led his horse toward her.

Show no fear, she reminded herself as he neared.

"'Tis good you came alone, Graeye," William said, a twisted grin upon his face.

"I have come to see Edward," she returned as his shadow fell over her. She hated the way his eyes sparkled with evil humor ... hated the rough hands that grasped her, pulling her toward him.

"Release me," she hissed, straining away from him.

He hauled her closer, then laid a bold hand to her belly.

She stilled, her breath caught in her throat. When his hand began a caressing journey over her firm roundness, she nearly screamed with revulsion. Just barely, she kept it behind clenched teeth.

"Do you resist, Graeye," he said softly, "'twill be your bastard whelp that suffers." His fingers dug into her flesh.

She could not stand it! Thrusting his hand away, she wrenched free and stepped back.

Surprisingly, he did not attempt to catch hold of her again as she feared he might. "And what business have you with the old man?" he asked.

Pulling her mantle closed over the evidence of her pregnancy, she stared into William's hateful face. "I bring him the Balmaine heir. 'Twill gain him all that he seeks."

Suspicion narrowed his eyes. "And what is it you seek, Graeye?"

Summoning the word she had used to learn of Edward's whereabouts, she lifted her chin higher. "Revenge." Would he believe her?

It did not appear so, but then he laughed. "'Tis not very godly of you." He shook his head with mock disappointment. "What did those nuns teach you at the abbey?"

"'Tis not what the nuns taught me," she retorted, "but what Balmaine taught me. I would see him suffer for the wrongs he has done me and my father."

"That he will," William said. Turning to his horse, he beckoned to her. "Come, you will ride with me."

"Nay, I will ride my own horse," she countered, moving to gather the nag's reins.

Suddenly, William was beside her, his hand cruelly gripping her arm. "Think you I am fool enough to trust you, Graeye Charwyck? Nay, you will ride with me."

She tried to dig her heels in, but to no avail. A sharp jerk had her stumbling after William.

"I have warned you," he barked, lifting her none too gently onto the back of his horse. "Do you defy me, 'twill be you to blame for the harm done your child."

Defiantly, she glared at him. "You speak nonsense, William. You would not dare see harm done me or my child."

He fit his foot into the stirrup. "'Tis Edward who would not take such a risk," he said, swinging up behind her. "And he does not yet know he is to be delivered the prize he seeks. So if harm should befall you, he would be none the wiser."

Fitting an arm around her stiffly erect body, he inclined his head and put his lips to her ear. "You see, it matters not to me what becomes of the bastard child, Graeye. Do you understand?"

Too much. "You are a cruel man, William Rotwyld."

"Aye, that I am. And you would do well to remember it, Lady Graeye."

Clearing a path for them, the followers of Edward Charwyck stepped aside, their voices falling low as they gazed upon the woman brought among them.

Some Graeye recognized as having been Edward's former retainers, but most were unknown faces belonging to men, women, and even dirty, ill-fed children. Villeins turned outlaw to satisfy the whims of a deranged old man. What had he promised them?

Cold swept her as William guided his horse to the center of the camp where Edward stood beside the fire.

Hands on hips, the old man watched their approach, his mouth a flat line. Had there been a breeze to move his long silver hair, it would have been the only movement about him, so still was he.

All the courage Graeye had gathered during her long journey seemed for naught when she looked down at him and met his feral eyes. Though it was certain William felt the tremor that coursed through her, she was grateful it did not manifest itself outwardly. She could not allow that, for Edward would use her fear against her. Holding herself rigid, she stared unblinking at him.

William broke the silence. "See what I chanced upon, my lord," he said, his pride evident.

With a twist of his lips Edward wrested his gaze from Graeye's and turned it upon his man. "She came alone?"

"Aye, my lord. I followed her for some time to be certain. She says she brings Balmaine's heir to you that she might have revenge upon the man."

Edward looked back to Graeye. "Is that right, daughter?" he asked, visibly distrustful of her. "You seek revenge against one you took as your lover?"

More than anyone, she had to convince Edward of the lie. "'Twas a mistake I made," she said with great bitterness. "Balmaine treated me cruelly and refused to wed me that his child would be legitimate. I would see him dead and all that is his become ours." Those last words deeply pained her, but they were necessary.

His jaw shifting side to side, Edward continued to stare at her. Then he nodded. "Come down from there, daughter," he said, raising his arms to receive her.

Though it was Graeye's greatest wish to vault over the opposite side rather than go into that evil embrace, she muffled the desire. Forcing her face to remain impassive she leaned forward.

At the first touch of those hands, she stole a sharp breath, only releasing it once she was set upon her feet and Edward had stepped back to look at her.

Throughout his scrutiny she held her head high, unflinching even when his gaze settled upon the stain.

"You should have died," he said. "Was it the devil that snatched you from the flames?"

The devil. Always it came back to this. So be it. Knowing Edward would do her no harm so long as she carried Gilbert's child, she defiantly tossed her head. "Aye."

Around her she heard the anxious whisperings that rose like a swarm of confused bees.

Edward reacted as if slapped, his head rocking on his thick neck; his body jerking violently. "You . . .

you ..." He stumbled back a step. "Where is your head covering?"

She folded her arms across her chest. "I no longer wear one."

His eyes widened. "You will in my presence," he spluttered.

She shook her head. "Nay, I will not." Purposely, she brushed the hair back from her face and tucked it behind her ear.

Edward's eyes flew to the stain.

"You fear me," she stated, matter-of-factly.

Her challenging words were enough to wipe much of the fear from his face, though he did not attempt to come any closer. "Fear you?" he spat.

Now that she had gained the advantage, she could not back down. "Aye. Think you a piece of linen will take the devil from me, Father? Nay, 'twill still be there."

He did not speak for several minutes. His hands clenched at his sides, he stared into the face of the woman who was not the same as the one he had known nearly nine months past.

"Come," he finally said, "I have something to show you."

Gathering her mantle against the cooling of afternoon, she followed him, passing shadowy figures and faces, curious and fearful alike.

Outside a crudely constructed tent, an older woman was seated cross-legged upon the ground, a babe suckling at her breast. Beside her was a basket, and within lay another infant.

Immediately, Graeye knew one to be Lizanne's child, but forced a frown to her face. Since she had first formulated her plan, she had determined it would be best if she pretended ignorance of the abduction.

A self-satisfied smile cracked Edward's face. Going down on his haunches, he lifted the sleeping baby from the basket.

Instantly, the infant awoke and began to fuss, its

whimperings growing ever loud as Edward clumsily turned it around for Graeye to see.

"Know you whose child this is?"

It was not easy, but she stilled the impulse to snatch the distressed infant from him. She stared at the small baby, noting its thatch of pale hair and chubby face, then shrugged. "Is it not the woman's?" she asked.

"Nay, she cares for it only when she is not caring for her own," he said, his mouth twisting viciously as the infant began to wail.

"May I hold him?" she asked, suddenly fearful Edward might do the child harm.

"Her," he corrected, though he did not relinquish his hold on the child. "And you may call her Gillian Wardieu."

"Wardieu," Graeye echoed, eyes wide. "Surely not."

He laughed. "Aye, 'tis. Took her from the cradle myself. Did you not know?"

"I heard naught of it. But why would you take this child?"

Idly, he fingered the infant's pale locks as it continued to cry its anguish. "'Twill bring me Philip's murderers."

The crying grew louder, the infant's face turning a frightening red as Edward held it upright.

"She is hungry," Graeye said, her hands itching to wrest Gilbert's niece from the evil man.

"I have no more to give her," the woman snapped, rising to her feet. "Me own child grows weak for all I have had to give that one." Her face angry, she swept past Edward.

Gracye watched her go. "Perhaps you should give the child into my care," she suggested, looking back at Edward.

"And who would nurse it then?" he asked. "You?"

Could she? Graeye wondered. "I believe I could."

He regarded her with mounting suspicion. "If 'tis true you seek revenge against Balmaine, why would you care what happens to this brat?"

The question unsettled Graeye. Knowing it had been unwise to insist so soon, she searched frantically for an answer that would appease him. It was a weak argument she came up with, but it was the only one close at hand. "Of what use is this child if she dies from lack of sustenance?"

He shrugged. "It will still bring me Balmaine and Wardieu."

"Perhaps," she returned, glancing at the child, who had calmed somewhat, "but should something go awry, 'twould be a powerful bargain you could strike with her still alive."

Edward's anger surfaced. "Naught will go awry," he growled. "My vengeance is assured."

Where she found her next argument, she could not have said. It simply came to her. "Aye, providing William does not turn on you."

He stilled. "What mean you?"

Pretending nonchalance, she shrugged. "He thinks you quite mad," she said, planting the seed and praying it would take hold and grow. "On the ride here he even boasted that 'twas he the people followed, not you."

Edward shook his head vehemently. "I do not believe you. You lie."

She stepped near him and placed a hand on his arm. "Do not let him fool you, Father. He deserted you once before when he took an oath of fealty to Baron Balmaine. He will do so again."

She had chosen her words well, she realized a moment later, for a hunted look entered Edward's eyes. Without another word he pushed the infant into her arms and hurried away, one hand worrying his long hair.

Graeye drew a long, shuddered breath. She had won this battle, but there would be more. Somehow she had to get Gillian away from here. Hardly able to believe she had come one step closer to achieving her end, she placed the child to her bosom, a great protectiveness assailing her.

Gillian continued to fuss, her fisted hands and stiff legs punching at the air until, at last, she found uneasy comfort in her protector's arms. Whimpering, she turned her face to Graeye's breast and began to search for the milk that would fill her rumbling belly.

It took Graeye a moment to realize her intent. Suddenly uncertain as to what to do, she looked around for privacy in which to explore the rituals of motherhood—rituals she had not expected to be introduced to for another fortnight or more. The woman's tent would do, she decided.

Crouching low, she entered the cramped interior. She was pulling the flap down over the opening when William pushed it aside.

"You may frighten the old man, but you do not frighten me, Graeye Charwyck," he said, squatting to view her where she sat.

"Do I not?" she tossed back, bestowing upon him the most venomous glare she could muster. "You would do well to be frightened of me, William Rotwyld."

With a harsh laugh he swept a savage gaze over her and the babe, then retreated.

Wondering at the depth of the well from which she had drawn the courage to face the two men she feared most, Graeye looked down upon the shadowed, angelic face nestled against her. "Ah, little one," she cooed softly, "all will be well."

Chapter 24

While Edward's brigands prepared for the coming battle, Graeye plotted, finding that pitting Edward against William was easier than she'd anticipated. And it did not take long to understand why. She had thought she'd lied when she'd warned Edward to be wary of William. Unwittingly, she had told the truth.

She could come to no other conclusion after two days of observing the happenings around her, which, prior to her arrival, Edward must have been too blinded by his madness to see. The old man was simply a figurehead, and one that William had very little tolerance for. Nearly every directive given by Edward was immediately countermanded by William, and it became apparent that the brigands did, indeed, follow the latter.

Now Edward also saw this, and Graeye knew it was only a matter of time before the confrontation that would give her the opportunity to escape with Gillian.

That evening, not until her belly began to gnaw with hunger, did Graeye finally emerge from her tent to the smell of freshly cooked venison. With a contented, slumbering Gillian propped upon her belly and clasped to her breast, she ignored the man who had been set to shadow her every step and crossed to where the food was laid out. As usual she found the leavings of the others modest, for she had not come soon enough to choose the best of the meal. Still, it would suffice.

As she settled upon a rotten log, the child in her belly kicked hard, reminding her that soon it would enter the world. Her sleep disturbed by the sharp movement, Gillian whimpered, then nuzzled back against the warm pillow of breasts and resumed her soft snoring.

The bread was hard, the cheese moldy, but the venison tender. As she had done with each meal, Graeye hid a portion of it in the small sack beneath her mantle. It would sustain her on the journey back to Penforke.

When she'd eaten her fill, she got to her feet and headed back to her tent. However, Edward curtailed her flight.

"I would see the child," he said.

Reluctantly, Graeye pulled the cloth back from Gillian's head and stepped sideways so he could see her.

Edward nodded, then reached to take the infant from her.

"Nay!" she protested, stepping away from him. What did he intend? He had not attempted such a thing before.

"The child, Graeye," he ordered.

She shook her head. "Why? What do you want with her?"

"I must send a message to Balmaine and Wardieu," he informed her with a twisted smile.

"Then send your message," she said. "It does not require the child."

"You are wrong. I require something of the child that my threat will be taken seriously."

"Something of the child?" she echoed, not wanting to read into his words the real meaning. "Send your message," she repeated, "but leave her be."

He reached again for Gillian and nearly succeeded in snatching her away.

Graeye stumbled backward, found her balance, then retreated.

"Give me the child!" he demanded, following her.

Surprisingly, it was William who stepped between Graeye and Edward. "The message has already been sent," he said.

A long silence ensued as Edward stared at the other man. "By whose order?" he finally exploded.

William crossed his arms over his chest. "Mine."

Recognizing this as the confrontation she had been waiting for, Graeye stepped quickly out of harm's way, just as Edward charged the younger knight. He threw his great bulk into him, sending them both sprawling in the dirt.

Immediately, the people rushed forward to surround the two men as they regained their feet.

"You think to usurp my power?" Edward roared. "I will cut you in two." He reached for his sword, but discovered it missing. Raining curses upon the air, he drew forth his dagger.

Though William had his own sword by him, he also took up the dagger. "Come, you crazy old man," he taunted, slicing the air with his blade. "Let us see if you can still wield a weapon."

Something in Graeye called to her as she watched Edward advance upon his opponent, but she did not act on it, harshly reminding herself that this man was her father in name only. Slowly, she backed away, her eyes searching out the man who had followed her earlier. With great relief she saw that he, too, was caught up in the excitement of the brawl.

Lunging forward, Edward laughed triumphantly as his blade sliced across William's ear. William bellowed and countered with a swipe that narrowly missed the other's chest.

"You are mine!" Edward shouted, but his dagger found no further contact.

As she continued her backward trek, Graeye looked away but a moment to be certain she was not followed.

In that fleeting space of time she heard Edward's cry of pain. Looking back, she saw the blood William had drawn from his upper arm.

"Have you no prayers to say?" William jeered. "Your death is not long in coming, old man."

The knight could not possibly have known how true he spoke, for in the next instant Edward fell to his knees, his hand clutching at his chest.

But William had missed his chest, Graeye thought. Hadn't he? A moment later she realized what had taken him down, for she had once witnessed the same thing with an elderly nun. His heart had given out.

Telling herself she cared not if he died, she looked beyond to the refuge offered by the bordering trees. If she could but make it . . .

"Lady Graeye," William called to her, "will you not tend to your father's last rites?"

Too late, Graeye realized with a sinking heart. The opportunity was lost. Would there be another before Gilbert arrived and she and Gillian were caught in the midst of the battle?

Dejected, she stepped forward, knowing that William had seen through her plans for escape. Clutching Gillian tighter, she knelt beside Edward's supine body.

He still breathed, his eyes wide as he held to his chest. "Bastard," he rasped, tilting his head back to stare at William. "I would have given you all."

"Nay," William snapped. "All would have belonged to the bastard growing in that whore's belly. There would have been naught for me."

Another fierce pain gripped Edward. Crying out, he shut his eyes and rolled his head side to side.

"At least have some dignity in death," William said scornfully, and walked away.

The others disbanded, leaving only Graeye with Edward. However, she was watched again.

Placing the slumbering Gillian on the ground along-side her, Graeye touched the old man's shoulder. "Do you accept the cross?" she asked as she lifted the relic from the neck of her gown.

His eyes opened and fixed dazedly upon her. "Alienor," he rasped, "is that you?"

Surprised to hear her mother's name upon his lips, Graeye could only stare at him. It was true she resembled her mother, though she was slighter of build and fairer of hair, but she had never thought to be mistaken for her. The depth of the old man's pain had brought on a delirium, she realized.

"Ah, 'tis," he breathed as he made to lift a hand to her face. However, it fell back to his side.

Graeye shook her head. "Nay, Ed—"

His weak, coughed laughter cut across her words. "See what I have done to your precious daughter," he proclaimed triumphantly. "You thought to close me out and punish me, but in the end 'twas I who won." A spasm of pain crossed his face. "Why could you not have loved me as I did you? I gave everything to have you. I sent Hermana away—forced her to the convent that I could wed you. And you hated me for it."

Shocked by his words, Graeye fell back on her heels. "Hermana ...," she whispered, seeing vividly the face of the woman who had plagued her days at Arlecy.

"Aye," Edward breathed. "Never did Philip forgive me for sending his mother away and taking you to bride. He hated me for it."

Graeye pressed a hand to her mouth. That Hermana had been Edward's first wife, and Philip's mother, explained so much that she had never understood. Philip's taunting ... Hermana's ill will ...

"But I tried to make amends to him," Edward continued, his eyes squeezing tight as he was shook by another pain. "I sent your darling child to live alongside that bitter old woman. And for a time it pleased Philip. But he always wanted more."

Graeye did not think she wanted to hear any more of it, but Edward was not finished. As his life ebbed away, his body eased of its pains and slackened. This time when he reached for her, he found the curve of her face.

"You should not have scorned me, untouchable Alienor—righteous Alienor, who, by silence, condemned me for everything," he murmured, his rough fingers caressing Graeye's cheek. "Had you but shown me some of the kindness you extended to all others, I might have accepted the devil's child you bore me, but you loved only her."

Graeye would not have expected it after all Edward had done, but she could not prevent the pity that rose within her. That this man had once been capable of such love, even were it manifested to the detriment of others, pulled at her emotions.

"Father," she said softly, leaning down to press her lips to his weathered cheek, "accept the cross that you might be delivered from this torture."

He pushed her hand away and, a moment later, expelled his last, shuddering breath.

Tears collecting in her eyes, her throat constricting, Graeye crossed herself and began her prayers.

A short time later, when she lifted Gillian and made to stand, her eyes caught the glint of the dagger that had fallen from Edward's hand and lay beside him. Her back to the man who stood watch over her, she secreted the weapon within Gillian's blanket and stood. What use it would be to her she was uncertain, but knew it might gain her an advantage later.

The advantage was to come far sooner than expected.

As night grew late, Graeye tried to rest her exhausted body—to find the sleep constantly eluding her. However, each time she found it, it was short-lived, for either Gillian awoke her, or her own child picked the inopportune moment to change positions.

At long last she fell into a troubled sleep marked by fitful stirrings and dark dreams that warned of danger. She saw Gilbert and blood, heard Gillian's cries, felt a hand close over her mouth, stealing the breath from her—

Her eyes sprang wide to stare at the shadowy form leaning over her. Was this part of her dream? Nay, she realized a moment later, she was no longer in it. This was real.

She thought to struggle, but then remembered that Gillian lay asleep in the crook of her arm. She would not see the little one harmed. Her heart thundering, she thought of the dagger hidden beneath the blanket she lay upon, and wondered if she could bring herself to use it.

"Ah, Graeye," a familiar voice slurred into the darkness. William's breath was so soured with alcohol, she nearly wretched against his hand. "Know you what I have come for?" he asked as he drew a crude hand over her belly to her breast.

She shuddered with revulsion, at the same time willing herself to lay a hand to the dagger. Moving slowly, she extended her arm and lifted the edge of the blanket.

"I have waited too long to have you," he continued, his greedy fingers kneading her flesh. "And now that the old man is gone, I will have the pleasure you denied me and gave to that bastard Balmaine."

Her searching fingers found the blade of the dagger, its honed edge slicing through her flesh before she realized her mistake. Suppressing a cry of pain, she inched her hand to the hilt and wrapped her throbbing fingers around it.

"I have warned you before," William said, "fight me, and 'twill be the child who suffers. Do you understand?"

Nodding, she was momentarily relieved to be freed of the pressure of his hand against her mouth. In the next moment, though, she realized his intent when he reached to remove Gillian from her arm.

Instinct told her to fight him, but common sense prevailed. Knowing it best to have Gillian out of the way when she found the courage to defend herself, she eased her hold and allowed William to set the babe aside.

Returning to her, he thrust away the rough blanket covering her and began to pull up her skirts.

In spite of the pain in her hand Graeye gripped the dagger tighter, but not until she felt the loathsome man's hand run the length of her thigh did she force herself to action. Though she could not bring herself to set the blade to his flesh, she swept her arm above her head and brought the hilt of the dagger squarely down upon his skull.

He did not immediately react, hovering above her before falling to the side with a muffled grunt.

"Heavenly Father," she breathed, unable to believe she had bettered the man. But then, she reasoned, he had been steeped in his cups from all the celebrating he had indulged in following Edward's demise.

Now what? Scrambling onto her hands and knees, she found Gillian in the darkness and crawled to the tent opening. It seemed too much good fortune to discover her guard absent, and she assumed William had sent him away.

Knowing there would never be a better time to escape, she quickly gathered the few things she anticipated needing for the return journey to Penforke—the sack of stale food, her mantle, a blanket, and the dagger.

Though a horse would certainly have speeded her flight, she knew it would be foolish to attempt acquiring one, and resigned herself to going on foot.

Emerging from the tent, she held Gillian close to her and crept toward the cover of trees. It seemed a long distance as she stepped lightly around the other tents and sleeping forms, but she made it without mishap. Now the only difficulty lay in getting past the sentries she knew were set around the camp.

She would have to go slowly, and pray that William did not too soon recover from the blow she'd dealt him.

Chapter 25

Thrusting his bloodied sword back into its sheath, Gilbert remounted, though not his own destrier. It had fallen in the short-lived skirmish of early morn when he had led the attack against Edward's brigands. A loss for certain, but the great white stallion had likely saved his life, taking the arrow that had been aimed at him. Shot from a crossbow, it would have easily pierced his coat of mail.

"There is no sign of either one," Ranulf said of Graeye and Gillian as he urged his destrier alongside Gilbert's. "Nor of William."

Gilbert swept his gaze over the destruction left by the clash between Charwyck's men and his. It was a pity the amount of blood that had needed to be shed ere the brigands had been defeated, but he was grateful to have lost so few of his own. But still he did not have that which he sought!

As they had trailed Charwyck's progress south, word had come from Penforke that Graeye had disappeared. It had nearly driven Gilbert mad as the old doubts about her had resurfaced, but he had not allowed himself to believe too long in any one of them. Now, however, testimony had been made of her presence in the camp by those of Charwyck's men who had survived. Too, they had told of the old man's demise on the night past. There was some relief in that, but not enough.

Why, Gilbert wondered, had Graeye sought out her father? It was not answer enough to learn she had cared for Lizanne and Ranulf's child while in the camp, for he could not believe she would endanger their child to protect another's.

Mayhap she had simply been biding her time to find an escape from him, had lied when she'd declared her love. . . . Nay! He violently rejected the thought. He could not—would not—believe that, either.

There was always Mellie's confession to consider, he reminded herself. Believing Edward wanted the Balmaine heir, Graeye might not have considered herself, or their child, to be in any immediate danger. It was possible she had left Penforke to seek Gillian's release. But what had driven her to such desperate measures?

Immediately, Gilbert knew the answer to that last question, and it pained him to know he was responsible for the burden of guilt placed upon Graeye's shoulders for the wrongs her family had done the Balmaines. He would make it up to her, he vowed.

"Think you William has her . . . and the babe?" he asked.

Ranulf ran a weary hand along the back of his neck as he stared up at the new sky the sun had penetrated only hours ago. "'Tis likely," he said.

Her face drawn and weary, Lizanne urged her horse alongside her husband's. "I do not believe it," she said. "Methinks Graeye must have escaped with Gillian during the night and William set off after her."

"How come you by this?" Gilbert asked.

She shrugged. "If all you tell me is true about the woman, then 'twas her intent to take Gillian from here. Mayhap she succeeded. 'Twould certainly explain why William was not here when we rode upon the camp. As the new leader of these brigands, he would have no reason to flee."

"Yet he told no one of her escape?" Gilbert said.

"None that survived," Lizanne pointed out. "Also, he may not have thought it too difficult to find her and bring her back."

"Then we must find her first," Gilbert concluded, and motioned for his men to regroup.

Tempting as it had been to follow the river so that she would not become lost, Graeye had known it would be to her detriment, especially once the sun had risen. It was what William would expect, after all, and she had no intention of aiding him in her recapture. Instead, she paralleled the river as best she could, occasionally turning in to catch a glimpse of it to assure herself she had not strayed too far.

How long and how far had she walked? she wondered, her legs and back aching with the exertion. A dozen hours or more, she guessed, and throughout, Gillian had been patient.

Graeye was grateful, for a wailing baby would likely find them intercepted before they reached Penforke. And she had the feeling they were not far from that place. Most evident of this was the land's sudden incline. Until recently it had been gradual, but now it pointed the way to the great fortress situated upon its hill.

Not allowing herself to feel too much relief until she was safely within the castle's walls, she hurried her awkward legs beneath her. "Soon," she told herself when her fatigued body protested its aches and pains. Hearing the faint sound of running water, she veered away, still careful not to go too near the river lest she expose herself.

The first cramp that caught her midsection was not so bad, though it did take her breath away. Pausing, she drew her hand down over her belly. It was nothing, she assured herself as she thought of her child's entrance into the world. Nay, it was not yet time.

Continuing on, she was taken by another cramp not long afterward. Again denying it for what it was, she resumed her journey once it had subsided.

Over the next hour the pains grew more intense and frequent, but still she refused to succumb to their draw. If the child was readying itself for birth, that she reach Penforke quickly was that much more important.

Gillian's plaintive cries finally forced Graeye to stop that she might feed the little one. Truly grateful for the reprieve, though it would set her back some, she chose a place among the low-lying bushes that offered adequate cover and set herself to the task.

Gillian was not long into the feeding when a crashing sound brought Graeye's head swiveling around. Scooting farther back into the protection of the bushes, she drew her knees up and searched the wooded area for the source of the commotion.

Dear Lord, she prayed, let it be a wild beast ere it be William. That was not to be, for it was William who emerged a moment later on a heavily lathered horse whose hindquarters shook with exertion.

Praying fervently that she would not be noticed in her hiding place, Graeye slowly lifted the hood of her mantle to conceal her telling pale hair. Then, holding Gillian close, she peered at the man through the canopy of leaves about her.

Wild-eyed, his color high and ruddy, William pulled hard on the reins, forcing the animal to step a circle as its rider searched the area.

"Bitch!" he roared. "I know you are out there. I can smell you."

Smell? Graeye shuddered as he threw his head back and sniffed the air. He was nearly as mad as Edward had been, she realized, and he meant to kill her. Aye, he had not come to take her back, but to put an end to her.

Grumbling loudly, William guided his horse nearer

her refuge, his angry, narrowed eyes scrutinizing the undergrowth and surrounding trees.

Though it was her greatest desire to withdraw more deeply into the bushes, she forced herself to remain still, barely breathing for fear William might hear. It would be miracle enough if his ears did not prick to the soft sounds of the infant's feeding.

Of a sudden a bird took flight, drawing William's attention. A moment later a hare skittered out into the open, then disappeared from sight. The quiet of a wood warmed by the afternoon sun followed.

Graeye's fortitude was rewarded seconds later when, with a savage growl, William jabbed his heels into his horse's sides and rode off—in the direction of Penforke. As he went, he shouted curses that lingered long after the last of him disappeared.

Still unmoving, Graeye wondered what she should do now that William had overtaken her. To gain the sanctuary of Penforke, she would first have to get past him, which might prove impossible had he set himself to watching the castle. If he caught her out in the wide expanse of open land surrounding the fortress, he would have little difficulty capturing her. Mayhap nightfall would provide her the cover to reach safety—

Another lancing pain caught her unawares. Sealing her mouth with a fist, she waited for it to pass. It did, but left her more drained than ever.

Her child was coming, she accepted, allowing herself only a moment of wonder before resolving that she must reach Penforke without further delay. Be it by the postern gate or over the drawbridge, she would find a way.

Gillian content and dozing in her arms once again, Graeye emerged from the bushes and cautiously made her way forward. Though she believed William presented no immediate threat, she took no chances and veered even farther from the river.

Like a hunted animal, she was keenly alert to the goings-on about her. Every unexpected sound made her skin crawl and her breath catch, but she did not stop, except when the birthing pains overcame her and she was forced to wait them out.

With the sudden thinning of vegetation, she realized she was nearly out of the woods. Though she had not the energy to run, she pushed herself to a faster pace, drawing herself up short only when, through the sparse trees, Penforke rose before her.

"Merciful Father," she breathed, wiping the perspiration from her brow. Moving nearer, she scrutinized the fortification and saw that it was in a state of preparedness. Though it was still day, the drawbridge was raised, and atop the walls armed soldiers crossed back and forth.

Could they protect her? she wondered. Perhaps, but first they would have to know who she was. In a quandary, she searched out the fringes of the woods for signs of William. She was not surprised when she found none, for the man was not fool enough to make himself visible before he had her.

Knowing it safer to approach the castle via the rear, where the postern gate was located, Graeye decided she would use the cover of the surrounding woods to get there. Keeping the castle within sight at all times, she began the last leg of her journey with the same caution she had exercised throughout. However, with each pain came the desire simply to strike out across the open ground. Each time she suppressed it, but only just.

She made all sorts of promises to herself as she plodded on—a hot, scented bath, a day's long sleep, fresh fruit and warm bread, the comfort of Gilbert's arms about her ...

Noise intruded on her musings—not the clamor of a single rider, but of many. Her heart pounding heavily, she walked quickly to the edge of the woods and pressed herself against a tree. Looking around its girth, she spied the riders emerging from the left—near where she had first caught sight of Penforke.

The vivid colors the knights wore and the banners

they carried told her immediately it was Gilbert. Relief, quick and molten, shot through her as she settled her gaze upon the large figure riding at the fore.

Though an insistent voice warned she was not yet out of danger, she pushed it aside in favor of the safety offered by Gilbert's arrival. She could not risk being left outside the castle's walls with William still hunting her, especially with her child demanding its entry into the world.

Drawing from deep within herself, she found the strength to carry her forward. Though she could not have been said to run, neither did she merely walk. Almost immediately Gillian began to whimper, awakened by Graeye's jarring movements.

"Soon 'twill be over," she soothed. Pushing back her hood to reveal her hair, she raised her hand high and waved it in hopes of drawing attention to herself. She was about to lend her voice as well when she saw the riders turn toward her.

It was nearly enough to drop her to her knees in thanks, but still she hurried toward the man riding upon her.

Gilbert was but a few lengths from her when Graeye was taken by another pain, but it was not like what she'd been experiencing. This one burned, so much that it, not God, forced her to her knees.

A howl of fury rose above the pounding of hooves.

Thinking it must have been Gilbert, and wondering at the depth of rage that had produced such a horrendous sound, Graeye peered over her shoulder and saw a shaft protruding from her upper back. Seeing it only intensified the pain, and the hazy realization that it had been William who had shot it filled her with remorse.

"Ah, nay," she gasped as she looked back to see Gilbert nearing her in a measure of time that was not of the real world. He moved so slowly, she thought as the pain took her all the way to the ground, where she fell heavily upon her side.

Gillian was wailing now, her small fists pummeling

the air as Graeye fought to preserve consciousness. She squeezed her eyes tightly closed against the pain, and when she opened them a moment later, found Gilbert bending over her, his face distorted with the shifting emotions of anger, concern, and . . . was it fear?

"Our baby," she croaked as he lifted Gillian from her and handed the infant into waiting arms. "It comes."

Disbelief flashed across Gilbert's face, washing it of all color. "Dear God, not now," he rasped.

She nodded, lifting a hand to touch his unshaven jaw. "Soon," she breathed. Her hand fell back to the ground, and her lids flickered closed over her eyes.

Gilbert stared down at her, all the promises he had ever made himself not to allow her into his heart dissolving as if they'd never been. He could no longer deny it—he needed her, loved her as he'd never loved any other.

"Do not leave me, Graeye," he said, his voice deep and raw with emotion. "I won't let you." His hands going beneath her, he lifted her into his arms and stood.

Graeye pulled back from the rest she so desperately needed and looked up at him. "Never," she said, trying to smile, but failing.

"Gilbert!" Lizanne's voice intruded upon the moment. "We must hurry or she will lose too much blood."

The urgency of her words, and the meaning behind them, forced Gilbert to action. As he strode to where Ranulf sat astride his mount, he pressed his lips to Graeye's forehead. "I love you, Graeye," he said, then lifted his head to gauge her reaction.

Though her eyes were closed, a smile made it to her lips. "And I you," she murmured.

He savored those words, then with great reluctance handed her up to Ranulf. To leave her now was almost a sin, but he knew he must.

"I am going after William," he said. "There will be an end to all this today."

"Likely he has already been taken," Ranulf said.

Knights had immediately set off after the man when Graeye had been struck.

"Perhaps," Gilbert said, turning back to his destrier, "but 'tis not over till I have been satisfied."

"Then I will go with you."

One foot in the stirrup, Gilbert looked over his shoulder at his brother-in-law. "I yielded Philip to you," he said, reminding him of that day a year past when he'd been given a choice of two men to fight. Though it was Philip he had wanted all along, to ensure justice would be done, he'd had little choice but to fight the other man—Ranulf's twin brother. "Now," he continued, "it is my turn to know the sweetness of revenge."

Understanding, Ranulf nodded, saying nothing further.

Ordering those of his men still with him to return to the castle, Gilbert mounted and rode alone toward the woods.

One by one Gilbert had turned back the men who had gone after William. Now, as darkness hovered on the horizon, he alone sought the man who had taken refuge in his woods, and who waited for the opportunity to slay him.

Refusing to allow anger and impatience to interfere with his judgment, he rode weapon-ready through the trees. Always, though, he found his thoughts turning to Graeye and their child.

Was she well? he wondered in a moment of weakness. Would she survive both the wound and the birthing? Had their child arrived? Each time he forced the worries aside with a reminder of the capable hands he had entrusted her to—Lizanne's.

It was instinct that alerted Gilbert he was no longer alone. Readying himself for the attack he was certain would follow, he searched for a telling glimpse of William's clothing, but found nothing.

He was not disappointed, though a bit surprised, when the awaited assault came from above. Reacting quickly to the man's bellow of rage as he descended from the tree, Gilbert twisted around in time to throw up his sword and deflect the blade that aimed to sever the vital blood supply in his neck.

Still, the sudden force of William's weight propelled the two men from the horse and sent them crashing to the ground.

Gilbert was the first to gain his feet, though his impaired leg protested at the weight he placed on it. He swung his sword in a wide arc that had William stumbling away from its deadly edge.

"Now it ends," Gilbert said, standing his ground as the other man lifted his sword in challenge. "Have you a god, best you say your prayers now, for your death is not long in coming."

William laughed, his mouth twisting grotesquely as he stirred the air with the side-to-side movement of his sword. "I need no god to spill your blood, Balmaine," he said. "Soon you will join that whore and your bastard whelp in death."

That Graeye might even now be dead—and his child—fueled the flames of Gilbert's fury. Snarling, he leaped forward and took precise aim to end the man's life then and there. But it was not to be, for William proved to be endowed with quick responses, the suddenness of his retreat leaving his assailant with little more than air to exact his revenge upon.

Swinging around, Gilbert countered William's attempt to catch him unawares with a thrust that sent the other man back several steps. Secure in the knowledge that what he lacked in speed he made up for in strength, Gilbert followed.

Again steel met steel, and William was forced to retreat to avoid losing his balance. Then, suddenly, he was to the left, his guided swing catching Gilbert alongside the ribs. William got little satisfaction from the contact, though, for just barely did the blade pierce Gilbert's protective chain mail.

Still, William glorified in it, waving his sword before his opponent to show the blood that trickled the length of its blade.

"That is one, Balmaine," he taunted. "Two will take a piece of your flesh, and three will end your life."

Nostrils flaring, Gilbert stared hard at the man. Though the blade had done little more than scratch his skin, it deeply angered him to have lost the first contact to such a miscreant. "'Twill be the last of me you shall have, Rotwyld," he spoke between clenched teeth.

"You think so?" William laughed, moving quickly opposite, but gaining no advantage as Gilbert anticipated the move. "Were you not so lame," he continued, "I might believe you, but it takes more than strength to down your opponent."

Aye, it takes observation, Gilbert told himself, refusing to rise to the same taunt others had attempted to best him with in the past. He merely smiled, for he had discovered the key to predicting William's movements. It was all in the eyes—eyes that fell to his next place of attack a bare moment before his legs followed. Simple as it was, it gave Gilbert the advantage when William next moved, and earned his blade a taste of the man's upper thigh.

William let loose a loud cry, for there was naught to protect his flesh from the bite of the cruel blade. However, he immediately countered with a blow that missed Gilbert's neck by only the width of a sword.

"Now we are more fairly matched," Gilbert jeered, pushing William's blade off his. "Both lame."

"A slow death for you!" William shouted, lunging again to catch Gilbert's sword arm. His blade merely skittered over the links of armor while Gilbert took the opportunity to flay open the vulnerable shoulder presented to him.

Clapping a hand to the wound, William stumbled backward.

"Are you prepared to die, Rotwyld?" Gilbert asked, not bothering to follow.

William's pale visage brightened, the hand he had held to his wound going to the hilt of his sword that he might take a two-handed grip on the weapon.

"You will need it," Gilbert said, lunging forward.

Time and again William used his waning speed to sidestep Gilbert's attacks, but his awkward attempts to land a blow went mostly unrewarded.

It was not so with Gilbert. Many times he found his mark and, like a cat toying with a mouse, drew out the moment when all would come to a close. He wanted this man's fear—that same fear he had felt when Graeye had fallen before him, William's arrow protruding from her back. He wanted to savor these last minutes. This was the end to years of torment, and he intended to find full satisfaction in it.

Weapons crossed above their heads, Gilbert stared into the desperate eyes of his opponent and knew it was time to end the contest. Using his greater strength, he thrust his weight into his sword and sent the man toppling to the ground.

Though it would have been futile had he tried, William made no attempt to retrieve the sword that flew from his hands. He simply lay on his back, his breathing labored as he stared up at Gilbert. "Have done with it, you bastard," he rasped.

Prepared to do just that, Gilbert lowered his sword, its point hovering inches from the man's neck, but something stayed him. Though the warrior in him urged him to fulfill his duty and send William straight to hell, something else made him hesitate. Graeye . . .

He saw again her lovely, ravaged face when she had thought he had killed Edward all those many months past. But, he reasoned, the man had been her father. Would her compassion extend to one who was not of her blood? Who had sought her death and their child's?

"Think you I will yield to you?" William shouted, raising his hand to tear open the neck of his tunic and expose his throat. "Nay, I am no coward. I will die with honor—a knight."

It came to Gilbert then, and the realization that he need not soil his hands with the taking of this man's life, yet gain greater satisfaction otherwise, swept much of his self-destructive anger aside.

"You are a coward, William Rotwyld," he said, thrusting his sword back into its sheath and retrieving his dagger. "And a coward you will die." Dragging the man to his feet, he shoved him in the direction of his horse.

"What do you intend?" William demanded, turning back around to face Gilbert.

Fearful, Gilbert thought, looking at the man's drawn features.

His own face impassive, Gilbert pushed him forward again, and not until he had bound William's hands behind his back did he answer him. "'Twill be King Henry who decides your fate, William," he said, holding tight to the rope as he mounted his horse. "By his hand alone will you suffer the indignity of a coward's death, and all dishonor will fall upon your name."

"Nay!" William protested, shaking his head and attempting to pull free. "I am a knight. I shall die a knight."

Wordlessly, Gilbert urged his horse around and, with a shrieking William in tow, headed for the castle.

Chapter 26

Pray to God? Ask for a miracle that he would shortly find himself mocked for? Gilbert shook his head, but could not prevent his feet from taking him to the chapel.

Having handed William over to his men, he had waved away those who thought to tell him of Graeye's condition. Though he was anxious to know, the thought that he might learn he had lost her was something he was not yet ready to face. Good or bad, he had first to do what he had so long denied himself—and Graeye.

Entering the chapel he had spurned many years ago, he went directly to the altar and knelt before it.

It was where Lizanne found him an hour later. "You prayed well, brother," she said, laying a hand to his shoulder.

He had not known of her presence until that moment. Surging to his feet, he gripped her shoulders. "Graeye. She is well?"

She looked down at her hands. "Your son is healthy."

His fingers dug more deeply into her flesh. "And what of Graeye?"

"The labor was hard, Gilbert, but she did a fine job. The woman who will be your wife is very strong."

He closed his eyes. "And the arrow?" he asked. "What of that?"

She reached up and stroked his cheek. "It hit nothing vital," she said. "There will be a scar—naught else. She will recover."

He sagged with relief, but quickly drew himself upright. "I wish to see her."

"She is resting."

"Now."

Knowing she could not win this argument, Lizanne grimaced. "Very well," she conceded. "Come, then."

The solar was dim, lit only by a single candle beside the bed. Sinking down upon the mattress, Gilbert leaned over Graeye. A spot of color in each cheek warmed her skin, making her appear unlike the woman of earlier that day. Still, she was quite pale.

He feathered a finger across her cool brow, flinching at the soft moan that parted her lips.

"I have prayed, Graeye," he said.

Her lids flickered open. "You have prayed?" she repeated with a mixture of wonder and disbelief.

Smiling his relief, he brushed his mouth over hers. "What else can I do to prove my love?" he asked, drawing back only slightly. "What more to earn God's favor?"

So much joy filled Graeye, she thought she might burst with the strength of it. " 'Tis enough," she answered, a tired smile wreathing her lips as she laid her hand over his.

Nay, it was not enough, he thought. He had treated her badly from the start, and if it took the remainder of his life, he was determined he would prove himself worthy of her. "Can you ever forgive me for not trusting you? For those things I wrongly accused you of?"

"There is naught to forgive," she said, smiling at him. "You could not have known."

"But I did know. I just refused to—"

"Nay," she interrupted, "all is healed."

Feeling as if the burdens of his past had been lifted with her sweet words, he laid his forehead against hers. "Soon we will be wed," he said, "and naught will ever come between us again."

She touched his face. "What of William?"

Gilbert raised his head. He did not wish to speak of the man, but knew she needed reassurance. "He is imprisoned. On the morn he will be escorted to the king to receive his punishment. He will trouble us no more."

"You did not kill him, then?" Disbelief raised her voice.

"You thought I would?"

"Aye."

He sighed. "Though 'twas my greatest desire to do so, my love for you would not allow it. I knew 'twas not what you would want."

She nodded. "He is as evil as Edward," she said, "but it pleases me that 'tis King Henry who will decide his fate."

"Likely he will be put to death," Gilbert felt obliged to inform her. "His offenses are too great for anything less."

"Aye, but 'twill not be by your hand."

He leaned forward and kissed her again.

"Have you seen our son?" she asked when he drew back, her eyes lighting at the mention of the beautiful child she had given birth to.

"Not yet, but soon," he answered. "I had to come to you first."

"Then go now," she said, "and bring me news of his well-being." Smiling, she closed her eyes.

Gilbert placed a fleeting kiss to her lips. "I will not be long," he murmured.

His son was, indeed, healthy. Looking up at his father through eyes so like Graeye's, the babe gurgled and threw a tiny fist into the air.

"So small," Gilbert said.

"Nay, he is a good size," Lizanne corrected him. "The same as Gillian was."

He shook his head. "Still small. May I hold him?"

Chuckling, Lizanne passed the child into his father's arms.

The babe fidgeted a moment before yawning wide and letting his eyes close.

"Methinks he's bored with me already," Gilbert mused, very much liking the feel of the small, warm body in his arms.

Lizanne stroked a finger over the baby's cheek. "Nay, he is simply content."

"You think so?"

Her gaze lifted to his. "You will make a wonderful father, Gilbert."

Gone was the tormented past that had afflicted both their lives for so long, and in its place was a future neither had ever thought to attain. As they stood side by side, something silent passed between brother and sister, something only they understood.

Then, wanting to be with Graeye again, Gilbert smiled and carried his son from the room.

A sennight later Graeye and Gilbert were wed in the presence of Lizanne and Ranulf. During the exchange of vows, their newborn son was huddled beneath the pall with them, legitimizing his birth.

When they emerged from the chapel, a beautiful summer sky lay overhead, foretelling of the wonderful future before them.

About the Author

TAMARA LEIGH has a Master's Degree in Speech and Language Pathology. She lives in the small town of Gardnerville located at the base of the Sierra Mountains with her husband David, who is a former "Cosmopolitan Bachelor of the Month." Tamara says her husband is incredibly romantic, and is the inspiration for her writing. They have one child.